Drawing on the Dark Side of the Brain

DISCLAIMER: This book contains content of an adult nature. This
includes explicit sexual content and characters who may not conform
to your religious, political, or world view. The content is inappropriate
and in some cases illegal for readers under the age of 18.

Soulmates, February 2025. D.R. Peters, 'Doc' to his friends, is an artist. He paints portraits of women. Doc loves women. Many of the women he paints love him. Then smart and sexy Rita, his next door neighbor, asks him to teach her the art of love, which Doc is all too happy to do. He's not quite so sure, though when Rita, a research scientist, decides to start experimenting with the effect his relationship with his models has on his art. Doc is about to learn all about the science of the art of love.

The Art and Science of Love, March 2025. D.R. Peters, 'Doc' to his friends, is an artist. He paints portraits of women. Doc loves women. Many of the women he paints love him. Then smart and sexy Rita, his next door neighbor, asks him to teach her the art of love, which Doc is all too happy to do. He's not quite so sure, though when Rita, a research scientist, decides to start experimenting with the effect his relationship with his models has on his art. Doc is about to learn all about the science of the art of love.

Drawing on the Dark Side of the Brain. Artist Jett Blackburn's paintings reveal the soul of his subjects. They have the power to change the viewer, the model, and the artist. Sometimes emotionally, sometimes terminally. Join this digital native and his accumulation of girlfriends as they break the ties with their parents and move off to college and self-discovery.

Strange Art. Words just don't come easily to Art Étrange, if they come at all. His slow speech, self-consciousness, and shyness all combine to keep him isolated from his peers. He can only let his frustrations out on canvas. If it wasn't for his sister, Morgan, Art would not have survived school, but her love holds Art together through his toughest times and expands his horizons. This special Signature Collection Edition contains all three Strange Art books, ***Art Something, Art Project,*** and ***Art Critic.***

Bedtime Stories for Grownups. A collection of short novellas, perfect for night time reading. "100 V Days," "My Sex Slave," "Carousel," "My Brother Reads Incest Porn. zOMG He Writes It!" and for the first public release since winning third prize in the SOL 2024 Halloween contest, "The Key to Eve."

Schedule and Releases Subject to Change

Contents

Drawing on the Dark Side of the Brain

Devon Layne

ELDER ROAD BOOKS
LYNNWOOD WA

1
Life as a Digital Native

HIGH SCHOOL WAS a bust as far as I was concerned. You'd think that in four years I could have gotten laid at least once. My grandfather got more sex as a teen in the '60s than I did now. My parents, the great Xennials—sort of GenX and sort of Millennial—practically invented the terms 'hookup' and 'FWB.' My generation was likely to die virgins if high school was any indication.

"It's not that I don't want to have sex," Jasmine once told me. "Just not… you know… in person." Such is life.

So how do we deal with the hornies? Oh, we've still got them. My generation is as horny as any of the old toads in my grandparents' or parents' generation.

"I got so turned on during the movie," Jasmine continued. "I'm going straight home and rub one off. You should do the same."

I did. You see, we have something neither my father or grandfather had. We are digital natives. We have the Internet. Porn flows as freely into my bedroom as gin flows into my grandmother. And if we can't find a site that has what we want, we have each other.

"We could Skype when we get home if you'd like to watch," Jasmine whispered. "I'll put my laptop between my knees if you will."

Well, hell yeah.

I had nude photos of a dozen of my female classmates on my iPhone. Encrypted and hidden—we're not dumb. Jasmine was one of my favorites to jack off to. With. Watching her in real time was good for an immense come. For both of us.

Jasmine gave me a deep and passionate kiss when I took her home. My boner was trapped painfully in my jeans as she rubbed against it.

"I'll be thinking of what your tongue would feel like while you're watching me pet my snootch," she breathed just before she closed the door.

I rushed home and headed straight for my bedroom. Skype chimed as soon as I booted my laptop. I connected and saw Jasmine, already naked. She twirled around showing me her bouncing tits and tight ass.

"Like it? Are you still hard?" she asked.

"Yes and yes," I said, stripping out of my clothes as quickly as I could. "I can practically feel your mouth taking my cock all the way down your throat." My cock sprang out to greet her as soon as my shorts were down.

"I love your big boner," she said. "Let's get in bed and do it. I'm dripping down my thighs."

We were two miles away from each other, each getting into our own beds with laptops strategically positioned so the camera picked up our genitals. She did have a wet pussy. I had drips of precome beading out my piss hole. I used it to slick my cock and began stroking as I watched her spread her pussy lips and start rubbing her clit.

It didn't take either of us long.

"Thanks for a great date, Jasmine," I said as my cock began to wilt.

"Let's do it again soon," she responded. "I always get the best comes after we've been out." I closed my laptop and went to sleep.

⁖ ⟡ ⟫⟪ ☼ ⟫⟪ ⟡ ⁖

IF YOU'RE MY grandfather's age—or even my father's—you probably think this is all super frustrating. You're wrong. In spite of not having put my cock *in* a girl, I'd had sex with several. I knew Jasmine would be stroking another one off in the morning while she watched Derek's morning wood. In fact, Dee had told me to call at exactly nine Saturday morning to help 'get my vibrator started.' I didn't think Dee ever actually got wet when she used that thing, but I was sure she got off. I sure did.

And it wasn't like we were cheating on anyone. We usually went out as a group and only paired up for a little kissy face. We hardly touched otherwise. Dee has huge tits and I did feel her up one night. I couldn't believe how heavy and squishy they were. But otherwise, you know, no one was actually having sex with anyone else. We had our smartphones and laptops.

•○·❖ ⊃⊂ ·☼· ⊃⊂ ❖·○•

WHEN I WAS twelve, I started figuring out how my equipment worked. When I was fifteen, I convinced my dad to let me get a lock on my bedroom door so Mom would quit walking in on me. She caught me masturbating once when I was fourteen and dragged me out of my room to make me go wash my hands with anti-bacterial soap. She'd been doing that for years, whenever she saw me touch something she thought was dirty. That included other people. I wasn't sure how I'd ever been conceived.

•○·❖ ⊃⊂ ·☼· ⊃⊂ ❖·○•

So, WHAT'S IT mean to be a digital native?

The day I got home from the hospital, I was placed in a crib with a digital monitor nearby. Not one of those speaker things that lets a parent in a different room hear the baby cry. This was full video linked to my father's PC at work and my mother's laptop in the kitchen. Neither one of them accomplished anything for four weeks after I was born. They just sat and watched my babyness on their computers. Why didn't they just sit in my room and watch me? They didn't want to invade my privacy at such a young age.

I learned my ABCs watching YouTube videos on my computer. By the age of ten, I had my own iPhone. And I saw Kelly O'Rourke's bare breast on webcam the day she turned fifteen. All my homework through high school has been emailed to my teacher. My parents own a huge collection of music CDs. They have a clunky old player they put them in when they want to listen. All my music is in the cloud. I don't buy ten songs I'm not interested in for one song I like. I plug earbuds in when I want to listen and don't bother anyone else when I choose what I want to hear. I've got a laptop computer on my desk at home, but most of the time just use my iPad. It's smaller and lighter and I can type 50 words a minute. With my thumbs.

3

Sometimes, my friends and I get together on the weekend to play a game. We all log in and choose up sides. If we need another player, we can usually find one pretty quickly online. I've got more online friends than IRL friends. I've got about 50,000 photos and videos in my library and I post hundreds of them online for my friends. I send and receive over 15,000 text messages a month.

I'm eighteen.

Digital native.

⟿ ❯ ⟊ ☼ ⟊ ❮ ⟿

So, IT ALWAYS surprises my friends when I log onto a chat session or answer a Skype and I'm standing there in my underwear with a brush full of paint in my hand and an easel beside me.

"Yuck, man! Why aren't you doing that on a computer?" Rick asked.

"Your mom will kill you if you get any of that on the floor!" Charmaine laughs. She knows my mom. I have to stop and point the camera down at the newspaper I've got spread all over the floor.

"I'll give you twenty dollars for your tightie-whities if you'll paint them while you're wearing them," Kelly adds. She is one twisted girl. I put a red swirl on my right butt cheek. I buy jockey shorts at K-Mart for painting in. None of them ever see the washing machine. My mom…

I like paint. I guess in some ways it is my way of rebelling. Even if I'm chatting with my friends, I'm doing something non-digital. Like Rick should talk. He actually goes outside and plays baseball. Damn good at it, too. Jasmine has her Barbie dolls. Charmaine collects Pokemon. The cards, not the virtual game, though she does that, too. Kelly collects my painted underwear. Go figure.

The first time I picked up a pencil in pre-school, there was something magical about it. There was a physical response to a physical action. I could hold my primitive drawing in my hands. There was nothing to click to close it. If I wanted to get rid of the paper, I had to find a recycling bin.

So, I suppose you're wondering where I get newspaper to spread under my easel. Grandpa, my father's father, gets one delivered every day. Once a week, I go by and collect the bundle. I asked him why he didn't just read the news on the computer. He grinned and asked me why I

4

didn't paint pictures on the computer. Touché. Grandma rolled her eyes and he poured her another gin and tonic.

I collect his newspapers and spread them out under my easel. As soon as I finish painting, I hang my underpants in an empty part of my closet and clean my room. I make sure all the papers are picked up, folded neatly, and taken to the recycling bins. I take a shower and make sure I've scrubbed all the paint off my body. Sometimes the red I used on my underwear bleeds through the fabric. I shampoo, rinse, and repeat.

My mom still thinks that everything I paint should be displayed for the public, preferably at MMoCA, or lacking that on the refrigerator. Everything she gets her hands on, she scans and turns into a screensaver. It's cleaner that way. Most of my paintings I hide from her. My drawings are in a box under my bed. When Grandpa comes to visit, he pours Grandma a gin and tonic and then comes to my room to visit. I show him my drawings and paintings. He's not an artist, but it's like something he understands and we can share. The only thing he does with his computer is email and reading.

But he likes my art. So does Granddad—my mother's father.

"You've got a dark side," Granddad said about a painting I did of Mom. I like to visit him on the farm a few miles out of town. "Don't let it get you down, but don't show this one to your mom, okay? I don't think she could take it. And you really aren't cruel." I wouldn't show her anyway. But I was kind of proud of that picture.

It would only be a few months until I was out of the house and off at college. For a while.

•०•❖ ꛯꛯ ☼ ꛯꛯ ❖•०•

Everybody who has completed a high school education in America has heard of the *Mona Lisa*. I can't speak for the education of other countries because I don't know shit about it. Here, though, the *Mona Lisa* is the most studied portrait in history. Everyone debates whether she is happy or sad. There are technical discussions about how Da Vinci created the subtle blurring effects. There was an old movie starring Julia Roberts called *Mona Lisa Smile*. Granddad, who still listens to vinyl record albums on a scratchy turntable, has both the original Nat King Cole version of the song *Mona Lisa* and the one his daughter, Natalie, recorded forty years later.

As far as I'm concerned, all the debate misses the point.

Leonardo Da Vinci paints a portrait. Presumably, he has a young woman pose for the portrait. Like all his work, it's a technical masterpiece, but it captures something that perhaps no one else had seen.

My question is, 'What was Lisa Gherardini's response when she saw the painting of herself?' Did she roll her eyes? Did she lean over and kiss the old man softly on the lips. Did she slap his face and scream at him? Did she just turn her back and walk away? Did she simply hold out her hand to be paid her modeling fee? Did she make some inane comment like, 'That's nice?' Did she become a better person because she saw herself through his eyes?

Maybe I'm just inventing oddball concepts, but I can't help but imagine that seeing herself captured on the canvas had some profound effect on her.

⋯⊰ ❲❳ ☼ ❲❳ ⊱⋯

I'D HAVE NEVER thought about that seriously if it hadn't been for Jasmine. And my portfolio submission to UW. A portfolio submission isn't required for admittance, but it's recommended. I thought it might improve my chances of getting a scholarship because there was no way I could afford the $26,000 a year to attend. My parents' philosophy was that they weren't going to destroy their ability to live in our home to send me to college. Especially since they considered an art degree to be a waste of time. They wanted me to go into engineering or computer science so I could earn a living. I could get away with living at home and save fourteen grand on room and board, but Mom and Dad had fixed the value of my room and board at home at a thousand a month that I needed to come up with. I was screwed either way.

Besides, I wanted out of the house and to get a taste of living on my own.

⋯⊰ ❲❳ ☼ ❲❳ ⊱⋯

BUT GETTING BACK to Jasmine…

I had selected three drawings and three paintings to photograph and submit for review. The paintings included the one of Mom that

Granddad suggested I not show her. I was supposed to show my range in the portfolio and I had an abstract painting, a landscape, and a portrait. The drawings were pretty good, too, but something was just missing.

I knew what it was.

I could do a figure drawing from a photo—maybe one of the nudes my friends had sent. But to paint a figure… I really needed a model.

"You want me to go to a motel with you, take off all my clothes, and lie on the bed for four hours while you paint me? Right." Jasmine was skeptical, but she hadn't hit me.

"I was trying to find a place where one of our parents wouldn't constantly be walking in," I explained, as if the motel part of the proposition was the problem.

"I can just imagine that. My mother would rush me to a hospital and demand a rape kit and your mother would drag you to the bathroom to scrub your hands with disinfectant." We both laughed about the very accurate description of our moms. My mother would want to scrub and disinfect my jail cell when Jasmine's mother got me arrested.

It's not like we weren't both eighteen. Just our mothers… You've probably heard about helicopter parents who hover around their children all the time. I overheard Mr. Phelps talking to Ms. Boyer in school one day when he described Ford's mother as a 'Curling Mother.' She shoves a dumb rock down the ice and screams and yells at everyone to clear the way. Could describe any one of our parents. Except we're not really dumb rocks. We just live in a different world.

"Okay," Jasmine said. "But you can't tell anyone. If anyone asks about the painting, you tell them you did it over Skype."

"Great. Yeah, that will work. Saturday afternoon. I'll load the Mini and we'll go to the Super 8 out on the highway."

"God! That sounds so sleazy. I love it."

•०•⟡ ⟩⟩C ☼ C⟨⟨ ⟡•०•

THE MINI. IT's almost as old as I am. MamMam loved that car.

About the same time I was born, MamMam, that's my mother's mom, was having her first go at fighting cancer. That freaked Mom out. But MamMam whipped it. To celebrate, she bought a brand-new car—a

2000 Mini Cooper. Granddad was all for it and called it her 'Mini-Beemer' because they couldn't afford a real BMW. It was a classic hardtop hatchback. MamMam drove it for sixteen years before the next round of cancer beat her. I heard someone mention that they thought she should be buried in it.

"I took the car down to the dealer and had them go over it with a fine-tooth comb," Granddad said. "It's relatively low-mileage since, as much as she loved driving it, your MamMam only really drove around town for groceries, hair appointments, and church. It's the cliché of being owned by a little old lady who only drove it to church on Sunday," he laughed. "But she wanted you to have it, Jett. When the pain and the meds didn't have her down, we'd sit and talk about how she loved to drive you to school in it, or to the movies on your MamMam dates. She said that when she was gone, you should have her Mini-Beemer for as long as it would last you." MamMam had taken me to the DMV for my driving test in that car. That was less than a year before she died.

So that's how I came to have a car. I didn't drive it much because I had to pay for the insurance and gas. That took nearly everything I earned from doing graphics for websites. I got an allowance, but by the time I was eighteen it was only $50 a week and Dad had already told me it would stop on my twenty-first birthday.

I handled all my other income through PayPal or Bitcoin. That's how I prepaid my motel room—through a website with PayPal. They didn't even bat an eye when I registered. I guess they get a lot of university students who book a room for Saturday night.

2
Discovering the Dark Side

I'D KNOWN Jas most of my life, I guess. We met on a play date at a shopping center. Her mom was almost as weird as mine. I was glad I still had my grandfathers and could act pretty normally with them. Jas only had her mom. Still, we'd seldom been alone together for more than a little while. We'd slipped away from our group once or twice to do a little kissing, but as much as we—and all our friends—talked about sex and looked at each other online, neither of us was particularly experienced with the physical side of the human interaction.

So, when we got to the room, I busied myself with setting up my easel and looking at the lighting in the room. I pulled the drapes, but I let a crack remain so a thin band of light fell across the bed. That was pretty cool. I could just see how it would hit her when she stretched out. I pulled the comforter off the bed, but just pulled the top sheet back. I thought it would be cool to have the sheet partially draped over her. I turned around and Jasmine was still standing there, just inside the door with all her clothes on and her little bag clutched in front of her. I don't know. I guess I just assumed she'd get undressed while I was getting things ready.

"Jasmine? Are you okay?"

"I've never done this, Jett. I'm nervous."

"You don't really have to do anything. It's not like you'll be online and teasing your pussy while we both come. All you have to do is lie in one position for a while," I said.

"That's not what I mean. I've never undressed with a boy in the room. Or anyone else. I've never been naked with someone."

I hadn't thought about that. I was completely comfortable stripping off my clothes and even putting my webcam between my legs so she could see me come when she was showing me her pussy. But I'd never been naked in the actual same room with someone, either. Suddenly, I was embarrassed.

"God, Jas! I never even thought about it being different. I just thought you'd undress and we'd start working. I… I never thought about how I'd feel if it was me. I'm so sorry." I was afraid this was all a bad idea and I should just pack up my stuff again. There was a sparkle in Jasmine's eye and I went to her slowly and wiped away the tear that escaped before it could get to her cheek. "We don't have to do this. It was a dumb idea," I finished lamely. She held out her arms.

"Hug?" I walked into her arms and held her tightly against me. "It's okay. I promised to do this. I'm just a little nervous."

"I won't make you do it, Jasmine. I just never thought about how I'd feel if I were you. I mean, we do it all the time online, but this is different."

"I'll do it. Online it's different. I know you're looking at me, but I never really see you. I mean, I see your penie, and I know you're looking at my snootch, but we don't really look at each other. And there's always a goal, you know? In ten minutes, we'll both pop and shut off the computer. But here, I'm going to be naked in front of you and you're going to look at me… *Me!* For like four hours. I'm just nervous about that. Actually, I'm terrified."

"I guess I kind of have to look at you if I'm going to paint you. Do you…"

"Just don't watch me while I get undressed, okay? Like, go in the bathroom and I'll call you when I'm posed. Would that be all right?"

"Of course. If you're sure. Jasmine… God! They beat this stuff into us for the past eighteen years. I won't do anything to you. I won't try to make you do something. Anything. I'll… I'll just go into the bathroom until you say you're ready." I gave her a quick squeeze and ran to the bathroom. I closed and locked the door. As if she was going to come in and look at me! Fap! What a disaster.

I pissed and washed my hands and then just sat there. It seemed like it took her forever. And the more I thought about it, the worse it got. I was going to be in the same room with a naked girl! What kind of an idiot was I? What made me think that I could just look at a naked model and paint her? What if the painting sucked? What if it didn't look anything like her? *What if I just stick my head in the toilet and drown myself?*

"Jett? You can come out now. I guess I'm ready."

I opened the door cautiously and went straight to my easel without looking at the bed. I squeezed my eyes tightly until I started to see little shooting stars behind my eyelids. I finally took a deep breath and turned to her. She was lying in the bed with the sheet pulled up to her chin. It wasn't that she wasn't cute, but… Well, maybe it was better this way. I'd just paint the picture of the shape of her body under the sheet. I guess I was looking puzzled and hadn't said anything.

Jasmine took a deep breath and just kicked the sheet off her. She lay back like a dead person with her legs spread. I could see that even as nervous as we both were, Jasmine's bare pussy was pretty shiny.

"Um… I… Uh… Maybe you could roll to your side? No. The other side," I said as she moved.

"I can't… um… open my legs in this position."

"Jasmine, I'm not going to paint a picture of just your pussy. God! That would be a whole subject by itself. This is a figure painting. I'm going to spend as much time on painting your face as your breasts. I think. I mean…"

"I'm such a dope! I don't have any idea what I'm doing!"

"Neither do I," I said. We looked at each other and both started laughing.

"Okay. Well, that's comforting. Just tell me what position you want me in, okay?" she said. "For the painting!"

My eyes popped open and we busted out laughing again.

"Let's… have you scoot up in the bed a little and prop a couple pillows behind you so you aren't down flat."

"Um… Help me put the pillows where you want them. You want me sitting all the way up? So my boobs aren't squashed flat?"

"Oh. I didn't think of that. I was just trying to make you look comfortable."

"I was kidding. I think. Just show me what the artist wants."

"Okay. Let's put these two up behind you so you can recline gracefully. Then put this one in front of you to rest your hand on. You can even hold your iPhone if you want to surf," I said.

"That would be nice. I don't want to talk to anyone, though. I'm afraid of what I might say. It would be nice to look at their Snaps and Instagrams, though, since I can't really do anything else."

"I might ask you to look up for a few minutes while I do your face," I said. "But first, now that you are on your side, bring your left knee up a little."

"You won't even see my snootch!"

"I'll see your butt."

"Oh! Is it… you know…"

"It's beautiful. Um… Can you hold your phone in your right hand?"

"Of course."

"Here. Take this corner of the sheet and tug it toward you a little. Right there! Stop!" I reached over and tugged another part of the sheet down so I could see the arc of her butt and the streak of daylight falling across her. Wow! "That's beautiful. Can you hold that position?"

"I'm pretty comfortable. Except for having you stare at me."

"Jasmine, I have to look at you in order to paint you."

"I know. I'm still… Why didn't you have Kelly do this?" she asked abruptly. I was already sitting at my easel and sketching in the gentle curves. She really was beautiful.

"Oh. Well, I did a sketch of her. From one of the photos she sent me. But… I don't know how to say this without it sounding racist."

"You don't like the Irish?"

"Haha! That's funny." I drew the outline of Jasmine's breast, just above her left elbow. "She's so pale. I didn't want to run out of white paint. I mean, your skin is so beautiful and the color is so rich. I just thought it would be nicer to paint."

"Wow! That is kind of racist," she laughed. "Um… Do you really like the color of my skin?"

"Yes, really."

"Guys and girls have both told me they like my pussy and my boobs. One even said he liked my butt. You said you liked my eyes that one night we were kissing, but when we got home and Skyped, we weren't looking at our eyes. I don't think anyone has ever told me they like the color of my skin," she said.

"It's part of the racist stuff we're taught not to say," I said. "Lift your face toward me for a couple minutes, please?" She tilted her face up at me and I started drawing the eyes she mentioned I liked. I still did. "Mr. Williams made us do that exercise in seventh grade where he'd show a photo of a group of people and then ask us to tell him about the third one from the left, or something, and we couldn't mention their color or nationality. We could say, 'The tall dark-haired one with her arm around the short guy next to her,' but we couldn't say 'The black girl,' even if she was the only dark-skinned girl in the picture. We had to talk about the 'short girl with the black hair and straight bangs' without talking about the 'Asian' girl. It was a real pain, but I guess it got us thinking about other characteristics than skin color."

"Yeah. The problem is that you can't recognize skin color then," Jasmine said. "I like the color of my skin. I like yours, too."

I'd laid in my rough sketch and started mixing paints on my palette. Talking about the color of her skin made me realize that it wasn't just one color. There were places where it seemed much lighter and where the streak of light fell, it had spots that looked almost white. I wondered if I painted Kelly if I could see those differences in skin tone from one part of her body to another and if the variation was as great as on Jasmine.

"Um… Jett?"

"Yeah?"

"Don't you usually paint… um… in, like, your underwear?"

"Yeah. Mom hates it if I have paint on my clothes."

"So, why aren't you in just your jockeys now?"

"Oh… uh… well, I thought you'd be more comfortable…"

"I think I'd be more comfortable if I saw you like I do online when you're painting."

"Okay." Now I was embarrassed. I know I blushed a thousand shades of red while I stripped off my jeans and T-shirt. Jasmine giggled. "What?"

"It looks silly with your socks on."

"Oh. I forgot." I pulled the socks off and quickly turned back to the easel and started applying paint to my sketch.

We chatted while I painted and Jasmine became more relaxed. As she relaxed, so did I. I was completely consumed by putting my beautiful friend on canvas. Eventually, though, she fell silent, absorbed in her phone while I was focused on the paint. It was coming along okay, but I was spending too much time on the sheet instead of on Jasmine. The contrast between the white fabric and her mocha skin was captivating.

"Um… Jett? I need to pee. Can I get up and take a break for a few minutes?"

"Huh? Oh, god! I'm sorry!" I swung toward her and flicked a picture on my cell phone. "Go ahead. I never intended to keep you in one position for so long. You must be cramped."

"No. It's okay," she said, rolling out of bed. "I almost went to sleep. I just need to pee." She closed the bathroom door and I realized I needed to use the bathroom, too. And I was hungry. I'd packed us sandwiches and soft drinks, so I set them on the table and invited Jasmine to help herself when she came out of the bathroom. I went in and took a long leak. I started washing my hands and heard Jasmine singing outside the door.

"Twinkle, twinkle little star…" I kept washing my hands until the song was finished and I sang along with her. We were both laughing when I came out of the bathroom.

"Our moms should have taught us 'Tinkle, tinkle,' instead," I said. "Really, couldn't they have come up with a better handwashing song?"

"Oh, yeah. I can just imagine our Moms trying to teach us 'Slow Hands.' No wait, they'd need something from closer to when we were born, not contemporary. Yes! Yes! That's it!" She started singing an old Alanis Morissette song.

> *Ooh this could get messy*
> *Ooh I don't seem to mind*
> *Ooh don't go telling everybody*
> *and overlook this supposed crime*
> *We'll fast forward to a few years later*
> *And no one knows except the both of us*
> *And I have honored your request for silence*
> *And you've washed your hands clean of this*

It was about then, when we were laughing about the songs our mothers could have taught us to keep us washing our hands for forty-five seconds, that I realized Jasmine was still naked. I mean. I knew she was, but she wasn't over on the bed posing. She was just sitting right beside me and I was just in my underpants. I started thinking of her as a naked girl within arm's reach of me.

"We'd… better get started again," I said. I almost knocked over my Coke as I went to the easel. Jasmine picked up her napkin from where it fell to the floor as she jumped up. *Oh!* I'd never been that close to a wet open pussy. She jumped on the bed, bouncing everything.

"Okay. Get me in position," she said as she leaned against the pillows. I looked at the picture on my phone and directed her as she settled in. Of course, none of the folds and drapes of the sheet were the same, but there was nothing I could do about that. I'd spent enough time on it. I just made sure the same part was covered and that she gripped the sheet in her left hand just at the level of her pussy.

THERE WAS SOMETHING about Jasmine that I noticed in the next two hours that I'd never seen before. We didn't talk as much, but she seemed to lose interest in her phone and stayed focused on me. My boner never really went down and the more she looked at me, the harder it got. I caught a slight movement and saw that she'd clenched her butt cheeks a little. There was the tiniest indentation in the perfect roundness. I managed to capture it.

In the last hour, I'd captured little details about her that I'd never noticed. Some of them, like a tiny dark spot under her left ear, were just physical things. But what I was capturing felt like more of her personality. She was sexy, carefree, entertaining, and… I guess she looked passionate. I could imagine myself crawling beneath the sheet with her and… and…

"I think that's all," I said, laying my brushes and palette aside. I grabbed my cell phone and snapped a couple pictures of it and one more of Jasmine just before she stretched and got out of bed.

"Oh, good. I want to see."

She pushed in front of me, trapping me against the air conditioner with her bare butt pressed up against me. She reached back and caught my hand, drawing it around her to hold against her stomach. Her back pressed against my bare chest. Jas was breathing deeply. She pulled my other hand around her and rested it on her left hip. Her bottom clenched again and trapped my cock between her cheeks. I was holding naked Jasmine in my arms.

But that wasn't enough. She moved my right hand first, pulling it up to cup her breast. When her soft globe was firmly in my hand, she squeezed and let out a long slow moan. This was accompanied by her dragging my more than willing left hand down to her wet slit while still rhythmically clenching her butt cheeks against my cock. I was gasping for air and certain that I'd cream my jockeys in a few more seconds.

Jasmine turned in my arms letting go of my hands so they could slip around to her back and butt. She wrapped her arms around my neck and brought her lips to mine. It was not a passionate kiss… not at first. Her lush lips moved across mine, exploring to find the most comfortable match. When her little tongue touched them, it was like tasting to see if she'd like the flavor and when she decided she did, opening farther to probe more deeply. Her soft breasts pressed into my chest as I gripped her bare buns.

She pulled away from my lips so we could look into each other's eyes. There were tears in hers.

"You found me," she whispered. "You found the real me—the insecurities I hide behind bravado, the fear of letting go, the… lust. Make love to me, Jett. We have a hotel room and a bed and I'm naked in your arms. Make love to me."

It wasn't difficult to convince me. If she'd asked me to fly out the window like a bird, I would have.

She tugged my briefs down and tossed them to the side, touching my cock with her hand for the first time. I pulled her back to me for a kiss. For the first time in my life, I was holding a naked girl against my bare skin. My hard cock was pressed against her smooth taut belly. I kissed her hungrily.

She jumped away from me and landed on the bed, sliding under the sheet, and holding it again like she had in her pose.

"Are you sure, Jasmine?"

"Jett, I've wanted this for three years and never knew what it was I wanted. You stripped me naked in front of my own eyes. You brought me face to face with my desires. Holding the sheet like this, Jett… I'm inviting you… I'm begging you to come and make love to me."

I didn't just jump between her legs and thrust. I wanted to explore and love every part of her body. I wanted to kiss her and suck her turgid nipples. I wanted to touch her and weigh her breasts in my hands. I wanted to taste her juices off my fingertips and find where the sensitive spots were. I'd seen her get herself off in front of me on Skype dozens of times. I wanted to see if I could duplicate what she'd done and bring her to that same point of orgasm.

Jasmine was of like mind—not only about me exploring her, but about her exploring me. She touched me, tasted me, stroked my cock and both of us exploded before we'd managed to put the parts together.

"God! I'm sorry," I said. I'd just sprayed semen all over her stomach and her hands were drenched in it. My hands were likewise slippery with her juices. "I'll go wash and get something to clean you up with."

"Jett! Baby, relax. Your mom isn't here and we're about to get a lot messier." I hadn't softened much even as much as I'd come and Jasmine was still stroking the sensitive length of my cock.

"Really? You aren't disgusted by it?" In answer, she pulled her semen-covered hand up and looked at it. She grabbed my jockeys from the corner of the bed where they'd landed and wiped the big glops off.

"Nope. Not disgusted at all. Come to me, baby." I rolled on top of her and she gripped my cock again to guide it to her waiting pussy. Jasmine kept everything trimmed neatly and shaved bare on her pussy lips so she could show us when we Skyped. My cock slid between the smooth lips and with a little thrust I was in her. She pulled on me until our pubic bones were pressed together.

"You're in me," she sighed. "Really in me. I'm not a virgin anymore."

"Well, I didn't take your cherry," I laughed a little. "I watched you do that with a candle on Skype three years ago."

"I'm glad I did. It hurt. You don't hurt. You feel wonderful."

We moved together quietly, just enjoying the feeling of being coupled for the first time. I guess having just come, we were a little less desperate now and just enjoyed the feeling of our parts touching each other. We kissed and I looked into her deep brown eyes. We were so different from each other. But we fit together, perhaps *because* of our differences rather than in spite of them.

We rolled so I was on the bottom and managed to mostly stay connected. She pushed down onto me as soon as she was on top and I cupped her breasts in my hands, playing with her nipples as she rose again toward her peak. When she tipped over the edge, she took me with her and I had the delicious feeling of coming in a girl for the first time.

"Jasmine! We didn't use any protection!" I said in a panic.

"We were virgins. I get a shot every three months for birth control. I think we're protected enough. You *were* a virgin, weren't you, Jett?"

"Yeah. I don't think a guy can actually lose his virginity to a candle. Jas, this was so… I think I might…"

"Shh. Don't try to analyze it. Don't try to put words around it. Let's just do it again."

"Now?" I'd definitely softened and could feel myself slip out of her when she squeezed her pussy.

"We've got the room all night, don't we?" she asked.

"I guess. They don't book them by the hour here."

"Then let's not go home. Sleep with me and make love with me all night, Jett."

3
Aftermath

I HAD HELL to pay when I got home Sunday afternoon. Jasmine and I both sent text messages to our parents telling them we were spending the night with each other. Then we turned off our phones. That had to be the weirdest feeling ever. It was like cutting off the world. All that was left was in that motel room, and it centered on Jasmine.

We had enough sandwiches and drinks in the cooler that we didn't need to go out for dinner. We went next door to Denny's for breakfast in the morning but ran straight back to the room and had sex again. Then we did it in the shower.

Jasmine. Wow!

When we finally turned our phones on, there were a million messages. Half of them from our parents. Apparently, they didn't believe we were spending the night together because half the messages from our friends were asking if we were really spending the night together and if we were 'doing it.'

"I don't feel like telling everybody yet," Jasmine said. "I'm not ashamed or anything, but I just want to enjoy it being the two of us for a while, you know?"

"Yeah. I guess maybe that's why newlyweds go on a honeymoon. It's so they can just enjoy being with each other."

"Jett, I don't want to… I mean, like you are my best guy friend, but I don't want to change into boyfriend and girlfriend exactly." I started to object, but Jasmine put a finger to my lips. "Shh. Wait. I don't really know what a boyfriend and girlfriend are that we weren't already. But at the same time, I don't want to do this with anyone else. Not right now. I don't even want to Skype with anyone else. Can we just be…"

"How about if we're just with each other until after graduation in a couple weeks and then see how we feel?" I suggested. "Jasmine, I don't even want to think of anyone else."

"You got nude pictures this morning from Kelly, Lisa, and Charmaine that all had 'Me next' written on them," she laughed. "Are you sure you don't want to do them all?"

"If… If you're willing, I'd really rather just enjoy you and our friendship for a while. I don't know if we're in love. Like you not understanding what a girlfriend and boyfriend are, I don't know if I understand what love is. I know I want to be around you a lot and I want to do a lot more of what we did this weekend together. Just with you, Jasmine."

"Then kiss me again. I have to go in and explain things to my mother."

I HAD TO explain things to Mom and Dad, too. And Granddad. And Grandma and Grandpa Blackburn. Dad's father was pouring Grandma another bloody Mary. God knows how many she'd already had. It was already two in the afternoon. I managed to carry my painting to my room before I was attacked.

"Young man, take a shower and make yourself presentable to the family," Mom barked at me. "Don't come down here until you are clean."

I briefly considered just not going back downstairs, but I knew that would end up with everyone in my room. I'd just showered with Jasmine in the motel before we left. I shook my head and rinsed in the shower. Knowing Mom, she'd check to see if my towel was wet. It gave me a minute to pull myself together, though. You know what? I'd just spent the past night making love to my beautiful friend. I wasn't going to let this spoil my mood. I dressed in clean clothes and bounced down the stairs as if I didn't have a care in the world.

"Hi, Mom, Dad. Hi, Granddad. Grandpa. Do you need a refresher on your drink, Grandma?" I went to the bar and mixed a bloody Mary and took it to my mother. "Here, Mom. You look like you need a drink. Did you all have Sunday dinner together?"

"Would you care to explain yourself?" Mom demanded. "Where were you last night?"

"Didn't you get my text message? I spent the night with Jasmine. It was great, thank you."

"I called Jasmine's mother. She thought the two of you were here."

"No. We rented a room. Wait till you see the painting I did of her. She's so beautiful."

"Painting?" Granddad chuckled. "Is that what you were doing?"

"Well, not all night. I finished the painting before we did anything else, though. It was really great."

"Is that all you have to say for yourself after spending the night with some girl in a filthy motel room?" Mom exclaimed.

"First, yes, that's all I have to say. Second, it wasn't some girl; it was Jasmine. Third, the room was really quite clean and I cleaned up all my painting mess before we left this morning," I said. I saw that there was a big bowl of Chex Mix in front of Grandma and helped myself as I went into the kitchen to get a DP. I went back in to sit beside Grandma and have more of the mix. "What have you all been doing today?"

"We've been talking about you," Dad said. "You had us very worried. You turned off your phone."

"I really didn't want to be disturbed, Dad. I let you know I was fine and who I was with."

"You know you aren't allowed to stay out all night," Mom almost shrieked.

"Mom, you and Dad have been telling me for three months how things have changed now that I'm eighteen and I need to be taking care of myself. So, I'm eighteen and I took care of myself."

"You still live under this roof and you need to abide by our rules."

"You've told me that you'll be charging rent for me to stay in that little room after I graduate. I'll be moving out by mid-summer. Earlier if you really want me to. I have finals next week, but then we have a week clear before graduation. I can use that time to look for housing," I said calmly.

"How much rent?" Grandma asked leaning in toward me.

"A thousand a month," I whispered back to her.

"For a thousand a month you can have the whole lower level of our house," she giggled. That was an intriguing possibility but I was hoping to find something for around a hundred.

"It's not necessary for you to be looking for another place to live, son," Dad said. Mom started to interrupt, but Dad held up his hand to her. "Charging you rent was to give you a taste for the realities of life, not to punish you or to make you think you weren't welcome. We set the rent high so you'd realize that even though you were an adult, you were still a dependent."

"Thank you for finally explaining that, Dad, but my $50 weekly allowance won't even cover my lunches. I still need to go out and find a job and find a place I can afford to live."

"You can work off your rent here," Dad said.

"How?"

"You can cook, clean, do laundry, and yard maintenance," Mom said.

"Sounds like slave labor," Grandma giggled.

"He needs to learn responsibility," Mom declared.

"At what point did you learn that, Isobel?" Granddad asked. "My recollection is that you got your first job at twenty-five and were in it just long enough for Jack to marry you. And at that time, you were still living at home."

"Times have changed, Dad. Our generation doesn't have the benefits yours did. Everything is more expensive," Mom said. She cut off the conversation by turning it back to me. "This still doesn't resolve the problem of Jett running away from home for the weekend to have a sordid affair."

"That's not why we went away. We went where I could paint her picture without being interrupted. The rest just evolved."

"I'd like to see that picture," Mom declared. "I don't think you were painting at all."

That pissed me off and I left the room. I grabbed a display stand I used for letting my paintings dry and brought it downstairs to set up first. Then I went back to get the painting. As I looked at my room, assuming I'd be leaving it within a week or two, I decided to grab the three other paintings I was using for my portfolio review at the university. They were dry and I'd have to go back again for the wet painting of Jasmine. I'd do a full presentation since no one seemed to believe I was an artist.

I set the abstract painting I'd done on the easel. My mother rolled her eyes.

"Portfolio review for the university art program is to assess the range of the student's experience and ability. This is not the painting of Jasmine. This is my abstraction of a biology class. You wouldn't have liked the class any more than you like the painting, Mother. It was dirty and messy. Even though I wore latex gloves during the class, I still washed my hands several times after class that day. While painting this abstraction, I also wore latex gloves because I didn't want to get my hands in it."

Dad's dad got up and walked around it. Grandma kept bouncing in her seat trying to get up off the sofa and finally gave up and took another drink.

"I can see what you're getting at here," he said. "It reminds me of the butcher shop in the store. It's a little discomforting. Very good." Mom rolled her eyes again, but Grandpa was nodding.

"The second request was for a landscape or street scene. I focused on trying to capture details in the painting from memory. I confess that I've gone back to this painting half a dozen times to add something else I remembered."

"Like your Grandmother looking out the window," Granddad said as he got up and looked at the picture. "The tire swing. Her favorite flowers. A glass of tea on the porch. Thank you." He turned and gave me a hug. I switched paintings and my mother practically jumped out of her seat. She just stood in front of the portrait I'd painted of her. No one said anything, but even Grandpa helped Grandma up from her seat so she could get close enough to see.

"Portrait," I said simply.

Granddad had cautioned me about letting my mother see the portrait I'd painted of her but standing over her left shoulder, he nodded at me. Maybe it was a little mean of me but I had to show her. Dad put his arm around Mom. Tears were running down her cheeks as she stood in front of the painting. I'd never seen someone transfixed before.

While everyone was looking at the portrait, I retrieved the painting of Jasmine. When I returned, they were all still gathered around the easel. I removed the painting of Mom. Her eyes tracked it as I leaned it against an end table. I placed Jasmine's picture on the easel.

"Figure study," I said.

Grandma gasped and turned her head to bury her face against Grandpa's chest. He put his arms protectively around her. Mom did the same with Dad. Granddad sighed and I saw a tear in his eye.

"I hope that with this portfolio of paintings and a few of my drawings, I will be able to get enough scholarship funding that I won't end up a million dollars in debt by the time I finish school. Or even $100,000, which is pretty much the same thing." I picked up the dry paintings and returned them to my room. When I got back downstairs, everyone had returned to their places and drinks, lounging around the room. Mom looked up at me.

"You still love me?" she said. "Even after…"

"Of course I love you, Mom. You've always wanted what was best for me."

"Jett, when you've finished your portfolio review, I'll pay you $10,000 for the painting of my house," Granddad said. "That should pay for your first year's tuition."

"Really, Granddad? You like it that much?"

"It made me feel closer to Marta. Yes. I like it that much."

"I'll match that bid for the abstract," Grandpa said. "I want to hang it in the office. It just captures something." I was amazed. With $20,000 I'd only have to come up with another $5,000 to pay for my first year at the university. Trust my grandparents to come through for me.

"Same offer," Dad said startling me. "For the portrait." My mouth fell open. My parents were offering me $10,000 for school? That's all it could be. There was no way any of these paintings were worth what my parents and grandparents were offering me. I glanced nervously at the painting of Jasmine, still on the easel.

"I think you've already been paid for that one," Grandma tittered. Everyone started laughing. I guessed our family meeting was over.

⋯❖ ⅃Ⅎ ☼ ⅃Ⅎ ❖⋯

"What did your mother say?" I asked Jasmine at school the next day. Jasmine laughed.

"She thought we'd been having sex for two years! I told her I wished it was so," Jasmine said. "But seriously, Jett, it's going to be so hard to go back to virtual reality."

"We don't have to," I said. "Um… would you like to come home with me this afternoon?"

"Jett! You're kidding, right? Your mom would never put up with that."

"I think she's okay with it," I said. "She put two sets of towels in my bathroom last night." Jasmine smashed her lips against mine and I welcomed the kiss with passion.

"Hey, no fair," Kelly claimed as the rest of our crew arrived. "I'd have done it with you, Jett. Shit, I'd still do it with you."

"Not now, Kelly," I said. I returned to kissing Jas.

"You mean like maybe later?" I just waved my hand at her. Jas dug in the back pocket of my jeans, a pleasant sensation, and pulled out the painted jockeys I wore on Saturday. She tossed them in Kelly's direction without breaking our kiss.

"Hey, how about me, Kelly?" Derek tormented her. "I thought you wanted this handsome bod."

"You'd just be a consolation prize," Kelly sighed, looping an arm through his.

"Yeah, well, with Jasmine occupied it moves you up a notch, too," he said. Kelly swatted him with my underwear. "Uh, Kelly? Speaking as an expert on the subject, that's not all paint."

"Ewww!"

•०· ·❖))C ·☽·))C ❖· ·०•

JAS AND I weren't going to spend the whole week just fucking, no matter what our friends thought. We had finals and neither of us wanted to let our grades slip and endanger our scholarship chances. Having an extra thirty grand in my bank relieved some of the pressure, but I really wanted to attend more than one year of college.

I'm not sure what our parents expected. Maybe more than we were ready for. When we got to my house after school, the dining room table was already set for four. Mom was happily humming in the kitchen and the house smelled better than I could ever remember.

"Hi, Mom," I said, poking my head into the kitchen. It was, of course, spotless. "Jas and I are going to go up and study for our Calculus final."

"Certainly, dear," Mom said happily. "You go 'study.' Dinner will be ready at six. Please shower first."

O-kay. Jas and I had serious studying to do and were sprawled out on my bed with our laptops open and four others joining us by Skype to review for the final.

"Where's Kelly and Derek?" I asked as we got started. There were a couple of giggles and Charmaine exploded in laughter.

"If I had to guess, I'd say Motel 6. I recommended the Holiday Inn, but they cut the last half of today's classes."

"Really?" Jas asked. "They're going to do it?"

"You broke the ice," Rick said. "You're an inspiration to all of us."

"Speaking of which…" Charmaine started. Rick cut her off.

"Not until after finals."

Geez! All of our friends were pairing off and… Were they really all planning to fuck now that Jas and I had?

4

What the Fuck?

TAKING A shower before dinner almost caused us to miss the meal. We'd studied hard and then all of a sudden it was just Jas and me and we were naked. We stepped into the shower together and started washing each other like we had Sunday morning. I was still pretty much in awe that she would allow me to touch her… encourage me to touch her in ways I'd seen her pleasure herself on vid. And she wanted me… wanted to touch me.

If Dad hadn't pounded on the bathroom door and yelled, "Five minutes until dinner," we'd probably still be in the shower.

Well, that made dinner a little awkward since we were both kind of on edge. Mom and Dad were suddenly like foreigners I'd never met before. They just chatted away as if it was completely normal for Jas and me to be sitting at the dinner table with wet hair from our shared shower, hardly able to be polite because we wanted to be in bed. I wanted to be in Jas.

"When will you present your portfolio at the University, dear?" Mom asked.

"Oh. I sent the electronic files by email this morning. I don't know if they'll call me in for a live interview or just a video chat. If they like the pictures, that is. I got an email receipt thanking me for sending them over," I said.

"What are your plans for school, Jasmine?" Dad asked.

"I've been accepted in the School of Business," she sighed. "Not as exciting as Jett's art. But I think I'd be good at marketing and advertising. I guess we'll see."

"So, staying local. We can discuss remodeling your room if you want, Jett. I don't think the rent would go up."

"I… What?"

"It would still be cheaper than renting an apartment together. I know Sondra's apartment wouldn't have room for both of you. We can have the work done this summer so it won't interrupt your school plans."

Oh. My. God. My parents had already jumped to the conclusion that Jasmine and I planned to move in together. Live together. Did they think we were going to get married?

Way to kill the buzz, parents.

Jasmine gripped my leg so tightly, I could feel the moisture being sucked out of the atmosphere. Especially any that had been gathering between her legs.

As soon as dinner was over and we cleared the table, Jas grabbed her books and I took her home.

⋅∘⋅✦ ꓒꓵꓰ ☀ ꓒꓵꓰ ✦⋅∘⋅

"I'm sorry," I said when we got to her house. "My Mom… I can't believe Dad…"

"I know. Come in with me. Maybe we can at least make out a little, okay?"

"You know I'd love that."

We walked up to Jasmine's apartment and she unlocked the door, just walking in like usual, except I was right behind her. The place was kind of dark and she flipped the light switch on.

"Mom! I'm home. Jett's with me and we're going to go study. In my room."

There was a clatter in front of us and somebody rolled off the couch into the coffee table, knocking drinks all over. Jasmine's Mom jumped up and started tucking her shirt into her pants.

"Jasmine! I… uh… didn't expect you home… so soon. I was just having a drink with Ray. Um… my friend. Ray." A big dude stood up from the floor behind Mrs. Davis and he was fastening up his clothes, too.

"Oh. My. God," Jas whispered. "You… When did you… In the living room?"

"Well, you have a boyfriend now. I thought you were staying at his house tonight. I didn't see any reason…" Jasmine's mother stopped and looked at the two of us just staring. "Are you all right? Did you have a fight? Oh, baby. I'm so sorry."

"Forget it, Mother! I… have a headache. I'm going to my room." She turned to look at me with a look of total confusion on her face. "I'm sorry, Jett." She slammed her lips against mine and then shoved me back out the door. "We'll talk. Later."

•0•⟶ ⟩⟨ ⟩⟨ ⟵•0•

HALF AN HOUR later, I was in my room on Skype with Jas. She was as frustrated as I was and couldn't sit still. She was pacing around her room, shedding clothes, and then putting them back on. She'd take off her T-shirt and then turn around and put on a silk blouse. Then she took that off and grabbed a sweatshirt. The whole time she paced around, talking non-stop.

"I can't believe we walked in on my mother giving a guy a blowjob! What the hell did she think she was doing? She's my *mother*, for God's sake. She's never had a man in the house before. I'm telling you, I honestly thought she was a lesbian. I mean, I know my dad died in Afghanistan, but I thought she just didn't like guys. I've never even heard her speak to a man before. And I don't think he's leaving. I heard her bedroom door close. Not the apartment door. Just her bedroom door. My mother! Is having sex! With a man! In the next room! What am I going to do, Jett? I don't understand anything."

"Jas, honey, I don't know. My parents were acting all weird, too. How are we supposed to figure them out? I'm just… I'm here for you, Jas."

"I know, Jett. I was so turned on when we were in the shower and then they started talking about us living together and remodeling your room. I just freaked out. But then… Finding my mother with a man…"

"It's too weird," I agreed.

"I want your penie in my snootch," Jas cried. She finally stopped putting clothes back on and just stripped off everything she was wearing. "Show me, Jett. Please?" Well, that was almost getting back to normal. I wanted to be in her snootch as well but stripping off and masturbating together was familiar territory and it didn't take long for me to get naked.

•·•→))C ☼))C ←•·•

Jas avoided me at school. I saw her once at her locker, but by the time I got there she'd disappeared. I got a garbled text message that I interpreted to say 'Talk after school.' I was really worried that I'd lost my best friend, so I hardly noticed when Kelly bounced up next to me.

"Come on. Let's have lunch," she said, grabbing my arm. She started dragging me toward the front of the school.

"Kelly, the cafeteria is that way," I said, pointing behind us.

"Yeah, but since you broke up with Jas, I thought you could take me down to The Grind for lunch. Then we could go to my place and get it on."

"What? Wait!" I pulled up short and looked at Kelly. Kelly is one of my best friends—part of the inner circle. She's been right up there in my fantasy material for a long time. She's sent me such close-up photos of her tits that I could count the freckles and memorize their locations. But nothing was adding up—especially with the morning photo I'd received from her.

"What about you and Derek? The picture you sent me showed come dripping out of your twat."

"Yeah. Icky stuff. Dries like cement. Took me forever to scrub it off this morning. I should never have let it dry overnight, but I thought it would be sexy. Wrong!"

"Derek?" I repeated.

"One and done," she sighed. "He barely got it into me before he came. Then he was all in a panic that my mother would discover us. He jerked up his pants and ran. He chatted from Dee's house last night. You know how they do. They had all the blankets in the house stretched across chairs in the family room to make a tent and planned to spend the night there. They really don't want to grow up."

"Um… I don't know what to say. But…" I started thinking about what Kelly had started with. "What do you mean I broke up with Jas? I didn't break up!"

"Well, it's obvious you aren't with her, isn't it? Have you even talked to her today?" Kelly demanded.

"She sent me a message to meet after school."

"Come on, Jett. You've been blown off. Let's go to lunch."

"Maybe later, Kelly," I said. I turned away from her and headed toward the art room.

IT SEEMED LIKE my whole world had been turned on its head in the past four days. Twice. Friday night, I watched Jas masturbate on camera for me. And a few others in the group. Saturday, we had sex for real and discovered how much better that was. Sunday, my parents and grandparents looked at my paintings and promised me thirty thousand dollars for college after my mother finally settled down about my sordid affair. Monday morning, I found two sets of towels in my bathroom—a tacit invitation to bring Jas home with me.

Then all hell broke loose. All of a sudden, my parents were talking about remodeling my room so Jas and I could live together while we went to college. *Fuck!* We'd spent one night together and, as usual, my parents had our lives planned out for the next twenty years. To complicate matters, when we got to Jasmine's apartment, we found her mother wrapped up in the arms and other body parts of some guy Jas had never met.

Monday night, I watched Jas masturbate online. Just for me. And I came for her.

And Tuesday… What the fuck was happening today? Jas refused to meet me until after school. Kelly had sex with Derek who then went to spend the night with Dee. Kelly told me I'd broken up with Jas and asked me to have sex with her. And I was fucking confused!

I admit that I started by pretty much just throwing paint at the canvas. My friends and I all promoted the idea that we were independent thinkers, not subject to emo like the millennials were. We recognized that the world was fucked up and there was nothing we could do about it. Nihilists. But all at once I was caught in a torrent of emotions that I'd never had to deal with and didn't even have a vocabulary for. 'Use your words, Jett,' every adult in my life had said. I wasn't supposed to act out, I was supposed to use my words to describe what was bothering me. Well, why the fuck hadn't they taught me words to describe how I'd feel when the girl I'd just discovered sex with dumped me? What were the words that described how I felt about my parents interfering and manipulating my life? What were the words that were supposed to help me deal with my friends turning into real live sex fiends?

I built broad, angry, hateful, happy, loving, sorrowful, panicked, brutal, tense, beautiful shapes on the canvas. I scraped the tissue of my heart and spattered it on the painting. I poured out my frustration.

"That's it! Give 'em hell, Jett. Stick it to the man!" Rick yelled when he walked into the art room for final period. I'd spent the entire afternoon here. At least I didn't have any exams this afternoon, so my absence from class wouldn't really be noticed.

"That's so sad," Ariel said as she slipped past to her seat. Tears were streaming down her face. My generation's embodiment of emo.

"That does it. I'm just gonna kill myself," Lonnie said. "Everybody is against us. It's time to stop participating. Let them end the world without me."

Somehow, everyone was seeing something different in the abstract painting I'd managed to slop together in the past three hours. I covered it up so no one else could see it. I just sat there through the last period, staring at the cover I'd used as if I could see through it to the painting beneath.

•ᴏ••❖ ᴐᴎ ☽ ᴎᴐ ❖••ᴏ•

"Jᴇᴛᴛ? I ᴡᴀs waiting outside. I thought you'd really… that you hated me… and I thought you abandoned me… and that we weren't…" Didn't seem like Jas could finish a sentence. I turned toward her from where I was still staring at the cover over my painting. "Then Rick said you were in here and were probably getting ready to burn the building down, but Ariel said you were really depressed, and Lonnie said you were probably going to kill yourself, and I came running in here. Please don't hurt anyone, Jett."

"I won't. I was just confused. I guess I still am. Why did you avoid me all day?"

"Because I didn't want to have these moments with you in public. And it was only the morning and then you disappeared. And Kelly didn't come to lunch and I thought you'd gone off with her."

"I had to paint. I was… I guess…"

"Yeah. Confused. What did you paint?"

"I'm a little afraid to show it to anyone after the comments I heard in class," I said. Jasmine pled with her eyes and I pulled the cover off. She spent a long time just staring at the painting. It no longer seemed like anything special to me. Just a bunch of paint splatters on an expensive piece of canvas.

"I see what everyone else was seeing. Rick's been mad at the world since he didn't get a baseball scholarship. Ariel is like the original bleeding heart, and Lonnie's had suicidal tendencies for years. But it's not about any of those, is it, Jett? It's about confusion and heartache and growing and loving. It's about us."

"I guess you know me better than anyone," I sighed.

"I don't want to break up. Were we even going together? I… I just want to be us and not have everyone else making life-changing decisions for themselves or for us. Can we do that, Jett? Can we just ignore what our parents and our friends are doing and have fun together? Like sex? Like, maybe, right now?"

"You want to have sex here in the classroom?"

"I would if you wanted, but I was thinking that if we're just ignoring everything and everyone, we could do it in my bedroom or yours or go back to the motel."

"Jas, I'd love to have sex with you again. Right now. And I don't mind making it obvious that we're ignoring everyone else." I stood up and wrapped her in my arms so we could kiss. "You know what? Why don't we go to my house and make love? Then we'll take a shower and only use one towel. And when Mom calls us to dinner, we'll go to McDonald's." I kissed her again and she giggled.

"That's so devious. I love it."

"Oh, look. They're back together. Now maybe we can all play," Kelly said from the doorway. Half a dozen of our friends were standing in the hall with her. I looked at Jas and winked. She nodded slightly and kissed me again. I covered the painting and we walked out of the classroom, ignoring our friends. They all started talking, but I had a feeling no one paid attention to what anyone else was saying. Jas and I didn't. We just walked away without having acknowledged their presence and got into the Mini.

•◦•❖))C ☼))C ❖•◦•

Making love with Jasmine was like a hundred times better than it had been our first time and our sessions of watching each other masturbate didn't even register by comparison. We silenced our phones and didn't even hear Mom when she called us to dinner.

"Jett, I… Oh, God. Yes! Right there. I really… again! Really like sex with you. Oh, yes!" I knew Jas was trying to say something significant, but I was so taken over by the feeling of my cock sliding in and out of her that I couldn't even begin to make sense of it. Everything! Everything about moving in her, touching her, kissing her, just revved my engines. I knew I was close again. I didn't even remember how many times either of us had peaked.

"Jas…"

"How can you keep going, Jett? My God! I'm going to. Suck… suck my nipple some more. No! The other one. That one's too sensi… yes! Do it, Jett. I want to feel you do it again. While I'm coming. Can you…? Yes!" Jas screamed as I started pumping inside her again. I felt like I was emptying my whole life into her and she'd carry me around inside her forever.

Forever. That was a hell of a concept. What did I know about forever? All I really knew was right now and right now, Jasmine's pussy was clasping my cock and draining me of the essence of my being.

•◦•❖))C ☼))C ❖•◦•

"I tried to say something, but my mind turned to mush," she sighed as we cuddled together. "Do we have to get up?"

"Not unless you are hungry," I said. "I'm not sure I can move yet."

"Maybe we should just sleep for a while and then decide. You know?"

"That's good with me. You make me feel so alive and then you exhaust me so much."

"What I was trying to say… you know, just before that last orgasm. Oh, God, Jett. I think I love you." My breath caught in my throat. Did I love Jas? Well… "Scratch that. I mean, I know I love you. I just think that I always have. You know? Since the day we met at playgroup and your Mom wiped my hands with a disinfectant wipe before she'd let me play with you. Do you suppose it was really a love potion? Wipe her hands with the dew of this flower and the next one she touches will be her heart's desire for the rest of her life." Jas was trying to be theatrical with her voice, but she was so sleepy that she could hardly get the words out and my befuddled head was showing me some woodland fairy scene with magic sprites squeezing some kind of… Mmm. That was my hand, but the magic dew was oozing out of Jasmine as she kept my hand pressed against her pussy.

"I know I love you, too, Jas. But I don't know what it means."

"Yeah. Isn't that the dumbest thing ever? That's what was on your canvas today. It was like it said, 'Here it is. What are you going to do with it?' And everybody saw it and it was different for them. Here's what you've held in your heart since you were a preschooler. What are you going to do with it?"

"What are *we* going to do with it, Jas?"

"I'm going to let it wash over me, overwhelm me, consume me, and see what's left when it sets me free."

"Do you really think I'll ever be able to set you free?" I asked. I was surprised when Jas started crying.

"Don't talk about forever," she sniffled. "We're eighteen. We're about to go to college. We don't know anything about the world. I think you will be a very popular lover. Even with Kelly. I know she acts like a slut and like she doesn't care about anything but getting laid, but I also know she's wanted you for a long time. If there is one, there are others. Just love me now and let's let the future fend for itself."

Jasmine cuddled in my arms and was soon asleep. Even as tired as I was, she gave me a lot to think about before I went to sleep. I'd never really thought about the future before—not more than sending college applications off.

Eventually, I went to sleep, too.

5
Lockdown

WE SLEPT straight through and woke up starving. We got cleaned up and made love in the shower. It was hard to stop fucking when every glance showed me a new side of Jas that turned me on even more. The little dimple at the base of her spine. The difference in the color of the sole of her foot from the top of her foot. The one slightly crooked tooth on the far right side of her smile. Everything I discovered made me want to have more sex with her. And she seemed to agree. It was only our hunger that got us dressed and out of the house.

We didn't bother to even greet the parents. We just packed our book bags and ran downstairs and out the door. We drove through Starbucks and got coffee and breakfast sandwiches. Then, of course, we had to stop at Jasmine's apartment so she could change clothes since she had nothing to change into at my house and didn't want to do the walk of shame at school.

"Jasmine, honey, I wanted to explain about Ray…" Sondra started as soon as she saw us. She was carrying a huge mug of coffee and looked like she hadn't slept the night before.

"Not now, Mother," Jas snapped. "I need to change clothes and get to school. The Calculus final is this morning."

"But we need to talk," Sondra whined.

"Later, Mother!" We went into her room and Jas stuffed a nipple in my mouth as I sat on her bed watching her change clothes. "Just a little to tide me over," she whispered. Then she popped it out of my mouth and wiggled into her bra. In three minutes, she had scooped up all her makeup into a bag along with clean underwear, T-shirt, and jeans. We were off.

"We should really talk, Jasmine," Sondra cried as we closed the door.

"We really should, you know," Jas said as soon as we were in the Mini. "I just couldn't do it now. I have to chill first."

"Calculus final should do that."

⋯∘⋅⋄❯ ⅅⅭ ☼ ⅅⅭ ❮⋄⋅∘⋯

JAS SPENT WEDNESDAY night with her mother, after we tried to see how many orgasms we could have in an hour after school. We needed a little break anyway and when we Skyped later on, neither of us could get up the energy to masturbate. What I discovered, though, was that I really missed cuddling up to her as we fell asleep. Nobody, in all our sex-ed and online exploration, had said that sex wasn't the only thing we were missing. For the first time in my life, I wondered if my mom and dad cuddled up to sleep at night. And did my mom bathe him with anti-bacterial wipes before they did?

It was Friday, though, that all hell broke loose. I was in the middle of my Social Sciences final, the last official class of my senior year, when the school went into lockdown.

Fuck!

Our school had lockdown and active shooter drills more often than we had fire drills. It was a way of life. The chances that there would be an active shooter in the school sometime during our education had risen to one in six hundred during our lives. The likelihood for kids born today is one in three hundred. We practice lockdowns four times a year.

Mr. Kennedy calmly walked to the door and locked it. He cross-checked attendance and picked up the room phone.

"Kennedy, room one-one-seven. All twenty-one students enrolled in this class are present and accounted for, as well as the teacher. We'll stand by."

We all looked at each other and breathed a sigh of relief.

"We will be under lockdown for at least half an hour. That means you get an extra fifteen minutes to finish your exam. If you feel a need to let your parents know you are safe, please do so now."

You couldn't have had a precision drill team work more in unison than twenty-one students reaching for their cell phones. We'd been taught this, too. Send a quick text message to the parents to let them know the school was in lockdown, then silence all alarms, alerts, and ringtones. If there was a shooter, you didn't want to accidentally clue him in on where you were hiding. Of course, once you had your cell phone in hand, you couldn't help but check the news, meaning Snapchat, Facebook, and Instagram to see what was happening.

"Oh, my God! No!" We all jerked around to look at Sarah Lynn. "It's Lonnie! He's going to kill himself."

"Is that why they have us locked down?" Rick asked. "Lonnie wouldn't hurt us. We're his friends. We need to call him and talk him down."

"I can't get an answer," Charmaine wailed.

We all started sending messages to Lonnie asking him to call us and talk. It didn't help. There was no response.

FELLOW GRADUATING CLASSMATES. This is it. The end of school. The end of life. Today is my eighteenth and final birthday. You all deserve to know why it has to end this way. So, I'll tell you.

We're doomed. If it didn't happen today, it would happen later. The only thing you could do would be to delay it and I've chosen a time and place where you won't be able to do that. Look around you while you still have time. There is nothing here for you. We can't afford to live. All those things that our parents and grandparents held out to us as symbols of a successful life are out of our reach. We will never own a home unless there is a total collapse in the real estate market. The only way that a total collapse can occur is if there are more homes than people by a significant margin. Then, perhaps, the value of property would come down far enough that common people could afford to buy. Common people, but not us. We will still be living with our parents because our college debt is so deep a hole that our paychecks, should we be fortunate enough to get a job, is shoveled into it with no hope of ridding ourselves of it. And if we don't go to college? We will be living in boxes under the abandoned railroad trestle because even entry level positions require a degree.

This is no dystopian romance we're in. No band of brothers will win this war. No alien invasion will be repelled. No happily ever after awaits us. It's too late to stop it now. But there is one thing left that I can control. I can decide the way I die. Goodbye.

"WE'RE STANDING OUTSIDE Carney High School where students are just being released from their ordeal of being locked down while their classmate held them in terror," the newscaster said. "We've heard so much about school shootings and the traumatic stress induced by these senseless acts of violence. Were you frightened while you were locked in your classroom?" The reporter shoved a microphone at our group, not really specifying who should answer.

We pretty much all muttered, "No." I sure didn't feel like talking about our friend's suicide.

"You weren't frightened about this mentally ill man threatening to kill you all?" That did it. Charmaine stepped up to the microphone and laid into the reporter.

"Lonnie never threatened us," she started. "He was our friend. He didn't leave a threatening note, he told us why he was committing suicide. We tried to reach him, but he didn't answer his phone. We're all just sad we couldn't help him in a way that would let him live in this tainted world any longer."

"Our reports say an armed teenager made threats against the entire school."

"Armed with what? A bedsheet? Lonnie hated guns and was afraid of them. His parents kept all sharp knives in a locked drawer. I'm sure there was no rope. We've known Lonnie was suicidal for ten years. We just kept trying to include him with us and be friends. It's all that was left to do. You should really try doing some research instead of making up your facts to suit the story you want to tell."

"If what you are saying is true, why wasn't he under the care of a psychiatrist?" The newscaster wasn't giving up on this. She was making me pretty pissed.

"Why? Is there another drug they want to experiment on him with? What's this one supposed to do? Elevate his mood? Even out the swings? Numb his consciousness?" I yelled. "Didn't you read his note? He sent it to each of us. A copy must have made it to you. What kind of psychiatric counseling is going to cure an economy that is in the toilet? What pills give you hope for the future? What kind of doctor does it take to make gays, trans, women, and minorities feel safe from harassment and discrimination? What kind of fucking pill does it take for you to tell the truth about what we see every day. There is no hope for our generation. No homes and families and two-car garages. My first year of college will cost thirty-five thousand dollars. At a school that's supposed to be a public state-supported college. Private colleges and the best colleges cost two and three times that. You know why there are so many so-called foreigners coming to our colleges? Because they are the only ones who can afford them. Don't give us crap about mental health unless you've got a healthcare solution. We're eighteen and out of high school. How many of us are ever going to afford to go to a doctor or a dentist again? Lonnie was just more sensitive to that than most people. He's seen it coming for years and couldn't cope with the reality of the world he saw. Everyone has known that one day we'd turn and he wouldn't be there any longer. Why don't you go find some news to report on?"

•○•◆ ⊃⊂ ☼ ⊃⊂ ◆•○•

We sat in a cluster at the city park trying to find a place where we could grieve without our parents rushing us to preachers and counsellors. If we showed emotion at home, we'd end up as drugged out as Lonnie had spent most of the past ten years. We just needed to be sad for a while.

"Maybe we should all follow Lonnie's lead," Rick said. "At least State U. has invited me to practice this summer. They didn't offer a scholarship but said they'd give me a chance to walk on."

"I don't have Lonnie's courage or Jett's words," Charmaine sighed. "I'll just keep going forward blindly. Maybe a miracle will happen in our world."

"I cybered with Lonnie last night," Kelly whispered. We all leaned in to hear what she was saying. "He seemed so… I thought he was actually happy. We both had really good comes. I mean, I know what mine felt like and I could see the fountain he sprayed into the air. He said nice things to me. Even hinted that he'd like to go out on a date sometime. I never imagined that when we shut down it would be the last time I saw him."

"I'm sure you depressed him so much he killed himself," Dee said. "Get real, it's not your fault. We've known it was going to happen for a long time, just not when."

"Maybe he like, just wanted the image of you coming to be the last memory he carried into…" Derek started. "Is there an afterlife?"

"If so, I hope it's better than this one."

"You know, all week, or at least the past couple of days, now that I think about it, Lonnie seemed really calm," Sarah Lynn said. "I don't know. Wednesday we were in the Calc final and when we came out, I asked how he did. He grinned at me and said, 'Aced it.' And you know Calc wasn't his best subject. He just seemed really alive—like he had something to look forward to."

"When he came into art on Tuesday, he said, 'I'm gonna kill myself.' Maybe that was when he made his decision," I added. I thought about the painting I'd done and what it meant to different people.

•o•⇒))C ☼)(C ⇐•o•

Lonnie's funeral was Thursday. Commencement was Friday. Jas and I spent as much time as we could fucking each other and ignoring the world around us. And I painted. Jas was becoming my favorite subject to paint. She posed on my bed, out in the park, sitting on the swings at the elementary school, and shopping at the mall. Of course, I couldn't cart all my paints to each location, but I drew her and then painted at night, sometimes with Jas in my room cybering with our group and sometimes by myself. Kelly stopped by to give me a twelve-pack of new underwear to paint in. I wondered what she was going to do with all my painty drawers. But I figured that was her kink. I always got paint on myself and just smeared my tighty whities with whatever colors I was using.

Jasmine stayed with me Thursday night after the funeral and we just cuddled together in bed and held each other all night long. We were both naked, but neither of us wanted anything but the comfort of the other. We kissed. We cried. We went to sleep.

In the morning, she had to go home to get ready for commencement. Her mom wanted to make it a 'special day' and take her to a day spa. Jas consented. I mean, say 'spa' to a girl and see if you ever get rejected.

I was just setting up to paint one of the sketches I'd done when Kelly texted me and asked me to Skype. Sure. I could stand to see Kelly's sexy tits on my screen for a while.

"Aren't you going off to get your hair done and makeup and all before commencement?" I laughed when I saw her. She was still in bed and her hair looked like a small animal had nested there overnight.

"It's commencement, not prom," Kelly yawned. "I'll shower and dry my hair." We chatted for another minute or so and then she got right to the point. "Jett, we're out of school. I'm going to start work at Donaldson's, but I'm taking a week off. Or I should say 'another week' since I've done nothing this week but lie in bed and watch you paint your underwear. Um… I was wondering… Jett, will you paint me once, like you did Jas? I'm not trying to put the make on you. Though if you want to fuck afterward, I will. I don't even mind if Jas is there. She's obviously your girlfriend and I'm just the neighborhood slut. Maybe you want a pose of her and me doing each other. But… None of us know what happens next in our lives. I'd just like to know that somewhere I've been immortalized on canvas. Will you?"

"Sure, Kelly. I have to do some job-hunting next week and see what I can get that doesn't involve me working in grandpa's grocery store. Though I'm guessing that's where I'll end up. Let's talk tonight at commencement and figure out when is good," I said. Somewhere in the back of my mind I was thinking that I should talk to Jasmine and make sure it was all right to have Kelly model for me, but it wasn't really her decision.

"Um… Jett? Would you like to… you know… cyber for a while? I haven't done sex for anybody since Lonnie and I'm kind of horny." She pushed her sheet down and positioned her webcam so that I could see her naked body stretched out. "Would you? Please?"

"Yeah, Kelly. I'd like to see you come."

"I'd like to watch you, too. You know?"

I knew and stripped off my underwear so she could see that I was already hard for her. Our conversation was limited after that. She had a webcam she could detach from the laptop and hold in her hand while she scanned her body. I'd always loved looking at Kelly's tits. They were so pale with the little spray of freckles across the top. And her nipples were just made for sucking. I stroked myself and absently wished that a guy's tool was as interesting as a girl's equipment. My only task was holding off my come until she was ready.

•◦•◦❖ ⊃⊂ ☽ ⊃⊂ ❖◦•◦•

KELLY AND I had logged off when my email chimed. That was unusual. We hardly ever use email. I mean, why should we when we've got text? I glanced at it, expecting some kind of advertisement from Amazon or something. Instead it was a message from the University asking me for an interview in the art department next Wednesday.

Hell, yes!

I sent a text to Jas as I shot downstairs to tell my parents. Then I turned around and ran back to my room to put pants on. The parents were suitably pleased and I went back to my room to get dressed for Commencement. I kept getting distracted trying to decide what I should take to my interview on Wednesday, but eventually I got ready to go.

6
Commencing our Lives

MY MOTHER ACTUALLY made me open up my gown to show her I had clothes on under it. I suppose she was a little bit justified. Jasmine had sent me a picture showing me she had only a bra and panties on under her gown. Not to be outdone, Kelly sent a picture showing that she was wearing only a garter belt and hose. It's a good thing I did have trousers on. I'd have been tenting out my gown.

There was something like three hundred in my graduating class. Carney High isn't a huge school, but there are enough people that it isn't possible to know everyone. They tried to get us to line up alphabetically, but we didn't have to walk across the stage or anything. They would read the names of the graduates and we'd line up to shake the principal's hand and get the fake. They just give you an empty folder with a flier in it that says 'Congratulations! You're a graduate!' So, it doesn't make any differ-ence what order we go up in. It's just so there will be a picture they can sell us when we get our diploma in the mail.

So, of course, our little clique managed to all sit together. All except Sarah Lynn. She was valedictorian and had to sit on the dais so she could give her speech. She'd had to give the speech to the principal and her adviser and have her slides approved earlier in the week. It was timed and had to be over in five minutes. The motivational speaker who was brought in for the keynote went before her and had half an hour of us yawning. I don't think he had a single original thought in his speech.

As Winston Churchill once said, "Do not let us speak of darker days: let us speak rather of sterner days. These are not dark days; these are great days – the greatest days our country has ever lived; and we must all thank God that we have been allowed, each of us according to our stations, to play a part in making these days memorable in the history of our race."

As Steve Jobs who invented the computer so many of you carry around said, "No one wants to die. Even people who want to go to heaven don't want to die to get there."

And as the great influencer of your childhood, J.K. Rowling said, "It is impossible to live without failing at something, unless you live so cautiously that you might as well not have lived at all— in which case, you fail by default."

You get the idea. As the snoring students said, "STFU!"

We finally got to the student recognition part and Sarah Lynn stood at the podium and attached her smartphone to the projector. The first slide was a picture of a bunch of us in first grade. We were all lined up in front of the school sign with our mothers hovering over us.

"Remember this? When we were all young and innocent and ready to take on the world? Well, most of us made it through twelve years of school. We're sitting here ready to receive our diplomas—one more attaboy in the long list of awards and prizes that our parents have told us now that we have to pack up and take with us. I've saved a place for my diploma on top of the participation award for freshman cheerleader tryouts."

The slide was a box of crap that had been given out over the years. I had one pretty much like it. Ribbons, plastic trophies, and certificates. There was even the mortar board all decorated up for our kindergarten graduation.

The next picture showed the box closed and taped with 'Goodwill' labeled in big letters across the top. I don't know about the parents, but all of us sitting in caps and gowns thought it was hilarious.

"That's what all that stuff is worth now. Now we have the real prize. The high school diploma. We are now fully qualified to take orders at McDonald's, pull shots at Starbucks, and pump gas at Shell. Or to go a hundred thousand dollars in debt to get a college education. We might not be able to get a loan to buy a car, but we can get one to go to college."

She had a clever graphic that showed an old-time scale with a Tesla on one side and a scroll on the other.

"You'll notice that my choice of car is a socially responsible electric vehicle. It's good for the environment and cheap to run because it doesn't use gas. Not only that, it's perfect for me because I never got around to getting a driver's license and this vehicle is self-driving. That's what we've all been taught the past twelve years. We've been taught how to let someone else drive us around, feed us, educate us, entertain us, live life for us without us ever getting to live life at all. Where do we go next?"

Her next slide was of Derek and Dee in their infamous blanket fort. We'd all played that where we got all the chairs and sofa cushions in the family room surrounding us and spread blankets over the top so we had a tent. But Derek and Dee had never grown out of that stage. They often ran home after school, even as seniors, and built their little blanket fort and huddled under it to study. When we chatted online, it wasn't unusual to see them there, using flashlights to illuminate their faces.

"Got news for you, guys. Our comfy secure little blanket forts are going to turn into cardboard boxes under the overpass. Basically, everything we've been taught and told over the past twelve to eighteen years has been lies. There's no happy ever after waiting for us after graduation."

She showed a picture of the honor society that had been taken just a couple weeks ago. While it was displayed, a circle appeared over Lonnie's face.

"You all know that there is someone missing today and I can't finish my spiel up here without acknowledging my best friend and fiercest competitor, Lonnie. We drove each other. We compared test scores after every class. We drilled each other to memorize all the states and capitals, practiced for the spelling bee, had math flashcard contests. We always wanted to show that we were just as good as the other. A few years ago, Lonnie cut himself, so I did, too. He got really mad at me and told me that there were some things that were meant for him that I couldn't have. That I had to find my own way. Lonnie wasn't depressed suicidal, he was committed. He believed that the only thing he truly had control over was his death—that he could choose when and how he would die. So, he hung himself.

"We were told that he was dead when police arrived. They lied."

The slide changed to a feed of Lonnie in his room. We all gasped because it was obvious that Lonnie had sent a stream of his suicide to Sarah Lynn. He had the rope around his neck, but before he dropped, the door to his bedroom burst open, knocking the stool out from under him. He swung away and then back and his body jumped as a splotch of red erupted from his chest. His leg pulled up and his back arched. I closed my eyes.

"You lied to us. You took away the one thing he thought he could control. Lonnie didn't commit suicide. Police killed him. Thirteen shots as he was swinging by his neck."

The people on the podium, of course, had their backs to the screen. They'd reviewed Sarah Lynn's valedictorian address and it took them a minute to realize she was off-script. When the principal turned and saw Lonnie's body jumping, he was so shocked he fell as he jumped up to stop Sarah Lynn. But she'd already unplugged her phone from the projector and stepped away from the podium.

"I hate you! I hate you all! You lied to us for eighteen years. I hate our parents. I hate the police. I hate the school and the teachers and the principal. I don't even want your fucking diploma!" With that, she threw her mortar board down and ripped her robe off. She stood in just her bra and panties—what I suspected most of the girls wore under their gowns—and marched off the dais. "I hate you all!"

Sarah Lynn marched down the aisle as the room watched in stunned silence.

I don't know what came over me, but I dropped my mortar board and pulled off my gown as well. Jas caught my eye and did the same, we headed for the aisle and followed Sarah Lynn. There was a general move in the auditorium as many of our friends dropped their caps and gowns and left the room as the principal tried to get order restored with all kinds of threats and pleas.

Not everyone left. Not even half. Face it. Most of the people in my graduating class were drones. They probably thought the video Sarah Lynn played was an animation. I heard two guys near the aisle talking and one said, "What a fake." But there were enough of us who left that there were big holes of empty seats in the auditorium.

•∘• ⇨ ⟩⟩⟨ ☀ ⟩⟨⟨ ⇦ •∘•

"WE NEED A place to go," Jas said. Kelly, Rick, and Charmaine were piled into the back of the Mini and it was groaning as it pulled away from the curb. She had a good point. Where were we going?

"I need to paint."

"Can we watch IRL?" Kelly asked. I don't think anyone but Jas had watched me paint in real life. And she was modeling. But I had an image burned in my head from Sarah Lynn's commencement address. I wasn't sure anyone would want to watch me paint that.

My phone buzzed. I had it on silent through commencement. I handed it to Jas and she answered. I noticed she was sitting, all prim and buckled in, in nothing but her bra and panties. Both very skimpy and almost transparent. I jerked my head back to face the road.

"Hi, Granddad! Are you mad at us?" Jas had always liked my mother's father and took up calling him Granddad like I did years ago. I don't think she knew her own grandparents. "I'm so relieved," she continued. "We're in the car now, but we need to find someplace to go.— Really? All of us?— At least five. Maybe twenty."

"And paint," I said.

"And Jett needs to paint. He'll have to drop us off so he can go get his stuff.— Thank you, Granddad. You're so sweet. We'll see you soon." I'd already made the turn out to the country road where my granddad lived. "Granddad says to come to his place. He has room for all of us for as long as we need. You'll need to drop us off so you can go get your paint. Um… Would you mind picking up a T-shirt for me? I shouldn't run around in a bra and panties in front of your grandfather."

"One for me, too, please," Kelly said. I glanced in the rearview mirror and saw that she was still in her gown, piled on top of Rick and Charmaine. "I… um… didn't wear a bra and panties. I had the gown unzipped in the auditorium before I remembered."

We all got a laugh out of that. I don't think Kelly ever wore clothes unless she was out of the house. Well, that was a pleasant thought, anyway.

"I'll just pick up as much clothing as will fit with my art supplies," I said.

"I just sent a text to Derek and Dee," Jas said. "Who else should we tell?"

"Sarah Lynn. Be sure to include Granddad's address."

"Of course."

Fifteen minutes later, I pulled in the long gravel drive at Granddad's. It took a bit to unpack everyone from the limited back seat of the Mini. I reached in to help Kelly off the top and found my hand held snugly inside her gown against her bare breast.

"After you paint, I want to take your briefs off you myself," she whispered. I groaned as my cock responded to the feel of her skin beneath my fingers. She moved aside so I could reach in to help Charmaine. I expected play like that with Kelly, I guess. I didn't expect it with Charmaine. The feel of her skin under my hand sent a jolt through my body. She had a bra and panties on but having her breast in my hand did nothing to relieve my erection pressed against her.

She gave me a kiss and whispered in my ear, "What she said." I wondered if she knew what Kelly whispered. I glanced across the top of the car and saw Jas locked in a kiss with Rick and his hand petting her breast. Then they broke apart laughing and Jas yelled for our friends to come to the house and told me to get moving and get back. I got in the car and headed home.

• ❖ ❖ ☾ ❖ ❖ •

"Your mom's in bed with a migraine," Dad said when I walked in the house. He held a finger to his lips and then replaced it with a glass of bourbon that he took down in one long swallow. "You are still welcome to stay here," he said. "We're not going to throw you out. Jas is still welcome. We're just a little shocked, you know?" A tear ran down his cheek and he turned to refill his glass. I didn't think the one I saw him drink was his first. "And Jasmine, too. I don't think she'll have a problem with her mother. I worry about that poor Sarah Lynn, though. We'll need a copy of that video when we picket the police station. We just can't do it today. We just can't."

He patted my shoulder and turned away. I ran upstairs and started transporting the stuff I thought I'd need. I figured that I could come back for more clothes, but I grabbed all my underwear, socks, T-shirts, and jeans. I piled them in the back of the car with my painting supplies and half a dozen blank canvases.

"We'll be at Granddad's for a while," I said to my father when I was loaded.

"He called. It's okay. I talked to Grandpa, too. He's arranging a grocery delivery." Dad stood and looked at me with such a mournful

49

expression that I reached out to hug him. He pulled me tight into his embrace. "When I saw that clip, all I could think was that it could have been you. What terrible parents have we all been?"

"Dad, I'm sure you were no worse than your parents. And you survived. So will we. I love you."

He didn't respond to that, but just patted me on the back as I headed out to the car.

•○·◦❖ ⊃⊂ ☽ ⊃⊂ ❖◦·○•

I FELT MY phone buzz again as I was getting into the car and realized I'd never turned up the ringer. I checked it and saw about five messages from Sarah Lynn. I opened the most recent.

"Please?" That was all it said. Shit, I didn't have time to look at all the other messages. I just called her.

"Sarah Lynn, what do you need? I'm sorry my phone was still on silent. I only saw your last message," I blurted out.

"Please pick me up, Jett."

"Where are you?"

"I'm at Starbucks on Fifth. They won't let me come in."

"What? Why not?"

"I don't have any clothes on."

"Shit!" I said as the car lurched forward. "Sarah Lynn, stay on the phone with me. I'm on my way. It's about four minutes from here. How long have you been there?"

"Not too long. I'm getting cold, though. I didn't think this through very well."

"Where were you ever since you left the auditorium? We looked but didn't see you. You know a bunch of us walked out."

"I went to the park. I just got so upset. I didn't think I'd show it until I hit the play button. Now everyone hates me."

"We don't hate you, Sarah Lynn. Not even the parents. My dad wants a copy of the video because they're planning to picket the police station tomorrow."

"God! Just give our parents an excuse to demonstrate against something. I almost erased it."

50

"How could you stand having it for so long?" I asked.

"I… When I saw the stream on my Snap I just saved it. I couldn't bear to watch. He set it up to stream so I wouldn't try to copy him. He knew me too well. I didn't look at it until last night after the funeral. How could I… I never… God, Jett, I'm so fucked up."

I pulled up in front of Starbucks and opened the door. A shivering Sarah Lynn jumped in the car. I reached behind me and grabbed a T-shirt for her from the stack I'd piled there.

"Not that I mind looking at you," I said, "but you're cold."

"Thanks. I'll let you look when we're someplace warmer," she said as she pulled on the shirt. It was long enough that she could pull it down under her butt and over her legs. We didn't talk much on the way to Granddad's. She leaned her head back against the seat and closed her eyes.

•○•⇨ ᗜ ☼ ᗜ ⇦•○•

I don't ignore my friends.

Friends. Those are like people you'd do anything for. I'd do anything for my friends. Except I needed to paint. That's when I found out my friends would do anything for me.

"Do you need a model or anything?" Kelly asked. "You know I'm willing."

"She's so willing she hasn't put clothes on yet," Jas laughed.

"Um… No. I mean, I know what I need to paint. I don't need a model."

"I still get your underwear," Kelly said. "Make sure you smear a lot of paint on them before I take them off of you."

"Kelly…"

"Jett," Jasmine interrupted me, "you know you need to give her what she wants. If you can't tonight, that's okay, baby. Just know that… well, I don't think she's going to put clothes on until you've fucked her."

"But, Jas, I don't want anyone but you."

"Really? We're eighteen, Jett. How do we know what we want?"

"Well… I mean… Are you going to fuck Rick?"

"Maybe. Probably. But not tonight. We're all too fucked up to do sex tonight. But sometime. Yeah. It doesn't mean I don't love you. No more

51

than doing Kelly will mean you don't love me. Hell, I might do her, too. And look around. Granddad brought us air mattresses and bedding. He just gave us this big family room down here, expecting we'd all be in it together. No one is wearing anything more than underwear and some aren't wearing that. Eventually, Charmaine is going to jump your bones. And I think, somehow you lit a fire in Sarah Lynn this afternoon. I think Derek would do us both, but then he'd crawl back into his little blanket fort with Dee. Ariel is going to pine away if someone doesn't show her some love soon—she's so emo. Don't worry, though. I think Ford is all over that one. For now. Just paint and see what comes up." Jas lifted on tiptoe and kissed me. "And when it comes time for Kelly to remove your painted underwear, don't let her use her hands," she whispered.

7
Catharsis

THERE WERE ten of us in the room. Five others had joined us earlier but decided they needed to go home. A couple of us weren't sure if we'd be welcomed back at home. Everybody sat around talking while I started putting charcoal on my canvas and then laid in broad colors.

That moment. Just before I closed my eyes while the recording of Lonnie's death played in the auditorium. That moment when the first bullet hit. We couldn't see his face—it was just out of the frame. As soon as the door knocked his stool out from under him, his hands grabbed for the cord around his neck. But before he reached it, the red spot appeared on his chest and his leg jerked up. That moment the choice was taken away from him.

•·•✦ ⟩⟨ ☀ ⟩⟨ ✦•·•

"DO YOU NEED to see it again?" Sarah Lynn whispered from behind my left shoulder. I had hesitated before adding the splotch of dark red that I'd been mixing on my palette. It wasn't that I didn't know what came next. It was more like I knew that painting that stupid red splotch was painting Lonnie's last breath.

"I don't need to see it again," I said. "I know what comes next." I turned toward her and wrapped an arm around her. She pressed her face against my chest. She twisted slightly and pulled my hand under the T-shirt I'd given her earlier. When I gave it to her, she was wearing panties and a bra. They were gone now. She rubbed my hand all over her breasts and torso, then down into her trimmed pussy hair and damp slit.

"I know you see with every part of your body," she whispered, "and I promised I'd show you mine." She stepped back away from me and watched while I turned to the canvas, dipped my brush, and attacked.

53

◦-◦-⬦ ⟩⟩⟨⟨ ☀ ⟩⟩⟨⟨ ⬦-◦-◦

Her wail when I stepped back was joined by others in the room. Some in pain and some in anger and some just in frustration. There he was.

Dead.

◦-◦-⬦ ⟩⟩⟨⟨ ☀ ⟩⟩⟨⟨ ⬦-◦-◦

Granddad knocked softly on the door but when no one answered, he stepped into the room.

"Are you okay?" he whispered.

We were all clutched together, collapsed on the floor in front of my easel, crying. I don't think we'd cried so much at Lonnie's funeral the day before. We just hung onto each other and cried. Granddad looked over at the painting and tears sprang from his eyes as well. I held out an arm and he joined our group hug. We all wept.

◦-◦-⬦ ⟩⟩⟨⟨ ☀ ⟩⟩⟨⟨ ⬦-◦-◦

It took a while. Granddad pulled away first and with a whispered, "I love you kids," he left the room. We all settled down a little, still squeezing each other and brushing fingers across lips or kissing the hair on someone's head. Then we started talking. Eventually, someone cracked a joke about the difference between dying and an orgasm being that an orgasm lasted longer.

"What are we going to do?" Dee asked in a very small voice. It wasn't a whisper, exactly. It was like she was a little child.

"Lonnie told me…" Sarah Lynn started. She stifled a sob. "He told me that this was his choice. Whatever I decided, the one thing I had to do was live. I couldn't copy him."

"So, I guess what we do is live," Rick said. "I might envy Lonnie a little sometimes."

"I think I'm going to take this painty underwear," Kelly said. Jas looked at me and smirked.

"Yeah, well okay, Kelly," I said. "You can have the underwear if you can take them off without using your hands." Her gasp was so loud that I think she might have come. But just about everyone gasped.

54

"Hell, if that's the rule, I think I might start collecting painted underwear," Sarah Lynn said.

"I'll share the next one," Kelly said. "But not this pair."

She shoved me in the chest and I fell back on the mattress. Then she started to crawl toward me from my feet. I've seen Kelly naked more than just about anyone online. I've started almost every morning for the past year with a photo of her breast or her pussy on my smartphone. Just this morning, we'd cybered together and had a really nice come.

But to have the flesh and blood naked girl crawling toward me with her teeth bared just lit a fire in my cock. I wasn't sure she'd be able to pull the elastic waistband out far enough to get it past my erection. But she was a long way from doing that.

And everyone seemed as intent on her as she was on me. I know there were pictures being taken and probably a video running. People were all cuddled up and touching each other while they watched the live sex show in progress.

Kelly didn't just go for the waistband and try to tug my briefs off. She went for the elastic around my left leg first. She bit at it and tugged at it. Mostly at the elastic, but nipping at me plenty, too. She worked her way around my leg until her nose was buried in my crotch and she was tugging the elastic away from my balls. All told, she probably moved it down about half an inch.

Then she attacked the other leg with the same fervor only it seemed like she was nipping at me through the fabric more and once pulled down on my nut sack. It was a little scary, but she didn't hurt—just tugging enough to let me know her teeth were nipping at my balls.

She gnawed her way up my cock and I thought that was going to be the end of it for me. She spent a long time chewing around the head of my prick until I was going crazy with the need to come. Then she stopped and grabbed the waistband, but not in the middle. She dragged it down my left hip, then switched and did the same with the right. She gave me a nudge with her nose and I got the message that I was to roll over—most of the way. As soon as she could reach it, she dragged the waistband down over my butt and rolled me back the other direction.

I was lying on my back again with my flagpole tenting out the front of my briefs while the rest was dragged down below it. Still, she didn't go for pulling the waistband down. Instead, she worked on getting her nose inside it.

She twisted around until her bare pussy was over my mouth and her tits were dragging across my stomach as she worked the waistband up and licked my stomach down as far as my pubic hair.

I'd seen Kelly's pussy in a hundred different closeups online and in pictures. But it was right there above my face while she kept nudging at my cock with her nose. I lifted my head just enough that I could lick the entire length of her slit. Her moan brought her head up and I licked again, finding the little bud of her clit that she'd shown me so many times online.

Licking Kelly's fiery red crotch was heaven but when she came, she slammed her pussy down on my mouth and her mouth down on my cock so far that I erupted. I might have passed out a little bit. Well, I couldn't breathe and all the air was sucked out of my lungs in the explosion. Fortunately, Kelly rolled off me with a groan and I struggled back to full consciousness. On my right, I saw Jas immediately dive in to kiss Kelly deeply. Maybe she was trying to get my come from her, but I was so deep in Kelly's throat when I came that I doubt there was any in her mouth. On the other hand, Sarah Lynn went to work cleaning up my face and probing my mouth with her tongue. Kelly had spewed so much juice on me that I was pretty sure Sarah Lynn was getting a good taste. And since she'd made sure she was in a position so that I could get a hand in her pussy, Sarah Lynn was getting her cookies, too.

"You know, I think body fluids are another thing our parents lied to us about," Kelly sighed. "Yum."

"Wasn't that, like, gross? I mean his stuff from his penis in your mouth?" Ariel asked.

"Well, I didn't get that much in my mouth until the end. If his real name wasn't Jett, I'd nickname him that. Zoom! Right down the old throat!"

We heard Rick groan and looked over to see Charmaine with his cock in her mouth bobbing up and down. His eyes rolled up in his head and he fell back on the mattress.

"Yeah. What she said," Charmaine giggled.

"WHAT ARE WE going to do?" Dee sighed. We'd kept expanding her blanket fort until we had a tent that would hold us all. Most of us had underwear on, with Kelly and me being the notable exception. Sarah Lynn started the rest of the girls putting on T-shirts and discarding their bras and panties. There were a lot of tangled limbs as we sprawled every which way.

"I've got a week off before I start work at Donaldson's. I can go back to live at home, I guess," Kelly said. "My mom is probably upset over everything, but I don't think she's mad at me."

"I'm not very enthused about leaving everybody," Ariel said. "It's so sad."

"Well, I can't go home," Sarah Lynn said. "My mother already screamed at me on the phone and told me that I was possessed by a demon and not welcome in her house."

"God, Sarah Lynn. Why are parents like that? You can stay here. I'll check with Granddad, but I'm sure it will be okay."

"Are you going to stay here, Jett? I mean, how long are we going to be welcome here? Your other grandfather brought over a bunch of food. Your Granddad said he'd cook tonight, but then we had to figure it out for ourselves," Derek said.

"Yeah. Well, a few days. Dad said Mom was taking it pretty hard and thinks she and all the other mothers are failures. Granddad said she'd be okay once she figured out it wasn't all about her," I laughed. "I think I want to give Dad a chance to sober up. He doesn't usually drink like he was doing this afternoon."

"My mother hasn't rented out my room yet but I'd sure like to pretend I was out on my own. Even with college. Does anybody know if we'll still get our diplomas? I'd hate to have to retake something in order to go to college," Jasmine said.

"You don't actually have to have a diploma to get into college," Sarah Lynn said. "They can't refuse to release your transcript."

"It all comes down to money," Rick said. "I got some financial aid, but no baseball scholarship, the jerks. We'll be stuck living with our parents if they'll have us."

"My folks said my room would rent for a thousand a month," I said. "They did say Jas could live with me at no extra charge, though."

"Would they take the rest of us?" Charmaine asked. "I know it would be a little crowded, but we're doing okay in this little tent."

"Let's wait and find out who snores," Ariel giggled.

"You know, it's not a bad idea," Sarah Lynn said. "I mean living together. We'd really need more room than this tent, but I bet we could find a space where we could all contribute toward the rent. I understand there are a lot of houses over by the U that sort of ignore the maximum capacity rules."

"That would reduce expenses," I said. "All we have to do now is increase income."

•◦•✦))⊂ ☽ ⊃((✦•◦•

My phone buzzed me awake. How weird is that? I'm lying here stark naked with nine other people. Jasmine on my left and Sarah Lynn on my right started the night with T-shirts on, but they were both kind of wadded up under their armpits so I had a naked boob on each side and a wet pussy on each thigh. And still, my smartphone is under my hand.

I lifted it up and managed to move it to where I could see it without completely waking Sarah Lynn up. She just kind of ground her pussy into my thigh a little more. *A text message from Kelly?* I glanced around and saw her lying naked on the other side of Jas with her phone held up in front of her. I opened her message with a photo of her wet pussy showing on my screen. While I was looking at it and glancing across Jas to see Kelly, the phone buzzed again and I advanced the message to see a closeup of her left nipple. I've seen them often enough that I can tell it's the left nipple because there's a little dark spot on her areola just beneath the nipple. She glanced over and caught me looking at her. She quickly tapped out a message and my phone buzzed again.

"You can come get a closer look if you want."

I clicked a picture of my morning hard cock trapped between Jas and Sarah Lynn's thighs as both of them now pulsed to rub their pussies against my legs.

"A little occupied right now." I sent back after I'd sent the photo. Kelly giggled.

"You have to lick my snootch before you can have the cock again," Jas muttered to our friend.

"Really?" Kelly gasped. "Okay!" Kelly was in motion and wedging herself between Jasmine's thighs, nudging her pussy away from my leg. I heard Jas gasp and saw a mop of red hair bobbing up and down between her legs.

"Oh, good. That other girl was preventing me from getting my leg all the way across you," Sarah Lynn said as she moved until she was lying on top of me. "Do you mind if I help myself?" I wasn't sure if she was talking to me or Jas, but Jas kind of waved her hand and I just stroked Sarah Lynn's side with my hand. She lifted herself up and notched my cock into her pussy and shoved.

If you'd have asked me yesterday, I'd have said there wasn't a chance in a million that the second pussy my cock had ever been in would be Sarah Lynn's. She didn't start fucking, though. Once I was fully in her, she laid her head on my chest and I'd have sworn she went back to sleep if it weren't for the rhythmic pulsing of her pussy surrounding me.

We all lay there, not disturbing the other six sleepers in the blanket tent. The only real sound was Jasmine's low moaning that she stifled with the back of her hand as Kelly lapped at her pussy. I closed my eyes and lost myself in the sensations.

My phone buzzed again and I lifted it lazily as Sarah Lynn kept up the gentle pulses on my cock. Kelly. This time it was a very closeup photo of Jasmine's pussy with Kelly's tongue on her clit. I chuckled a little and I guess my cock jumped because Sarah Lynn caught her breath and started moving her pelvis along with the pulses from inside. I tried to lie really still and just let Sarah Lynn control what was happening. She managed to keep lying tightly on top of me as just her pelvis moved. I could feel a hum from her against my chest, though, and it was quickly joined by one from my own lungs.

Just as I knew I wasn't going to last any longer, Sarah Lynn's hum got louder and her pussy started fluttering around me. That was it for me. I let out a long low groan and emptied myself into her.

8

What Do We Do Now?

"**I THINK I'LL BECOME** a stripper," Kelly said. She held up a flier she'd picked up when we were all wandering around on Sunday. I was just thankful the place was closed until evening. We'd all returned to Granddad's basement family room except Derek and Dee. They had to go face the parents. It took Kelly about fifteen seconds before she was naked again.

"Um… Kelly? Don't you have to wear clothes to become a stripper?" Charmaine asked.

"Huh?"

"Isn't the idea of stripping tantalizing your client by teasing him? Building the expectation that you are *going* to take off your clothes? You can't be a stripper if you're just going to run around naked all day," Jas joined in.

"Oh, fuck."

"Besides, this flier says that the place is just topless. You wouldn't be happy if you couldn't show off your little fire crotch," Sarah Lynn piled on.

Kelly swayed over to me and began to rub up against me as she unbuttoned my shirt.

"I thought being a stripper meant that I could take off *their* clothes," she whispered while looking me in the eye. "Don't you think I'd make a good stripper, Jett?"

"If that was the definition, I'm sure you'd do great," I said. She started rubbing my cock and I pinched her nipples gently. We both moaned as she pressed her lips against mine and explored my mouth with her tongue.

60

"You really want to do this in a smelly bar with a bunch of random dudes who couldn't get a date?"

"Eww. You mean I couldn't choose?"

"No, and it would get very up close and personal," I said as I dipped a finger between her legs. I always loved how wet Kelly's pussy got when she sent me photos or we cybered. It was better with my finger there.

"They'd touch me?"

"You can count on it. These places don't make money by throwing guys out for little indiscretions."

"Oh, Jett. Push my little button. Are you going to paint me today? I'm so ready. To get painted, you know."

"Mmm. Yeah." I kicked my jeans off and took two hands full of Kelly's ass as we ground against each other.

"What position do you want me in?"

"Besides bent over the arm of the sofa?" Jas laughed. "You two are going to have to screw pretty soon or we'll all be dripping on the floor."

"Paint first," I said. "We'll get around to the other eventually. Weren't you just saying that the purpose was to tease?"

"That was for strippers, not for painters," Jas said. "Besides, if you don't tend to my little snootch soon, you'll be painting a picture of Kelly licking it."

"We aren't going to be able to live together if all we ever do is sex," Sarah Lynn said. "We'll all starve and flunk out of school."

"What a way to go," Ford said. I noticed that he and Ariel were still fully clothed, but she was sitting straddling his lap and they'd only just come up for air from their kissing.

I reluctantly let go of Kelly so I could put a fresh canvas on my easel and arrange my paints where I wanted them. Jas and Sarah Lynn both moved in to kiss Kelly. I saw a dark finger disappear in her red thatch.

"This is like performance art," Charmaine said. She cuddled up on Rick's lap and watched the antics of the three girls. "We should sell tickets for people to watch Jett paint his girlfriends. Just getting them ready to pose would be worth a few bucks."

"It's that whole teasing thing," Rick agreed. "Seeing those fingers at work makes me want to use mine." He leaned forward and kissed Charmaine's ear, which caused her shoulder to reflexively come up.

"Keep that thought. My cootchie is still cherry, though, so don't go breaking anything. Much as I like the thought, I'm not ready yet."

I turned to the threesome of girls who were now just giggling and talking to each other. Sarah Lynn licked Jasmine's fingers and then looked at them curiously.

"Your polish is chipped," she said. "I mean speaking of painting, we should get our polish out. It looks like your fingers have been soaking in a pussy or something."

"Yeah! Polish party," Ariel said, turning around and jumping off Ford. "Sorry, Ford, but I *never* get to do this with a bunch of girlfriends. Nobody ever wants me."

"We want you, Ariel," Kelly said. "You don't need to cry about it. You're so emo."

"I can't help it. Everything just affects me more than other people. Can I join your polish party?"

"Of course! What do we have in the way of colors?" Jas asked. "Charmaine? Are you in?"

"Yes! If I don't move soon, Rick's going to be in, too." The girls all went to their bags and started talking about the colors of polish they wanted. My painting was quickly forgotten. Rick said he was going out to play some ball. Ford looked at the girls lost in their own world and said he'd go, too. I don't think Ford had ever played anything that wasn't on a computer. I waved them on.

I stood at the easel and let the scene take shape before my eyes. There was a lot of giggling and comparing. Eventually, they settled into the serious business of painting nails and talking softly.

Kelly was sitting on the arm of the sofa with a towel under her so she wouldn't spill any polish on the furniture. Her left leg dangled down as her right foot was pulled up almost to her butt on the arm. She bent forward and started to paint her toenails. I snapped a couple of pictures on my phone and then started sketching the scene.

•·•·◆ ⟫⟪ ☼ ⟫⟪ ◆·•·•

IN SCHOOL, WE were taught all about dimensions. One dimension is a point. Two dimensions is a plane. Three dimensions is space—x, y, and z axes. Supposedly you can plot any point in space if you know the coordinates.

The canvas is a flat surface—a plane. So, we call paintings two-dimensional. That's a little like saying the eye only sees two dimensions. After all, the human eye is nothing but an array of light receptors on a concave surface. Still, we see life in three geometric dimensions. But in art, there are actually five dimensions. Shape, color, texture, depth, and focus.

Shape is usually the first thing I put on the canvas. Charcoal or graphite is used to sketch in where things are. It's a cartoon of where I see objects. I can see her butt contrasted against the back of the sofa. I see the shape of her knee under her chin. I see the casual elegance of her leg hanging over the edge of the arm. And I see the shapes of her friends in the background. Cartooning a painting is different than making a drawing. I don't need to capture everything with the graphite—it will just get covered up anyway. I only need the outline of where the shapes are in the composition. And after I've cartooned the painting, I don't really need the models to stay in the exact same positions.

Then there is color. I usually start by laying in broad areas of color, looking for the dominant hue, tint, or tone. I love color. I had a virtual rainbow of flesh tones in front of me. Jasmine's mocha skin started with a base of raw umber. Charmaine's lighter cinnamon coloring started with just a touch of brown ochre. Ariel's light Asian skin started with transparent gold ochre. Sarah Lynn bore a healthy tan that I started with copper. When Kelly's skin was contrasted to the white towel she sat on, it was obvious that her pale skin was not pure white, but rather an iridescent pink on which I would carefully paint her transparent red ochre freckles and nipples. Color. The first pass just laid in the basics.

A lot of the difference between surfaces we see is in the texture. There is an inherent texture to the substrate, canvas, that I have to deal with. Sometimes it is more pronounced than others. I can overcome it completely by using thicker paint or let the texture of the canvas enhance textiles. A light stippling of the terry cloth towels the girls were using, for example, differentiates it from the swirls of the sofa upholstery.

What brings a painting to life is depth. In traditional parlance, it's called chiaroscuro. This is where I spend the greatest portion of my painting time, capturing the way light plays against surfaces. How shadow falls between her breasts defining the shape as three-dimensional rather than flat. Painting the light is what shows the slight hollow at her hip, the curve of her eyes, the shine of her lips.

Painting the depth is how I made love to Kelly.

And that changed the focus. Some art tries to mimic a camera. Everything is in uniform focus. There is as much detail and light and depth in background images as in foreground. Other artworks show a complete disregard for the background as an afterthought to the detail in the foreground. I think that's why so many artists put drapery around their models. Otherwise, the background becomes too distracting.

I handled it a little differently. Everything around Kelly, the other girls and the furniture and the room, was there in the painting but a little less detailed. It made you believe that if you shifted your eyes, it would come into focus. But the detail and care I took with Kelly's pretty figure and intense concentration on her toenails held the eye and did not let it escape into the background.

•○·◦❖ ⅛C ☽ ⅛C ❖◦·○•

"I wouldn't mind if it was just the five of us," Sarah Lynn said. I gradually tuned into their conversation as they variously held their hands with fingers spread or placed cotton balls between their toes while the polish dried. "I mean us five girls and Jett. The six of us could live together pretty easily, don't you think?"

I wondered when it was that Sarah Lynn had become so well integrated into our little group. And Ariel. I would have placed both of them on the periphery until this weekend. As I came out of my painting trance and became aware of her voice, I could still feel my cock sliding in and out of her as she rode me Saturday morning. She had felt… natural. Her motions weren't frantic. She'd settled onto me and just held me in the embrace of her vagina until we both came. We hadn't repeated it. Yet. I was looking forward to the next time, though.

"That would be fun. I wouldn't close the doors on the others, though," Jas said. "We've been close to Derek and Dee for years."

"They've always been a couple, though, you know?" Kelly said. "I mean, it was never like they excluded anybody else. Derek jumped at the chance to fuck me. But as soon as he popped, he ran home and cuddled in a blanket tent with Dee. I don't think they've ever done it together, but you can't think of one without the other."

"Did that make you feel bad… that he ran off after you made love?" Ariel sighed. "I'd be crushed."

"Um… Well, I guess I kind of used him. I was horny and he was handy. The only bad part was that I didn't get off. He left and my pussy was still drooling, mixed with his come running out of me. I worked myself over with my vibe to about three good ones before I even left the motel. I didn't even think of him while I was coming."

"Yeah. We know who you were thinking of," Charmaine giggled with a quick glance in my direction. I just kept making little touches on the canvas, pretending to be focused on my work and ignoring them. "What's with that, Jas? Are you going to share Jett out with the rest of us when we're horny?"

"I think Jett gets to decide. You know, I almost made it with Rick last night," Jas said. "He had his fingers up in me and he's a pretty good kisser. When he hit my clit with his thumb, I jerked and came like a freight train, which was when I noticed his come squirting up between my fingers on his cock. It felt good. He was spent. I think someone had drained him not long before I got to him." She looked meaningfully at Charmaine, who just giggled some more. "But, like Kelly, it wasn't Rick I was thinking of when I came."

"As much as I like Jett and really want to make love to him again, I have to admit that when I came Saturday morning, it wasn't Jett I was thinking of," Sarah Lynn said. "I mean… It was, sort of. But in the back of my mind it was Lonnie's voice chanting, 'Live. Live. Live.' And that was what I wanted to do. I wanted to live and that's what I was thinking when I came."

"The little death becomes the little life," Jas mused. "Did you paint something new, Jett?" she called.

•○•⇨ ꭂꭃ ☀ ꭂꭃ ⇦•○•

KELLY WAS SITTING curled up in a ball on the sofa crying while the other four girls cradled her and soothed her. I looked at the painting. Damn

65

it! I didn't think it was *that* bad! Maybe I should just grab my scraper and scrape the canvas. I could put white fixative over the top and in a few days, I could paint something new on it. If I ever decided to paint again. *Crap!* What a fiasco.

"And everybody thought *I* was emo!" Ariel said as she put her arm around me and stared at the canvas.

"I don't know what I did wrong," I moaned. I looped an arm over her bare shoulders. *Bare?* I tore my eyes away from the canvas and took in Ariel's naked form pressed up against my body. *When the hell did **she** get naked?*

"It isn't wrong," she said. She took my hand on her shoulder and pulled it down onto her breast as she slid in front of me. "Sometimes it's hard for us to see the truth. When I look at this, I see Kelly. Really see her. It's okay for me because I see the whole world as pathetic and hopeless. Seeing Kelly is like a breath of open honest air. She's beautiful. I never realized how much. Someday, I hope you paint a picture of me. I think. It scares me, too. I think I'd rather have sex with you."

She pulled my other hand around her and pushed it down into her moist pussy. She just held it there while she rocked back and forth on it. That did some pretty wonderful things to my cock, trapped between her butt cheeks, even though I still had my jockeys on. I closed my eyes and just focused on feeling her. She pulled away.

"Not today. But sometime. I have to decide which would hurt me more—having sex with you or seeing your painting of me. I need to prepare myself." She turned in my arms, dislodging my hands but pressing her little breasts into my chest as she lifted her lips to kiss me. "You are really the only one who can comfort her. You should go to her now."

Great. The tip of my erection was poking out the top of my shorts and I'd just smeared precome all over Ariel's stomach and now I should go comfort Kelly. *Oh, hell.*

"Um… Can I sit with you, Kelly?" I said when I got over to the sofa. Jas and Charmaine moved over so I could get between Jas and Kelly. Kelly immediately turned her head toward my chest and wrapped her arms around me. I sighed. Sarah Lynn pulled my arms around Kelly as if I didn't know what to do. Well, I didn't.

"You didn't paint my pussy," Kelly whispered against my chest. "You only painted a hint of my nipples pushed against my arms. I don't look like I'm going to come or like I want to have sex with you." She raised her head to look at me, smearing tears and mascara all over my chest and her cheek.

"I'm sorry, Kelly."

"Sorry? For looking at me and seeing something other than sex? You're sorry for that? You're sorry that you painted me as if I was a real person and not a Snapchat sex queen? Why would you be sorry for seeing more than I think I am? I love you, Jett. Thank you. Thank you for seeing a me I never thought to look for."

"Kelly, you're so beautiful and sweet, how could I show you any other way?"

"I'm going to make love to you, you know. Probably the next time Jasmine lets me close to this beautiful cock. But I'm not in a hurry now. I don't want to just get it over with," Kelly said. "When we make love, I'll know that you aren't just making love to the pussy and tits I've been showing you since we were kids. And I won't be able to just fuck your cock. Not the first time. The first time I'll be making love to all of you, Jett Blackburn. I'll be making love to your heart, your soul, and your mind. Because I know you'll make love to all of me."

Jas reached across me and kissed Kelly. It was sweet and gentle at first, but the two girls reached for each other and I could feel their rising passion as their faces pressed together against my chest.

"When you're ready, sweetheart," Jas whispered. "When you're truly ready."

9
Interviews

WEDNESDAY WAS A big day for me. I'd futzed around all day Monday and Tuesday selecting paintings to take to my interview in the Art Department at the University. The biggest problem was that the canvases weren't all dry. Notably, the paintings of Lonnie and Kelly. I definitely wanted to take both of them.

I understand that old fashioned artists used to stretch canvas on a frame, size it, gesso, wait for it to dry thoroughly, and paint. It takes a lot of skill and precision to build a frame to stretch the canvas on. It needs to be perfectly square at the corners. Some classic artists would use the same frame over and over by waiting for their painting to cure and then removing it from the frame, rolling it up, and stretching a new canvas.

Of course, now you can just go to Blick's and get a pre-stretched canvas that's already been triple gesso'd and is ready to paint on. But for a young artist—especially one who has to buy his own supplies—pre-stretched canvas is expensive, even if you only get medium quality. A sixteen by twenty will cost around twenty bucks. On the other hand, you can get a heavy-weight stretched canvas laminated to an eighth-inch board for about three-and-a-half dollars. So, guess what I paint on.

The problem is that a wet board is really hard to handle. There's nothing to grip it by. No frame. No handles.

I talked to Granddad and he helped me create a corrugated box for them and we used duct tape on the back of the board to hold it in place so it wouldn't slide around and damage the paint. Those two pieces, I'd carry on the front seat of the Mini with the others carefully boxed in the back.

I woke up slowly on Wednesday morning. We were still sleeping on air mattresses in the basement of Granddad's house. Things had shifted during the week. Several people stopped in and we met others when we were out. Rick and Ford had returned to their homes. Derek and Dee didn't return after they went to Dee's house, but we Skyped every day. It had boiled down to the five homeless girls and me. Well, Jas and I could have gone home any time, but why would I want to stop sleeping with five sexy and often naked girls? And why would Jas leave me to them?

It's funny, though. Even though we were all pretty touchy-feely, Jas had been the only one I had sex with before this week. And not all that often. Starting Sunday night, the girls started rotating who was sleeping next to me. One night it would be Jas and Ariel. Another night Kelly and Charmaine. Tuesday night it had been Jas and Sarah Lynn. There had been quite a few shared orgasms as we settled down at night, but the only one who did a show online was Kelly. And every morning, my phone would chime with another picture of her. Or a body part of her.

I sleepily raised my phone to my face and looked at the morning's offering. It was definitely Kelly's pussy with the tuft of bright red hair above her slit, but the finger rubbing her clit was dark brown. "Guess who's getting me off!" I grinned. Jasmine's butt was up against my left side and Kelly was sprawled next to her. On the other hand, when I lifted my head slightly, I saw Charmaine beyond Kelly. Hmm.

But that meant the hand on my morning erection was not my girl-friend's. I turned my head to the right and saw Sarah Lynn looking at me. She smiled. Then, in a very uncharacteristic move, she wiggled her way higher under my arm and kissed me. We'd had sex the morning after commencement but I'd heard her say it wasn't me she was thinking of. And we hadn't kissed. In fact, there had been a few little pecks and an occasional tongue twister among us, but mostly none of us had done much kissing except Jas and me.

Sarah Lynn's kiss was unexpected and intense. I pulled my left arm out from under Jas and wrapped it around Sarah Lynn as she continued to move over me. My right hand was on her butt and it looked like we were headed for a rematch. She made that clear when she pulled her lips away from mine for a second.

"Can we make love?" she whispered. "I want to do it looking into your eyes so I know for sure that it's you and not a fantasy. I want to feel you come inside me and know that you are the one filling me up and focused on just me. Can we make love, Jett?" I answered her with another kiss and a little pressure from my hand on her butt to move her over me.

She still had a grip on my cock, so when she lifted up, it was easy for her to rub it up and down her slit, mixing our lubrication. The whole time, though, she was looking at me. I moved my left hand up to touch her cheek and let my fingers trace her lips. She opened her mouth slightly and sucked my fingers in. They probably still tasted like Jas from the night before but Sarah Lynn didn't seem to mind as she laved them with her tongue. She held them in her mouth as she directed my cock to her opening and slowly sank down on it.

I could feel her moan on my fingers. She let them loose from her mouth when she was fully on my cock and lowered her face to kiss me again. We continued to hold still while joined together for a while. I don't know if she was controlling the pulses in her vagina or if it was just something that naturally occurred in her. Nonetheless, I knew that if we did nothing more than kiss and stay connected, I would come in her. I wouldn't be able to resist.

She lifted up again and looked into my eyes. My hands came around to the front and I cupped her breasts, playing a little with her nipples. That started little pelvic thrusts. It wasn't like sawing in and out. I don't think I came out more than an inch each time she pulled her hips forward and then slid back. She wasn't bouncing on me, just that little thrust that I fell into rhythm with.

"Sarah Lynn, I don't know how or why we got together, but I hope it continues. You are like an anchor that I didn't know I needed. I love making love to you."

"Jett, I just fell on you the first time, letting all my sorrow drive our coupling. I want you to know that I've found something special with you—with you and Jas and Kelly. And I think with Ariel and Charmaine. I think we can all anchor each other," she said. "But right now, I just want to feel you in me. I just want to feel it building. And when it builds enough, I want to feel it take over my whole body and soul. I want *you*, Jett."

It got pretty hard to talk after that. I could feel every muscle in my body vibrating. And every one of Sarah Lynn's muscles creating harmonics with mine. Her whole face was quivering when she finally let go and the ripples in her vagina turned into spasms. I felt moisture on my cheeks before the first tears from her eyes dropped. I pushed myself firmly inside her and just let my prostate do the work from that point, pumping and pumping until I thought I'd pass out.

She lowered herself to my lips again and we kissed softly, caressing each other with our mouths and tongues. She kept her pelvis wedged tightly down against me, preventing me from fully softening and sliding out. Her lips eventually parted from mine and she hugged me tightly as my arms encircled her. Her lips didn't quite reach my ears, but I heard her whisper.

"I might be falling in love with you, Jett. I hope your heart is big enough for all of us."

•0• •◦❖ ⊃⊃⊂ ☽ ⊃⊃⊂ ❖◦• •0•

I NEEDED TO get ready. It was early, I knew, but I was antsy to get to my ten-thirty meeting at the U. I hopped in the shower and as the water beat down rinsing shampoo from my hair, the shower door opened and a slick body pressed herself up against me.

"What shall we name the baby?" Sarah Lynn asked. I slipped on the shower floor as I turned and would have fallen on my ass if she didn't have a grip on me.

"What?"

"The baby. You know. You just shot four hundred thirty-two million a hundred eighty-seven thousand two hundred seventy-one sperm against my ripe cervix. I counted. I think I felt every one of them hit."

"Sarah Lynn! I thought... Aren't you protected?"

She stared into my shocked eyes and smiled. "Yes. But you didn't know that. You need to think about these things, even if the girl is willing or aggressive. Like me. There are four more girls out there who want this beautiful penis in their warm wet vaginas. I know you had this discussion with Jas. Kelly is probably protected. My guess is that Ariel and Charmaine have never even thought about it. An unplanned pregnancy could put any one of us on welfare, in an abortion clinic, or—God forbid!—on the street."

"Christ, Sarah Lynn! You scared the shit out of me."

"I don't see any on the floor, but maybe I should soap up the area, just in case."

"Why'd you do that?" I scrunched my eyes together as she soaped my ass and used the detachable showerhead to make sure I was thoroughly rinsed. My cock was not quite rigid, but close enough that she felt it was necessary to soap it up, too. She kept stroking as she talked.

"We've been unfair to you, Jett. We've taken advantage of your good heart and friendship. We run around naked and tease you—not intentionally teasing most of the time, but we can tell the results pretty obviously. And you let us have our fun. But what you don't realize is how much we've come to depend on you. Not just since my disaster of a commencement speech, but it's been growing for a few years." I was panting as I got closer. She hadn't stopped stroking my cock and I was getting close. "Rinse this off," she said, turning me around.

She got the soap off my cock and her hands then turned me back. She sank to her knees and took my cock in her mouth. It was way too much and for the second time this morning I came inside her. A lot. It dribbled out the corners of her mouth and she spit the remainder out as she popped off of me. She grabbed the spray head and rinsed me off then pointed it into her mouth to rinse and spit some more. I just sagged against the wall of the shower and looked at my second lover.

"I'm not crazy about the taste. I appreciate that Jas and Kelly like it, but I'd rather have you come in my pussy."

"I won't object to that. Um…"

"Oh, yeah. About what I was saying. You called me an anchor while we were making love. That's sweet. So, you should understand how we feel about you. Of all of us, you are the closest to normal. Whatever that means. I know I wasn't as close to your inner circle in high school. I guess Lonnie and I invested most of our time in each other. But even Lonnie was drawn to you. Maybe we won't all stick around forever, but we all want to be with you… if you'll have us. I don't just mean sexually with you. Rick isn't interested in you that way. I don't think Derek knows what he's interested in. Dee either, for that matter. But we all still want to be near you. You balance us."

"Wow!"

"Yeah, a lot to take in, huh? Dry my back?" I took her towel and carefully dried her back and legs. "If you'll have me, Jett, you'll see a lot of this body in the next few years. Um… I didn't ask earlier, but can I catch a ride to the University with you? I need to go to the financial aid office and see if I can get some more funding now that my parents have said they're disowning me."

Sarah Lynn carried the boxes with the two wet paintings in them, which was no small task in the little Mini. I dropped her at the administration building and hunted for a parking space near the Art building. With the two new paintings, the four that were cured, and a portfolio of my drawings and sketches, I gingerly made my way from visitor parking to the entrance. I was trying to figure out how to get the door open when a pretty blonde opened it from the inside.

"Excuse me, could you hold the door for me, please?" She looked at me like I was crazy and then saw the boxes and portfolio I was carrying. Her look softened.

"Portfolio review for admission?" she asked as she held the door.

"Yeah. Thank you."

She followed me back into the building. "Are you any good?"

"I guess so. There are some things I'd like to learn, though."

"I'm not a professor. You don't have to play meek and humble. I'm in the art program. I'll come along to your review."

"You can just do that?" I asked. I figured my review would be with a professor or adviser or something.

"Portfolio reviews are open to students. We're supposed to learn something from the professors' comments and suggestions. Frankly, those of us who focus on watercolor are kind of second class artists. You do oils?"

"Yeah. Some acrylic, but mostly oil. My mother hates the fact that it doesn't wash out."

"Does she have rotor blades?"

I laughed. "Are you a pilot?"

"Yeah. Actually, I am."

"That's a good description. Mostly, she wants to make sure that my environment is sterile. She sneaks into my room and wipes down my easel and brushes with disinfectant wipes. I'm Jett, by the way."

"Eva. My mother was upset that I traveled across the country to go to college. Mostly, I think she was afraid that without all my ribbons and awards that I'd lose my self-esteem."

"Awards for your art?"

"Awards for everything. Out East, you only have to show up for something to get a ribbon or a trophy."

"I understand. I think those things reassure our parents that they are raising a child as precious as they think. It just taught me that awards were meaningless."

"Cool. Here's the presentation room. How many easels do you need for the paintings?"

"I brought six paintings. Two of them aren't cured yet, so I'm not sure I'll be able to display them on an easel."

"Well, let's see. You can lay out drawings and sketches on the table over there while I get display easels for you."

"Thanks. You're really being a big help."

•○·◈))C ☼))C ◈·○•

Eva was a little miffed that I was there half an hour early for my interview. She glanced quickly at my drawings and told me she'd come back when the show was ready to start. I carefully opened my boxes and set the dry paintings on the easels then debated how to show the wet ones. I had tape in the car, so I used my pocket knife to cut the flaps away from the cardboard boxes. They were only an inch deep, so I was able to set them on the ledge of the easel and fasten them down. It was like a shadowbox. Really cheap framing.

About two minutes until time for my interview, a guy came into the room with a clipboard and zeroed in on me.

"Jett Blackburn?" he said after glancing at his notes.

"Yessir."

"You found easels. Good. I'm running a few minutes late. Welcome to the Fergusson Art Center. I'm Dr. Lawrence. We were impressed with your photos but wanted to see some originals so we could look at your technique and help figure out your program. First of all, let me tell you that this does not affect your admission to the university or to the art school. You are admitted as a candidate for a BS in Studio Art."

"I was planning to go for a BFA," I said.

"We don't do BFA admissions until after the second year. Everyone is admitted as a BS candidate. Ah, here's Dr. Anders."

I got introduced to the second professor and a woman introduced as Professor Wells. A few other people came into the room and I saw Eva but they weren't introduced. As soon as the three professors were gathered, the interview started with a review of my drawing technique and skill. Then they started on the paintings.

"Tell us about the abstract first," Professor Wells said. And with that I was off with the same basic presentation I'd given my parents and grandparents a few weeks ago. I didn't expect the same emotional response that I got from my family and friends. These were art teachers. They would look at fine details and techniques.

"I apologize for the display of these last two pieces. The paint is not yet cured and it is difficult to handle them. You may have heard about the reported suicide of a local teen two weeks ago. I saw the video of what really happened. After the first shot was fired by the police, killing my friend, I closed my eyes. But I saw in that moment—that instant—his spirit leave his body. I had to capture that instant. For his sake. And for the sake of his friends."

"Jett, if you would give us a minute, please," Dr. Lawrence said as I was moving to the last painting. I stood back and the professors approached the paintings. I was thrown a little because I had a very nice narrative, I thought, to go with the last painting of Kelly. The professors examined the paintings closely, each moving at his or her own pace and not all looking at the same one at the same time. Dr. Anders went so far as to pull out a magnifying glass like some super sleuth to examine the brush strokes on the painting of Jasmine. They returned to their seats and whispered together. I approached the painting of Kelly to resume my presentation.

"You won't need to present that one," Dr. Anders said. "One of the things we hope to teach you in the next four years is effectively presenting your work. There is a story to each of your paintings and we want to help you capture it, even if you do not do a live presentation. One of the things you will learn is when to end the presentation, which means how to order the pieces as part of the overall story. Like in Greek tragedy, if I may be blunt, when you have reached the catharsis, you need to sit down and shut up."

I guess I glared at him a little until I saw Professor Wells dabbing at her eyes.

"Jett," she said, "correct me if I'm wrong. I believe you painted four of the works from memory or inspiration and the two of the young women from live models. Correct?"

"Yes, ma'am."

"I'm further guessing that you did each of them in one sitting."

"Um… Mostly, yes, ma'am."

"You did a great job of capturing intense emotional content in a short period of time. One of the things we'd like to help you with is to slow down. Not every time. The death scene, for example, I'm sure had to be captured immediately. The passion had to be lived in the moment. It's a remarkable painting, by the way."

"Thank you."

"Look at the portrait of the older woman—your mother, I believe you said."

"Yes, ma'am."

"You captured essentials that told the story, especially in the set of her mouth and the hardness of her eyes. But this is a painting you should have come back to. Perhaps you will do another of her. The care you took with the eyes and lips is missing with other features, like the hair, nose, and ear. It makes the picture look somehow unfinished."

"I did come back to the painting of my granddad's house several times," I said. "It took about a week."

"An excellent touchstone," she continued. "It's the little things in that painting that made it come to life. The face in the window. The glass of tea. They show that you thought about the details of the painting as well as the scene. I'm sure, for example, that as you look at the paintings of the two young women, you will begin to remember details that you wish you had included. A reflection in her eye? The bottle of polish she was using? Even the floor or ceiling. You have a raw talent here that is filled with emotion and passion. We don't ever want you to lose that. We want you to expand it to every detail that you paint. If you can do that, you will not only be a fine talented artist, you will become a master."

"I'll do my best, ma'am."

"Jett, we don't want to change you or your painting and style," Dr. Lawrence took over. "Too often, we encounter talented artists who do not want to move forward. They are happy where they are and won't grow. We want to give you additional tools, sharpen your eye, and hone your skills. The art. The talent is what you bring to the table. Will you let us help you perfect it?"

"Um… Thank you for your comments and criticisms, professors. I am torn about college in a way. I might not be able to afford four years. It's expensive, even at a state university. I don't want to waste my time with unnecessary courses because the curriculum says that's what I should take. But I wouldn't come here at all if I didn't think I could learn to be a better artist. To that end, I'll devote myself completely."

"If you will accept me, I will be your freshman adviser," Professor Wells said. "You can always change later if we don't work well together. I can see from your high school transcript that your AP classes may allow you to skip some general curriculum courses that would normally be required of first year students. You may have to interview with the concerned professors before they let you out of the requirement. I'll do my best to work with you on that. At the same time, the University is a business that produces degrees. There will be some pressure to have you on a degree program and not to merely give you classes focused entirely on your art. Just know that I'll be your advocate."

"Thank you. I accept."

•○•◦⟡ ⊃⊂ ☼ ⊃⊂ ⟡◦•○•

"GREAT PRESENTATION, JETT," Eva said. "Can I help you pack up?"

"Sure, thanks. Um… I need to get tape from my car. Can you watch things for a few minutes?"

"There's people who want to look at the art and probably talk to you. Is it safe for me to get the tape from your car while you talk to your new fans?"

"Sure. It's on the floor of the passenger seat. I have a red Mini in the visitor lot." I handed her my keys and she took off. *Shit! I just gave a strange girl the keys to my car!*

It turned out okay. There weren't really that many people who wanted to talk, though everyone wanted to look closer at the paintings. It was neat to hear other artists try to pick out the things the professors mentioned.

"I'd love to meet your models," one guy said as he stared at the painting of Jasmine. I got a little jealous and protective but managed to just smile and say maybe. In a couple minutes, Eva was back with my tape and I started packing things up. She carried my portfolio—and my keys—as we took things back to the car.

"Uh… Jett, I know we just met and you probably have a ton of models falling over each other to pose for you, but… uh… if you'd like… I mean… I'd like… Would you paint me sometime?"

I grinned at her. "Eva, something I didn't know about myself until a few weeks ago is that I almost never turn down a girl who wants to undress for me."

"God! I can't believe I volunteered to get naked in front of a boy I just met. Um… Here's my phone number. Call. Um… Anytime."

10
Paint Me

I'M NOT much of a literal thinker. I'm an artist. I interpret things. I'm not as bad as Charmaine, who can turn anything into a dirty joke. But I turn things into an artistic expression.

I drove over to the admin building after I left Eva, figuring that Sarah Lynn would be finished soon. I'd have to make an appointment soon and see if I could get my financial aid increased. Not likely, since even though they aren't helping pay for my education, financial need is based on the parents' ability to pay. How sucky is that?

I pulled into a visitor spot near the front entrance of the admin building. Lucky it was summer and there weren't too many students around. I reached for my smartphone and sent a quick text to Sarah Lynn that I was waiting. Two police cars pulled up in front of the admin building and I thought it was odd that they just stopped half blocking the street without their emergency lights on. I opened the door so I could stand beside my car and snapped a few pictures of the officers as they got out. Just then Sarah Lynn came out the front doors and after checking a paper in front of them, the two officers approached her.

"Sarah Lynn Jamison?" one of them said. I clicked my phone over to video.

"Shit! What do you want? Don't I have to hang myself before you use me for target practice?"

"There's no reason to be confrontational here. We've been looking for you for several days," officer one said. "We'd just like to take a look at your cell phone."

"No."

"We are asking politely but will frisk you and remove the device if you force us to. We believe it was used in the commission of a crime." Sarah Lynn folded her arms across her chest.

"Naughty cell phone. I do not consent and if you touch me inappropriately, I will sue you, Officer Brennan and Officer Richards," Sarah Lynn said, reading the names from their badges. "And your department."

"You leave us no choice. Place your hands on the hood of the car and spread your feet apart." Sarah obeyed and I zoomed in as the officer went straight to her back pocket where the phone's outline was obvious.

"Good girl," the officer said as he turned the phone on. "This is password protected!"

"Duh!"

"Give us the password."

"I refuse to say anything further without the presence of my attorney."

"We just want the damned video," Officer two said.

"Are you nuts or really that ignorant? If you want the video, it's on about fifty share sites."

"Then why don't you unlock your phone for us."

"No."

"Jack, this was supposed to be a simple open and erase. We either need to take her in or let her go."

"Yeah. You're free to go, Miss Jamison."

"My phone, please."

"This phone is considered evidence in a crime. You can inquire about its release after the hearing," officer two said. He handed the phone to the other officer, who dropped it in a plastic bag. They got in their cars and left Sarah Lynn standing on the street as they drove off.

"Fucking thugs!" she screamed after them. She turned and ran to me as I turned off my recording. "Did you get all that?"

"Every bit. Thanks for speaking up. Now what?" We got in the car and pulled away.

"Let me borrow your phone," she said. I handed it to her after I unlocked it. She tapped a few things out and then her thumbs started flying over the keypad. Finally, she exited and handed the phone back to me.

"You bricked it, didn't you."

"Yeah. When Lonnie gave us that talk on security and set up the phone blanking, I really thought he was going overboard. I figured, what's the chance that someone would steal my phone? Well, now I know." Tears were running down Sarah Lynn's cheeks. "Damn it! I miss him! The fucking son of a bitch!"

On the way back home, we got her a new iPhone and a prepaid plan. She got a new phone number and we wondered how long it would take her parents to figure out she was no longer using the phone on their plan.

•o•◦❧ ⟢⟣ ☼ ⟢⟣ ❧◦•o•

KELLY WAS HANGING onto me a lot as we moved into the weekend. It seemed like whenever I was in the big room at Granddad's, Kelly was naked and close enough to touch me. Not that I minded. Having naked Kelly close enough to touch all the time was heaven. And it didn't seem to be a conflict with the other girls. Jasmine had me on my back and was riding her pony when Kelly settled her sweet red pussy over my mouth. As much as we'd shared touching and even getting each other off, it was the first time I actually had two girls sexing me at the same time. I liked it and if the quantity of juices poured over my cock and my face were any indication, they liked it, too.

When Kelly crawled into my lap Sunday afternoon, though, I knew something wasn't right. She curled up in a little ball, buried her face against my chest, and cried.

"What is it, baby?" I asked. "Did I do something wrong?" I guess the first thing a guy thinks when a girl cries is that he did something. It didn't make sense, though, since she was hanging onto me like her life depended on it.

"No," she whispered. "Jett, I have to leave. I have to move back with my mom."

"What? Why? I thought you liked living with all of us."

"I do. I don't want to go."

"Then…"

"I start my new job tomorrow. I love living out here with you all, but there's no bus. I have to move back so I can get to work."

"I'll take you to work," I said confidently.

"I know you would, like tomorrow," she said. "But you couldn't do that every day. It isn't fair to everyone else. You are the only one of us with a car and it won't even hold all of us. It's not fair."

"She's right, Jett. I'm thinking of making nice with my parents, too," Ariel said. "I love living with everyone, but we won't even be able to get to school in the fall if we stay out here. And we need to start making more of a contribution to your grandfather than just cooking."

"We really have to get started on a place to live," Jas said. "I've been looking through housing ads and it's expensive. I found a five-bedroom five-bath townhome for just a thousand a month. Turned out they expected to rent each bedroom for a thousand a month. What a rip!"

"Geez. If we don't find something soon, we'll be moving into that box under the bridge sooner than we thought," I said.

"Mom already told me I could move home," Jas said. "Um… Charmaine, I know home's never been all that great for you. You could come with me if you want."

"Oh, Jas. You've always been my bestie. If I had a sister, she'd be you. Thank you!"

"So, Kelly and me can go home," Ariel said. "As long as it's temporary. My parents won't say anything as long as they hear me practicing the piano for a couple of hours a day."

"That leaves Sarah Lynn," I said. "Um… Jas?"

"Yes, Jett. Do it."

"Sarah Lynn, you can stay with me until we all find a place to move to."

"Really, Jett? I don't want it to look like I'm shutting everyone out or claiming you for just me," Sarah Lynn said. "Really, girls, I'm not trying to trap Jett."

"If you hadn't eaten my pussy last night, I'd be worried about that," Ariel laughed. "God! Why can't I give myself that kind of orgasm?"

"Okay. We've got a stop-gap plan. It's temporary. The goal is to get us a place to live together as soon as possible," I said.

"We should consider all options," Sarah Lynn said. "Dorms, condos, houses, fraternity/sorority, co-ops. Whatever we can find."

"I'll put together a shared spreadsheet so we can all put in the numbers of what we think we can afford to commit to," Charmaine said. "I'll try to create a budget for housing and food and we can test it with each other. If we can find a place to live by the first of July, we should be in good shape. I'm excited about this."

WE HELD THINGS together in pretty good spirits Sunday night. We didn't have a real meal in the evening. Granddad had made a big pan of lasagna for lunch. In the evening, we ran the air popper half a dozen times and I sat with Granddad to watch a baseball game while we ate ours. He opened a beer and handed it to me as he settled in with his own.

"I see the numbers downstairs fell off this week. Do you want to just rent this place for the future? I can probably make a better deal than your parents offered," he said between the second and third innings.

"Um… We talked about it. Problem is that we're a long way from the university and we only have one small car. We've got to get Kelly in to work tomorrow and I think everyone else will scatter. We'll all be gone in a day or so, I guess."

"Well, that's sad. It's been fun having you all here. Probably not a good long-term solution, though. What comes next?"

"Um… Charmaine and Sarah Lynn can't go home to their parents. Sarah Lynn's just flat-out disowned her after commencement. You know her father's a fireman, and her mother thinks she is demon-possessed. Charmaine's never had a very good homelife and doesn't want to go back there. She's going to stay with Jas for a little while, until we can get the housing figured out," I said.

"And Sarah Lynn?"

"I need to talk to Mom and Dad. I think she'll stay with me."

"Mmm. Probably. Your mother will want to disinfect her." We laughed.

"Ariel and Kelly will go back to their homes. Ariel's parents are mad at her, but she says that as long as they hear her playing the piano two hours a day, they won't say anything."

"She's very talented. It's been enjoyable to hear her play up here. That old piano of ours hadn't been played since your grandmother passed away. It brought back good memories," Granddad said wistfully. "And Kelly?"

"You know, her mom is kind of weird," I laughed. "She joined Dad Monday, picketing the police station. It wasn't a very big demonstration. Nothing's going to happen. They'll all go scot-free. Kelly's got great space where her mom lets her do about anything she wants to. Except she wants to be with us. The six of us want to find a place to live together."

"None of the other boys?"

"Ford's headed out of state. I think Derek and Dee are going to live at her house together. Their parents have assumed the two of them would be married for the past ten years or more. They raised them to be a couple."

"Parents always talk about the benefits of an arranged marriage but you don't often see one working out."

"I still don't know that they'll get married. They're more like brother and sister. They might be the least mature of all my friends."

"Time will tell. What about that other boy who was here at first?" Granddad asked.

"Rick got a surprise call Thursday night and found out he'd been drafted. He figured that since none of the colleges he applied to would give him a baseball scholarship, the majors wouldn't be interested either. He says he has to report July ninth. He expects he'll play during the winter somewhere in South America and then be called for spring training. He figures that he'll end up playing rookie ball or Class A minors for a year or two before he gets cut loose. He's just going to save as much money as he can and go to college afterward."

"Good for him. I've never believed people had to rush off to college as soon as they finished high school. Like you, for instance. What are you going to learn in college? It's obvious to all of us that you are an artist. Are you looking for a fallback position?"

"Um… no. I'm not even looking for a degree—which seemed to shock the professors at my interview Wednesday. I'm going to power load as many courses as I can that will improve my skills and make as many contacts as possible. If I run out of money in two years, I'll call it quits and not worry about letters after my name. Doesn't make a difference," I sighed.

"And that brings us to the elephant in the room. Whoa! Stand up double with two RBIs! Nice." I waited for Granddad to continue as we settled down after the sudden home team rally. "How are you going to earn money to pay for an apartment or whatever you live in? How are you going to eat or pay tuition?"

"Well, the money you and Grandma and Grandpa Blackburn and Dad gave me will cover two years' tuition if I can get my living expenses covered. I was offered a student loan for ten grand that would cover some of it, but I just can't see borrowing that kind of money. I keep hearing horror stories of people who are paying on student loans at the minimum and never touch the principal for years," I groaned.

"We didn't give you money," Granddad objected. "We bought paintings. They were worth every penny we paid for them. The problem with making a living selling art is that art is only worth what a buyer will pay. You probably have some priceless works among your masterpieces. Those are works no one would buy at any price. That doesn't mean they are bad, but that the market isn't there. The death scene, for example. It was very liberating to look at that painting and release all the sorrow and grief we felt. It is a wonderful painting. But would Lonnie's parents ever buy it? Not a chance. It is too painful today. In ten or twenty years, someone may want it."

"You know they keep saying to do what you love and the money will follow. All I want to do is paint, but at the same time, I don't know that I want to be dependent on painting for a living. I'll get a job."

"Any prospects?"

"Two. Grandpa said there was a summer job for me at the grocery store. He wants me to learn to cut meat. Butchers don't make much, but it's pretty dependable work if you are willing to work for a processing plant. Seems stores are cutting back on their butcher shops."

"Well, it's a skill as long as you aren't squeamish. What's the other choice?"

"I've been doing all my own maintenance on the Mini. I enjoy it and thought I might see about going to work as a mechanic. I guess it doesn't really make that much difference what kind of job I get. I'm just going to leave at five o'clock and paint all night."

⋅⋅◦⋅❖⟩⟩C⋅☀⋅C⟨⟨❖⋅◦⋅⋅

"ARE YOU SURE?" I asked again. "Do we need protection?" I might have been asking Kelly but I also might have been asking myself.

"Yes, I'm sure. And I'm protected. Do it. I can feel you. Push," she whispered. "Oh God, yes! Jett, we're finally doing it! I'm so… stretched. Ah!"

We'd been playing around all evening. Not just Kelly and me, but the other four girls as well. Nobody had any clothes on. Ariel looked like she was enjoying riding Jasmine's mouth and Charmaine and Sarah Lynn were locked in a sixty-nine. Kelly and I had rolled toward each other and after spending an eternity kissing, I found myself poised above her with the wet tip of my cock steeping in her pussy juices. I pushed and felt her hot tight glove slip over my cock.

I moved slowly, dragging back and moving forward a little at a time in order to fit myself into her. When I was finally all the way in, she wrapped her ankles around my back. We stayed that way, just connected as deeply as we could get.

"I can feel your heartbeat," I whispered. "I mean inside. I can feel it beating against my penis."

"You're so deep, you're probably touching it. I just want to stay like this forever. Did you come?"

"Kelly, we haven't even started yet."

"Really? I mean… well, when Derek did it, I don't think he ever got all the way inside. Then as soon as he came, he got dressed and ran home to Dee. Can you stay in me like this?"

I responded by pulling back and thrusting into her hot core again. She moaned and I repeated the thrust. If it hadn't been for Charmaine demonstrating her newly acquired blowjob skills earlier, I'd have popped almost as quickly as Kelly said Derek had. We'd been teasing and playing with each other all week, since I painted her picture. It wasn't the first time my cock had slid through the wet folds of her sex, but this was the first moment that I went inside.

"It's so different. I have a little vibrator I use. Mostly on my clit, but inside a little. I'm always afraid that I'll get it so slippery that it will

86

shoot out of my fingers and into me and then I wouldn't be able to get it out unless I got someone to help me. I'd be lying there with my bullet vibrating in my cunt, helpless."

"I'll try not to get stuck. Kelly, you are so fantastic."

"Move some more. Oh wow! I feel every time you touch my cervix."

"Does it hurt? I can back off."

"No! It's like a little tickle when you slide over it. It's the most sensitive part deep inside and no one has ever touched it before. Everything is tingling, Jett. I'm going to… come!" Kelly gripped me tightly in her sheath and the pulse I'd felt earlier was overridden by the milking convulsions of her orgasm. I'm not sure how I delayed, but I held still until she'd calmed down a little and I kept kissing her and thumbing her nipples as I tried to keep my full weight off her.

"You okay, redhead?" Jas asked as she rolled toward us and put a little kiss on Kelly's cheek.

"He's still hard. He's still in me. Oh God! Jas, thank you."

"Hey, you don't need my permission. As long as Jett has a little something for all of us, we're in this together."

"Can you stay in me, Jett? This feels so good."

"Honey, we've hardly started," I said. I started moving in and out again.

"Oh, fuck! Yes!" Kelly cried. "I didn't know you could keep going like that."

"I haven't come yet," I laughed a little. "I want to stay connected to you as long as I can."

"You mean… Oh shit! Here it comes again!"

When her convulsions died down this time, I rolled to my back so I wouldn't collapse on her and brought her over on top of me. She kissed me again and then sat up, groaning as she forced me farther up her channel. She looked down where we were joined.

"Look! Look! You can see him go in and out of me," she said as she raised and lowered herself. "Quick, grab my phone. I want a picture. I want to see him going into me. This is so exciting!" Jas handed Kelly's cell phone to her and Kelly started snapping pictures and putting video on Snapchat. Jas took the phone and got a little of the action from behind Kelly's butt. It gave me a couple seconds to slow my heartrate down, but

Kelly started getting intense again and moving faster. I had both hands on her pretty tits and wished I was flexible enough to get one into my mouth while we were connected like this. Kelly was a lot shorter than either Jas or Sarah Lynn and smaller in the chest.

But when she started pumping away seriously, I got lost in the action and could feel the come boiling in my balls.

"Oh, Kelly, baby. I'm going to come. I'm going to put all my semen in your hot little vagina."

"Yes, Jett. Yes! Put it in me. Let me feel it. Oh! Me… I…" Kelly started convulsing again and this time there was nothing I could do to hold back. I could feel the whole path of the come as my body propelled it from testicles to prostate to penis and into Kelly. I pushed up as far into her as I could and my body locked into place with my butt off the floor as pump after pump of come spat into her.

I finally collapsed back to the mattress and Kelly fell forward onto my chest.

"I felt it! I felt every gush against my cervix. It's going to run out of me for days! I'm going to work at Donaldson's tomorrow and smell like sex all day. I'll have to wear a tampon to keep from leaking down my legs. I need a picture of it!" She started to rise up off me but I clamped my arms around her to hold her down on my cock. I was still half hard and didn't want to come out of her pussy until there was no choice.

"You've had a picture of come dripping from your pussy," I said.

"Yeah, but it wasn't like this. This is Jett's come."

"You should sign it, Jett," Sarah Lynn said.

"Good idea," I laughed. "Get me my Sharpie off the easel." I rolled Kelly and me over again so she was on her back and I made a few more little thrusts into her. I wasn't going to get to full erection again so soon, though, and could feel myself slipping out. "Got your camera ready?" I asked her. I pushed myself up and she shoved her phone down toward our crotches as I pulled out and up, my cock dripping into the trimmed curls of her red pubic hair. Jas handed me my pen. Kelly kept filming her dripping cunt as I signed my name on her mound.

"You painted me! You signed this work of art. I love you, Jett."

"I love you, Kelly."

11
A Body of Work

I **PLANNED TO GET** a lot of work done Monday morning. I'd made a couple of sketches during the week that I wanted to develop, so I gave Sarah Lynn the keys to my car and she packed Jasmine, Charmaine, and Kelly into it to take into town. Jas and Charmaine were going to move in with Jasmine's mother for a while, though they were warned that they couldn't freak out if Sondra had her boyfriend over for the night. Kelly went to her house to select clothes for her first day at work. Sarah Lynn, Charmaine, and Jasmine spent most of the morning hunting for a place for us to live.

It was really nice to hear Ariel playing the piano upstairs as I started filling in some of the details in my sketch. I'd already started trying to apply some of the things the professors said in my interview. I figured one of the things that I could do was explore more different styles of painting. The simple exercise of having to submit an abstract, a landscape, a portrait, and a figure for my admission had started to stretch my techniques.

I thought about Ariel playing the piano. Her dad was Chinese, but her white mother had completely adopted the role of dragon lady. She dominated the household, riding her children to success. Ariel was the oldest and it might have been hardest on her, but her two younger brothers were also given the choice of piano or violin and forced to practice two hours a day while still maintaining 'A's in every class in school. The only reason Ariel didn't end up in the top five in the class was that she took fewer AP classes. The kids were spaced a perfect two years apart and would be a freshman and a junior next year.

I set aside the sketch I'd been working on and chose a sheet of Bristol. Once I had a place of my own, I was going to put in more different kinds of supplies. For what I wanted, I needed rice paper. And genuine Chinese paste inks. But I had a short set—four bottles—of acrylic artist ink. This stuff was great because it could be mixed with water and applied like watercolor, but it dried quickly and was water-resistant when set.

I moistened the board and chose a #20 round brush. It wasn't exactly a sumi brush, but it was the best I had. I dipped it in black ink and began painting. I have no idea how to write Chinese characters, but I decided that I'd start drawing musical figures with a kind of Chinese style. As the music played, so did I. I wasn't going for any great composition on the Bristol, but just focusing on the individual shapes. I thought about the hours of practice Ariel had put in since her third birthday when she started. And she didn't consider herself a musician! She was going to study to become a mechanical engineer. I think that was another choice her parents gave her. Medicine or engineering. Her father wasn't paying for any other kind of degree. I added some structure beneath the notes I'd been drawing.

"Wow!"

I hadn't even comprehended the fact that Ariel had quit playing. I stood back from the paper and saw her removing her panties—the last article of clothing she had on.

"You painted me!" she said. I laughed.

"Not yet." I dipped my brush in the ink again and turned to start painting musical notes on Ariel's chest. She startled a moment and her eyes got big, but she didn't move. It was fun and fortunately, Ariel wasn't very ticklish. I just continued the drawing I'd started on the Bristol board onto the girl.

Ariel is the shortest of the girls—probably about five feet or maybe five-one. She has bigger breasts than Kelly, though, who has the smallest and I'd have to say perkiest little titties of my five… girlfriends. Charmaine had the largest with Jas and Sarah Lynn about even between. I circled Ariel's nipples with half notes and a triplet running between her breasts. I painted her navel as a whole note with a fermata. I turned a staff of music into a suspension bridge as I stretched it from hip to hip, resting on her bush. I drew girders and piers down her thighs. She spread her legs a little and I couldn't help dragging a finger up between her lush pussy lips. She moaned and pushed toward me.

Instead, I had her turn and started painting on her butt and then the small of her back. I painted gears and levers—a kind of Rube Goldberg contraption that I didn't think through very well in terms of what direction things could and couldn't turn, but as I approached her shoulders, I let musical notes emerge from the mechanical invention. The notes turned into birds.

I looked at my work on her body and signed her right butt cheek, then put the brush to soak in a dish of water. She was standing still, her breath coming in deep gasps, her feet still held more than shoulder width apart. I blew across her back and butt to make sure the ink had dried enough not to smear and then reached between her legs. Ariel moaned and grabbed my stool to support her weight as she leaned forward and I thrust my fingers into her wet pussy. Bending over like that just made my target easier to get to.

Unlike Jas, who is shaved smooth, or Kelly, who shaves all but the mons of her bright red pubic hair, Ariel has a dense black bush. She trims it down enough that it all fits in the skimpy underwear the girls wear, but the hair covers her puffy outer labia. It made a nice frame for the pink gash revealed when I spread them with my fingers.

"Are you going to fuck me now?" she gasped.

"Not quite," I said. "I don't have a condom and we already established that you aren't on the pill or protected."

"I'm going to a clinic as soon as I can get there."

"That's good but doesn't help today. Lift up on your toes." When she complied, it not only made her legs and ass look like they'd just arrived from paradise, it served to angle her pussy back toward me more. I buried my face between the gears painted on her cheeks and started licking. I reached forward between her legs and grabbed both breasts, rolling her nipples between my fingers. Her butt cheeks started quivering so violently that I thought I might be ground to dust between those gears. I just kept licking, finding the little bud of her clit between the soaking curls. Her high-pitched keen and collapse let me know she'd reached her fulfillment.

⋅∘⋅◈ Ⅻ ☼ Ⅻ ◈⋅∘⋅

"YOU NEED TO frame her!" Sarah Lynn exclaimed when she saw us curled up on the sofa. "I love the whole gears into music theme!"

Ariel lazily rolled onto her back in my arms. "What do you think of my bridge?" she asked.

"Oh my God! I could walk right across your pussy. And I love your half notes." Sarah Lynn leaned forward to kiss the nips of our little Asian lover. "I won't smear it, will I?" I shook my head and Sarah Lynn slurped first the left and then the right nipple into her mouth, switching back and forth as Ariel moaned her approval.

"You could float your canoe right up under my bridge," she sighed. "Just, yeah. Right there." Her pussy was still glistening from my oral treatment, but Ariel lifted her head to kiss me as she spread her legs so Sarah Lynn could lick her. It only took a minute of the two of us working on her for Ariel to peak again. Sarah Lynn fed me juices from her lips as we kissed and Ariel recovered.

"I need to take some pictures," I said. "As soon as you can move, I want you to stand by the painting so I can make photos. That is, unless you are okay with just being framed with it."

She laughed. "Yeah. We should take the pictures before I shower all this off and go home." She stood shakily and walked over to the easel while I grabbed my camera.

"There's too much background here. Let's move everything over to the blank wall." Sarah Lynn helped us move the easel and set the scene. I snapped a couple of pictures and then Sarah Lynn insisted that I get in the picture with Ariel as the artist and fake like I was still painting her. It worked pretty well. Ariel headed for the shower, but Sarah Lynn delayed me.

"I didn't see or taste any sperm. Did you fuck her?"

"No. She's not protected and I didn't have a condom."

"Good. But after all that excitement, you must be in pain. I'll bet she never thought about doing you, did she?"

"I guess not. It was really all about her. I was just lost in the painting."

Sarah Lynn pushed me down on the mattress and pulled my briefs off. I was stiff and watching her take off her clothes made me stiffer.

"You gave something special to our girlfriend without asking any-thing in return," she whispered. "Now lie back and let me give to you. Without asking anything in return." She kissed me and started working her way down my body with kisses making sure to cover everything but not really going down on me or sucking me. When she had kissed me to her satisfaction, she straddled me and sank down on my pole. It was that perfect fit kind of thing and she started gently rocking back and forth as her pussy muscles rippled around my cock. "Just think. One day soon, your cock will be buried in that sweet little Asian pussy. You'll have to be gentle with her so you don't break her by accident. She's so tiny. But based on how much she loves tongue in her pussy, when she gets your cock there, she'll go wild."

"Sarah Lynn, I'm in *your* pussy now. I'd like to focus on that," I whispered. It was confusing for me to think of one girl while another fucked me.

"When we move over to your house, will I have to sleep in a guest room or can I sleep with you?" she asked as she picked up speed. "Because I think I'd like to do this a lot and I'd hate to have to sneak across a hall or something."

"If there's a problem with it, we'll come back here. But I told Mom that there would be two of us and sometimes an extra. Her only problem will be that it isn't Jasmine living with me. She'd already started designing wedding invitations, I think."

"Is that what you want?"

"No. It's not what either of us want."

"What do you want, Jett?"

"Right now, I want to come in your pussy. I can feel it. Sarah Lynn, I'm going to…" She'd worked up the speed to a frenzy and I couldn't hold back. I held her boobs in my hands as I let go with all I'd stored up while playing with Ariel. Sarah Lynn slammed down on my hard dick and held me deep inside as her muscles milked my cock for everything I could give her.

I passed out.

"You tattooed me!" Ariel said. "It doesn't wash off."

"Shit, Jett. I know it's not a real tattoo, but how do you get the stuff off?" Sarah Lynn asked.

"Oh, fuck! I didn't even think about that. I was just painting on the paper and then she walked up and I kept going. Damn it! Let me look it up." I fumbled with my phone and found the manufacturer of the inks with directions for removing it from skin. "Okay. Here it is. They say the quick way is to use vegetable oil and then wash with shampoo to cut through the oil. If there is residue left, then clean it with alcohol. I'm sorry, Ariel. I never thought. I'll go up and get the oil."

"No," she said firmly. "Now that I know it isn't forever, I want to leave it on. We're moving away from each other for a while. At least I'll have this to remind me that I belong with you."

"But, what about your parents?" I asked.

"I don't usually undress in front of my parents!" she said, her eyes getting big. "I'll just keep clothes on while I'm home. It's my pervy little brothers who always try to sneak peeks at me. I'll just be careful not to flash them."

"We'd better get you home, then," I said. I was a little sad. When the rest of the crew left this morning, there was so much going on that it didn't seem so lonely. I'd spent an intimate day with Ariel, though, and watching her walk up the steps to her home brought a tear to my eye.

"It won't be for long, Jett," Sarah Lynn said as I drove away. "We have a fragile new relationship among us. We need to nurture it and get us all together as soon as possible."

"I was really surprised," I said. "First that Jas wanted to make love. Then you. I knew Kelly was always horny—or at least she talked like she was—but I always figured she was all talk. And then Charmaine and Ariel attaching themselves. I didn't know all you girls liked girls so much."

"Hmm. I guess I've always known I was bi. I love the taste of a girl's pussy. I love having your cock in my pussy. Kelly is kind of omnisexual. It wouldn't surprise me if she tried it with a dog. Jas is just so compassionate that she does whatever the people she loves need. I think Ariel might be a little more girl-biased than into boys. She likes to have that hairy little pussy eaten. Doesn't make too much difference if it's a boy or a girl down there. And what a tongue. I think she's given me more orgasms the past week than everyone else combined."

"And Charmaine?"

"Yeah. Well… Charmaine is really needy right now. I think she'll do anything to be held and comforted. Safely. She wasn't safe at home. You know she wasn't in the top twenty percent of our class, but she loves numbers. She plans to go for an associate degree in accounting. But what she really wants is to not go back home. Period. End of paragraph."

"I don't want to take advantage of her just because she's needy," I said. Charmaine was first and foremost a friend. I knew she'd do anything she could if I was in need. That's what I'd do for her.

SARAH LYNN AND I spent the evening cleaning house. Oh, we'd kept the place tidy while we were all living there, but we wanted to make sure that Granddad didn't regret having us as houseguests. We cleaned the space where the girls and I had lived for a week and then went upstairs and cleaned the rest of his house. I disinfected all the countertops, the bathroom sink, the shower, and the toilet. Sarah Lynn vacuumed and got down on her hands and knees to scrub the kitchen floor and bathroom tiles.

We wished Granddad goodnight and went downstairs for one last night in his house before we faced the world. We were so tired that we snuggled up in spoons and went straight to sleep.

WE PACKED UP the Mini with everything we could fit but I would need to make a second trip. Sarah Lynn still hadn't been to her house to get any of her personal things, but that would have to change soon. Instead of moving straight home, we went to the grocery store and filled out job applications. Grandpa Blackburn immediately took me to the butcher shop and described what I would be doing.

I know some people get squeamish with the thought of cutting up dead animals for people to eat. A lot of people disconnect so much from the idea of eating animals that they don't even recognize that steaks were once a part of a cow. Or that milk comes from a cow. Or bacon comes from a pig. Or eggs from a chicken. We don't see the animal when we shop for groceries. All we see is what goes on the grill. So, Grandpa told me I'd be trained as a meat cutter. That's not the same as a butcher. It's mostly about cutting existing slabs—what Grandpa calls primal cuts—into smaller uniform pieces and packaging them to meet customer requirements or to look good in the case.

I guess the way I was raised, in a state where cattle are a major industry, even though most of them are dairy, makes me less sensitive to it, though I'll have to think hard before I consider taking up Grandpa's offer to pay for my certificate education if I want to progress to becoming a butcher. Not sure if I want to deal with the whole slaughter and carcass thing. Still, it would be a dependable source of income. As long as I could live on $20-25,000 a year.

When I was finished, I found Sarah Lynn getting a tour of the front of the store. The supervisor hired her immediately and she'd work first as a courtesy clerk while she was trained as a checker. We were both employed and would start full time work in the morning.

•∘•⇨ ⊃⊂ ☽ ⊃⊂ ⇦•∘•

MOM WAS SKEPTICAL when we arrived. Nearly everything in the Mini was mine except some clothes Sarah Lynn had borrowed from Jasmine.

"What about Jasmine?" Mom asked. "Have you broken up? Oh, Jett, I like Jas."

"Mom, Jas and I didn't break up. We were never engaged except in your mind. But I understand. You like her. I like her. I probably like her a lot more than you do. So, if you are worried about Sarah Lynn, don't think of it as leaving one and being with the other. Think of it as Jas and I expanding our family to include another," I said. "Or others," I whispered.

"And Jasmine is okay with you and Sarah Lynn?"

"I expect she'll be over later this afternoon for some quiet time with us. She's out hunting for an apartment big enough for us to live in while we're in school."

"Sarah Lynn," Mom said, "please don't think I don't like you. I'm just worried. It's a mother's prerogative. I was very impressed with your speech at commencement. And very sad."

"Thank you, Mrs. Blackburn. I guess my parents were very impressed with it, too. Just not favorably. All my mother has been able to say was that I had snuff porn on my phone," Sarah Lynn said sadly. "The really hard part is that I miss her, you know?"

"Oh, sweetheart, come sit beside me here." Mom immediately reached out and pulled Sarah Lynn into a hug. "I understand. I really do. My mother and I didn't get along all that well. She was very critical of me and absolutely doted on Jett. Some days, I thought she wished he was her son and I was out of the way."

"Mom!" I said. "Mammam loved you."

"I know she did," Mom responded. "And I loved her. There hasn't been a day since she died that I didn't reach for the phone at least once to talk to her before I realized she was gone. That's what I'm saying, Sarah Lynn. Just because you don't see eye-to-eye on this doesn't mean you don't love each other and miss each other. Time will heal all wounds."

I was impressed with my mom. I hadn't seen that side of her in a long time. Or maybe I'd become inured to it. It seemed like she always wanted to control me, sterilize my environment, and criticize my life. I'd painted a harsh portrait of her. But seeing her comfort and hold Sarah Lynn made me aware that, despite her controlling ways, she had deep love for me and concern for my well-being and that of my friends.

12
Slumming

I BORROWED MOM'S SUV the afternoon Sarah Lynn and I moved home. Jas and Charmaine met us at Sarah Lynn's house and we went in to pack her things and move them. Her mom stood in the kitchen with her arms folded glaring at us.

"Your phone doesn't work."

"It was confiscated by some police officers. They probably shot it," Sarah Lynn said.

"Showing a pornographic film at commencement doesn't prove anything against the police," Mrs. Jamison said. "They came here looking for you and I didn't know where you were. What kind of mother does that make me look like?"

"The kind who doesn't know much about her daughter," Sarah Lynn sighed. "I didn't come to argue, Mother. I just want to pack my things and leave. You can reach me at Jett's house until we find a place to live."

"One boyfriend dead and you are already shacking up with another. The devil has his claws in you. Get your things and leave."

The four of us went to Sarah Lynn's bedroom and followed her in. She crumpled to the floor. Jas and Charmaine jumped to kneel beside her and support her. I pulled out my phone and started snapping pictures. The room was a mess. Her dresser was empty with drawers pulled out. The clothes from her closet were tossed on the floor and boxes were lying open. All her makeup cases, nail polish, and creams were open and dried out. The bed was stripped and the mattress shoved to one side. It looked like one of those movie sets where the mob comes in and ransacks a room looking for the missing diamond.

Sarah Lynn wailed.

She shook Jas and Charmaine from her and shoved me out of the way as she barged out the door and back to her mother.

"What did you do?" she cried. "Why did you destroy my room?" I reached her in time to hold her back from assaulting her mom.

"I didn't do anything. Those nice policemen asked if they could search your room. They said they suspected you were in collusion with that nasty boy and were probably dealing in drugs or pornography. I let them in to search. They took your computer with them, so you'll probably be arrested as soon as they get here. I already called."

"Did you get names? Badge numbers? Were they in uniform? Did they have a warrant?" Sarah Lynn demanded.

"They were police. They had every right to search."

"You are so stupid, Mother. They had no right to even enter the house without your invitation. You're despicable. I hope they do come to arrest me. I'll make sure you and your mothering are on trial," Sarah Lynn spat. She turned in my arms and pushed me away as she marched back to her room.

As Jas, Charmaine, and Sarah Lynn started cramming stuff in boxes we'd picked up from the grocery store, I called Granddad. I figured he'd know what to do if the police showed up. I knew I couldn't interrupt my dad because he'd have some patient with jaws locked open and a dental dam in place. I learned early in life that I couldn't just interrupt a dentist.

"I'll be there in a few minutes. Just refuse to answer any questions until you have a lawyer present. Unfortunately, we can't plead that you are all minors any longer. But I don't think you will have difficulty. The four officers who were involved in the shooting have all been suspended for investigation. The department will be pretty cautious about approaching Sarah Lynn. Don't get in the way." I breathed easier when Granddad hung up and I knelt to help the girls.

"Jett, why don't you go entertain yourself by sorting and packing my underwear," Sarah Lynn sniffed. She was obviously trying to make a joke and I kissed her cheek. Then I did as she said and started putting her underwear in a peach crate we'd picked up at the grocery store.

"This is all a mess," Jas said. "What do you want us to do with the boxes of stuff from your closet?"

"Just pack the clothes. I'm going to quickly sort through the open boxes and grab the few things from my life that I want to remember. The rest I'll just leave here for her to clean up."

•◦•⇒))C ☼))C ⇐•◦•

GRANDDAD WAS WAITING next to the SUV when I carried the first couple of boxes out. He stayed outside by the car and didn't try to come in. When it came down to it, Sarah Lynn didn't have that much to pack. It was mostly clothes and shoes. She had a few books, like her entire collection of Harry Potter books that were hidden in the closet because her mother believed witchcraft was evil and the books were tools of the devil. That just made them more precious to Sarah Lynn.

She also took a painting of mine off the wall. I didn't even know she had one of my paintings and it took a minute before I recognized it as something I'd done as a freshman.

"When did I give you this?" I asked.

"You gave it to Lisa Nolan."

"And she gave it to you?" I asked.

"Well… sort of. Jett, this is embarrassing. I had a really bad crush on you as a freshman. I guess I never completely got over it. After all, I'm loving fucking you. But I couldn't let you know, so I convinced Lisa to get you to give her a painting and give it to me. It was never for her in the first place," Sarah Lynn said.

"You are devious," Jas said. "Just about as bad as the rest of us."

"Well, I never masturbated on Skype," Sarah Lynn laughed. It was good to see her recovering from the shock. "I did take a picture of my breasts and sent it to Jett after Kelly did. I never signed it and it didn't show anything but my breasts. I don't think you knew my phone number back then," she giggled. "I felt so wicked! Lonnie teased me for days, the jerk."

We took the last box out to the car and found Granddad talking to a guy who just had 'police detective' stenciled all over him.

"Jett, let me introduce you to Detective Lebowski," Granddad said. "He's the detective conducting an internal review of the four officers involved in Lonnie's death. Sarah Lynn, you don't need to say anything

100

but you should know there is someone on the force who is taking this whole thing seriously."

"More than one," the detective said. "The whole force is pretty upset. Some on one side and some on the other. The important thing I want to tell you, though, is that we are investigating the officers, not you. You are neither accused nor suspected of any crime. Releasing the video of Brennan and Richards shaking you down for your phone was the straw that broke the camel's back and got them suspended. You can pick your phone up from the main station."

"It's a brick," she said. "What about them ransacking my room?"

"Is this something new?"

"I just came here to pack up my belongings and leave only to find that my mother let two police officers in to 'search' for drugs and porn. They tore it to pieces and took my computer. My mother, of course, just let them and believed I was guilty of anything they said," Sarah Lynn said. The detective sighed heavily.

"I guess I should go talk to your mother. Is there a number I can reach you at if we need to talk?"

Before Sarah Lynn could answer, Granddad broke in. "They've been staying out at my place since graduation. Here's my card. Just give me a call and I'll track them down."

"Andy, I appreciate the contact. Are you still selling eggs out there?"

"No, I still have some chickens, but a few more Sunday dinners and they'll all be gone." They laughed and the detective went up to talk to Mrs. Jamison. We thanked Granddad and got out of Dodge.

•·o·•◈ ⊃⊂ ☼ ⊃⊂ ◈•·o·•

The rest of the week went by in a blur. I had a new full-time job that started at six o'clock in the morning. Yuck! I was already reconsidering my choice of employment. Sarah Lynn worked at the same place, but our hours were completely different. I got off at three. She didn't start until one and worked through dinner.

We barely had enough energy to crawl into bed at night, but we still managed to make love. Jasmine felt comfortable leaving Charmaine alone and spent Tuesday night with us. That was a real round robin as

Jas and Sarah Lynn were into each other as much as either was into me. Thursday night, Kelly showed up. Sarah Lynn kissed her sweetly and then left, saying she was spending the night with Ariel.

Kelly. *Sweet Mother of God!* I'd been cutting chickens up all day and then had gone out with Jas to look at a house she found. I was exhausted but seeing the look of longing in Kelly's eyes when Sarah Lynn left revived me instantly.

Mom and Dad had adopted the strategy of retiring to the family room after dinner each evening and intentionally not paying attention to who arrived or went up the stairs to my bedroom for the night. I found out later, though, that after Dad and I went to work in the morning, Mom often had long talks over breakfast with my girlfriends. Maybe my relationship with Mom would have been better if I'd been born a girl.

Kelly was carrying most of her clothes by the time we reached my bedroom and her panties hit the floor a second after I closed the door. I took the naked redhead into my arms and we kissed with such deep passion that I nearly passed out from lack of oxygen.

We managed to slow down enough for me to get undressed and I led Kelly to the shower where we lovingly washed each other. We did a lot of touching to make sure everything was clean, but we were both careful not to make the other come. Without saying much of anything, we let each other know that we wanted that saved for making love.

"Did I really shake so much when I signed your pussy?" I asked, looking at the signature I'd placed there with a Sharpie when we last made love.

"Um… It was fading. I wasn't with you and I sort of touched it up so I'd still have you on me," she confessed. I shook my head.

"Little redhead, that is forgery." I got a bottle of alcohol and a cotton swab and carefully wiped away the ink. "Now. After I've painted another masterpiece in your pussy, I'll sign it again. Anytime you needed it signed, you'll have to come to me for another painting."

"How about now, Jett? Will you make love to me?"

"Would you mind terribly much if I made a little snack of this tender morsel before I filled it?"

"Oh, yeah!"

I went down on that sweet little pussy like it was my last meal. Kelly wasn't satisfied until she'd maneuvered us around until she could get hold of my cock, too. I had a head start, though, and she had to keep pulling her mouth off my erection to moan and howl. I just loved parting those little folds surrounding her opening and darting in and out between licks of her clit. Before I let her get me off, though, I moved around between her legs and plunged my cock into that hot love tunnel.

"Oh! Oh, God! Yes!" I started to worry as I remembered how loud Kelly could get and I captured her mouth with my lips and drove my tongue into it. We battled there as wave after wave of pleasure washed over us, culminating in me driving as deep into her as I could and unloading a full measure into her tight pussy.

We managed to slow down a bit and our kissing became less desperate, even as her muscles and my continued thrusts kept me hard.

"Jett… do you… um… do you want to uh… come in my bottom?" she asked. She was turning so red her freckles blended with each other.

"What?"

"Um… anal? Do you want to fuck me there? In the ass?"

"Oh. I… Gee." I hadn't really thought about it much. Sure, there was a passing idea when I was tonguing her, but it wasn't like I set out to do that. It would be cool. But her pussy was so tight and hot that my cock was fully recharged and I really didn't want to pull out, even for a moment to plunge into something else.

"If you don't want to it's okay," she whispered. "I just want you to know that anything you want, I'll give you."

"I'd love it… sometime," I said. "But Kelly, you have to know that being in your pussy like this is the most intimate and delicious feeling I've ever known. You're… I just don't want to stop what we're doing."

"I love you, Jett. When you want it, I'm yours. Let me on top. Please?"

We rolled over so Kelly could sit up and post on my erection while I fondled her tits and reached around to pet the ass she'd just offered me. The flush of sexual excitement spread fully down onto her breasts, almost concealing her pale nipples against her normally milky skin. My fingers traced down her long torso and over her sucked-in navel and tummy. I played with her trimmed red bush and she pushed forward far enough for me to wiggle a finger between us where I could stimulate her clit.

"I'm so close, Kelly," I whispered.

"Good. I'm going to be quieter this time, I promise. I just want to feel you coming in me."

"Oh God! Can you hold right there?" I gasped. I knew I was buried as far as I could get up her because I could feel the hard ridge of her cervix against the tip of my cock. She held still as I continued to pulse my finger against her clit and her pussy squeezed and relaxed around me. Then it was there for both of us. We weren't thrusting or driving, so in the stillness we could both feel every quiver in the other's organs. It was amazing to lie still, gazing up at this petite beauty, and just feel my come shooting into her. And feel her response. Her vagina spasmed around me. It convulsed on my cock as she climaxed. We kept looking into each other's eyes through the whole peak and I saw tears running from them.

Finally, she lowered herself against my chest as she kept squeezing my softening dick.

"Jett, I um… don't want to do this with anyone else."

"Is anyone asking you to?"

"Yes. Well, not exactly. Derek said he'd like to try again, but we both agreed that he wasn't really interested in me. It's just that Dee won't fuck yet and he wants to feel it again. But… online… there are guys that want to watch me come. A lot of the time they say they want to fuck me. I'm just not interested. It's intense to hear guys talk about it or read their text messages while I've got my vibrator on my pussy, but nothing compares to this."

We snuggled in and hugged as we settled for sleep after I finally slipped out of her. She's light enough that I could probably sleep with her on top of me, but we lay on our sides kissing a little as she continued.

"I'll still do girls. I never thought I would until Jasmine told me I had to lick her if I wanted your cock."

"She was kidding, you know."

"Yeah, but it was like a challenge and I just dove in and discovered how yummy she is and then she was down between my legs and that girl can really munch a muff. I don't know where she learned it, but I'm confirmed now."

"I think you were her first."

"Unbelievable. I just want you to know that I'm good with all the girls in our little group. Even others if you bring someone else in. But yours is the only cock I want. You're the only boy."

We fell asleep breathing each other's air.

⋯∘⋅⇨ ⅢⅭ ☀ ⅢⅭ ⇦⋅∘⋯

"Seriously? This is where you think we should live?" Ariel asked in disbelief.

"How much is this going to cost?" Kelly added. "Do we have to clean it first?"

"Look at the bright side," Jas said. "Complete independence from both the college and our parents."

"It needs some fixing up, but I agree that it is within what we planned to spend," I said. Jas, Charmaine, and Sarah Lynn spent a lot of time doing research and establishing budgets for us. "Let's tour it and see what it has to offer, then sit and discuss the costs."

We went into the house with the rental agent who was apparently used to dealing with student renters in the slums. Technically, we don't really have a slum here. There are neighborhoods of questionable safety and economic value. This one was filled with homes built in the late thirties, just as the country was recovering from the Great Depression. It looked almost exactly like all the other boxes on the street. The difference between this and any modern subdivision was the size of the lot. There was enough room on either side of the house to walk through to the back yard. It was set only about ten feet back from the sidewalk. I guess one of the advantages was that we wouldn't have too much to shovel clear of snow.

In back of the house, the lot was about the same size as the house and included a rickety garage and a place for garbage cans on the alley. There was an old rotary push mower in the garage, but the back yard didn't look much like it had ever been used.

The agent took us in the front door onto a small enclosed porch. The porch covered the right half of the house when looked at from the street.

It was deep enough for a chair and a tray for winter boots. Then we walked into the… mess. The previous tenants had evacuated after school got out, apparently not caring if they got their cleaning and damage deposit back.

"The agency will have this shoveled out," the agent said. Beer cans, cigarette butts, even pizza boxes were on the limited furniture. There was no carpeting and the hardwood floor was scarred and stained. To the right was a small office, about eight-by-eight. The living room was a pretty good size and looked like the central social area of the house. Off to the right, behind the office, was a large dining room with some built-in buffet cabinet that had most of the glass missing. The kitchen was greasy. I couldn't tell what color the appliances had once been. They were about the same color as the rust-stained fixtures in the three-quarter bath next to the mudroom.

We headed up the narrow stairs and found three pretty good-sized bedrooms and a full bath. Aside from being dirty, it looked okay. Kelly immediately started running hot water in the tub and waiting to see how long it took to heat up. She was pleasantly surprised.

"Years ago, when the owner decided to rent it out to college students, he did some improvements so there would be adequate hot water, including an on-demand heater and new kitchen appliances. He had great plans," the agent said with a sigh of exasperation. "He only lasted a year, though, and when he died his son just assigned it to a rental agent and said to fill it. He never does anything to it and we do minimal maintenance. What you see is what you get. What you make of it is up to you."

It was obvious to me from the tone of her voice that she was used to dealing with the lowest level of college students—often those who came to school to party and needed a place off-campus to do it. Each of the bedrooms had two single beds and two desks in it, pretty much like dorm rooms would be. The closets were pretty tiny, though, and I wondered how the girls' clothes would fit.

"What's this?" Kelly asked, opening a door, and seeing more stairs.

"There's an attic room. If you need to store things, you can use it. It isn't heated, though." We went upstairs and found a low-ceiling room with two dormers. It was pretty big and very dusty, but it didn't look like the last tenants had put anything up here, so there was no trash. I watched as the girls mostly took a glance and left. Kelly kept wandering around, though, and noted there were four outlets in the room.

"I want this," Kelly said. "I could plug in a space heater to keep it warm. These circuits look comparatively new and are grounded."

"I'll have to check that," the agent said. "The original owner planned to live up here, I think, but he moved into a nursing home before the first students moved in. He was crazy to think that he'd live up here and use the three-quarter bath on the main floor as his bathroom. I think the circuits will support a space heater, but you'd be required to have a safe porcelain electric heater. No hot coils and no gas heaters."

We headed back downstairs and looked around at the amount of work we'd have to do. I could tell the girls were interested, if skeptical. Kelly had been sold when she walked into the attic.

"What about internet and utilities?" I asked.

"Utilities are included in the rent," the agent said. "Usually, this place is rented out to six individuals and dividing utilities up evenly is just too big a hassle. So, water, electric, and garbage are all included. So is gas heat unless you exceed the utility company's estimate on heating costs, based on their historic services. Unless you all have to heat the house above the norm or if there is an abnormally cold winter, you won't have to pay extra. I would advise keeping that attic door closed, though. The house is wired for cable TV, but that's not included. You can contract with the cable company for internet service and get a wireless modem. Or you can just use your cellular hotspots." The agent paused. "I'll tell you one other thing. We usually rent to six individuals and charge each one five hundred a month on a nine-month lease. That's total rent of three thousand a month. We could get more if the owner authorized a general fix-up. I don't usually see a group that's committing together, but if you will sign a single twelve-month lease with one person, or at most a couple, who is responsible, I can cut one-fifty off the cost. Each. Total rent would be twenty-one hundred a month. That's a big discount I wouldn't offer most people."

We left with a lot to think about.

13
Commitment

BY SOME miracle, none of us had to work on Saturday night. We'd just started working this week and some of us hadn't even finished training yet. I was sure that our schedules would get screwed up pretty soon. Sarah Lynn and I were both working at the grocery store. Kelly was at Donaldson's. Charmaine and Jas had both landed waitressing jobs at Applebee's. Only Ariel was still unemployed and I wasn't sure what she'd be doing. I just figured this was the last chance for a while that we'd all be able to spend the night together, so I called Granddad. He agreed we could use the lower level room for an overnight campout.

We needed a meeting. The house we'd toured was beginning to grow on us. I think we could all see possibilities that would require a little work over the summer but would give us a pretty decent space to live in by the time school started. The big question was whether we could afford it.

"Three grand sounds like an awful lot for that dump," Ariel sighed.

"Even twenty-one hundred is a stretch," Kelly agreed. "But I like it."

"Here's a question before we all start shooting it down," Charmaine said. She was usually the quietest of all of us, so when she spoke, we listened. "How many of you originally intended to live in a dorm this fall?" All except Kelly raised their hands. I know she was intending to just live at home and commute by bus to the campus. I wasn't sure what Charmaine had planned to do since she was doing the polling and didn't raise her hand. "Now, have you looked at the cost of dorm rooms? They cost between nine and twelve thousand for the school year. Keep in mind that is room and board. You get meals at some level. The very cheapest rooms are what they call expanded living. Nice name, but it means that instead of two in a dorm room, there are three. Same room-size, just more crowded."

"Ten grand for a year of room and board doesn't sound so bad," Sarah Lynn said. "And there are janitors. You only have to clean your own room, not the bathroom and kitchen."

"Not like the former tenants in our house ever cleaned," I jabbed.

"I agree that ten thousand dollars a year isn't a bad rate for the services, but it isn't for a year," Charmaine continued. "It's for the school year, September through May. And not even all of that. You can't stay in the dorm over winter break. There's a month that the school expects you to go home to mommy like a good little girl."

"Wait. So, we pay ten grand for eight months?" Kelly asked.

"Yeah. Twelve-fifty a month and you still have to deal with winter break and summer," Charmaine said. "When you look at that, even the five hundred a month is a bargain. At three-fifty, it's a steal—though we have to do our own cleaning and cooking."

"If we showed Jett's and my moms that place, they'd hit it like an atom bomb. Everything would be clean and sterilized in a week," Jas said.

"What about food?" Ariel asked. "Do we all just buy our own, or do we pool the money and create menus?"

"That would be most efficient," Charmaine said, "but maybe everyone isn't willing to do that. I checked the USDA website and it says that the monthly food cost for a nineteen-year-old is between two-eighty and three-seventy-five. At the top end, you have a male who eats out part of his meals—or orders pizza." We looked at the empty pizza boxes in front of us and started laughing.

"So, what you are saying, if I have the number right in my head, is that we'd pay twelve-fifty a month for eight months of campus housing and food, or we'd pay a maximum of eight-fifty and we could get it down to six hundred a month for twelve months of living independently with each other," Sarah Lynn said. "I'm in."

"Me, too," I said.

"There's only three bedrooms," Jas said. "Who gets to be roommates? And can we get a double bed for Jett's room?"

"We should get a king-size bed and use the other two rooms for overflow," Ariel laughed. "I'm in."

"I have a request," Kelly said.

"Go with it, girlfriend," Jas answered.

"Um… Not that I don't want to room with any of you, but I need to earn a lot more money than I do to pay for school and housing. That's why I was going to live at home. But I've been experimenting a little with some help from one of my co-workers at Donaldson's. She uses her job there just so she can answer the question, 'Where do you work?' without admitting she's a stripper."

"Kelly, are you still thinking of becoming a stripper?" I asked softly.

"Not exactly. I told you something Thursday and it's still true. You're really the only male I want to be close to—in any way. Delilah doesn't work in a club. She does it all online. I mean, we've been doing that with each other for three years. You've probably all seen me come a million times. Why not add a few anonymous viewers who will pay for the privilege?" she said.

"Can you really make money that way?" Jas asked.

"Yeah, but please don't go into competition with me," Kelly laughed. "Delilah says that in a slow month, she makes about a thousand dollars. During her birthday month this year, she made five thousand."

I could see where this was going at last. I had no strong feelings one way or another about Kelly doing sex shows for online viewers. What she needed, though, was a broadcast space.

"That's why you are interested in the attic," I said. "You would have your own private studio."

"Yeah. I'd need a few things to make sure I could do a good quality broadcast. For example, I'd need a broadband connection that was stable and had unlimited high-speed internet. The agent already told us that I'd need a space heater. Maybe some lights and stuff," Kelly said.

"How are you going to pay for the startup costs?" I asked. "I mean, we do okay with our short sessions and WiFi, but aren't you going to need a more powerful computer and camera and stuff for this?"

"Um… You know my mom is a single parent, right? Well, Siobhan has always been very upfront with me about sex and men and all. She's got a nice secretarial job now, but when she was my age, she was a stripper. Exotic dancer, as she says. Exotic enough that she got knocked up and I came along. That changed a lot of her career. Anyway, she knows I do stuff online with you. And it's one of the reasons I've had this birth control implant since my first period," Kelly giggled. "Anyway, she doesn't make enough to pay for college, but she said that if this is what I wanted to do, she'd invest in new equipment for me and give me tips."

"Your mom is so cool," Charmaine sighed.

"I don't mind Kelly having the big room, but I think Jett needs a room, too. Maybe not his own bedroom by himself because we all want to sleep with him," Jas said. "But Jett needs somewhere to paint and not be limited by studio hours and availability at the U."

"That one should be obvious," Ariel said. "What would we do with that office space off the living room? If it's not too crowded for you, Jett, would that work as a private space to paint?"

"Yeah. That would work. I don't have much more room than that in my bedroom at home and there wouldn't be a bed in this room," I said.

"Which brings us to the lease," Sarah Lynn said. "Do we each sign separately, or have just one or two of us sign with the others subletting?"

"A hundred and fifty bucks a month is eighteen hundred a year," Jas said. "We could bank that and all go to Florida for spring break."

"Who should sign the lease?" Kelly asked.

"Jett and me," Charmaine answered. We jerked our heads around to look at our quiet friend. "It makes sense. Jas and I found the place, but when we toured it, the agent addressed all her comments to Jett. It's just a reality of the world. She just figured we were his harem."

"We are," Jas giggled.

"So why you?" Sarah Lynn asked.

"Because I'm going to be our group's accountant and treasurer," Charmaine answered. "Jas is studying business and marketing which will always be helpful. Ariel is in engineering. You're doing rocket science and brain surgery as a double major or something. Kelly is doing sex. Jett is doing art. I'm the only one who is doing numbers. I should write the checks for our rent and groceries and such."

"Char, do you have any idea how much you mean to all of us?" I asked. The other girls nodded. I'd been about to object to having my name on the lease, but her simple and selfless declaration made me change my mind. We had a lot of things to work out, but we had found a place to work on them.

Charmaine and I went in to the agency Monday after I got off work and signed the lease. I paid the damage deposit and first month's rent. Well, if this didn't work out, I'd just signed away most of the thirty thousand I had in my account. The agent said they would have the house 'mucked out'—like it was a horse stall—by the end of the week and we could have the keys, even though it was still a week before the first of the month.

The next day I met Char after work again and we went to the bank with seven hundred fifty-dollar checks from each of us. We tried to open a business account and were told we needed to create a business first. I had about thirty-five thousand in that bank, so they were really helpful and showed us the options. She helped us set up a co-op and navigate the state registration process. Then, we could open a checking account for our club. All the checks were made out to me but, because I had a healthy checking account at the bank, I was permitted to endorse the checks payable to our co-op. We set it up as a basic food co-op with the house as our location. We could now pay the rent and pay for food from the co-op account. Charmaine figured out that because I paid the damage deposit and the first month's rent, I didn't need to pay my 'dues' for six months. She was registered as the treasurer and I was registered as the president of the co-op.

"God! I feel like I just married you!" Charmaine said. "Can we go on our honeymoon now?"

"With all our four other wives?" I laughed.

"Yeah. There is that. Um… Jett?"

"Are you okay, Charmaine?"

"Yeah. I guess. I really do want to make love to you, you know?" Char hesitated for a few seconds and I wasn't sure if I was supposed to answer. "I'm just not quite ready."

"We didn't put anything in our registration that said members of the co-op have to have sex with Jett," I said. "We're going to live together and I hope you will let me hug you, you know? But you don't have to have sex with me or any of the others in order to be with us."

"I really want to. But I'm scared and I'm not really ready. With you. Not all the way. I kind of liked blowing you. I love it when Jas or Ariel eat me. I gladly return the favor. But, I'm not on anything and I don't want to take any chances. And… I'm just not ready yet."

"Char, I meant it when I said I love you. You know I haven't had sex with Ariel either. It's just not a requirement. Okay?"

"Thank you, Jett. I love you, too."

I dropped Charmaine off at Applebee's so she could go to work and went home, not really sure who would be in my bed that night.

⚬∘⇨ ꞊ ☽ ꞊ ⇦∘⚬

"I'm glad to see all the paint came off," I said when Ariel undressed in front of me. This was just a 'friendly sleep-over' according to Sarah Lynn, with the three of us sharing my bed. We all needed our fix of each other on a regular basis. I'd prefer that we all slept in one big pile like we did at Granddad's, but there just wasn't room in my bedroom. And tomorrow we'd begin going to the house to start our own clean-up.

"Yeah. I'm not sure I'm happy about it, though," she said. "Getting painted was intense. Wearing the paint for a few days, though, kept me on edge. Um… My mother knows."

"She what? Ariel, do I need to be concerned that there's some Ninja contract out on me?" I asked. I thought she was going to keep the paint covered up until she removed it.

"Ninjas are Japanese. Besides, the Dragon Lady is white. She just adopted Chinese ways when she married my father."

"So, she knows about the paint job and hasn't kicked you out of the house?" Sarah Lynn asked. The three of us were sitting cross-legged on my bed facing each other. It was a distracting sight, but I'd had close-up encounters with both girls' breasts and pussies, so I was mostly relaxed. Mostly. "I wish my mom was like yours," Sarah Lynn sighed.

"Really? I know I complain a lot about my mother, but when I see

113

what yours did to you… Oh, Sarah Lynn, I'd make you my sister any day. And you were our valedictorian. My mother would be so pleased. She'd make you play piano or violin, though." The two girls embraced and shared a very unsisterly kiss and some fondling that that changed my mostly relaxed into not relaxed at all.

"Um… How did the Dragon Lady find out? About the body painting?" I asked when it looked like the girls were settling down.

"Oh. Well, I didn't want to risk washing the paint off, so I didn't shower. I did sponge baths and made sure I didn't start to smell, but Mom caught me washing my hair in the sink and making a total mess of the bathroom. Once she started to question me about why I wasn't in the shower or soaking in the tub, I couldn't evade her. I tell you, the CIA needs to have my mother interrogate terrorists. They'd never have to resort to torture," Ariel laughed.

"What did she say about it?"

"She demanded to see it. I haven't undressed in front of my mother since I got my first period! It was very embarrassing and she kept walking around me and turning me so she could see. Then she says, 'You can't wear a bikini.' I got all defensive and said I was proud of the art and would be happy to show it off. My mother laughed. She said, 'No. A bikini would cover too much. You have to go naked.' I about died."

"Fuck! I didn't know your mother had a sense of humor," I said.

"We had a really good talk after she washed my hair and allowed me to get dressed. She said you are a very good artist but what are you going to do for a living?" Ariel laughed. "She expects you to become a doctor so you can take care of me properly."

"Tell her I'm training to become a surgeon and am getting very good at cutting up dead animals."

"I'm so impressed with your mom. She's okay with you moving in with us?" Sarah Lynn asked. Ariel shifted position so her left arm was toward us.

"See this?" She wore a small bandage on the inside of her left arm above the elbow.

"Did you hurt yourself?" I asked.

"I got an implant."

"For birth control?" Sarah Lynn asked.

"Yep. Dragon Lady says that if a boy is getting that familiar with my body, he'll get more familiar soon. She took me straight to my doctor and she shot this little rod into my arm so I'm covered. Um… Jett? I don't want to just lie down and let you fuck me because I'm protected. That's not too romantic and I'd die if it was just a fuck. But sometime when we're being all sexy and turned on and we're ready… Well, you don't have to worry about stopping to get a condom and coming in me. Okay?"

I was a little dumbstruck and just nodded. When my head nodded, I guess my erection did, too. Both girls noticed but ignored me as they returned to a mutual embrace and kissed.

"What about me?" Sarah Lynn asked. "If we get all sexy and turned on and are ready, can I fuck you?"

"Sarah Lynn! You've already fucked me! And you're welcome to do it again and again," Ariel said. "Now!"

"How about if we double up on Jett and both get off while we're kissing and touching each other?"

"You mean…?"

"You take his mouth and I'll take his cock."

And that was about all there was to that discussion. It didn't take long before Sarah Lynn was posting on my cock while I filled my mouth with Ariel's pussy.

-o-·❖ ɔɔc ·❈· ɔɔc ❖·-o-·

I woke up in a guy's dreamworld. A soft head of hair was on my shoulder and I could feel Sarah Lynn's breath on my chest. And Ariel's mouth on my erection. I reached down enough to touch her hair and let her know I was with her as I moaned softly. Sarah Lynn raised sleepy lips to touch my cheek and then my lips. As we teased each other gently, Ariel kept up her rhythm on my cock.

"I'd get up on your face, but it's so nice to just kiss," Sarah Lynn sighed. Our kiss deepened and I wiggled my hand down to where I could touch her pussy. Her sigh became more vocal, causing Ariel to lift her head slightly off my dick to look at us. Her gentle hum around my cock as she returned it to her mouth told me she was content with this arrangement.

115

Sarah Lynn edged her way up far enough that I had a better angle at her pussy and could get one of her nipples in my mouth. She preferred a gentler touch on her nipples than, say, Kelly, who liked to have them chewed on a bit. But Sarah Lynn was very sensitive and a little bit of sucking and tonguing got her started pretty quickly. Shortly, she was humping on my fingers as I slid them over her clit and into her steamy center. I knew the tension was mounting for both of us and it was a near thing, but I beat her over the precipice. Ariel didn't try to deep throat me but kept the tip of my cock between her lips as she stroked me to completion. The reflexive jerk of my fingers against Sarah Lynn's clit sent her over the edge just behind me.

We all three just lay limply in that position, my softening cock in Ariel's mouth and my fingers in Sarah Lynn's pussy, as we came slowly back to earth.

"We have a girlfriend who hasn't gotten hers yet," Sarah Lynn said. "You got to taste her juices last night. Why don't you go take a shower while I show her I love her, too?"

It was difficult to move away as the two girls rolled toward each other, but I gave them their space while trying to touch every bit of their bodies on my way out of bed. By the time I made it to the bathroom door, Sarah Lynn was between Ariel's thighs and our little Asian girlfriend had already begun her ascent.

The girls squeezed past me as I got out of the shower and they got in, both with happy grins on their faces. I'm pretty sure my face reflected their happiness. I dressed in my grubbiest clothes and went downstairs for breakfast.

This was a big day. We were going to claim our house.

14
Shacking Up

THE MOM brigade arrived at the same time we did. Sondra Davis brought Jas and Charmaine. Siobhan O'Rourke came with Kelly, and my mom and dad followed Ariel, Sarah Lynn, and me. It was a little sad to realize that my dad was the only father who was active. Charmaine's abusive father was part of the reason she never wanted to go home again.

Ariel's mother showed up looking the part of a professional house-cleaner. Her father was friendly with other adults but considered dealing with 'children' to be the women's work. And Sarah Lynn's father was probably the reason her mother was so hysterical about Sarah Lynn being devil-possessed and disowned. We'd be watching carefully if he showed up as it would mean trouble. Jasmine's dad was killed in Afghanistan when she was little and Sondra's new boyfriend, Ray, just hadn't been around much yet. Then there was Kelly, of course. She'd never known a father at all.

"We need before and after photos," Charmaine said. "And make sure your date and time settings are on."

"What gives?" I asked.

"You put up over two thousand dollars for a damage deposit, Jett. We need to make sure that you get it back. I like our agent, but I still wouldn't put it past her to claim as much of the deposit as possible because something was left dirty. I want evidence of what it looked like when we moved in compared to how we leave it."

"Wow, Charmaine. You think of everything," Ariel said.

"Just money things," she laughed.

The women attacked. If there was one thing Jasmine's and my mothers knew about, it was cleaning and sterilizing a house. The Dragon Lady seemed to be on the same page. Among them, they had buckets, mops, cleansers—all organic—and gloves for everyone. Siobhan carted in a huge vacuum cleaner and I grabbed it to follow her all the way upstairs to the attic. The room was empty but covered with dust and cobwebs.

Dad and I assessed the physical maintenance chores and headed to Home Depot to get a few gallons of off-white paint, brushes, rollers, and paint trays. At the last minute, he decided we were going to need a step ladder at the house anyway, so he bought two and a plank to put between them so we could paint ceilings more easily. We picked up a plaster kit and sandpaper as well. We'd seen pretty serious gouges in the walls of two of the rooms. When we got back, Granddad was carrying out a garbage bag filled with debris he'd picked up from around the house. He'd brought rakes and his lawn mower in the pickup.

Dad and I started filling nail holes and cracks, working from the upstairs bedrooms down. Kelly thumped down the attic stairs with the vacuum cleaner and attachments, grabbed a gallon of paint, and headed back upstairs. They were moving quickly up there but had a lot of surfaces to cover.

By the time Dad and I finished spackling the holes, Sarah Lynn and Charmaine were in the first bedroom sanding the rough edges and running the vacuum. Dad and I set up the step ladders and I started with the ceiling. I hadn't noticed how dingy it was until I put a fresh coat of ceiling white on. I was just thankful that it was only lightly textured and not one of those popcorn ceilings they say are illegal now. Something about Styrofoam or asbestos or something.

I moved the stepladders and plank into the second bedroom and started on the ceiling while Dad was joined by Mom to paint the walls. Jas and Sondra were cleaning the oven and appliances in the kitchen downstairs while Ariel and the Dragon Lady scrubbed a year's worth of gunk out of the upstairs bathroom. Someday I was going to have to find out her name. I suppose I could just call her Mrs. Chen.

I could hear the mower running outside when someone yelled that we should come downstairs for lunch. I'd only managed to get two ceilings painted.

WE DIDN'T GET finished that day. Or that weekend. By Sunday night, the six of us were exhausted. Fewer parents had shown up on Sunday. They had other things to do. It was nice of all the moms to take a break from their busy schedules to help clean, but they weren't really into painting. Sondra and her boyfriend Ray had planned to go on a dairy tour in the next county. They called it a wine and cheese tasting. My parents had plans with Grandma and Grandpa Blackburn like they did most Sundays. Siobhan went to church in the morning but came back to help us in the afternoon. Now that Kelly's room was clean and painted, they were working as hard on the rest of the house as anyone. The Dragon Lady brought us lunch, but she had things to do with her other two kids.

That left the six of us. And Granddad.

"I don't mind helping you when you are all working so hard. You kept my house spic and span when you stayed with me," he said.

"The work you did in the yard yesterday probably improved the value of this place by ten thousand dollars," I said.

"At least a hundred beer cans. And some of them had been crushed into the ground long enough that I could tell they'd been there longer than a year. The one thing you can be thankful for is that no pets have been allowed. I'd be in a different mood if I was cleaning up dog shit," he said. "Now, I'm going to work on the doors. The porch door is almost off its hinges and the downstairs bathroom door doesn't close right."

I was thankful that Granddad took on the fix-it jobs. I can sling paint but rehanging a door would take me about three times as long as it took him. I think I could do it, but it wouldn't be fast or pretty.

BY THE END of the second weekend, we were all getting a little surly and on each other's nerves. None of us realized what a big project just cleaning this house and getting ready to move in would be. We all had jobs, too, and none of us was used to working full time. I know. World's tiniest violin. My heart bleeds for you. Poor little privileged kids getting a taste of real life. Nobody said it would be easy. *Yadda-yadda.*

"I want to go to the festival next weekend," Ariel whined. "I'm tired of all this work."

"Aren't you going to move in?"

"I don't have that much to move. And we don't have to do it all at once."

"So, because you have a nice secure place where you could live all summer, you're not going to help anymore?" Sarah Lynn demanded. "That's pretty fucking selfish."

"Knock it off! Nobody made you president, Sarah Lynn," Kelly snapped. "Maybe you're smarter than the rest of us, but you didn't work any harder."

"Says the girl who gets a private room away from everyone else," Jas sniped at her.

"Nobody said anything about it until it was clean and nice," Kelly said. "It's not like you'd live in the attic. It's hot in the summer and cold in the winter."

"Which won't stop you from getting naked and whoring your pussy to anybody who'll pay," Ariel said.

I could feel our whole little family crumbling around us and had no idea what to do. I felt the same way. I hadn't painted a picture since we split up and left Granddad's. And forget about sex. We were all too tired for that. Everyone wanted private time and this was supposed to be the great fun summer between high school and college. It sucked.

And to top it all, Charmaine was crying.

"Char, honey, it's okay. What's bothering you?"

"We sound like my father and brothers. I thought we'd be something better," she sobbed.

"Fuck! You're right. Sounds just like my family, too," Sarah Lynn said. "I'm sorry. Of course you should go to the festival next weekend, Ariel. That was stupid of me. We should all take a break."

"I'm sorry, Kelly," Ariel said. "I think you have a very pretty pussy and I miss licking it."

"Me, too," Jas said. "I mean, I'm sorry, too. I mean, I miss licking your pussy, too. But, I mean…"

"I get it, Jasmine," Kelly said. "Thank you. I didn't mean to grab a private space and exclude you all. It should just be our fourth bedroom so we can have one more option."

"Honey, you do need space to perform," Sarah Lynn said. "I hope you'll invite us up to be with you sometimes, though."

"Or come down to be with the rest of us," Charmaine said. "But we agreed before you signed the lease that you could have the attic. I just want to be with you all and not be fighting."

"We're so tired. And it's shark week for me," Ariel said. "I'm already cramping."

"Oh, God! Are we all going to get on the same cycle? Now that you mention it, I smell blood in the water," Jas said. "Who are you texting, Jett?" I tried to stay out of most of the conversation while the girls were ripping each other to shreds. I'd avoided being attacked so far but wasn't willing to risk it.

"Um… I was trying to think of something nice to do for my girl-friends because we're all stressed out," I said. "I texted Ford and I'm going to run over and pick up a lid. I'll pick up food, too."

"Yeah. I could stand a good high," Sarah Lynn said. "I'd spread my legs for a joint."

"You'd find me between them," Ariel said. "I hope you weren't counting on a cock."

"Jett, you're so sweet," Jas said. "Can we have Chinese food?"

"Right here," Ariel said, pointing at her crotch. "Ordinarily, I'd be highly offended at your suggestion, but if we're going to get high, we need lots of noodles and rice."

"Carbs!"

"Can you bring some chips, too?"

"And chocolate."

"I'll go with Jett," Jas said. "We're asking too much of the sweetest lover we could want."

"Why don't we fix up a place where we can… um… relax," Char said.

"You mean get naked?"

"Yeah."

With that, Jas and I made the rounds of Ford's house, the grocery store, and Wok & Roll. When we got back to the house, it was eerily quiet.

·o·◆))C ☼))C ◆·o·

AFTER YELLING FOR people, we finally heard Char come downstairs. She met us without stepping out of the shadow as she was naked and we didn't have blinds pulled on the downstairs windows.

"Let me help take some stuff and come on up. We're meeting in Kelly's Kat House."

"Her what?"

"That's what we've decided we need to call the attic room. It's going to be fun!"

What a change from the mess of girls we left earlier. We climbed the stairs with a case of pop, chips, and boxes of Chinese food.

What a great room this was going to be!

"Wow, Kelly! When did you do all this?" I asked.

"Mom and I have been doing a little bit each night. She says she's jealous and wants to come perform here, too."

"No kidding?" Jas said.

"No offense, Kelly, but if your mom performs, I'm going to tune in," I said. "She's a total MILF. Who wants a hit?"

I had the bong filled and we started passing it with the lighter while I looked around at Kelly's Kat House. She had a large futon bed with a soft foam topper and it had been made up with new sheets and pillows. She had a window fan, too. That was going to be necessary as the weather got hotter this summer. It was already pretty hot just with the six of us sitting around. The temperature had been in the eighties earlier and wasn't cooling off outside very fast.

It was obvious that the room wasn't finished, but she had shelves made out of crates with a curtain over them for a dresser. There was a clothes rack next to her desk where the computer and camera would be.

"How'd you come to name it Kelly's Kat House?" I asked.

"I registered as a performer on nood.tv. I needed a screen name and didn't want it to be anything like my real name or heritage. I decided to call myself Kat Mon Dieu. So, this became the Kat House."

After the second hit from the bong, we dove into the food. Sarah Lynn and Ariel took charge of getting Jas and me naked and then Ariel

122

proceeded to eat a spring roll off Jasmine's mound.

"No hot mustard!" Jas screamed. We all took that to heart and didn't eat anything real peppery. We all had thoughts of eating at the Y later. In fact, while Ariel knelt between Jasmine's legs to eat her roll, I crawled up behind her and took a good long lick of her…

"Ariel! What happened to your hair?" I asked. "Your slit is bare as a baby."

Ariel wiggled her butt, encouraging me to take another lick. I obliged and heard Jas echo Ariel's moan.

"Oh, God! I'm glad the flow hasn't started!" she groaned. "The Dragon Lady happened. When I got my implant, my mother found out I was still a virgin. Which led to a lot of questions that I ended up answering about our sex lives. 'You make your boyfriend and girlfriends wade through all that hair to give you pleasure?' she yelled. Tuesday, I found myself stretched out naked in stirrups while this Vietnamese woman ripped my pussy hair out by the roots."

"You got your pussy waxed?" Jas exclaimed. "I want to do that. I'm sick of shaving every day."

"It hurts," Ariel warned. "But fuck! Jett's tongue on my little bare lips feels so… I didn't know I had so many nerves down there!"

None of us actually planned to spend the night in our new home, but by the time we'd eaten, smoked, and fucked, we were all too exhausted to leave. We just piled onto Kelly's bed however we could and went to sleep.

•ᐧ❖ ⏾ ☼ ⏾ ❖ᐧ•

I WAS AWAKE and just lying there in a bed filled with girls. Cute, lovable girls who said they loved me and each other. We'd had a close call the previous night when exhaustion and tempers created enough friction to heat the room. I was contemplating how to keep us all in tune without making orgies while we're high into a regular thing.

And I was enjoying the position I woke up in. Charmaine's cinnamon skin was pressed against me in spoons. My morning wood was lodged between her lush ass cheeks. Her ample tits, the largest of all the girls, were held in my hands with hard nipples pressing against my palms.

Char shifted a little and I felt the pressure between her cheeks relax some as her hand found the opening between her legs. She started rocking

123

back and forth against me, which felt just fine. I joined in, not making any big thrusts because I wasn't sure if anyone else in the bed was awake. I felt Kelly's lips softly kiss my shoulder from behind and her hand creep down between her own legs.

I'd woken up in various positions with Sarah Lynn, Jasmine, and Kelly over the past few weeks but if we woke up turned on, we got right to business fucking. If I woke up with Ariel, it was usually with her on top of me or sucking me. It might sound strange, but we were all still pretty inexperienced when it came to sex. It had just been five weeks since Jas and I broke the ice. And so far, Jas was the only one I'd done doggy-style. So, sawing my cock back and forth between Char's cheeks was a new experience for me and I was enjoying it immensely.

Then I ran into her asshole. I didn't go in or anything. I just made contact with the tip of my cock. Char jumped with a whispered scream. I backed off.

"Sorry," I said. "Didn't mean to hurt you."

"Didn't hurt," she gasped. "Didn't hurt at all. It's real… you know… sometimes Jas licks me there and I go crazy." That was a new data point. I'd have to try that.

"Do you want me to lick you?" I whispered.

"Yeah… um… no. I want… you to do it again." *Do it again?* Oh! She meant run into her asshole again. Yeah, well, that just meant that I could continue sawing between her cheeks with my cock spreading precome all over to make them slippery. I pulled back and pushed forward, snagging the tip of my cock on her anus again. I could feel it fluttering and it drove my cock crazy. Char already had a hand between her legs and reached through to pull my cock down there. She dragged it back and forth between her labia and I was getting ready for her to position me so I could thrust in for the first time. Then she shoved me back, grabbed a handful of her own juices and smeared her butt, and held my cock at her tiny hole while she pushed back against it.

When the head of my cock popped through the tight little ring, I nearly shot off right then. I was gasping for breath and Char was whining as her hand flew over her clit. I wanted to pull back and thrust again, but only the head of my cock was in her, so I pushed forward more instead.

Her whine came in tiny gasps and I thought she'd hyperventilate, but her fingers never slowed down, so I just kept pulling back a bit and pushing in some more.

Char came. I wasn't ready yet and kept thrusting into her bottom. She came again. I was getting close and pulled all the way back to the head of my cock and pushed again, burying myself in her butt as my semen started pumping out and I saw stars. Char came again.

I heard a couple other orgasms around me as our bedmates reached their climaxes. Then my cock started to shrink out of her and she jumped.

"Oh, God! I think I'm pooping." She threw off the light sheet and ran for the stairs.

"Shit," Kelly said as I rolled to my back. "She's right. Come on. You need a shower." Kelly grabbed my hand and dragged me all the way to the main floor three-quarter bath and shoved me in the shower. "Fuck! I'll have to change my sheets already. That girl can't sleep in my bed if she shits it."

"Um… She didn't, Kelly."

"Huh?"

"I uh… fucked her ass. What she felt was me pulling out."

"Holy…" Kelly grabbed soap and began vigorously scrubbing my cock. My balls. My ass. I think she was trying to be rough as she scrubbed with her hands but… well… soapy hands on a teenage cock. Pretty soon, Kelly had her hands full. She looked at my cock and then up at me. "Did you… want to do that with me?" she squeaked.

"Um… Not right now, Kelly. It really took me by surprise. If you want to try sometime, we can but you know how much I love being in your pussy." She rinsed my cock and examined it carefully.

"You think it's clean now?"

"With the way you were scrubbing it, I can't imagine how it wouldn't be," I laughed.

"Then put it in my pussy," Kelly said. She bent forward with her hands on the shower wall and thrust her ass out. I had to bend my knees down and Kelly stood on tiptoe but between us we got my hard-on notched into her pussy and pushed. Again, I'd made love with Jas in the shower, but Kelly's ultra-tight and ultra-hot little pussy pounding back against me as I squeezed her cheeks was a new experience.

Eventually, we both got our release and I shrank out of her to rinse my cock again. She held her pussy lips open as the shower water beat down to rinse our come from between them. I finally turned off the water and Kelly turned in my arms to kiss me.

"Maybe someday, Jett," she sighed. "But for now, I like having your cock in my pussy too much to waste it somewhere else. Except my mouth sometimes, but I know that if you come in my mouth you'll just last longer in my pussy. Oh, look. Somebody brought us towels."

15
Back on Canvas

BY THE weekend, we'd all managed to get moved in. There were still a few things of mine and Sarah Lynn's at my house. Charmaine had less to move than the rest of us. She'd always had a limited wardrobe. Her dad had plenty of money, but he was stingy as all get-out. He didn't figure women needed money and he'd have to pay to get her married someday, so he wasn't about to waste it on her now.

We had several big deliveries. We chose the biggest of the bedrooms, which was about twelve-by-twelve, and bought a king-size bed for it. We took the two twin beds out to the garage and wrapped them in plastic. We'd put them back when we moved out. We kept the two twins in each of the other two rooms but put new mattresses on them and had the mattress company cart away the stinky old ones. I've never seen so many body fluid stains on a mattress. Guys must have been coming on them for twenty years.

The other really big delivery was a piano. Not like a baby grand or anything. It was just what they call a console, I think, but it was good quality and Ariel started playing almost immediately. *Sweet!*

We weren't going to replace all the furniture in the house, no matter how disgusting most of it was. We bought slip-covers for the sofa and chairs, a couple of plastic tablecloths for the dining room, started stocking the kitchen cabinets. Charmaine kept a record of everything we bought—even down to having checked the receipts for the cleaning supplies the moms bought and the paint Dad bought.

"These are things that apply to the cost of living here that exceeds the rent. If we ever get a complaint, all we need to do is show all our receipts and threaten to charge the landlord for improvements to his property."

She loved the numbers and had a dozen different spreadsheets that included a breakout of what each of us had contributed and our share of the balance. She even included the value of our labor at both minimum wage and average local "painter's helper" wage, which was somewhat higher.

We all managed to go to the festival on Saturday and heard some great bands. We were beginning to feel like we were a family and had our own home.

•◦•✦))C ☼))C ✦•◦•

I FINALLY MANAGED to get some time in my new studio. Well, that's what we were all calling the little eight-by-eight room at the front of the house where my painting things were. At first, I was going to just spread newspaper around on the floor like I did in my bedroom at home, but Jas convinced me to get a canvas tarp to spread on the floor.

"This way, the hardwood is protected and you won't have to worry about picking up newspapers every day. Once a week, we can take it out and shake it, or just run the little vacuum cleaner over it," she said. After the tarp was down, we moved my equipment in on top of it and realized right away that we wouldn't be moving everything out of the room once a week to shake the tarp. Vacuum it was.

"Do you want to sit for a painting?" I asked. "Maybe we could make love after. Or during." I kissed her and she melted into my arms like a kitten.

"I hate to delay you but could we make love first?" she whispered. "And again after?"

"Yeah. I'd love to do a painting of you with that just-fucked look." And that was what we did. No one else was home, so we fucked right there on the tarp-covered floor. Then I painted her with that slightly bemused expression she gets and her glassy eyes. I knew that my instructors in school were going to teach me to slow down, but the paint just flowed onto the canvas as I got lost in that smile. There was probably a lot of detail work that I'd want to get finished later, but I only took an hour and then bent Jas over the stool she'd been sitting on and slid smoothly back into her snootch. God! She even had me calling it that.

"I hope you never get tired of fucking me," Jas said as she turned in my arms and laid another kiss on me. We'd both gotten off loudly and were thankful no one else was home.

"You sure gave a show to the street and the house next door," Sarah Lynn said from the doorway. So much for having been alone.

"What?"

"Your windows are open. It wasn't quite so visible from the street because of the porch, but I walked around next door and they had a clear view."

"People saw us?" Jas squeaked.

"Just me. The house is still empty and probably will be until September," Sarah Lynn soothed her. "It just shows that we need to get some drapes up on these windows and remember to pull them when Jett's painting a model. Either that, or charge admission to the show. Let me see the painting."

She didn't wait for an answer but just walked around the easel to look at the painting. I returned to kissing and fondling Jas. Hell with the windows.

"You're an exhibitionist," Jas whispered.

"So are you."

"Only online, mostly."

We stopped our whispered conversation just short of me penetrating her wet pussy again when we heard a deep sigh from Sarah Lynn, still in front of the painting. Her eyes were closed and her head was tilted back as one hand fondled her own breast. I guessed the hand I couldn't see behind the easel was in her pussy. I saw that same look cross her face that I'd painted on Jas and wondered if she was mimicking the painting. After a couple more squeaks and a long sigh, her eyes opened and Sarah Lynn moved around the easel to approach Jas. The kiss they shared told me all I needed to know about why our little group worked.

"I hope it was as good for you as it was for me," Sarah Lynn said. "I've never felt so… satisfied after getting myself off. It's just… You looked… Satisfied is the only word I can think of." She turned enough to kiss me deeply. "Thank you for making love to us. We love you."

•◦•◦❖ ⟨)(☀)(⟩ ❖◦•◦•

As BIZARRE AS the interaction between Jas and Sarah Lynn had been, it felt good to be putting paint on a canvas where it belonged instead of on the walls. The girls went upstairs to take a shower together and left me naked in the little studio. I looked around for my briefs and finally found them next to the paint cabinet. I pulled them on and smeared a bit of paint from my palette on them. Kelly would be disappointed if she found I'd been painting and didn't save the underwear for her. Her new room with its camera and computer and toys had one sloping ceiling with my painted underwear tacked to it.

I was still trying to figure out what to do with my walls. Bare white wasn't really my taste. I didn't want to tack up a bunch of posters or nails for hanging pictures, though. The ceiling was higher than the room was square. Old houses, I guess. There was molding about a foot below the ceiling and the windows met it. That gave me an idea. I'd make a few hangers that I could hook on the picture rail and hang paintings from to dry. With that decision made, I kept applying paint to the canvas, filling in little details in the initial painting. Each time my brush touched the canvas it revealed more depth and meaning.

◦·◦❖ ❩❨ ☽ ❩❨ ❖◦·◦

THE SUMMER GOT boring real fast. We were all working more or less full-time jobs. I had the most regular hours at the market where I worked from six in the morning until two in the afternoon. Grandpa was 'promising' that I would be at a level of being able to work alone soon, but I still needed to finish my certification as a meat cutter. I was trying to figure out how I was going to do that.

I was fortunate to live in an area where there was a meat-cutting certificate program. That was what it was called informally. Formally, it was the Sustainable Farm to Table: Modern Meat Production. It had 26 credit hours and I was going to try to complete it in summer and evenings. Fortunately, the lab portion of the Protein Identification, Fabrication, and Utilization course was what I was learning at the market. Grandpa said he thought he could make a case for having me get the Retail Butcher Shop Operation and Sales credit from the market, too. It was still going to take me a year and a half to complete the other courses and over four thousand dollars in extra tuition. Grandpa was a devoted mentor, though, and the market was picking up all the extra tuition.

Sarah Lynn worked at the grocery store, too, but checkers got shuffled around a lot. She never knew from week to week what hours she would work and whether she would have a full forty, twenty, or fifty. While normally rare, overtime was more common in the summer as all the checkers with kids needed extra time off and it was a popular time for vacations. When a bunch of college students came in wanting jobs in the fall, it was more common for the store to hire people for ten to twenty hours a week and Sarah Lynn could expect a reduction in hours as more people were available.

Charmaine and Jas were experiencing some of the same issues. Now that they were no longer trainees, they had to check the schedule every week to find out what shift they'd be working each day. They were getting a lot more lunch and weekend hours when tips were lower and the work was just as hard. Kelly had finished her training, as well, and found herself working a regular thirty-hour week that included eight hours each on Saturday and Sunday. The other fourteen hours were Friday and Monday, so she had three days off in the middle of the week. That wasn't prime time for camming, but she was just getting started and wasn't worried about putting in long hours online until fall.

Ariel surprised even the Dragon Lady when she got a job doing childcare. She was like a nanny who worked each day while the kids would normally be in school during the fall and winter. It was a little less than full-time, but the pay was good and her three little kids grew to love her quickly. The only bad part was that she was even more emo when she got home than she normally was. She was either worried about Johnny's runny nose or upset that Karla had been pushed on the playground. Or she was furious that the parents had been late getting home and she'd run out of things to do with the kids and life was so horrible.

So, summer was a drag. I was getting my Principles of Sanitation and Pasture to Plate lectures out of the way in the evenings, working forty hours at the market, and worrying about having to attend a Slaughtering course one day a week in the fall.

My paintings—what few I could work on—were beginning to get bloody.

THE BIG DAY for Kelly's grand opening as a camgirl came at last. None of us realized that it wasn't just a case of flicking on the computer and sitting around naked. She actually had a training course she had to complete before the site would let her go live. That she had to pay for, of course. She'd also created three intro videos that were five minutes long. They were carefully scripted; were mostly tease, but they all showed my favorite Kelly-bits.

Kat-bits. The other five of us had also been training. Kelly did not go online. Kelly did not do porn videos. Kelly did not spread her legs and use a huge vibrator to come on camera for anonymous tippers. Kat did all that. Kelly was absolutely exclusive to our little family. Sure, she ran around naked like she always had. She sometimes waited in my bed for me to get home from the market before I had to go to class. I often heard her name moaned out by one of the other girls—especially Jas.

But if the camera was on in her room, she was Kat Mon Dieu.

The attic room where she performed had been transformed into a kind of Bohemian flat. She could stretch her hands over her head in the center of the room and place her palms on the ceiling. There was about ten feet of flat ceiling and then it sloped down until a little half wall dropped to the floor.

She had several props scattered about the room. A desk where she could study was against one wall with what looked like typical girl knick-knacks on it. But on closer examination, the desk lamp cover was shaped like a breast, complete with nipple. The teddy bear was a slipcover for her big vibrator. The poster on the sloping ceiling above the desk featured a drawing of a girl on a horse, but the closer you looked at it, the more you realized the entire drawing was made up of penises and vaginas.

There was lots of other stuff, of course, and we'd see bits of it revealed during her shows, but it included a kind of wheel-of-fortune with various acts or products on it. And there was the one sloping ceiling covered with my painted underwear. She had arranged it in such a way that, from the camera's angle, it almost looked like wallpaper. I was impressed.

Speaking of the camera, Kelly's mom had truly come through with top-of-the-line equipment, including a fast computer, high-res video camera, huge monitor that Kelly could see from any position in the room, multiple microphones so she didn't have to be beside the computer to talk and be heard, and even a few small lights that she could control on a dimmer to set the mood for her performance.

Our four girlfriends and I sat in the living room two floors below Kat's studio with our laptops and logged in to her site. My log-on was 'Kat's Coal'. The girls thought that was a clever pointer to my real name of Jett Blackburn. What's jet-black and burns? Coal. Okay. It worked for me. We all bought tokens to tip her in her first hour-long session.

She'd been building an audience through Twitter, Snapchat, and Instagram for the whole month she was in training, so there were a couple of dozen people who logged into her chatroom right after she started.

"Hi, guys. And girls," she started. "I'm new. I am so excited! Just as I started the camera, I started feeling my juices wetting my snatch and my nipples just popped out, hard as a rock. I could really use some good loving." She went on from there to welcome each of the people who came to her chatroom by their screen-name as she danced around in a pair of ultra-short cutoffs and a crop-top. "This is my one-hour introductory session tonight. I'm not going to get completely naked, but as a special welcome to my room gift, each member here can request one of my teaser videos for free. You can have the strip tease," she said as she unsnapped and lowered the zipper on her shorts, "the blowjob demo," she pulled a dildo off a shelf and slid it into her mouth, "or the red-snatch masturbation vid. If you want all three intro videos, you can get them tonight for 100 little tippy tokens. Don't forget to give me the addy where I should send the clip. So, let's talk a while and get to know each other. RaginCagin, are you from down south? It's close to eighty here. Does it get lots hotter where you are?"

Wow! I couldn't believe how much energy Kat Mon Dieu put into her show. She managed to get comments from nearly half the people in her room. When she pulled her shorts off to show her cute little butt with a thong running down her crack and barely covering her pussy, she got a bunch of tips. She kept up the chatter as if she were talking to them face-to-face. She smiled and bounced around her room, giving a tour and what she'd be doing during future cam sessions. She got another round of tips when she shed her top and showed her tits encased in a sheer nylon bra so we could see her nipples through it.

"Look at how frickin' wet my pussy got tonight, just talking to you guys," she said, pointing between her spread legs. Her camera zoomed in on the wet spot on her thong as she fingered herself. "It's time for my one-hour opening special to end, but I'm really horny. Mmm. I love touching myself. As soon as this camera goes dark, you should know that I'm going to get my boyfriend to plunge his cock into me until we both come hard. Just think about that for a while. This week there will be cam sessions at eight o'clock Central time on Tuesday, Wednesday, and Thursday. Come back and see more of me, 'kay? Night now!"

The camera went dark and we all closed our laptops. I was hard as a rock and imagined everyone who watched Kelly was off stroking the meat. Jas, Sarah Lynn, Ariel, and Char were all leaning back with their hands in their panties.

"Jett!" we heard as Kelly came thundering down the stairs. "Fuck me! Now! Please!" She came running into the living room as my pants hit the floor. *Fuck her? Hell, yes!* She threw her little bra at Char and was wiggling her thong down over her butt as she crossed the room. I didn't give her a chance to do or say anything else. I grabbed her around the waist, bent her over the arm of the sofa, and plunged my cock into her hot, wet cunt. She wasn't kidding about how wet the broadcast had made her. "Yes!"

Ariel got the edge on the other four girls and got her pussy under Kelly's mouth. Her instant cry told me Kelly got right to work licking that cute little snatch. She was working her pussy muscles, too, and I wasn't going to last long. I felt a hand gently massaging my balls and realized Jas was behind me waiting for her turn at our girlfriend. At the other end of the sofa, Char and Sarah Lynn were locked in a sixty-nine. Kelly whined as loudly as my own bellow when I came in her. I'd scarcely finished pulsing when Jasmine pushed me aside and out of our girlfriend and started licking that inflamed cunt. Kelly went off again.

Kelly got an orgasm from each of the ladies and gave as good as she got before she finally came down.

"I know it won't always affect me like that but damn, that made me horny. I needed you. I needed all of you and I love you," she cried.

16

Getting Framed

"**OKAY, BUSTER. IF** you tip me again, I'm going to ban you from my room."

"Um… you can do that?" I asked my redhead girlfriend.

"It's one of the ways we have of protecting ourselves against harassment," Kelly said.

"But, how does tipping you mean harassment?"

"Do you pay the other girls for sex?"

"I don't pay anyone for sex."

"You're paying me! It makes me feel like a whore. You tip me fifty bucks a week and I trot right downstairs and fuck you. I don't want you to tip me!"

"I… I guess I sort of understand. Kelly, I never thought I was paying you for sex. We fuck because we love each other."

"And because I sometimes need release after three hours online playing with myself. Jett, I don't ever want money to be part of our relationship. If you can't watch me online without tipping, then I'd rather ban you from my room."

"I just thought of that as completely different. Like how many times you bought my painted briefs—for way more than they were worth, by the way. You're doing your job and that's what I was paying for. I'm sorry. I didn't realize what it would seem like to you."

"It gets complicated. I've been sending you pictures and masturbating with you online for three years. When I'm camming, it's different. I have to meet a certain level of expectation. People pay me to do that. You never demanded anything from me. I did it because I got turned on with you.

Some guy tipped for me to fuck my pussy with a dildo last night. I didn't feel like it, but it was on my tip menu. I was dry as a bone and still had to cram that plastic cock up my cunt for ten minutes and pretend to come."

"Can't you refuse?"

"Maybe once or twice. If guys start thinking that I won't perform for the tips they give me, they'll stop tipping. I just don't want anything about us to be like it is in the chat room," Kelly sighed. She leaned into my shoulder and I petted her hair. Eventually, we fell asleep.

⋅∘⋅ ⇨ ⟩⟩⟨ ☀ ⟩⟨⟨ ⇦ ⋅∘⋅

A WEEK BEFORE school started, I finished my first term in meat cutter school. Fall term wouldn't start until mid-September and I'd only have the Friday class in slaughtering. I wasn't really looking forward to it. I scheduled my art classes first, sort of hoping I wouldn't have time for a class at the tech school, but apparently, artists at the U don't like Fridays and I ended up with no class that day. How convenient that the three-hours a week slaughtering class only met on Friday morning. We had to go over to the slaughterhouse and learn the process as part of the Farm to Table certificate.

It was also my last week full-time at the grocery store. All six of us arranged to be off work for Saturday, Sunday, and Monday, Labor Day Weekend. It was the first time we'd all have extended time together since before we moved. Classes started Wednesday but there were some freshman orientation events on Tuesday. That meant we had three days to just loaf and make love.

Hah!

There were still a few dozen tasks to be done around the house that we never got around to before we moved in. I'd managed to mow the small yard once a week after Granddad got it all cleaned up before we moved. But the girls had wanted flowers in front of the house. They did a great job of directing me in where to dig and exactly how to plant what they bought. It did look nice, but we hadn't paid much attention to them after they were planted and the flower beds were covered with weeds. As the resident male, it looked like I was going to be assigned all the guy-tasks.

137

Whoever decided men should work outside and women inside should be hung. Why should a guy be the one to push a lawn mower, run an edger, trim bushes, weed flowerbeds, and… *Whoa!*

"Hey! Nice digs. How'd you manage to score this? Our place is a pigsty!"

Three girls in bikini tops and shorts were on the sidewalk looking at our place. And at me. I guess I'm not that bad to look at, but these chicks were in their predatory mode. I'd been slinging animal carcasses around the butcher shop all summer. I was in pretty good shape and was just wearing shorts and sandals. It was mid-morning and already hot. Summer's last flare-up before snow flies.

"Um… Hi. It wasn't any different than the others on the block when we moved in. We just did a lot of work," I managed. All three girls were blondes, with straight hair in identical cuts. The major difference that my practiced eyes could discern was the colors of their skimpy bikini tops. Why the heck would girls be out walking around on the street in so little clothing? It hadn't gotten that hot yet.

"You mean you bought the place?"

"No. We're just renting."

"Why would you do a bunch of work on a place that you don't own? What a waste!" Okay, second difference in the blondes. This one had a whiny voice and big round sunglasses. I just shook my head.

"Didn't want to live in a pigsty," I said.

"We already pay too much in rent and have a tiny room we have to share. I'm not giving the creep who owns the place any more than I have to." Number three. Pink sunglasses, pink patches of fabric that barely covered her nipples, and teeth that betrayed her perfection by being slightly too big for her mouth. "Could you come and cut our grass? We're just two houses down."

"Um…" Shit. Why is it I always feel obligated to help others. Especially when it's three stacked blondes standing almost topless on the sidewalk.

"Jett, honey, I brought you a Coke and came out to help with the flowerbeds," Kelly said from behind me. The blondes' plucked eyebrows shot up as they took an involuntary step back. I turned and grinned at

Kelly. She hadn't stopped with a bikini top. She had string-tied bottoms on and was barefoot. It wasn't quite a thong, but if Kelly moved around much, the back of her suit would creep right up her crack.

I took the Coke from her and pulled her to me for a kiss. "Thanks," I whispered.

"You two live together?" Blonde One said. The one with the blue top and a floppy hat. She wasn't looking straight at us. She was looking at Kelly's crotch. I glanced down and saw my signature, not quite hidden by Kelly's bikini. I sort of snorted.

"Us and four others," Kelly said brightly.

"Are they couples, too?"

"We're more like a sextet," Kelly said. I thought she overdid the emphasis on that, but who was I to argue.

"Do we have company?" Jas asked from the doorway. I looked up from Kelly and saw Jas and Sarah Lynn come down the steps. They were both in bikinis and flipflops, too. It was quite a sight. Both girls had a bit more boob and ass than Kelly and their bikinis were straining.

"I guess these are neighbors a couple doors down," I said. "We hadn't gotten around to names yet. I'm Jett. This is Kelly, Jasmine, and Sarah Lynn."

"Oh! Yeah. Sorry we didn't introduce ourselves. I'm Barb. This is Terri and Syl. Um… we were just wondering if we could borrow your houseboy to cut our grass." Well, she might as well have shit on the sidewalk. There was no way I was going to help them out. I definitely didn't like their user attitudes.

An arm slipped around me from the side and I glanced over to see Char next to me. Char's a little more full-figured than the other girls, and a little more modest. Her bikini was designed to cover more territory, but it was still stressed to contain her big tits. I was wondering where Ariel was. Then I saw her in the doorway.

She outdid all the others. I'd grown to expect some outrageous behavior with Ariel. She'd been surprising us all summer while emerging from her emo-goth girl persona. The first had been showing us how enthusiastic she was about oral sex—giving and receiving, male or female. Then discovering that her mother suggested she get her pussy waxed for all our greater enjoyment. After I painted her body, she'd become almost as much of an exhibitionist as Kelly, even though she was still technically a virgin. She had breasts a little bigger than Kelly's but less ass. And her shaved pussy was very puffy and it spilled over both sides of the tiny strip of fabric that went between her legs and disappeared in her crack. It was a one-piece suit and the strip between her legs split into two narrow bands that stretched up behind her neck like suspenders, barely covering her nipples.

"Jett, the radio said today was going to be the nicest day of the weekend. It's a shame to waste it on yardwork and cleaning. We thought maybe we could convince you to go to the beach today. We'll all help get everything ready for winter tomorrow? Okay, sweetie?" Ariel stepped down toward me and my other girlfriends parted to let her through. She stood on her tiptoes and I bent to kiss her.

That was an event all by itself. Ariel's kisses had gotten better the more she practiced—and she practiced a lot. I found my hands on her bare buns and lifted her until she wrapped her legs around my waist. She ground herself against my very erect cock.

"Please?" she whispered into my mouth.

"We'd better go inside before this turns into a sidewalk orgy," Sarah Lynn laughed. I looked around. The blondes were gone but there were three guys on the porch of the house next door watching us. I didn't put Ariel down as I led the girls back into the house.

"Jett? Just continue up to the bedroom, okay?" Ariel said. "We got you a Speedo to wear. I'll help you get it on."

Getting it on with Ariel was definitely on my mind and she didn't relax her grip with her legs, so I didn't relax mine on her butt. As soon as I flopped back on the bed, though, Ariel scrambled around so she could push my shorts down and swallow my dick. I pushed the little strip of fabric between her legs to the side just in time for her pussy to touch my lips. As worked up as Ariel had gotten us while we were kissing, it didn't take long for either of us to flood the other's mouth.

I gave her one more long swipe with my tongue from the top of her slit to her asshole and she shuddered before rolling off me. I flopped back and looked at my five girlfriends in their skimpy suits. Ariel, curled up next to me, hadn't rearranged her suit, so the strips of fabric now did nothing to cover her pussy and titties.

"We're sorry about all that, Jett," Sarah Lynn said. "Kelly saw those blonde bitches working their way up the street and went into action. We had to go out and sort of establish our territory."

"If you want to play with someone else, we'll try to understand, Jett. We're only eighteen and none of us have promised a lifelong commitment to each other. But by God! No fucking bitch is going to come around here and call you our houseboy!" Jas almost screamed.

"And if you're turned on and need relief," Kelly said, "among the five of us, we have fifteen holes, ten titties, and ten hands. At least one is going to be available to you at any time."

"I know Ariel and I are a little slower than the other three," Char said. "But we love you. And we love each other. I mean all of us. We never want you to feel like you are a hired hand around here."

"It was pretty obvious those bitches were going to treat you like that and they only have one currency to pay with," Ariel sighed.

"Are you all really going to the beach like that?" I asked. What I wanted at the moment was pretty much to line them all up and fuck each one, but even I have limits.

"No," Sarah Lynn laughed. Her top suddenly dropped and her magnificent boobs popped out on display. "I mean, we want to go to the beach, but these particular suits we bought just for our mutual entertainment. We didn't really mean to even… um… expose them to anyone else."

"You know what? I really love you girls. Let's get ready for the beach."

Getting ready included a deep passionate kiss from each of the girls and a lot of fondling. They made sure that before we were fully dressed again, I'd touched or been touched by all thirty-five of the offered sources of relief. It was a good day.

•·•❖ ⟫⟫ ☀ ⟫⟫ ❖•·•

By Monday, we'd managed to go to the beach, finish all the cleaning and repairs on the house, talk about our schedules for school, and lay out clothes for the first day of classes. Don't ask me. I had a pair of baggy jeans and a T-shirt. The girls didn't just throw 'any old thing' on and call it good. They did provide quite a show while trying things on and checking my opinion, though.

So, anyway, Monday morning after making love with Jas in a sweet encounter that just reminded me over and over of the first time we got together, I went into my little studio and got out some materials I'd been intending to experiment with but hadn't had time. After I'd painted Ariel's body, I'd started reading up on body paint. There were two kinds of specialized paints that were commonly used—water soluble and 'permanent'. The permanent body paint was more like the acrylics I used on Ariel in that they didn't wash off in a quick shower. They could be cleaned off with an alcohol solution or would wear off with normal showering in a week or so. I'd bought a bunch of both and an airbrush. I got a piece of Bristol board and was pretty much just experimenting with the flow settings and how to control the width of the stream. There was nothing about what I was doing that could be called 'art'. I just wanted to play.

I guess I was in there for a couple of hours before Sarah Lynn walked in with a Coke for me.

"What's that?" she asked, looking at the board. Her eyes were all scrunched up as she tried to decide if I had actually painted anything.

"Just an experiment," I said. "Trying out my tools." I put the airbrush down and took the Coke in one hand while pulling her to me with the other. She was wearing a baggy T-shirt and, I discovered, nothing else. As we kissed, I ran my hand up her thigh and under the shirt onto her bare butt. She squashed herself into me.

"You haven't painted me or Char yet," Sarah Lynn said. "Do you need a model?" She pushed away from me and stripped off the T-shirt. As usual in my studio, I was painting in just a pair of briefs. I had only a couple seconds to appreciate Sarah Lynn's body before she pressed her bare skin up against me and returned to our kiss. I still wonder where this girl… I mean… It seems like she just came out of nowhere last spring and suddenly I couldn't get enough of her.

I loved Jas and we made love as often as feasible when there are six people all trying to get it on with each other. She was calm and stable and sexy and willing and everything else a guy could want in a girlfriend. A look from her could turn me on and she looked at me a lot.

Kelly was just plain sex-on-a-stick. Preferably my stick. She'd been sending me naked photos and sexting with me for three years. She was a little taller than Ariel but thinner with little titties that I loved to suck at every opportunity—and she made sure I had lots of opportunity.

But Sarah Lynn… She was strong and a leader for our little group. You'd probably have to add all our IQs together to equal Sarah Lynn's. She wasn't the prettiest of the girls and knew it. The fact she didn't care didn't mean she was sloppy about her looks. She was just happy with them. As I was. When I held her in my arms, things just seemed to fit together, whether we were alone or with one or more of the other girls. Just standing in my studio kissing her with a Coke in one hand, I had the other in her pussy as she stroked my cock.

"I didn't come here to distract you like this, Jett. If you want to, we can. I was really volunteering for a painting."

"I can't help myself when you are with me like this," I said. "If we stop now, can we continue later on?"

"As much as we want."

"Are you game for some sexy painting?"

"Of course!" She kissed me lightly again and pulled her hand out of my briefs as I dragged my finger through her wet folds one more time with a sigh from both of us.

"See if Char wants to play paint, too."

Sarah Lynn ran out of the room with her tits and ass both bouncing and I started setting things up the way I wanted them. I moved the easel out of the way and grabbed an easy chair from the living room to drag into the studio. We'd put slip covers on all the furniture, debating over whether the gross stuff should be wrapped in plastic before we even did that. I draped a canvas drop cloth over the chair and tucked it in so I wouldn't damage the slipcover.

Char happily bounced into the room with Sarah Lynn and I saw the other three girls looking in to see what we were doing. I seated Sarah Lynn on one arm of the chair and Charmaine on the other. Sarah Lynn faced the seat and Char faced forward, straddling the arm of the chair. Mmm. I loved the way that position spread Char's pussy open but I tried not to get distracted. Again. Once I got the two girls leaning in toward each other with their arms linked on the back of the chair, I grabbed the experimental painting I'd been doing and positioned it between them. One of Sarah Lynn's breasts was in front of the painting and she reached across to the inside of Char's thigh with her hand, partially blocking the bottom of the painting. One of Char's massive mams was behind the painting, but the other was tucked up against it, slightly bulging over the edge. I stepped back and snapped a few pictures on my cell phone.

"I've got this," Kelly said. She came into the room behind me with her video camera. "I was Skyping Lisa and she wanted to watch. Rick, Ford, Derek, and Dee are on, too. Figured I might as well record it." Jas and Ariel had pillows they threw in a corner to watch me paint. I had no idea what people thought was so fascinating about watching me put paint on a canvas. But they were all surprised when I didn't pull my easel and a fresh canvas out. Instead, I loaded the airbrush with the first color I wanted and approached the girls.

"Unlike the paint I used on Ariel, this is temporary and is *supposed* to wash off in the shower," I said as I began. I started inside the painting and streaked outward across Sarah Lynn's left arm and side. She screeched a little when the cool paint mist touched her skin. A second streak went across the canvas to my left and over Char's shoulder.

"You're painting us!" Char said. "I hope you intend to be in the shower washing us when we're through."

"It will be my pleasure," I said. I couldn't stop myself before I used my left hand to reach between her spread legs and smear a little of her moisture over her exposed clit. She moaned and I got down to seriously painting.

•○• •◇ ⟯⟯⟮ ☼ ⟯⟯⟮ ◇• •○•

THE PAINTING ONLY extended in a couple of limited areas onto the girls, as if it had broken through some kind of invisible barrier from the canvas onto their skin. I could see exactly what was needed to finish it, though. I carefully held a straightedge along each side of the painting as I created a frame on the girls' skin. The frame was broken at the points where the paint seemed to flow out of it onto them.

I made sure the overflowing paint spilled down onto Char's exposed pussy which got her juices flowing so strong that the canvas on the chair was soaked beneath her. Part of the fun of painting my girlfriends was touching them while I worked. I slid a hand down Sarah Lynn's back and into her butt crack. She started to squirm and I whispered, "You need to stay still. You'll spoil the painting." She moaned.

I stepped back to look at the finished work and Kelly stepped forward to video it from every angle. Including a closeup of the paint on Char's pussy lips. I got my cell out and snapped a bunch of still photos. For just being an experiment in how to use my airbrush and body paints, it had turned into a couple of fun hours and a very sexy painting.

We finally told the girls they could get up and they grimaced a little where their skin was stuck to the canvas or each other by paint. The pain was short-lived and we got them to stand together as we took pictures of where the paint went and what they looked like without the painting held between them. Those pictures were also cool and informative regarding where the mist of color had gone. Sarah Lynn had one painted nipple and one just naked. The contrast was even sexier.

After everyone had petted and examined the two girls and we got comments from our online friends, I took Char and Sarah Lynn to the downstairs shower and cleaned them thoroughly. It wasn't really big enough for three of us, but we crammed into it together anyway.

17
Frightening the Specters

OUR NEXTDOOR neighbors were creeps. Not the dumb blondes from two doors south but the guys who moved in on the other side of us. The first party ran most of Labor Day weekend. We ignored them as much as we could, but when we went out to orientation Tuesday, there were beer cans in our yard and vomit on the sidewalk. The girls were royally pissed off and were going to start picking up the cans and throwing them back in the assholes' yard.

"Hey, wait," I said. "Don't touch any of their garbage without gloves. I hate to say it, but they could have all kinds of crap in there. Maybe even needles, condoms, and body parts."

"But they trashed our yard!" Jas screamed. "They can't do that!"

"And the sidewalk," Ariel agreed. "Gross!"

"I'll pull the hose around and wash the sidewalk," I said. "When we get back this afternoon I'll go have a talk with them. I doubt anyone is awake or sober this morning."

I sprayed down the sidewalk and managed to not get any of their shit on me. We walked down the middle of the street anyway to the next block where we could catch a bus to campus.

•∘•◈ ⊃⊃⊂ ☀ ⊃⊂ ◈•∘•

ORIENTATION WENT FINE and we stuck together most of the day. Of course, there were portions that were departmental specific and we headed off in all directions for a couple of hours. Ariel headed off to the College of Engineering, Jas and Char to different parts of the School of Business. Kelly hadn't declared a major yet but decided to investigate the

Digital Studies Department. I figured Sarah Lynn would go to medicine or nuclear physics or something, but instead she headed to the College of Arts and Letters to receive orientation for a Political Science degree. That girl was going to change the world one day. Of course, I headed for the Department of Art.

"You never called," Eva said, falling into step beside me.

"I haven't been available this summer," I answered when I recognized her. "You aren't a freshman. What are you doing at orientation?"

"Work study. We get a stipend for leading tours of the department and taking people over to the Art Lofts. So, you still want to paint me?"

"The way I remember it, it was *you* asking me to paint you," I chuckled. I wondered if Eva would fit in with our group or if the girls would tear her a new one. "We should talk about it now that I've got a place to work."

"Yeah. Well, you've got my number. Use it, okay? I gotta run to my group. See you!" She turned off toward a different studio and I went into the lecture hall where we spent an hour getting the rundown of how the department was organized and what the expectations were for first year. Then we divided into small groups for a tour of the facilities. I didn't get Eva's group.

After a day of touring and getting class schedules and requirements, I spent two hours in line at the bookstore spending over five hundred dollars on supplies. And two of the books I bought were used!

⋯∘⋅◈))C ☽))C ◈⋅∘⋯

"Assholes," Sarah Lynn said quietly as we walked down the street on the way home. Kelly sent a text that said she went home early and would put the casserole we made up yesterday in the oven. Jas said she needed to rearrange her work schedule and was going to Applebee's. Char and Ariel were walking behind us sharing some excitement over being on their own in college. I looked at the weekend worth of beer cans in our yard.

"We'll figure out a way to deal with them," I said. I wasn't sure what it would be yet, but it had to do with gluing the cans to their hands and foreheads. Wish I could figure out a way to do that.

"Hmm. Maybe you could do the same thing for the jerks in Poli Sci," Sarah Lynn said.

"Bad?"

"Men outnumber women five-to-one in my major. Apparently, one of the women is really ugly because I had six men stuck to my ass all afternoon."

"I hope you mean figuratively!"

"There were a couple of not-so-accidental touches," she fumed. "And one guy is going to lose his arm if he puts it around me again. The worst, though, was the rich kid. 'Hey, let's take a drive in my Boxster and put together our strategy for the term. You and I would make a great pair.' He didn't even know my name yet!"

"Hmm. Maybe we should have a contest tonight to see who got hit on the most at orientation," I laughed.

"You didn't! Of course you did. How many girls—or boys—were stuck to your butt today?"

"Just one. And she couldn't stick. She was leading another tour group. But she wants me to paint her."

"Oh, dear. Did she use those words, Jett?"

"Yeah."

"And you're thinking she's going to be a canvas and not a model," Sarah Lynn laughed. "Is she cute?"

"Sort of. She's a little geeky, like most art students. We aren't exactly known to be the models and athletes of the school."

"You could fuck her when you paint her," Sarah Lynn said. "Make her hold the pose while you do her."

"You have a mean streak! I'm not looking for anyone else to fuck, Sarah Lynn. After last night, I'd just as soon move in and live in your pussy."

"Well, I liked the way you decorated it. But Jett, really. We've got to keep our options open and not get tied to each other. I mean that for all of us. We are just going to get emotionally screwed over if we get too invested in each other. Kelly fucked Derek before you. Jas gave Rick a farewell blowjob before he left for baseball camp. I've got six sticky Poli Scis on my ass and one of them—not the rich kid—is pretty cute. You've got a girl that wants to get naked in front of you and painting is a good excuse. I don't know. I think Ariel and Char are just holding out to tease you."

"Jas gave Rick a blowjob?"

"Shit! You didn't know?"

"She told me she was going to fuck him, but when we all moved over here, I never heard anything about it again. I guess I thought she'd decided not to."

"She did. She decided a blowjob would be enough to settle her curiosity. It was during the three weeks we were all living in different places trying to find our little paradise here. But the point is that none of us have made exclusive commitments, Jett."

"Yeah. I know. I guess it just caught me by surprise. I'm still not really interested in screwing around."

"Say that when the opportunity actually presents itself. Like the blonde bimbos did Saturday. I bet you could get the three of them to pose naked together. Get them into a position with their asses in the air and do all three of them, then paint them together," Sarah Lynn laughed.

"You are truly an evil woman," I said as we walked up the steps to our front door.

"You know what?" she whispered in my ear and then licked it. "I bet you have time to decorate my pussy again before dinner. I mean… since you've moved in and all."

⁘⟡ ⟠⟡ ☽ ⟡⟠ ⟡⁘

As IT TURNED out, the casserole was in the oven with a note on the door that said, "Ready at six." There was a note on the door to Kelly's attic that said, "Camming until six." We knew that meant not to disturb her. Ariel and Char followed Sarah Lynn and me to the big bed in 'my' room and helped us fuck each other. Sarah Lynn rode me in a reverse cowgirl with Ariel between our legs licking my balls and her clit. Char mounted my face with her arms wrapped around so she could play with Sarah Lynn's tits. When Char finished on my face, I didn't want to let go of her cinnamon hips. I just kept stretching my tongue into her pussy as far as I could get it. By the time Sarah Lynn clamped down on my cock and I started spewing into her, Char had peaked again.

Ariel crawled from between our legs and lay down beside me with a sigh.

"You didn't get off, did you?" I said, tracing circles around her nipples with my index finger.

"Not yet. I know you'll all take care of me. I just… I was down there licking where I could see and feel your cock going in and out of that yummy twat and thinking that if I wasn't such a chicken, you'd be pumping in and out of my juicy cunt. I'm just… I'm the only virgin left and just can't believe that huge cock is going to fit in my tiny Asian pussy."

"Hey, Tiny," Char said. "I'm a virgin."

"What? All yesterday afternoon after the painting we could hear you all over the house screaming, 'Fuck me! Fuck me!' Didn't he do it?"

"Well, my pussy's still virgin."

"Really? You… He was… You mean…"

"As good as he feels in my ass, I'm in no hurry to lose my vaginal cherry," Char sighed. "His tongue in my pussy ain't bad, either."

"Oh. Oh!" Ariel gasped as Sarah Lynn rolled between her legs and took a swipe at her slit. "I… Maybe I should try that. I could feel how big it really is. Um… you wouldn't hurt me would you, Jett?"

"Of course not. I love you just the way you are. Don't feel pushed to do something more than you're ready for," I said. Ariel started to answer but squealed as Sarah Lynn zeroed in on her button.

•◦•◈ ɔɔɔ ☾ ɔɔɔ ◈•◦•

ALL SIX OF us stood at our neighbors' door when I knocked. Our front porch was enclosed with storm windows but theirs was just open. It was still hard for all of us to approach the door because they had the porch full of empty boxes. Our neighbors were slobs.

"Hi. I'm Jett from next door," I said when a tall skinny guy wearing a pair of boxers and nothing else opened the door. "These are my housemates." He scanned the girls.

"Shit! You guys should come party with us. We're doing body shots tonight," he said. "You girls would be perfect!" I could hear groans behind me. Beyond the guy, I could see one of the blonde bimbos from a couple doors down stretched out naked on a coffee table with a lime in her mouth. Maybe I *would* paint her!

"Um… No. We're not really into the party scene," I said. The guy looked really disgusted. "Not that we object to it. We're not going to complain about your parties, even if they're loud in the middle of the night. That's not our thing either."

"Oh. That's cool."

"We'd like to ask just one thing, though. Please don't toss your empties into our yard and try to keep the vomit in front of your own house." He looked at me blankly. "I've got five delicate girls living with me. Like fresh blooming roses. So, I work my ass off trying to make things nice for them. They like a clean yard. They even planted flowers in front. Beer cans and puke upset them. When they get upset, they turn from delicate flowers into raging dragons. It's not pretty. Understand?"

"Yeah. Uh… Right. You'd rather have them pretty instead of bitchy. I'll tell the guys."

"Hey, if it makes things easier on you, I'll get one of those big garbage cans and line it with plastic bags for you. You just wouldn't believe how friendly my girls are when things are neat and tidy."

"We'd like 'em friendly," he said with an open leer.

"Well, it looks like you've got a friendly one on the table right now, so I won't delay you getting back to her. You know, I read that the best way with a girl like that is not to just salt her nipples and put a lime in her mouth but pour the tequila in her navel. It really gets 'em hot!" He glanced behind him at the bimbo on the table. While we were talking, she'd subtly changed her position so her open legs were pointing at the door.

"Yeah. Good idea. Thanks."

•0• •◦➤))C ☽))C ◦•❮◦ •0•

"How DO YOU know so much about body shots?" Sarah Lynn demanded as soon as we were back inside our house.

"Oh… uh… well… I read something. And seeing one of the blondes stretched out on their packing boxes sort of gave me an inspiration. I made it up."

"I want to try," Ariel said.

"We don't have tequila," Jas said. "Can we pour Dr Pepper in your navel?"

"Sticky!"

"I think the idea is that someone is supposed to lick until the sticky is gone," I laughed.

"You can lick me!"

"It would all just run down my sides off my big belly," Char sighed. I frowned. She didn't have a big belly. She was rounder than the other girls but I was beginning to love every inch. I'd lick about anything off her navel. I reached over and pulled her into a hug while the other girls kept discussing what could be poured on their bodies that others would have to lick off. Or eat. Or smoke. *Smoke? Oh, Christ!* I tuned out.

"Char, please don't make bad comments about your body," I whispered as I held her. "I love that you are softer than the others. I love cuddling with you and loving you."

"I've just been told for so long how fat and ugly I am, I sort of believe it," she sighed.

"I love you just like you are."

"Even though I'm still a virgin? A vagina virgin?"

"I would never pressure you for any kind of sex. But…"

"My butt. Do you really like it when we do that?"

"God! I love fucking your ass. I can't believe you want me there."

"If fucking my pussy is better than my ass, I'll die when I come. I'm sorry I'm so slow about the other. It seems so stupid, but my father keeps threatening me."

"What? When?"

"He called me Friday and said I'd better still be a virgin. He was negotiating some kind of marriage deal."

"Char, that's terrible. It's not like some honor killing, is it?"

"That's Pakistan, not India," she huffed.

"I'm sorry."

"But Indian families also have a long tradition of arranged marriages. My mother was light-skinned from New Delhi. My father paid a lot for her and was terribly disappointed that my skin turned out so chocolaty. After four children, he berated my mother so much for her inability to have fair-skinned children that she decided to take me and return to her parents in India," Char said.

"But you are still here."

"My father caught us at the airport and snatched me away from my mother. He was being disgraced by her leaving and was determined to make it as bad for her as possible. All through the last year of school, I've been thinking that I should see if I can find her again. Father blamed her for all the bad things in his life."

"Of course it couldn't be his fault. What is with this whole fair-skinned thing?"

"It's an Indian thing. A woman could weigh two hundred pounds and have warts on her nose but if she is fair-skinned, she's considered beautiful. I pray to Ganesha to free me from my father and his influence."

"That's like the fat little Buddha with the elephant head, right?"

"Please! Don't call him a Buddha! Jett, you need to get educated! Ganesha is the son of Shiva and Parvati. Well, Parvati was taking a bath and didn't want to be disturbed, so baby Ganesha guarded the door. Shiva had gone away when Ganesha was a tiny baby, but the baby grew really fast. When Shiva got back, they didn't recognize each other and the boy wouldn't let him in to see Parvati. Shiva got so mad that he cut the boy's head off. Parvati was unhappy and demanded that Shiva save her son. The first head Shiva could find was an elephant's head and he put that on the boy to heal him," Char said. All the time she'd been edging me toward the stairs and we left the other girls still in the kitchen trying to figure out what kind of shots they could drink off each other's bodies.

"Are you really Hindu?" I asked.

"Yeah. My mother was devout. My father worships money. I became fond of Ganesha because he is the Lord of Obstacles and Difficulties. I hadn't been praying to him for long when Sarah Lynn's little stunt at commencement gave me the opportunity to escape from home and join with my wonderful lovers. I figure it can't hurt to keep praying to him."

We stopped at the head of the stairs and kissed. Char rubbed my erection through the shorts I was still wearing.

"Go get naked and in bed, lover," she whispered. "I'll be in as soon as I take care of something in the bathroom."

···⋄⟫ ⟫)⟪ ☼ ⟫)⟪ ⟪⋄···

I KNEW THAT when Char needed to 'take care of something' before she came to bed, she was cleaning things out so we could make love. That was confirmed when she climbed into bed naked and snuggled her bottom up against my hard cock. I wasn't just going to fuck her ass, though. After a few licks of her ears and pulling her toward me to kiss her, I managed to get her on her back and started working my way down. She has fat dark nipples and they stood proud and erect after I'd finished tonguing and sucking on them. I loved those big beautiful breasts but I didn't stop there.

Since she'd made a big deal about liquids spilling over her belly from her navel, I stopped there and spent a long time kissing and licking her stomach and navel. By the time I reached the top of her slit, she was leaking thick milky lube. I went straight to her clit and she found her first orgasm waiting at the tip of my tongue. I scooped up as much of her fluid as I could on my tongue and pushed her back so I could get to her little asshole with it. I deposited it around and in the little star that kept pulsing in and out as if it would gobble me up. I used a thumb on her clit as I continued to stimulate her asshole and she rose to another peak.

Pushing myself up onto my knees, I crawled between her legs and pushed her thick thighs back against her chest. Her eyes popped open when she felt my cock rubbing up and down her wet pussy.

"Jett, don't…"

"Don't even think I'd do that without your permission and cooperation," I said. "I'm just getting slippery." When I was working her over with my tongue, I'd seen the evidence of her virginal state and I wasn't about to damage it.

"Do you want me to roll over?"

"No." I slipped the head of my cock down her crack, gathering moisture, until I lodged against her pucker. "I want to look into your eyes when I enter you, Charmaine. You are my lover and I want to look at you while I love you."

"Really?" she squeaked as I pushed. I'd gathered enough lube in my adventures, both on my cock and her asshole, that it didn't take much for the head to slip in. A beatific smile crossed her face as she sighed, relaxing and letting me slip farther into her depths. "Really. If fucking my pussy is better than this, I'll die from the pleasure. Oh! Jett, fuck me. Fuck my fat ass." I smacked the ass in question with my open hand as a rebuke to the fat comment. She jumped and drove herself farther down my shaft. "Yes. Yes. Oh, god! Yes!"

This orgasm was sustained until I thought she'd pass out. I pulled back and thrust in to the maximum depth, unleashing a torrent of my come in her.

If fucking her pussy was any better than this, I might not survive either.

18
School Days

I CHECKED MY class schedule and saw that two of my classes in the Art building were back-to-back on Tuesday through Thursday. Both were lectures in the same room at ten and eleven. Then I had to truck halfway across campus for my Literature and the Arts course. My last class of the day wasn't until three o'clock and was the only 'art' class I had. At least what I considered art. That was my Drawing Concepts and Methods class. My last class was the Colloquium in Art and it met irregularly, based on when lecturers were coming in. We were told at registration not to miss the first session next Tuesday at five in the afternoon.

By the time I got to my drawing class, I was pretty discouraged. I wasn't going to be painting and making much art this term. In fact, I was going to be reading and writing papers. 2D Design would have a few studio projects, but according to the syllabus, the first four weeks were focused on a survey of 2D art and color theory. Foundations of Contemporary Art was a lecture on principles and ideas in the various movements of the past century. I guess we were supposed to fit into one of them or something. And the Western Culture course, Literature and the Arts, was going to start with Akhenaten's Egypt. Professor Merck was pretty cool, though. Just from his attitude and posture, you could tell he toked up before the lecture and really didn't want to be there.

"You've got a fabulously expensive text book that you picked up at the bookstore," he said, "so it would be criminal if I didn't make you read it. The ancient Egypt chapter is first. Your task in reading the chapter is to identify the heresy of Akhenaten and how it affected the development of the arts in Egypt of 1350 BC and changed its direction for centuries to come. This is going to take you some time to figure out, so why don't we cancel class for tomorrow and come prepared to discuss the subject on Tuesday next week. Class dismissed."

I wondered if he was always going to have short classes and cancel them. I checked his website and syllabus and the cancelled session was posted there with a more complete description of what he wanted us to cover in our reading. It looked like he actually expected us to get something out of it, so I figured I'd put some effort into my prep. Heck, I had almost a week to read and figure out what he wanted.

It was finally time for the class that I wanted—Drawing. I had my supplies and wondered what we'd be drawing first. This was the only class I had in a studio. Professor Blankenship, however, was not what I expected. I'd met three professors in the Art Department during my interview and thought they were all okay. Blankenship was a bastard.

"Children, sit down and shut up," he started at exactly three o'clock. "For some reason, you all think you can draw. Did any of you even bring a pencil? Paper? What do you need? Finger paints? Get something in front of yourself that you can draw on and get ready. This is your subject." He pointed to a plain black vase. "You have fifteen minutes and then I'll look at your doodles and tell you if there's any hope for you as an artist. The rest of you can switch over to computer graphics. Time starts now."

Shit! I wasn't expecting my one art class to be the worst on my schedule. What an asshole! I heard a sniffle and glanced to my right. A girl with dirty blonde hair and a baggy sweater was sitting with her art pad in front of her and tears running down her cheeks. Her hands were shaking so much I was sure she couldn't get a shape drawn on the paper. She looked up at me just as I glanced at her. Her scowl seemed to melt a little, though, when I just nodded and mouthed out the words, "You can do it." She nodded back and bent to her drawing.

That left me to mine. Dr. Anders had said they were going to teach me to slow down when I interviewed and here this jerk was giving us fifteen minutes to produce a drawing that our art careers were going to be based on. A drawing of a black vase. We could just scribble it with a crayon.

I looked at the vase and plotted out the major points of the shape. As soon as my graphite touched the pad, my soul lifted and I was drawing.

Fifteen minutes? Fuck him. I'm not going to rush through a drawing just to satisfy his stopwatch. The more I looked at the vase, the more I saw. It wasn't a flat black shape. It was shiny and reflected light. Of course, that was what would give it shape and turn it into a three-dimensional object. But there was more there and the deeper I sank into my drawing space, the more I saw. I could see the front edge of the pedestal it was sitting on reflected in the downward slope of the vase. In the midst of the highlight, I could see the girl who'd been crying reflected in a distorted way. I could see Professor Blankenship elongated and reflected on the other side. Suddenly the exact shape and contours of the vase no longer mattered. The vase was a canvas of reflections. I was lost in what I was seeing.

The bastard blew a whistle!

"Fuck!" I know mine was one of the voices that responded, but not the only one by a longshot. He started moving around the room immediately. There were eighteen of us in the class. As usual in Art, only four of us were male. It had been that way all the way through high school as well. Art is for sissies and no one wants to be a sissy. I didn't care.

"You need to work on perspective," Blankenship said, pointing at one piece of art. He moved to the next. "There's no depth." At another, "You should be a cartoonist, that's the only direction your art is taking you." "What the hell is that?" It seems like he didn't have a good word to say about anyone. He stopped behind me and just stood there for a minute. My drawing wasn't complete—not even close. In fact, there was only a hint of the outline. Instead, I'd focused on what I saw reflected. He cleared his throat. "Next time try drawing the vase," he said and moved on to the girl who'd cried. I could see her hands were still shaking. I wondered if it was just her nerves or if it was some condition she had.

Blankenship surprised her and me, too, when he reached out and touched her hand. It seemed to steady a little. "I'll show you how," he said softly. Then he went to the front of the room and turned to stare us down again. As far as I could tell he hadn't really said anything positive about anyone's drawing.

"So, what makes you think you're an artist?" he demanded. "Put your hands down. That was a rhetorical question. Look up the meaning. You undoubtedly all have mothers who still have your kindergarten scribbles tacked to the refrigerator. You've been told your drawings were good since the first time you stuck a crayon in an electrical outlet. Oh, you're so talented, you should become an artist. Let me tell you exactly what all that means. *Shit!* You couldn't run fast or play baseball or weren't big enough for football, so you should be an artist. You weren't pretty enough or couldn't cook or were a failure at math and music, so you should be an artist. Art is where you got shoved because you weren't good enough to do anything else. All the praise you got from your grandma, the awards you got at the 4-H Fair, the pictures on the refrigerator—none of that means shit. Accidentally drawing something that could be construed as looking like this simple black vase doesn't mean you are talented."

Blankenship was on a roll. I could see that every student in the class hated him already. He lectured and expected us to listen. Mostly he told us why none of what we knew or had accomplished meant anything.

"Limit your vision! Look at this vase. Find one thing about the vase and draw that. Not the whole vase. No! I'm not going to give you an example. Figure it out. Ten minutes. Certainly, there must be one thing about this simple black vase that you can draw in ten minutes. Ready, set, go."

Fuck! We were drawing again. I looked at the vase and turned to a fresh sheet of paper. There was an indentation near the bottom of the vase and then it flared out flat from there to the table. I started with that, but quickly realized that what I was looking at was the vase reflected in the table's surface. Reflection reverses the perspective. What was convex becomes concave. I found myself sinking into the drawing again.

Thankfully, the class ended before Blankenship blew his whistle. He had a big clock in front of the room and we looked up to discover it was five o'clock and he'd already left. Without saying anything to any of us. We all kind of looked at each other and then started packing up our materials. The blonde was gone before I could speak to her, so I just headed out to go home.

•·•◆ ⟩⟨ ☀ ⟩⟨ ◆·•·•

"So, you survived Blankety's first day," Eva said when she spotted me in the hall.

"Were you waiting for me?" I asked.

"Yeah. I wanted to check in and see if you survived. I was going to try to talk to you after orientation yesterday, but I had a tour that simply would not end. Our group was the last one back. So, how did it go?"

"Mostly okay, I guess. This class isn't what I expected, that's for sure. Does it get better from here?"

"No. It gets worse. Blankety never says anything positive about anything. I sometimes wonder how anyone can be so fucking negative about everything. You will never meet a student who likes him."

"Why call him Blankety?"

"It's short for Blankety-blank-blank. Somebody couldn't find enough obscenities," she said. "So, you want to get together this weekend?" Wow! That came out of nowhere.

"Uh… What do you mean?"

"I was just thinking of hanging out."

"I work six to two on Saturday." I wondered how the girls would take me meeting Eva to 'hang out' on the weekend. I wondered what she planned to hang out for me. But it gave me an idea. "Why don't you plan to come over around four and stay for dinner with my girlfriends and me?"

"Your girlfriends? Plural?" she raised an eyebrow and sort of sniffed. "Sure. Maybe I could find a few boyfriends."

"There's a house full of them next door if that's what you're interested in." I scribbled down our address and handed it to her.

"Party row, huh? I thought you were a serious student."

"It's up to you. Come and see. You'll be surprised."

"You invited your new girlfriend to dinner Saturday? Here? Aren't you afraid we'll, like, scratch her eyes out?" Kelly asked.

"I'd just come out of Blankety's art class from hell and was really tired of people doubting me. She says she wants me to paint her," I said. I recognized Kelly was pulling my chain, but somehow felt it was necessary to justify myself anyway. "I figure that if she isn't comfortable with all of you, she isn't suitable for the project I have in mind."

"Do you mind if one of us seduces her? Or two of us?" Ariel asked as she glanced toward Jas.

"Maybe all of us?" Jas giggled.

"You might not even like her," I sighed. "But give her the full treatment, whatever that is. I don't think we should have anyone else move into the house though. Can we at least agree on that?" The girls all started laughing.

"Jett, you are so much fun to tease," Sarah Lynn said. "You know where I stand on this. Paint her. Fuck her. Marry her, for all I care. Just don't leave us."

"That sounds so fucking weird."

"So does five girlfriends living with their boyfriend," Jas said. "I just accept that it's weird and fill my mouth with yummy snootch."

"What kind of project do you have in mind, Jett? You said that as if you already have a picture forming in your head," Char said.

"Yeah. Sort of. It's like I can see it but it isn't quite real yet. Remember when I painted you and Sarah Lynn as the frame?"

"Do I ever!"

"I think I might have come more times that night than ever before in my life," Sarah Lynn added.

"I've got this notion of making her a part of the canvas," I said. "I know I can't just glue her to it and hang it, but I'm thinking of a way to incorporate both the model and the canvas more… permanently… than just taking a photo."

"Performance," Kelly said. She was naked already and planned to go online in an hour. Her Wednesday night shows were bath shows so all the other girls were using my bathroom while Kelly set up her camera and lights in the upstairs bath. "You all haven't seen the video I did of Char and Sarah Lynn getting framed."

"It's like two hours long, isn't it?"

"I edited and used some special effects to speed the process. I've got it down to fifteen minutes," Kelly said. "It might even be a good idea to show it to this girl—Eva?—so she knows exactly the kind of painting Jett wants to do."

"I wonder if we could find a place where he could perform the painting," Ariel mused. "I'm thinking of a recital kind of thing. Live performance with a music video afterward."

"I love to paint while you're practicing, Ariel. I just don't think people would be comfortable sitting in an auditorium for three hours watching me paint," I said.

"I bet I could get subscribers for a videocast as well," Kelly said. "But I agree that a recital hall isn't the best venue. Besides, you need to figure out how you are going to handle things like potty breaks. You might be able to drop into a zone and stay focused for three hours straight, but Char and Sarah Lynn were about to burst when you finished the frame painting. I've got to go get ready for my bath show. Anyone tuning in tonight?"

"My only assignments are reading and it isn't due until Tuesday. I'm definitely going to watch my favorite redhead shave her legs and pussy and get herself off," I laughed.

"I've got reading to do," Ariel said. "I want to be finished so I can taste those smooth pussy lips and yummy juices when your show is over."

"Oh, girlfriend! If you can lick around Jett's cock sliding in and out, it's a date!"

•◦•⇨ ⊃⊂ ☽ ⊃⊂ ⇦•◦•

Thursday was a lighter day since there was no Literature and the Arts class. I was dreading going back into Blankety's classroom, but at least it was more interesting than the two lectures.

"Hey. I'm Jett," I said to the dirty blonde I'd noticed in class the day before. "You think today's class will be as weird as Tuesday's?"

"Um… Hi. I guess. I'm Mary. It was a little nerve-wracking. I might not make it."

"If uh… you need to talk or anything… let me know. I'm a little overwhelmed myself… But maybe there's safety in numbers," I said. She looked at me a little strangely, like I'd just grown another head.

"Th- thanks."

Blankety swept into the room at exactly three o'clock and started in on the proper use of different hardnesses of graphite and what paper texture was best. Then he put a teddy bear on the pedestal where the vase had been the first day.

"Two drawings. Fifteen minutes each. One is to be drawn with a 4H pencil. The other is to be drawn with a 4B. Capture what the graphite tells you to." He snapped a stopwatch and put his damned whistle between his teeth. We started drawing. I didn't have time to waste watching to see if Mary was okay. She was bent over her sketchbook. I drew.

I wasn't going to get any great revelations of reflections out of this drawing. This was a technical drawing lesson. He'd just lectured us on what each hardness of graphite was best for, and the 4H was definitely a drafting pencil. I sharpened it to a fine point and began laying in the outline of the teddy bear. I started with big features, the shape, the eyes, the nose, the white patch on the chest and bottoms of the feet. I was tempted to draw lines and label each part but decided that was too risky at this stage of the class. I didn't want to get a reputation as a smartass with a prof who was a bastard. It didn't take long to do the technical drawing though and I had several minutes left in my time period. It was tempting to lay the pencil on its side and fill in the color areas to be shaded. I resisted.

Instead, I noticed the contours of the bear and began drawing short straight lines from about thirty degrees from the left and used those short lines to do my shading. I was not quite finished when that damned whistle blew. I wondered if this guy had been a football coach in a former life. *Fucker!*

I grabbed a different sketch pad and my 4B pencil. This pad had a little more tooth and slightly lighter weight than the drawing pad I'd used for the first drawing. I didn't sharpen my 4B quite like I had the 4H. I laid in large areas with the side of the pencil and blended them with my thumb. I created highlights with my art gum eraser and then went back with my thumb to blend them. I could have used a blending stump and had cleaner hands. I thought briefly about what my mother would think of the graphite streaks I wiped on my khaki slacks. Oh well. When the damn whistle blew again, I had something that looked almost squeezable. I looked over at Mary and she was sitting there slumped back in her chair with her eyes closed. She was breathing in short bursts.

I recognized the signs. I guess that's one of the things my generation is known for. Anxiety and panic attacks. Ford had been diagnosed with asthma for five years before they realized his shallow breaths and gasps were panic attacks. But we were raised with kids like that and understood—at least some of us understood—that it was as real and as painful as asthma. I reached over and touched Mary's sleeve. Her eyes popped open and she focused on me.

"Deep. Deep breaths, Mary," I said as I demonstrated inhaling and exhaling. "You aren't alone here. You can get through this. Deep breaths. Get in touch with what's around you. No one will hurt you." She made a short nod and worked on mimicking my breathing pattern.

"Maybe you should switch to technical school," Blankenship said over my left shoulder. My heart leaped into my throat as I realized he'd been working his way around the classroom criticizing people. "You press too hard." "Learn to blend." "What a mess you've made." And now to me. "Technical School."

Aside from that he looked at the drawings and nodded then went on to Mary. She tightened up again and I was afraid she would burst out in tears. He didn't comment on her drawings. He picked up her pencil and handed it to her. She took it and looked at him trying to figure out what he wanted.

"When you finish a drawing, don't put your pencil down. Hold it in your hand. Think about its texture. Smell it. Let your senses focus on the pencil."

Then he walked out of the room. It was five o'clock.

19
Test Drive

I HALF EXPECTED EVA to be waiting outside the door for me again, but it was Mary that stopped me.

"Thank you."

"Any time," I said.

"You've dealt with panic attacks before. I could tell."

"Like I said, you're not alone. My mother was susceptible, though not as much since I hit high school. I have a lot of friends, though, who picked up the slack. People are all different. I try to be calm."

"Girls must love you."

I chuckled. Oh, if she only knew.

"It's not just girls who have anxiety," I said. "I've helped my friend Ford down a few times. Others. We all have different ways of coping. If there are special things that help you, you can tell me about them and I'll try to incorporate them. When we happen to be in the same place. I've only met you twice and we didn't talk at all the first time."

"Yeah. Well. It's hard to meet people. I wouldn't have talked to you today if you hadn't been there to focus on," Mary said. "I've got to go. I guess I'll see you Tuesday."

I don't know what came over me. I spoke before I thought clearly. "I've got a house and five housemates. We're having dinner together on Saturday evening. Would you like to come?"

"Me and six guys? I don't think so."

"No! I'm sorry. My housemates are all female. We're… kind of a family. Oh. And there's another artist coming over who wants me to paint her. We're going to discuss the concept." *Shit! I forgot Eva was coming over. Well, so what? It isn't a date.*

"Um… Uh… text me the info and I'll see how I feel. That's a lot of people."

"All I can say is that we try not to be threatening. Everyone is different and we don't get in people's faces."

"Unless she's having a panic-attack?" Mary laughed. "I'll… What's your number? I'll text you and you'll have mine so you can send me directions."

⚜

"You already have a date Saturday night! What were you thinking?" Sarah Lynn exclaimed.

"It's not a date. I just invited a couple classmates over for dinner."

"Girls," Kelly clarified. "You invited a couple of girls over for dinner. On Saturday night. Date night. And they don't even know each other. They'll think you invited them over for a threesome."

"I think it would be an octet. I wouldn't leave the five of you out of it."

"Je-ett," Jas moaned out. "This could be serious. Text me their names and numbers so I can call them and make sure they're prepared. We were all going to slip out after dinner and leave you here."

"No! Don't do that. I don't want any more girlfriends!"

"Are we so bad that you don't want any others?" Ariel asked.

"Wait! That's not what I said. I love each of you. I don't need anyone else."

"Well, it sounds like at least one of them needs *you*. What you did in class today is just the kind of thing we love you for," Char said.

"Okay," Sarah Lynn said, taking control. "Jett has to work from god-awful until two on Saturday. That means we need to have the house cleaned up tomorrow and Saturday morning."

"I'll do it," I moaned.

"Wrong. You'll help. *We* are having guests Saturday. All of us. Will anyone be gone?"

"Char and I are working breakfast and lunch, so we won't be home any earlier than Jett," Jas said.

"I'm clear. I wanted to invite my mother over to hear me play Saturday morning. She always wants to make sure I'm practicing," Ariel said. "But I can do cleaning, too."

"I'm latest," Kelly said. "I work ten till six on Saturday. I'm just hoping to be home in time for dinner."

"Well, if everybody can take a room Friday night and do the vacuum, dust, and empty thing, Ariel and I can take care of the kitchen and bathrooms Saturday morning."

"Thanks for volunteering me, Sarah Lynn," Ariel pouted.

"Honey, I'll give you an orgasm on my tongue for every bathroom you clean."

Ariel bounced up and sat in Sarah Lynn's lap, giving her a steamy kiss that I thought might progress into advance payment. Sarah Lynn regained control.

"Two exclusions are Jett's and Kelly's studios. You each get a room to clean on Friday, but you're responsible for your own studios, too." We nodded. That was always assumed. We had private studio space and we were responsible for keeping it clean. "Jett. You are responsible for dinner at six-thirty sharp. The only thing that might delay it would be if Kelly has trouble getting home. Eight for dinner, unless one of us falls madly in love at school tomorrow and brings home our date." I started to say they weren't dates but she scowled at me. That shut me up. "Remember, you'll have guests to entertain as well. We'll trickle in and help with that, but dinner is your responsibility."

We all agreed to our responsibilities, but Jas wasn't quite ready to let it drop.

"Jett, honey, we love you. We know you didn't plan dates for Saturday night. We hope the girls will just become good friends, like our bunch back in high school. But girls think different than guys. I guarantee they both think they are your date. Having other girls living with you just means it should be a safe first date. But don't be surprised if one or both of them are still hanging around at ten, hoping for an overnight invitation."

Not a chance in hell.

•◦•❖ ⟫⟫ ☼ ⟪⟪ ❖•◦•

SLAUGHTERING 101. NOT my favorite course in the world.

Richelieu Processing Plant is not the biggest slaughterhouse in the country by a longshot. Big houses can process as many as ten to a hundred-fifty head of cattle an hour. Sound like a lot? Well, consider the fact that over thirty million head of cattle are slaughtered for food in the United States every year. Richelieu is capable of processing up to twenty-five head of cattle an hour, but seldom reaches that capacity. They also slaughter hogs and sheep. The number is dependent more on their staffing levels than on the capacity of the plant itself. There are over a thousand head in the feedlot.

We're lucky. The Richelieu family bought an existing operation back in the seventies. They'd heard a lecture by Temple Grandin and hired her to redesign the pens and slaughterhouse for the best in humane animal care. Look her up at Grandin.com if you really want the details of the process. I'll just say that the animals were calm when they were put down and the butchers were efficient. Our first class was a walk-through of the entire process from transportation through to hanging carcass.

I'm not squeamish about meat. Grandpa had been a meat cutter before he bought the grocery store where I work as an assistant meat cutter now. Once when I was little, I declared that steak was my favorite animal. I knew the relationship between moo-cows on a farm and hamburger on the grill. Like many people who are half-intelligent, I was amused by the Facebook meme that made the rounds in which an animal rights activist declared that hunting and ranching were evil and we should get all our meat from grocery stores where it's made. People are so disconnected from what they eat. They think it came from a *Star Trek* replicator.

Nonetheless, I viewed the process that first day with the awareness that sometime in the next few weeks, I was going to participate directly in the karma of my food. It was a sobering thought.

Thinking of the incredible serpentine path that the cattle follow to their death, though, reminded me of the rest of Temple Grandin's research and study. Geez, the woman is older than my Grandpa by a few years. She's one of the country's greatest animal behaviorists. And she was autistic! For years, she couldn't stand to be touched and crowds and strangers made her extremely anxious. She actually invented a hugging machine that was based on the same philosophy as the chutes she designed to calm cattle. A lot of what we know about dealing with anxiety came from her research.

When I got home after class, I showered first and then started work on cleaning. My responsibility was the dining room, which was kind of a give-away. Vacuum and dust. I put out two folding chairs for our guests the next day along with the six mismatched chairs that came with the mostly furnished house. When I finished vacuuming, I just carted the machine upstairs and did the floors in all three bedrooms to relieve Char and Kelly. In addition to dusting, they had to change all the beds and then Kelly had to do her upstairs studio, too. Of course, we all knew that it wouldn't take her long to do her studio. She kept it immaculate for her camming.

My studio was a little more complicated. I had a big piece of canvas on the floor and it was too loose to vacuum easily—at least with the big machine—and moving all the supplies and furniture off of it to take it outside and shake was a hassle. I swept it with a broom and made sure everything was dusted with non-allergenic dusting spray to clean all the surfaces in the room. I knew if the Dragon Lady was coming to listen to Ariel play the piano tomorrow, she'd run her fingers over every surface to check for dust—including the tops of the door frames.

With all six of us working Friday afternoon, the cleaning went quickly and was pretty much fun, too. We chatted and there were more than a few kisses shared with pats and fondling tossed in. I got to thinking, though, about what I learned at the slaughterhouse and the fact that I'd invited a high-anxiety girl to dinner with seven other people the next night. I was trying to figure out how we should prepare in case she had a panic attack.

On Saturday after work, I shopped for dinner groceries. It was only fair that I was springing for dinner since I'd invited the guests. But I didn't feel so flush that I could buy steaks and lobster for eight. Good old reliable meatloaf was on the menu. I did pick up four pounds of ninety-eight percent fat free ground beef. I bought baking potatoes and salad makings. I stopped by the bakery and picked up a chocolate and strawberry cheesecake. Even being conservative, dinner was costing me close to eighty bucks and I was thankful that we didn't drink any alcohol. Bottles of sparkling water were expensive enough.

I got everything ready to put in the oven at five o'clock, had the salad made and in the refrigerator, and had the table set before I heard the knock at five after four. I wondered which of the girls would arrive first. All my girlfriends were at home except Kelly but they were staying discreetly in different spaces so they wouldn't overwhelm the guests all at once.

They were both there. I hoped I'd managed to get the door before they started talking to each other.

"Hi, Eva. Welcome, Mary," I said brightly. Eva stepped forward and gave me a hug—sort of possessively, I thought—before Mary got through the door. I let go of her and had to sort of push her out of the way so Mary could get in.

"Hey, Jett. Nice place for the neighborhood," Eva said. I had a feeling she'd been down this street once or twice last year and was surprised to find our house neat and clean.

"Hi, Jett," Mary said softly. She didn't step forward for a hug or offer her hand. She just nodded toward Eva. "Is she one of them? Your housemates?"

"Oh, no. She's the artist I told you about that wants me to paint her. I thought it would be fun to get to know each other and talk about the concept, so she's a dinner guest, too." I was smiling but I felt like my heart was going to hammer through my chest. Fortunately, they both nodded and I led them on into the living room. Sarah Lynn stood up from where she'd been reading a book on the principles of aeronautics.

"Sarah Lynn, this is Eva and Mary. Ladies, my roommate, Sarah Lynn." I thought I did a good job of subtly switching from housemate to roommate. I'd let that one sink in a while before I started referring to them as my girlfriends.

"Nice to meet you," Sarah Lynn said. She held out her hand and Eva immediately stepped in for a hug. Apparently, she was the huggy type, not just with me.

"So, it's true and he really does live with a girl. You're okay with me being here?"

"Of course. And, you know, I'm only one of the girls. Hi, Mary. Welcome to our chaos. If you need anything, just let any one of us know." Mary had stepped just slightly behind me and nodded to Sarah Lynn.

"Thanks."

"Say, I've been dying to meet Eva ever since your interview last spring, Jett. Can I take her around to meet the others? Pretty please?" Sarah Lynn played it perfectly and all of a sudden Eva had a new best friend. I barely nodded before Eva had picked up the text Sarah Lynn had been reading.

"You're studying aeronautics? Cool! Do you plan to fly? Design airplanes? Work in aerospace?"

"Oh, no. I'm in Poli Sci. I had to have a science elective and this looked interesting."

"If you want a tour of the insides of an airplane, I'll take you out to the field with me. I was up this morning and it was beautiful. I'm so glad the weather is holding," Eva said as Sarah Lynn led her to the stairs and left me alone with Mary. She sighed.

"You're a pilot…"

•o··◆ ⫶⫶⫶ ☽ ⫶⫶⫶ ◆··o•

"You could have told me this was just a time to get to know your girlfriends," Mary said. "It would have saved me a lot of stress. I was afraid you were expecting me to date you."

"I did say there'd be others here," I defended myself.

"Yeah. That was almost worse. I dialed your number twice today to cancel and hung up before it rang. Thank you for holding them off so I didn't have to deal with everyone at once."

"The part where Sarah Lynn took off with Eva was planned," I said. "I wanted to talk to you and make sure you were okay with being here."

"Um… I guess. That Eva girl is sure… um… touchy-feely."

"I take it you aren't. That's fine. I wanted to let you know that if things get too tense and you want to leave, I'll take you home at any time. If you just need to be alone for a bit, all three bedrooms upstairs are available to you and you won't be disturbed. If you feel like you really need to hide and go to sleep, go all the way to the attic. Kelly says she doesn't plan to use her room tonight, so it's available to you. Nobody will try to touch you or hug you unless you initiate it. And like Sarah Lynn said, if you need anything, let one of us know. We'll do our best." I breathed deeply, having

171

gotten everything out in what seemed like one breath. It was me who was feeling anxious around her.

"I'm not fragile, so don't go overboard trying to accommodate me," she said. It was the strongest I'd ever heard her voice. She softened at once. "But thanks. It's nice to know I've got an escape route. Where's your studio?"

We were on comfortable ground for both of us when I led her into the tiny room. She unslung her shoulder bag and set it on the floor.

"Okay if I leave this in here? If I do feel something coming on, it helps if I grab my sketchbook."

"I understand that. I can block out just about everything when I'm drawing. I guess I learned to paint with a lot of distractions going on."

"This is a cute little room. I can see you spending a lot of alone time in here if you really have five girlfriends. That's bizarre," Mary said. She looked at everything in the room, touching my paints, easel, and drawings. It was strange that a girl who didn't want to be touched was so tactile when it came to inanimate objects. But each thing she touched gave her a point where she could ground herself.

"So, what do you think of Blankenship?" I asked as I watched her.

"He gets it. Like you do. Half the people in his class will be gone before the end of the semester. That's why he's such an asshole. But even though my first drawing was little more than a scribble, he didn't comment on it. He touched my hand. It wasn't creepy. His hand was cool and dry and it was like he just stopped my shaking. Then the next time he told me to keep hold of my pencil."

"Be thankful he isn't commenting on your drawing. I haven't heard him say anything positive about anyone's drawing yet."

"Yeah. I get that he's an asshole. I'll probably never like him. But I think I can survive his class now. As long as… Um… Did you mean what you said? About being there?" she asked tentatively.

"If there is anything I can do to help, I will," I affirmed.

"So, this Eva. Are your roommates going to let you screw her?"

I sighed. "It will be a small miracle if my roommates don't all beat me to it. Let's go to the kitchen. I need to put dinner in the oven."

"Ah, so let me get this straight," Eva said as we sat at the table talking. "When I said I wanted you to paint me, you decided that I didn't mean I wanted to model for you, but that I wanted you to put paint on my body? That is freakin' weird."

"Jett learned in automotive class. He wants to paint your chassis," Ariel giggled. She was sure acting a little squirrely. I bet she's waiting for Sarah Lynn to pay up on the orgasms she's owed.

"I think it's a cool idea," Mary said. "If I could hold still long enough, I'd volunteer. Jett would have my hand in one position and when he looked again it would be someplace else."

"So how would it work?" Eva continued. "I mean it sounds like it could be fun and sexy, but you couldn't really show your art anywhere. You might put paint on my body, but you aren't hanging me in a gallery."

"It would be a performance piece," Kelly jumped in. She hadn't really talked about what she did. I wondered if she was going to go into it with Eva and Mary. "I can show you the piece he did as a test with Char and Sarah Lynn. I video-taped two hours and then edited it down to fifteen minutes. I added some music and titles and now we can sell it online when Jett's ready."

"It wasn't a great piece," I said. "I was really just experimenting and getting used to the airbrush. In fact, I think we'd need to test the whole idea once or twice before we do it. So far, I've only painted that way twice. Ariel was the first and we discovered it took her all week to get the paint off. With Char and Sarah Lynn, I switched to water-based paint and we managed to scrub it all off after about half an hour in the shower."

"Half that time you were fooling around," Ariel said. "Besides, I liked wearing your art for a week. And Kelly still wears your signature on her mound."

"You what?" Eva asked.

"The first time Jett and I made love, I said he'd painted my insides. So, he signed me."

"You got it tattooed?"

"No! Jett told me that was forgery. The only art that is going to appear on my body is Jett's. He can paint me any time he wants. Inside or out," Kelly declared.

"Wow. Um… I guess we could try it once with the water paint. But filming? Me naked? I don't have that great a body. I knew you could make it look good on canvas."

"You're cute, Eva," Sarah Lynn said.

"That doesn't make me porn quality. Can we watch the video of Char and Sarah Lynn and see what you want to do to me?"

"If you want the whole experience, I'd suggest the upstairs shower. It's a little bigger and has hand holds," Ariel said brightly. Eva blushed.

So did I.

•∘•⟡ ⊃⊂ ☼ ⊃⊂ ⟡•∘•

WE CLEANED UP the dishes quickly. I'd have to wash them after the guests left. Kelly hooked up the video to our television and ran it. Then she showed pictures of the art I put on Ariel. Mary had a quiet smirk on her face as Eva watched with her mouth open. Kelly really did a great job with the video and the final painting even looked pretty decent. And I really loved the mechanics and music art on Ariel. Yeah, I was definitely going to stretch her out and paint her again.

"So, all you end up with is a photo and video," Eva said, still not convinced.

"Not quite," I said. I went to the studio and got the canvas that had been in Char and Sarah Lynn's arms. "The concept I'm working on will leave me with a finished canvas as well. I had this picture mostly all painted when I posed Char and Sarah Lynn. But in painting them into the canvas, I got this negative space image of the parts of their bodies that overlapped the painting." It wasn't a huge area with this painting, but I'd looked at it frequently. Char's arms and Sarah Lynn's left boob were clearly outlined by the mist from the airbrush spattering on the canvas as I painted them. I'd been thinking about it more and more as I looked at the painting.

"I've got a question," Mary said just loudly enough for us to hear. We all turned to her. "Um… Well, I was wondering if you could show some poses with a blank canvas so we could get a better visual of what she'd look like. Kelly could take a few reference photos. I wouldn't mind doing a sketch or two if Eva doesn't mind posing for a bit. Then you could

174

talk more about the way it would unfold. I'm betting that Kelly has an idea about making it a live performance—not just video. You could find out how Eva would hold up with just the other seven of us in the room watching her."

That was more than I'd heard Mary say at one time since we met. She was a different person when she was truly into her art. I nodded and turned back to Eva. "What do you think?"

"You want me to strip in front of all of you?"

"We could do the whole changing room and enter in a robe thing," Sarah Lynn said. "I mean, if that would make you more comfortable. It might be more fun the other way, though."

"Do you have any weed?"

20
Prepping the Canvas

IT TURNED out that even naked, Eva wasn't the star of the show. I\\ was thankful though that she got naked before Mary took her sweater off. It was one of those oversized baggy things that was sort of a dress, hanging down below her butt. Like the two times I saw her in class, she was wearing tights or yoga pants under it. That's what I *thought* she wore under it. When the sweater came off, we all stopped to stare. Eva's nudity was all but forgotten.

"God! You're beautiful!" Kelly exclaimed.

Mary blushed and her hands started to shake. She wasn't just wearing tights, but a full bodystocking. It hugged every curve and indentation, every peak and valley of her body.

"You wear those bodystockings all the time, don't you," I said. She nodded.

"I'll wear slacks or skirts over them in the winter, and I have some heavier weight ones if it gets really cold," she said as she picked up a pencil and pad. Once she put the pad in front of her and rested the pencil on it, her hands stopped shaking. "Polartec and Patagonia make great winter wear. Sometimes I wear yoga pants and leotards but I like the one-piece outfits. It's like… um… I like the feel…"

"It's like being hugged over all your body," I offered.

The smile she flashed at me as she nodded was brilliant. I tore my eyes away from the incredibly beautiful girl and focused on the almost as beautiful Eva. Eva had been demure as she stripped, keeping her tits and pussy covered with her hands. But when Mary pulled off her sweater, Eva lost track of where her hands were and just stood there fully exposed. I took her hand and led her to the stool where I'd draped a towel.

"What I've got in mind first is having you partially on and partially off the canvas," I said, drawing her attention to me. I scooted the easel with a two-foot canvas up behind her and started directing her into different positions. I'd move the canvas around and try her in different positions until either Kelly or Mary would say, "There! Hold it." Then I'd step back and just look at the composition, trying to see it in my mind's eye while Kelly snapped photos and Mary drew. Then we'd start again.

"I could do this if it was water paint," Eva said when I had her in a position where she was pretty much hugging the canvas in quarter profile with her cheek against the canvas and looking over her shoulder. "I don't think I could stand to have acrylic in my hair and on my face. I'll wear the acrylic on the rest of my body for a week, but not on my face."

"These that you've posed so far would do for tests," Mary said. "But eventually you are going to have to do a canvas big enough to get her whole body on. Any of those poses would have looked great as a full canvas."

"That's the problem with doing life-size art," I agreed. "There's also the problem of being able to take breaks and get back into the same position. It's even more critical than in a normal studio pose. The outline is painted right onto the canvas. You can't fudge it. Thank you, Eva. I think we have enough for tonight. It's been a long day and I have to work again tomorrow."

⋯⧫))C ☀))C ⧫⋯

My heaviest class schedule was on Tuesday. I had back-to-back lectures on 2D Concepts and Foundations of Contemporary Art. Then I had to dash across campus while I ate lunch to get to my Literature and the Arts class before rushing back across campus to Blankety's Drawing class. That didn't even end my day on Tuesday as I had a five o'clock colloquium in the gallery.

Literature and the Arts was interesting. After a ten-minute class last Wednesday, Professor Merck gave us the rest of the week off with our first discussion scheduled for this Tuesday. I was irritated that I had to take this class. I just wasn't into art history and looking at the developments of literature in ancient Egypt was something I thought of as completely irrelevant.

"This is a general studies class, so some of you are here from different disciplines. Art, writing, history, and drug abuse," our stoner prof said. I swear his eyes were so glassy I could see the universe reflected in them. "Usually, a class like this would have a term paper or a test at the end of each segment. I hate reading term papers and grading tests. But I like art and literature. What I'd like at the end of each of our units is an incorporation of the developments during the period we discuss into a creative work of your choosing. If you are a painter, paint incorporating your understanding of the period. If you are a writer, give me a short story, poem, essay, whatever. If you are a historian or political science major, I want to hear about how the subject affects the contemporary application of your area of interest. If you are just a stoner thinking this will be an easy class to get out of the way first semester, I'll expect to sit over a bowl with you while you discuss the philosophical implications of Akhenaten dancing on the head of a pin."

We all laughed at his joke, but it looked like a couple in the class might take him seriously. Well, anyway, maybe the class wouldn't be so bad after all. I'd have six drawing or painting projects incorporating ancient Egypt, Homer's Troy, Euripides' Athens, Virgil's Rome, Dante's Florence, and some printer dude named Manutius in Venice. Merck wasn't putting any restrictions on the project other than how well we incorporated what we learned into it. I might do more art in his class than any of my others.

MARY KIND OF smirked at me when I rushed into drawing class. She seemed calm today and she was wearing a shorter sweater than what I'd seen her in before. I reflexively looked down, but the tights she wore weren't the completely revealing kind she had on Saturday that showed absolutely every curve and indent. She had some kind of short skirt combined with shorts that came down a few inches below her butt. I didn't have time to say anything because at exactly three o'clock—about thirty seconds after I sat down—Blankety started lecturing about paper texture. We were expected to have half a dozen different grades of paper in our bags. The materials list for this class had cost a bundle.

The subject for the day was a bowl of fruit and we were to select a match of three different substrates and media to draw it. After he'd lectured for half an hour, he cut us loose to draw without a timer. It was still disconcerting to have him wandering around behind us commenting on the grade school quality of our drawings. "Is that an apple or a beach ball?" he asked as he passed behind me. Rhetorical question. He never expected any of us to answer him. I glanced over at him as he approached Mary.

"Work two-handed," he said. He picked up her art gum eraser and placed it in her left hand as she held the pencil in her right. "You should erase as much as you draw." I thought that was mildly insulting, but Mary nodded her head and started working on her drawing with both hands moving. I wouldn't copy her instructions in class right when she got them, but I was definitely going to try this. For Mary, she had to focus on what both hands were doing at the same time. Neither one was free to shake.

⋯•⋯⟩ ⅅⅭ ☼ ⅅⅭ ⟨⋯•⋯

WE CLOSED OUR sketchbooks at exactly five o'clock when Blankety walked out the door. I had five minutes to get to the gallery, but it was only on the other side of the building. Mary fell into step beside me.

"Colloquium?" I asked. She nodded. "That's a different look for you today. It's nice." She blushed and turned to look at me.

"Um… certain bodystockings I have to wear something over."

"Not that I have an opinion on that, but why?"

"Most bodystockings are crotchless." We walked into the gallery and joined thirty-some other students as some artist I'd never heard of was introduced to give a story of his artwork. It was mostly just about how great he considered himself.

Or maybe I was just too preoccupied with thoughts of Mary's crotchless bodystocking.

⋯•⋯⟩ ⅅⅭ ☼ ⅅⅭ ⟨⋯•⋯

WE'D SET UP a system with each of the six of us responsible for dinner one night. Obviously, Tuesday was not my night. I got Mondays because I had no classes and was off work at the grocery store at two. I was down

179

to three eight-hour days a week and it kind of wrecked my weekends. Monday dinner was the end of my 'work-week' and Tuesday morning started my 'school-week.' This past week, I'd switched off with Kelly for Saturday. We reserved Ariel for Friday nights because we were almost always all home for dinner and her Asian cooking was the most time-sensitive.

Tuesday night, I got home to find Jas finishing cleanup in the kitchen. I went to her and cuddled up behind her as she bent over the sink. She wiggled her butt into my stiffening cock and I cupped her breasts as I nibbled her neck. God, I loved Jasmine!

"There's a bowl of Sarah Lynn's jambalaya in the fridge for you," she said as she rubbed her head back against my shoulder. "It heats up quickly and is just as good warmed over as fresh." I kissed her again and she turned in my arms. "Unless you'd rather eat at the Y," she murmured.

"Maybe I could dine there for dessert if I fully brush my teeth after dinner," I said.

"Yeah. As much as I love Ariel's tasty little pussy, I'd rather have your come in my mouth. Or my pussy. Especially since I know Kelly loves to eat it out of me."

"Do you want just me?" I asked hesitantly. I'd offered to be her exclusive boyfriend before we all moved in together and she'd declined.

"I *want* you," she said, "but I'm not going to give up licking Ariel or sucking on Char's nips or double-dildoing with Kelly or…"

"You double-dildoed with Kelly?" Now that was an image I wanted to savor.

"Yeah. Last night. She got this new toy and it was way cool. We may need a few more for the house. Just think, Char could fuck your ass at the same time you're fucking hers." I shuddered and clenched my butt cheeks.

"I think I'd better eat something and then take my very first lover to bed for a while," I said.

"Agreed."

Everyone had something going on. Kelly cammed Tuesday, Wednesday, and Thursday. She'd developed a pretty good following. She was pulling down about three hundred a week. That might make her the biggest earner of all of us. Ariel's summer nanny job ended when school started but her parents were paying her rent. She'd picked up three piano students and that was getting her a hundred a week in spending money. Sarah Lynn's room and board were included in her scholarship and the full semester was paid into her bank account at the beginning, so she had no problem meeting rent. Jas and Char worked five shifts each at the restaurant. I knew Sondra supplemented her daughter's expenses but I wasn't really sure how Char was making it. Her father was trying to force her home and tied up every penny he could. She hadn't even been able to retrieve her personal belongings from her room.

I was pretty tired after my long day in class, but not so tired that I couldn't get into Jasmine. Literally. I kissed every inch of her that I could reach, including a couple inches inside her pussy where I could push my tongue.

"I love you, Jett. Put your penie in my snootch and fuck me into the mattress." That was an impossible request to turn down and I slid into her with one long thrust.

I'm not naïve. I know our parents had sex—probably most of them still do. Jasmine's mom, the Dragon Lady, and especially Kelly's mom are pretty hot women. I'm glad I refrained from becoming one of the assholes who called for a mother-daughter show in her chatroom. She blocked at least one of them a week. But as hot as those older women were for their age, I just couldn't imagine anything better than the teen pussy my cock was gripped in at the moment. Yeah, yeah. I know all the stuff about experience improving performance, but Jas and I were getting our own experience. Every time I slid into that velvety hot glove, I was getting a new experience.

And I've got a double standard. I admit it. I try not to let it influence anything, but if you don't admit your faults, you can't overcome them. I lived with five girls and my cock was regularly in three pussies, an asshole, and a mouth. I loved every one of them. And I knew that Jas had given Rick a blowjob—and maybe some of our other friends. But there was something about being the only cock that had ever been in her pussy that gave me a little extra charge. I wanted to make sure mine was the only one she ever wanted.

It was only slightly different with Kelly. Derek had taken her virginity, but she was the only one of my girlfriends who had point-blank told me that she was only mine for as long as I'd have her. Sarah Lynn had a couple of boyfriends in high school she went all the way with. She'd never said who, but I figured that Lonnie had been the one to take her virginity. There were still times when she got a faraway look in her eyes and I knew she was thinking of him.

But Jas. For more than two years we'd Skyped and watched each other masturbate and come. She'd given me an hour-long guided video tour of her erogenous zones, including well-lit closeups of every body part. For months, all I had to do was close my eyes to recall what the inside of her pussy looked like and I'd come.

Then one day, I'd asked her to pose for me. Something fell into place for both of us and when she looked at the painting I did, she took my hand and dragged me to bed to invite me into her hot passage. I no longer had to think of what the inside of her pussy looked like. Now, I thought of what it felt like and could pop an instant boner.

"I love having you in me, Jett. You find nerves inside me that I never reached with my fingers or a dildo. I love when we're getting close like this. I can feel more juices slicking my snootch. We slow down a little when we're about to come. That lets me feel your cock swell just before you spray. And if I can hold off coming long enough, I can feel your stuff spurt inside me. That's when it's just too much for my senses and I come. I come. I come."

I held myself inside her as tightly as I could. I felt every muscle in her vagina tighten as I swelled, knowing that I didn't have to do anything else. This train had already left the station. As she chanted, "I come. I come. I come," I unleashed a torrent in her depths and she rocketed over the edge in an orgasm we didn't bother to muffle. I wondered what Kelly's chatroom would think if they heard us from below. But who cared.

"Again, Jett. Move in me. Stay hard. I want to feel it all again!"

I softened a little, but Jas worked her muscles and I thrust a few times. What can I say? It was Jasmine's eighteen-year-old pussy and it was mine, all mine. We took longer the second time and it was even more satisfying.

"Would Mom ever know if I didn't get up to wash my hands and brush my teeth again before bed?" I asked sleepily. I could still feel her pulses around me.

"Who'd tell her?" Jas answered just as sleepily. "Stay in me as long as you can. And when you wake up in the morning… or anytime during the night… put it in me again. Put it in me again and again."

I didn't manage to stay hard enough not to fall out, but even shriveled up, my cock steeped in her pussy juices all night long. And in the morning, we fucked again.

•◦•❖ ⊃⊂ ☽ ⊃⊂ ❖•◦•

"Wait, Jett. Um… give me a sec to catch my breath," Mary said after class on Thursday. I just couldn't figure out how Blankety managed to make each class more stressful than the one before. He was in a rare mood today and actually laughed at our drawings. It wasn't just his normal "this isn't good" kind of comments. He actually made a joke out of every drawing. I wondered how he came up with so many denigrating one-liners and finally decided he had Lenny Bruce writing for him.

"Hey, Mary. Got plans for the weekend?"

"Yeah. That's what I wanted to talk to you about. Can you get free of the girlfriends to go to a movie Sunday afternoon?"

"Um… You mean like…"

"I know it sounds like a date but… Well, it probably is, technically. But I don't plan to fuck you. I mean…" Her hands were shaking. I reached over and put my fingertips on one. It calmed as she held my eyes.

"Yes," I whispered. "A date between friends. I get off work at two."

She took a deep breath and let it go. Then smiled.

•◦•❖ ⊃⊂ ☀ ⊃⊂ ❖•◦•

"That took guts," Sarah Lynn said. "I expected that Eva would be first to invite you out for some hanky-panky. In fact, she called and asked if it was okay to do a painting with you next weekend."

"She called and asked you?"

"Apparently, she figures that I'm head bitch. I told her it was okay with the women but not to expect that we'd be dressed all the time either. Then I told her she'd have to discuss with you whether you wanted her naked body under your fingers."

"You told her that? No wonder she hasn't contacted me," I laughed.

"That girl is naturally brash. I don't mean that she didn't see something in your paintings last spring that made her want you to capture her soul on canvas. But I think she saw something in you that made her want to capture your body in hers. I'd expect her to want the full treatment of wash and wax after you paint her."

"It's not like that with Mary, you know," I said.

"Yeah. But if you can get that bodystocking off her, you'll have five breathless observers," Sarah Lynn said as she dragged me to the bedroom. She started pulling my clothes off and I joined in the fun. It wasn't unusual for Sarah Lynn to want sex, but it was unusual to see her so excited about it before we actually got going. "You know I'm mostly hetero," she continued. "I love the girls in our house and wouldn't deny one of them access to my pussy or tongue. Nothing satisfies quite like having your cock buried in me. Still… I could see myself swearing off men if that was a condition of having Mary."

I sincerely hoped it wasn't as she pulled my erection into her wet folds. Sarah Lynn and I didn't have the same kind of chemistry that I had with either Jas or Kelly, but we came together like that was where we belonged.

For an instant as we lounged in the afterglow, almost asleep, I had a flash of wondering if Mary would wear a crotchless bodystocking Sunday.

21
A Fantastic Woman

"Is this a test?" Jas asked.

"Only sort of," I explained. "It's a class project. We're supposed to create a work of art that captures, in some way, the effect of Akhenaten's changes in ancient Egypt on today's art. You are perfect for my Egyptian canvas. Will you do it?"

"You'll use the water-soluble paints so I can shower it off afterward?"

"Jas, sweetheart, I will personally bathe you and massage you until all trace of the paint is erased from your body."

"Bathe and massage? I'm in. I'm out of class at two tomorrow."

"It's a date, lover."

•○•❖ ⊃⊂ ☽ ⊃⊂ ❖•○•

I'd been thinking about this since Tuesday when Prof Merck explained the assignment. It was a little risky, but he wanted original artwork. I checked to see if he would accept a photo of the art and he kicked back in his chair.

"I suppose it is too much to ask your model to show up for our class, so I will accept a high-resolution photo. I want to be able to display it for the class." He was vaping cannabis as we talked and I thought I might be getting a little high just from being in the same room.

I'd managed to talk to Jasmine over dinner Thursday night and was thinking I might give her a down payment on her night of loving, but Kelly had other ideas.

"Come up at nine when I go offline, please? I think I'm going to be very horny tonight." Let me think. What's the proper response to that suggestion? Kelly had some very interesting ideas to share with me.

"I'M GOOD WITH videoing the whole thing, if you are," Jas said.

"As long as we all remember that the main thing I need is the pictures of the finished project for my class, okay?" I was a little nervous about where Kelly wanted to take it. Not that there weren't plenty of videos of me playing with and even fucking my girlfriends. But this was going a step beyond family playfulness. Everyone agreed. We had about four hours to work before Ariel called us for our Friday night stir fry.

I positioned Jas on the stool with one leg on the rung and the other stretched out. I wanted her in a comfortable position that she could hold for a long sitting and could get back into after a break. The position of her legs meant that her pussy wasn't gaping open when she turned her torso toward me.

Damn it! I liked the position so much that I considered just painting a picture of her and embellishing it with the symbology I wanted, but maybe I could get her to pose for me like this again for a serious portrait. She was so damned beautiful.

Of course, the price Kelly was extracting for the video was that I wear and paint a fresh pair of white briefs. *You know? Whatever floats her boat.*

Once we were set and the camera was running, I started with yellow body paint in my airbrush and created a sunburst on her torso. After all, the number one thing that Akhenaten did was mandate worship of a single deity, Amon-Re, the sun god. The curling rays emanating from her core were a little fanciful for the period, but the real Egyptian theme was what would appear inside the sun. Still, I loved curling flares of the sun around her nipples and into her thin pubic hair. As I hoped, the contrast between the yellow sun and her chocolaty skin was intense.

Using a finer nozzle and contrasting blue paint, I created a pyramid pointing up between her breasts, but cut off at the top. The Great Pyramid of Giza pre-dated Akhenaten by a thousand years, but the radical pharaoh had built upon what came before him, just as my art was building something new with his tools. At the apex of the pyramid, I painted a glowing eye framed in a triangle. I loved the eye resting in the center of Jasmine's chest, seemingly supported on the foundation of her breasts.

With the fundamental elements laid in, I started feathering in a glow around the pyramid and then out from the sun as well. I could hear a sigh from both Kelly and Jasmine when I sprayed her nipples, which promptly popped out erect and required that I touch them up again. When it was finished, Jasmine's torso looked like it was a gate into the past, opening to an Egypt hidden within this goddess.

But so far, Jas had just been a canvas for the art. My plan was to make her into the art itself and this required a steady hand and a lot of trust on her part. It wasn't just paint. I used makeup to highlight her eyes and create dark outlines that had flourishes onto her cheeks. The eyes themselves seemed to glow when I was finished. I shaped her cheeks and deepened the red of her lush lips. Then I returned to the airbrush and created a third eye of Horus on her forehead. The final step in the process was to position her hands.

Steve Martin had a classic routine Granddad loved about King Tut. It took some of the same elements that I'd incorporated into the painting and posing of Jas and turned them into a comic dance. With Jas, though, positioning her right hand so her arm was bent and the palm was held out flat. The other arm pointed the opposite direction and the palm was held low and flat. This was the hardest part for Jas because no matter how it looks in hieroglyphics, it's not a natural position to hold your arms and hands.

The idea for this whole scene hit me on Tuesday in Merck's class, so as soon as I could manage it on Wednesday I went to the local Spencer's and picked up a couple of glo balls. I grabbed these now and activated them. I placed one in each hand. I stepped back and started snapping pictures. Kelly moved in and did a full survey of Jasmine with the video camera. I'd had to ask her to loan me her digital SLR to take the pictures because Prof Merck wanted better photos than I could get on a cell phone. I loved the way Jas looked. So elegant. Our other roommates applauded from the doorway.

I took the glo balls when Kelly said she had enough video and I felt I'd captured about every possible nuance in photos that I could. I had closeups and composites. I took pictures from different angles to make sure I got just the right amount of her face and then I set up one of Kelly's studio lights behind Jas and took a series of backlit shots that made it look like the glow was all around her. I offered my hand to Jas and she stepped off the stool and into my arms. The kiss she gave me melted my heart.

"I feel like the Mona Lisa," she sighed. "Or maybe Venus Rising from the Sea. Like I just stepped off the canvas and into the real world. I think I can actually see through the third eye."

Her eyes were moist and Kelly rushed up to dab them with a tissue so her tears wouldn't cause the makeup or paint to run.

"I wish I'd had you paint it with the acrylics instead of the water paints," Jas continued as she looked at herself in the hall mirror. That was one of the things we'd added early on. The girls all wanted to look at themselves before they went out the door in the morning and that required a full-length mirror right beside the door to my studio. "I don't want to wash it off. I want to live as an Egyptian goddess."

•°• ⋅❖⟆ ⟊⟊⟆ ⟆⟊⟊ ⟆❖⋅ •°•

ACT TWO OF our little performance came after dinner. We went to Kelly's Kat House. Kelly was becoming quite accomplished at videography and editing. Granted, nearly everything she recorded was classed as porn, but she was making as much money selling the solo videos she released each month as she was getting tips for her online performances. If I didn't know better, I'd think she had a cameraman working with her to get some of the shots she managed. The one thing that was chafing at her was that all her videos were shot in her little chatroom. She wanted to get out where she could perform in different settings.

She also looked at me meaningfully every time she mentioned wanting to do a boy-girl video. The two-minute cell phone video of her fucking me the first time—it only showed where we were connected and my hand signing her mound—was her top seller. I had to admit that I'd watched it a hundred times. If there wasn't always a cute teen girl in my house who wanted to suck me or fuck me, I'd have put that video on endless loop and masturbated to it. It sent a shiver down my spine to think that was exactly what a thousand faceless guys were doing.

I wasn't crazy about performing, but the only part of me that would be seen was my cock. Sarah Lynn and Char were enhancing Jasmine's makeup. They were good at it and it would take photo recognition software to identify her when they were done. Kelly kept tinkering with her camera angles as I lay on the bed. Ariel was doing a great job keeping me hard with her tongue.

"You know I want to jam this down my throat and drink you," Ariel said when she popped off. "I never thought I'd consent to being a fluffer."

"Well, I'm just a stunt cock for Kelly's big experiment. Jas is the star," I laughed. My cock slapped her in the cheek and she took a long lick up the side.

"Ready?" Kelly asked.

"Ariel, Jas needs a little help, too," Sarah Lynn said. Ariel leaped into action, leaving my hard cock waving in the air. In a second, she was between Jasmine's legs, making sure my girlfriend was extremely well-lubricated. Kelly left her camera long enough to take a few licks on my cock and make sure I stayed hard.

"If this works, you know I'm going to want you to fuck me on camera," Kelly whispered to me. "Maybe that will be when I give you my anal cherry. I bet I could get a subscription to watch that live in a private show while we're taping."

"God, Kelly! I can't believe my girlfriend is a porn star."

"So far, it's all been solo, but I'm definitely going to get a girl or two involved with me. You wouldn't believe how many other camgirls have contacted me wanting to do a show with me!"

"I'll bet plenty of guys have contacted you, too."

"Yes. But you are the only guy I want in my pussy, Jett. I'm a sex-crazed lunatic, but I'm a selective one."

"We're definitely ready," Ariel said, emerging from between Jasmine's legs. "If this girl was any wetter, she'd slide right off."

That meant it was time for action. Kelly had hung drapes around the bed so it looked a little like a harem tent. I guess a little mix of metaphors was okay. My head was kind of in the folds of the tent so you couldn't see my face. The shot started with Jas entering through the tent flap and stopping to stare at me, lying on the bed. When she'd established Jasmine in the room, Kelly panned from my toes up my oiled legs and torso. She circled around my cock to catch Jas approaching the bed.

I knew a lot of the video was going to be of Jasmine and the painting that had turned her into something mystic and goddess-like, so I was a little worried that my erection would flag before she needed it. Every time it was out of the camera frame, though, Sarah Lynn would snake her hand out and gently stroke me. With this kind of attention, I wasn't going to flag.

Jas finally straddled my chest and took over the attention to my cock. There was no dialog in our little movie but as it progressed, there were an increasing number of moans. The goddess above me worshiped me. By the time she sank onto my pole, a lot of the moans were mine. My concern changed from being afraid I'd get soft to being afraid I'd come too quickly. I could already feel Jasmine's snootch, as she called it, fluttering around my cock in her first moaned orgasm.

I couldn't see a lot since my head was in the flimsy curtains and most of my attention was held by Jasmine's gorgeous ass as she pumped up and down on my cock. When I saw the camera move up Jas's body to capture her face thrown back in ecstasy, I felt Sarah Lynn reach in again. Instead of stroking my cock, she squeezed the base painfully. All thought of coming fled for at least thirty seconds. Jas was just too hard to resist.

This time, Kelly scanned down Jasmine's body as Jas continued to undulate on my cock. She focused on each nipple to show how the paint wrapped the precious points and then down her torso to show closeups of the different features of the painting as Jasmine's tummy flexed in and out with her movement. Before long, the camera was focused on our joining and Jas started fucking with intent. My own voice rose to match hers. A near match. When Jas is truly worked up, no one gets louder than she does. My hands were on her butt and I was bouncing up from the mattress into her when we both reached our climax. It wasn't a short one. Before we finished, I could feel our combined juices running out of her and over my balls.

The last scene was of Jasmine slowly leaning back until she was lying on top of me and my cock, even though still pretty hard, pulled out of her. Kelly panned from the come running out of Jasmine's pussy up across her belly and then pulled back to show her lying back in sweet repose with one of the glo balls held at her side in each hand and her head turned slightly. It was a nice reflection of the final pose I had her in for the painting.

Mostly, while we were shooting, I was only aware of the attention Jas was giving to my cock and fucking her. It wasn't until Monday that I finally saw the edited video with cuts from my painting of Jas and music provided by Ariel on the piano. Once we'd watched the ten-minute video together, Jas and I fucked again.

I CUT OUT of work Sunday afternoon as quickly as I could and picked up Mary at her dorm. I'd come to expect the kind of baggy sweater that hung down almost to her knees with the tights under it. I went to her door to collect her and we drove over to the Pyramid Art Cinema.

Every town needs a movie theater like this one. Still, I don't understand how they stay in business. They specialize in showing foreign, independent, and art films. I've never seen the theater more than half full unless they happen to get one of the real popular ones during the International Film Festival. There have even been a few protests outside the theatre when they showed foreign films that would have been rated NC17 in the US—if anyone had submitted them for rating. But the theater owner stubbornly refused to shut down the '20s era movie house. I'd heard that before they started showing movies it was used for burlesque. There was supposed to be a whole stage behind the screen. The architecture was filled with Egyptian motifs that made me think about Jas. I mean about my Literature and the Arts class. *Right.*

"This is supposed to be a great film," Mary said. "It's about a Chilean singer who falls in love with an older man. Soon after she moves in with him, he dies and his family is mean to her. They even take away the dog he gave her. It won the Academy Award for Best Foreign Language Film. And I won't say anything else because that's all the blurb said."

We found seats and watched previews for half a dozen other films that would be shown in the near future. A couple of them looked interesting and one looked extremely sexy. I wasn't sure exactly what my relationship with Mary was, so I didn't try to put an arm around her or hold her hand. We just sat companionably as the movie started.

What the blurb she gave me didn't include was that Marina Vidal, the singer, was a transgender woman. What I first thought was just a sad love story took on a new dimension as we witnessed even the police who investigated Orlando's death try to pin it on her. The nastiness of the family directed at the young woman was just because she was trans. I started to get angry. Not at Mary, but at the society that did this to people because they were different. The woman in the film was beautiful, talented, loving, and smart. She didn't deserve what they did to her.

I'm not sure anyone deserves the way she was treated. Still, that was how my little household was formed. Charmaine was treated terribly by her father, who was still trying to sell her off in marriage. Ariel's father was pretty much a sperm donor who considered it the mother's job to raise the children and his to go make money. He was only concerned that she not disgrace him. And Sarah Lynn's dad… Well, her mother was a total fruitcake, but her dad was cold. He was a fireman and held his loyalty to his fellow first responders above his loyalty to his daughter. He hadn't spoken to Sarah Lynn since commencement.

Yeah. We all had our little crosses to bear, as Grandma would put it. But it seemed like some people had more crosses than others. That image set something in my mind moving and my fingers began to itch. I wanted to draw a scene—paint it—of a transgender Jesus. I'd need a model.

Mary's fingers touched mine on our armrest and I could feel her low tremor. I rolled my hand over and our fingers interlaced.

Mary.

Oh. My. God! Was that why she wanted me to see this film?

•०•⇨ ᗃᗡ ☽ ᗃᗡ ⇦•०•

"Seeing things like that makes me angry and sad and afraid," she said as we walked to the car. We continued to hold hands all the way to the door and I opened it until she was settled in the Mini. As soon as I was in and started the car, she continued. "I like to see foreign films because they take me places I'll never go and inspire me to paint things I'll never see. Santiago, Chile. The idea of going there is as remote as going to Mars."

"The movie made me want to paint."

"I could feel your fingers twitching."

"It happens like that."

"Describe the painting."

"I'm thinking a classical crucifixion scene but with Jesus portrayed by a trans woman. Then paint the characters—not the same ones as the movie, but the archetypes of them—surrounding the cross. You'd have the politicians, the friends, the family, the religious hypocrite, and whoever else."

"Grotesque."

"Yeah. I'll probably do a sketch but realizing a full painting like that will probably take years. First, I'd have to find a trans model who would be willing to work with me." I just let that hang in the air. We pulled up in front of her dorm. I was still holding her hand and turned toward her so our eyes could meet. The light came on.

"Oh, my God! You think… Because I suggested that movie… You wonder… I didn't…" I was completely surprised by what she did next. Her hands had started to tremble so much that I could barely keep hold. There isn't much of a console in a Mini, so nothing obstructed her when she pulled my hand to her lap and pushed it up under the sweater, straight into her crotch. "Check and see. Find out if I have a cock and balls."

She was nearing that state of panic I'd learned to recognize with other friends where she'd hyperventilate until she passed out, but she wouldn't let me pull my hand away from her very bare and rapidly moistening pussy.

"Mary, I didn't mean to imply anything. It's okay. You don't need to…"

"Of course you thought I was trans. I bear all the signs and I took you to a movie sympathetic to trans women. What else would you think? I just want you to be sure!" She started rubbing my fingers up and down her slit. One question answered—a crotchless bodystocking. Second question answered—Mary was all woman.

I was more concerned about Mary's anxiety than about whether or not she was trans. But her breathing pace changed. She still didn't let up on the pressure against my hand on her pussy and I reflexively started stroking my fingers through the gathering moisture. Her mouth opened slightly and a soft moan issued forth.

"You don't have to do this, Mary," I said.

"I'm not going to… I wasn't going to have sex with you. Today. But… I think you should keep exploring a few minutes. Explore that spot… right there. Mmm." That spot was obviously her clit. I shifted slightly and leaned in to kiss her. Her eyes flew open when our lips touched and then she relaxed into the kiss, her parted lips giving easy access to her tongue. And it heated up from there. She pulled her right foot up so her heel was on the edge of the seat, opening herself further to my questing fingers. I made sure I complied with her demand that I explore thoroughly, inside and out. Mary stiffened and whined her orgasm into my mouth.

"I… Oh, God! I'd invite you to my room but we wouldn't be alone. I'd invite myself to yours but we wouldn't be alone. I don't want to give you a blowjob in the parking lot. It's so crude. Says the girl with a boy's fingers still pumping in and out of her. I'll… Oh, God, Jett." She finally pulled my hand away from her sex. She'd never let go of my wrist while I was finger fucking her. "I'll make it up to you. After I talk to Sarah Lynn."

Mary pecked me quickly on the lips and jumped out of the car to run to the dorm door without looking back.

22
Facing the Muses

"**YOU ASKED** her if she was trans? Are you an idiot?" Sarah Lynn yelled at me. What could I say. I felt like an idiot, especially facing her wrath.

"I didn't. I just wanted… I thought she must have some reason for wanting me to see that particular movie with her," I whined.

"Couldn't you see the way that bodystocking hugged the curves of her pussy when she took the dress off in the studio?"

"I was really trying hard not to stare. It's fine for other girls to stare at a girl, but it's not right for a boy to stare. Even if the other girls want take her to bed," I accused. Somewhere I read that a counter-offense is the best defense. *Idiot.*

"So, I suppose you didn't notice that she has bars pierced through her nipples, either."

What the fuck? How could I have missed…? Her nipples are pierced?

"She does?" I brilliantly asked.

"With five pair of nipples *constantly* at your fingertips, you think hard, tight, luscious nipples are naturally shaped like that?"

I was in a corner and had nowhere to flee. I really didn't want this fight with sweet Sarah Lynn. I clammed up and hung my head. She wasn't finished.

"Just what would you have done if you'd found a cock and balls when she shoved your hand up her dress?"

That gave me a second's pause. I'd never met a male that sparked the least bit of interest in me. We'd had group chats on Skype when the guys all had their cocks out stroking them as the girls fingered their pussies.

It was pretty hot. But I'd never thought once about them. I was totally focused on Kelly or Jas or even Dee. But Mary…

"Sarah Lynn, I'd have done exactly the same thing I did. I'd have stroked her to the best orgasm I could give her. I'd have kissed her just as passionately. I doubt I'd have wanted to fuck her the way that I admit I want to fuck Mary. But she's my friend. I mean, really my friend. And I made a commitment to her. I told her I'd be there if she needed me and *damn it!* she needed me. I could feel it. Deep down inside, I could feel how much she needed me. I'd have done exactly the same thing."

Sarah Lynn stepped back and stared at me. I was sure I'd just driven a wedge into my little household that I'd never recover from. I'd never get laid again, that was for sure. I was ashamed of my behavior. I'd just told my girlfriends that if I'd found a cock and balls under Mary's dress that I'd have jacked her off. I was pretty sure, by the way they were all staring at me, that I was sleeping alone tonight. And every night for the foreseeable future. But what the fuck. I didn't do it to get myself off, even though I was still hard as a rock, despite Sarah Lynn's rant. She'd already talked to Mary by the time I got home from my date. I closed my eyes and waited for the tirade.

"I hope you've got five loads of come in you," Sarah Lynn whispered. "You are going to get so fucked tonight."

•o• •❖ ❭❭❈ ☼ ❈❬❬ ❖• •o•

Okay. I'm clueless. I'd confessed as soon as I got home that I fingered Mary to an orgasm or two. I thought I was prepared for the wrath of my girlfriends. I wasn't prepared for being stripped of my clothes and fucked within an inch of my life.

What makes girls tick? I was pretty sure that if I could answer that question, I would become the world's most popular guru. The guys next door would pay a year's tuition for the secret and the hos down the street would be selling themselves for a quarter on south Main.

When Sarah Lynn pushed me down on the couch, I was almost prepared for her to mount me. That means not prepared at all. She sank onto my cock and the silk glove milked me for all she was worth.

"I love you so much, Jett. I knew you were the man for me. I knew it

196

from the moment you picked me up after commencement and gave me a T-shirt to wear. Jett, I love you and I love making love to you. You are everything I imagined you'd be. Everything that Lonnie said." *What the fuck? Oh, fuck!* Sarah milked me until I thought she'd drained the life force out of me.

But Char was waiting. And she was ready. I don't know when she'd prepared herself, but I slid into her buttery ass like I was built to mate with her. It was a little slower this time, but… Char's ass. *Oh, my God!*

I got a little reprieve after I'd filled my dark lover and she'd come a couple times as I fingered her clit and Jas and Ariel sucked her nipples. Kelly dragged me out of the living room and upstairs to the shower. She made sure I was scrubbed and sanitized and then led me to the big bed. The other girls met us there and fed us fruit and cheese and crackers. Then Kelly pulled me on top of her and wrapped her ankles around my neck as I plunged into her fiery cunt over and over again.

It was after midnight when Jas perched on the bed with her ass waggling in the air, begging me to get behind her. She didn't have to beg too hard before I was behind her and sawing into heaven's own pussy while Ariel lay below her and licked Jasmine's clit and my balls. I was dead. There was no way I could service all five of my girlfriends in one night. I pretty much passed out on top of Jasmine's beautiful chocolate ass.

I didn't think that… well, I didn't think. Period. But Ariel's tongue and mouth had me hard again by two in the morning and she rolled me onto my back so she could rub her little virgin pussy against my cock. I let her have her fun, knowing full well that I would never pop a fifth time in one night.

"This is it, Jett," she said as she leaned forward to kiss me. The difference in our heights meant that the tip of my cock slid past her clit and into the moisture beyond. "I've known for months that this was what I wanted and I have no idea why I've waited so long. I love you, Jett." With that, she pushed back and I sank into the tightest little pussy I'd ever experienced. Even as hot as all the girls were, it took a while before Ariel had me fully inside her.

I'd dreamed about this moment. I'd licked the bald pussy and sensitive clit of this Asian beauty a hundred times or more. Every time I licked her, I thought about what it would be like to actually have my cock inside her. Nothing I imagined even came close to Ariel pushing herself up and down my cock. It took us half an hour or more before I felt the tightening in my balls that let me know the climax of all those dreams was near.

"I want you to paint me again. Use the permanent acrylics and make my body your canvas. I'll wear the skimpiest clothes I own for as long as a trace of the paint is visible on my body. I'll parade myself on Kelly's webcam for the world to see. You own my body and soul. Let me feel you come in me and claim me as your own."

I couldn't disappoint this little beauty. I did as she commanded.

I BARELY DRAGGED myself to work Monday morning. Grandpa saw the condition I was in and wouldn't let me near a knife or power slicer, even with cut gloves on. I was thankful. I took a nap before anyone else got home Monday afternoon and then spent the evening working on the photo imagery of Jas for my Literature and the Arts class.

I'd intentionally kept a neutral backdrop as I painted Jas and it took me about two hours to remove the background and place her backlit, glowing image on a scene I'd found on a free photos site. The scene was a rock at the shore of the ocean with the sun rising. I'd intentionally positioned Jas so her seated position could be transferred to the rock. It took some tricky editing to remove the glow from where it would be blocked by the rock and keep it where it would naturally appear against the sky with the backlight of the sun. I'd taken photos from a lot of different angles in order to get the one that fit correctly with the scene.

I'm pretty sure there were people who could do a better job of photo composition and editing than I could. Kelly for instance. But we'd all had a digital editing class in high school as an elective and I still had a student version of some high-end software. I was pleased with the result and prepared to compress it to send to my prof.

Kelly bounced into the dining room where I was working about ten with a copy of the digital video she'd edited. I don't know when she had time to do the editing, but she said she was using the same file for her video editing class.

"Wow! That's great, Jett," she said. "I wondered what you were going to do with the backlighting. Jas will be stoked about this. Watch this and then package it with your project. Your prof will love it."

We watched the video of me painting Jas. Kelly had cut it together and sped up sections so the whole painting took only ten minutes with music from Ariel playing a scherzo as I painted. Kelly sat on my lap as we watched and I slid a hand under her T-shirt to find there was only Kelly there. She bounced on my finger as the video played and I did my best to show her how much I appreciated her work. When it was finished and we switched to the scene of Jas on the rock, it was twice as beautiful.

"Now stop finger-fucking me," Kelly panted. "Jas wants to watch the other video with you. Don't include it in your package to the prof. Jas! We're ready."

Of course, it wasn't just Jas that came into the dining room to watch. All the girls gathered around, but Jas sat on my lap. She started out dressed the same way Kelly was, but lost the T-shirt before the video was over.

"Undress for the next one, Jett," Kelly said. "You aren't going to want to be confined."

Jas and I watched the edited video with cuts from my painting interspersed with the unbelievable sex and Ariel's piano music. I couldn't believe the way Jas just glowed with pleasure. It was like the sun I painted on her skin was lit from inside her. Once we'd watched the ten-minute video together, Jas and I fucked again with all four of our lovers touching us and joining in.

◦•◦✦))C ☼))C ✦◦•◦

"Jett…"

"Mary…" we both began at once when I saw her in class on Tuesday. We blushed and I saw Mary's hands begin to shake. "Are you okay, my friend?" I asked.

"Yeah. I'm okay. Thank you. I mean for Sunday. I mean… really… thank you."

"I feel like I'm the one who should be saying thank you," I said. "Not only for the movie."

"Yeah. About that. Um… Thank you."

Blankenship interrupted anything else we might have said after that and we had to focus all our attention on the task he assigned. Today we were focused on highlights. He had us cover an entire page with graphite and then use an eraser to just tease the highlights out of the darkness. It was pretty cool, but I couldn't see actually creating something entirely like this. Maybe it would be useful on something else.

•◦•⇨ ⊃⊂ ☼ ⊃⊂ ⇦•◦•

"Jett," Eva said when I stepped out of class. I was going to talk to Mary some more, but she waved goodbye to me as Eva joined me. There was no colloquium today as our next one was scheduled for Wednesday next week. That class jumped around based on the availability of the special speakers.

"Hey, Eva. How are you doing?"

"Yeah, good, good. Do you want to do a test this weekend? I mean, paint me? I figure it would be a good idea to… um… practice a little."

"Eva, I don't think I'll be ready to do the actual project for several weeks. I'm still trying to get the concept together. I'm not very experienced with this body paint thing. Especially with integrating it with a live painting. But I'd love to practice with you a few times. We can use water paints instead of acrylic."

"Don't get any ideas about what I want to do to your body," Eva answered, "but getting naked for you has kind of filled my fantasies lately."

"Eva, having you naked has appeared a few times in mine."

"Yeah. So, this weekend? I checked with your boss and she said the women would be okay with it."

"Sarah Lynn isn't actually my boss," I huffed. How did I even know she was talking about Sarah Lynn? "I actually have a will of my own."

Eva rolled her eyes.

"If I want to spend any kind of time with you, I plan to do it without offending the FIVE women you live with. Sarah Lynn might not be your boss but she is a gateway that I'll willingly pass. Jett, do you want me naked in your studio to paint? I by God WILL get Sarah Lynn's permission first."

"I think you already did," I growled. "But understand this. Once you are in my studio, all decisions are between you and me. If I want to undress you, that's between you and me. If I want to suck your nipple to a hard little point before I paint it, that's between you and me. If you want to drag my fingers through your juicy wet snatch, that's between you and me." I was right up against her ear and could see the gooseflesh rising on her arms as I blew my words at her.

"I just want you to paint me," she squeaked.

"That's between you and me. Be at the house at three-thirty sharp Saturday afternoon."

"Okay. Or should I say 'Yes, sir'?"

"That's between you and me."

⋅∘⋅⋄⟩⟩⟨⋅☼⋅⟩⟩⟨⟨⋅∘⋅

I WAS A little pissed that both Mary and Eva seemed to consider Sarah Lynn to be my boss and that we had to get permission from her for anything we'd do. I already had permission.

Aw, shit!

What am I talking about? I'd never have moved beyond having, loving, and dating Jasmine if she hadn't given me permission to do so. Hell! Encouraged me. Kelly accepted me with no boundaries and no restrictions. She claimed she was mine but didn't try to make me hers. Sarah Lynn had never given or asked for any kind of commitment. Ariel and Char were just there to be part of what we had. Char with her willing ass and Ariel with her active mouth.

And pussy.

I thought about waking early Monday morning after the marathon sex with my girlfriends to find Ariel slicking my pole with her juices and then sliding me inside her again. Just the thought was getting me hard. I breathed deeply and imagined her scent was still in my nostrils. I'd really begun to think after four months that Ariel was going to stay a virgin except with her mouth. While she was always active in pleasuring me and getting pleasure from me, I was sure she did the same with one or more of the girls every day. She liked her face glazed with pussy juice.

I had a ton of work to do in order to be prepared for painting Eva on Saturday, not to mention the fact that we were supposed to read the first book of Homer's Iliad for class on Thursday. At least Merck wasn't a sadist about what he expected us to read. Book one is about five hundred lines. It was going to be hard enough to understand the translation of a very stylized Greek of approximately the seventh century BC. He also provided a link to a recorded version in Greek with music that we could listen to so we'd get the feeling of what it might have been like to listen to old blind Homer reciting the epic.

But that wasn't what had me concerned. I'd talked about doing a test painting with Eva, but I don't like wasting art. Sure, there were exercises that we did in drawing class. There were painting exercises, as well. But what I was interested in was a creative exercise that would yield something… meaningful. I guessed that was the only way I could describe it.

'My philosophy of art is…' That's what we were given for an essay in Foundations of Contemporary Art the first day of class. It wasn't supposed to be a long essay, but one to five sentences—not to exceed a page—that described our personal connection to art. There were people in the class who weren't art majors and took the course as an arts elective. There were also people from nearly every discipline of the arts. I only had to write one sentence and it was one of the hardest assignments I've ever had.

My philosophy of art is an opening of the senses to a universe beyond the merely sensory. While appealing to the senses, it should stimulate the soul. The artist should engage the viewer in a personal relationship, even if the two never meet or are separated by centuries.

I scratched it out and rewrote it a dozen times. I still wasn't sure I agreed with myself. How the fuck am I supposed to build a personal relationship with a viewer in 3018? What do I have to open that person's senses who might be out exploring a physical universe that is beyond my imagination, let alone my experience?

Well, artists have engaged in that for thousands of years, just as storytellers have. Listening to Homer's Iliad on my computer, even though I didn't understand a word of the ancient Greek, filled my mind with images of gods and goddesses using human heroes to enact their contest for supremacy on Olympus. They dared not oppose the supreme Zeus directly, but they could cleverly set obstacles in the way of his goals, perhaps even thwart them through human treachery.

The image of Athena came to mind. Thousands of images of the warrior goddess had been created over the ages and even the most ancient inspire a sense of awe and wonder today. In classical art, the goddesses—even Aphrodite—seldom had more than a breast bared. The Renaissance changed that and most of the goddesses, even Athena, were shown nude.

I had in mind, a picture of Athena armed for battle with one breast bared—kind of a hybrid of the two styles. She would have her iconic shield, spear, and helmet. Only my model, my canvas, would be completely nude. I would paint the clothes and shield on her. Her right arm would be her spear. I set to work creating the canvas. At my interview, my professors told me I needed to slow down. This was a scene of such utter complexity that I doubted I would finish it. I could only ask so much of Eva. Trying to keep her for more than four hours would be inhuman— even with breaks every half hour.

•o•◦➧ ⫯ ⫯ ☽ ⫯ ⫯ ◄◦•o•

"It's getting late, Jett," Ariel whispered. "I don't mean to interfere in your creative process, but everyone has gone to bed."

I'd definitely been in a zone. I didn't remember eating dinner, though there was an empty plate and two empty Coke cans on my cabinet.

"Wow! I'd better get to bed, too," I sighed. "I'm exhausted." The two-by-three canvas board in front of me still didn't have any paint on it. It had one of the most elaborate sketches on it that I'd ever done before applying paint. I'd changed perspective twice, changed the background, changed the scale. Nothing that I started with in the initial drawing remained save the general pose of the goddess. I turned to look at Ariel. She was ready for bed, meaning she was stark naked.

"That is intense. Is that how you are going to paint Eva?"

"More or less. I'm incorporating this into the painting."

"You don't have underwear on." My normal painting mode was to wear white briefs and paint them for Kelly as I went. But I wasn't painting today and when I went to the studio to draw, I just stripped out of my clothes.

"My keen observation says that you, too, are without clothes."

"I'm naked. Nude. Bare. Undressed. And very horny." Ariel turned away from me and approached the posing stool that was about waist-high on her. She positioned her hands on either side, spread her feet, and bent over it. "I would be helpless if my boyfriend decided to plunge his thick cock into my tiny Asian pussy."

Now that she mentioned it, maybe she was. I knelt behind her and began stroking her butt and thighs with my hands. Then I leaned in and licked up her fat pussy. It sprang open like it was on a hair trigger. I dipped my tongue into the sweet nectar and found her clit.

"Oh, Jett. Please fuck me!" It was a great invitation, but in this position, not only was her pussy wide open, but her anus was fluttering. I decided to apply my tongue to that. "Oh! God! Oh God! Jett! Are you going to fuck my bottom?" There was genuine alarm in her voice but she made no effort to change her position or protect her tiny hole. I continued to bathe it with my tongue and she squirmed beneath me, rising to her first climax.

"I *am* going to fuck your bottom, my little Asian beauty," I said, leaning over her and reaching for her dangling breasts with my cock resting in her crack. "But not tonight. It was only two nights ago that I first entered your tight wet pussy. I want it again." I pulled back and my cock bounced down to her opening. I began to slowly push through her tightness. "I want your pussy tonight. I will want your pussy many times before I am finally ready for your ass. But one day…" I was fully seated in her core and pushed my thumb against her asshole. She screamed with her second orgasm. "One day, it will be my cock that presses its way into this tight sphincter. Until then you can look forward to it."

23
Cutting the Beef

BLANKENSHIP'S DRAWING class continued to be a pain in the ass. Thursday, he wanted detailed drawings of our fingernails. I guess I was learning things. I think my drawing was improving. You couldn't tell by his comments. "You're supposed to draw your thumb, not your big toe." Fuck.

We survived the class and Mary was waiting for me outside the door.

"Um… Sorry I ran off Tuesday before we could talk. It looked like Eva wanted your time." She slipped a slightly shaky hand into mine and I relaxed.

"We're getting together Saturday afternoon for our first painting session. We needed to work out the details."

"You're going to paint on her like you did on Jasmine?"

"Yeah. Merck stopped me after my Literature and the Arts class to congratulate me on that work and asked if I was going to do similar works for each of the periods. He liked it. So, I'm painting Eva up as Athena for the Homer segment."

"She's already a piece of work."

"I've never had a canvas talk back at me as much as she does," I laughed.

"Could I… stop by and join you?" Mary asked. "I'll stay out of the way, but you seem to be the only person in our class who has an unending supply of figure models and a private studio. Maybe I could draw one of your girlfriends if it's too crowded in your studio with Eva."

I found that we'd left the art building and were walking in the opposite direction of my bus stop. We were headed toward Mary's dorm and

I was just letting her lead me along. Her hand was calm in mine and I didn't want to remove it.

"Mary… You know that all five of the girls I live with are my lovers, right?"

"Yeah. That's pretty hard to miss."

"I guess… We aren't really a house of hedonism but sometimes it seems things get a little out of control. We don't have alcohol in the house, but we do get a little high sometimes and clothes don't seem to have a lot of meaning then. I mean, I'd love to have you come over. It's going to be a long, intense painting session. But I like you and I don't want you to feel obligated to play with people—even if I play with Eva a little."

"Do you think you'll 'play' with her instead of painting?"

"Not instead, but sometimes one thing leads to another. I just don't know where her head is."

"I bet you know where other parts of her are," Mary laughed. We were almost to Mary's dorm when she stopped and pulled me around to face her. "Jett, I function pretty well. I know you're aware of my anxiety and panic attacks and I really appreciate your calming influence in class. But I'm working at overcoming a lot of the problems I have and I can't do that sitting alone in my dorm room. The shaking in my hands isn't all from anxiety—in fact, it contributes to my anxiety. I've had mild essential tremors since I was a toddler. It made school a frustrating experience. Teachers were sure I was being abused at home and tried to get me taken away from my parents. It seemed that every year there was another ignorant do-gooder who was concerned for my well-being."

"Damn, Mary, I had no idea. That must have been hell."

"Yeah. But when the doctors could only prescribe sedatives and tranqs, my parents found a specialist in bio-feedback. It's not a hundred percent effective, but I'm able to control about eighty percent of the tremors by drawing and painting. The doctor found something I loved and linked it to my bio-feedback. When I don't have time or lose control, then I end up multiplying the effect with my anxiety. God's truth, Jett. You and Blankety are the only people I've known in four years who could get me down from that point without Prozac."

"Any time. I don't know what kind of relationship you want… or even what kind of relationship we have… but if you want to come and draw or paint with me, any time. Any time at all."

"Thanks, Jett. I don't know about the relationship thing either but I'm a big girl and might even get turned on if I see you 'playing' with Eva." We giggled a little at the image. I had a feeling that by the time I was done with her on Saturday, Eva wasn't going to be interested in any playing. We were all going to be too tired.

"I've got to head home now, Mary. Thanks for talking to me. You know, I really enjoyed our date Sunday and I'd like to do it again sometime."

"Believe me, I'd like you to do it again sometime, too. I… um… don't usually have anyone else's fingers up there. It was pretty damn nice." Mary reached over and pulled my head toward her for a sweet kiss. "See you Saturday, Jett."

∘₀∘ ∘⇨ ꀀꀀ ☽ ꀀꀀ ⇦∘ ∘₀∘

I WAS TEMPTED to cut my slaughtering class Friday morning, but we were going to be studying the grading of beef on the hoof and I felt like I'd never understand it if I didn't participate. I shifted gears as fast as I could Friday afternoon, though. I still had a ton of work to do on the canvas Eva would pose with. Detail work on the figure would have to wait until the painting of Eva was finished. I had another ten days before the Homer project was due. But enough of the image had to be complete that I could blend the edges with the living canvas.

Ariel and Kelly got home about two o'clock and both stopped to give me a very sweet kiss that ended up with them naked. Of course, that was kind of their normal attire within five minutes after getting home from classes. I just appreciated the fact that I got to help get them there. I didn't mind the little break. Ariel headed for the kitchen to start getting Friday night stir-fry ingredients prepared and Kelly headed upstairs. I went back to painting.

About an hour later, Kelly came back into the studio with her tripod and video camera.

"You know I won't be here until after dinner tomorrow when you're painting," she said. "I've got the camera set up with a terabyte external storage device. You just have to route it through your Mac. There should be plenty of room for the action but turn it off when you take breaks. It just wastes space to let it run. I'll worry about editing and splicing later."

"Kelly, you're a sweetheart. I feel bad about you spending so much time on my projects. I need to pay you for…"

"Shut your fucking mouth!" she snapped at me. "You don't pay me, Jett. Ever. I thought we settled this. I'm a whore for my art, but I will never be a whore to you. I am yours, body and soul. Don't ever offer to pay me!"

There was only one thing I could do. I kissed her. She was still a little angry and stiff when I pulled her into my arms, but she melted as soon as our lips touched. There was a quiet longing in that kiss. I wanted it to go on forever. Kelly needed my reassurance and I needed to accept the conditions.

"Red, you are not my whore and I will never think of you as a whore in any circumstance. Please forgive me for misunderstanding and be sure that I love you. I love you, Kelly."

She moaned into my mouth as she ground her crotch against me. I'd been wearing briefs to paint in as I usually did and my cock poked out the top as it hardened and was moistened by her pussy juices. "Come upstairs and sleep with me tonight?" she pled. "No cameras, no one else. Just you filling me over and over. I love you, Jett." I quickly agreed and with a date to consummate what we'd just started, we were able to back off a little while she set up the camera.

"You know I'm using these as projects in my video editing class. My prof is impressed with the footage I bring in. She's giving me tips on videography, too. And Jas and I have made five hundred dollars off her Nubian Goddess video. We aren't starving here."

"You are clever. I'm glad Jas is earning something but a little surprised that she was willing to sell something she could be recognized in."

"Between the paint and the makeup, there is no way anyone would recognize her. She absolutely glowed in that vid. When she started working her abs on you, it was like the entire scene you painted came to life."

"I don't think you can do that with Eva."

"No. She doesn't want her first time with you on video. I respect that."

"Wait! Her first time with me?"

"I'm not saying that you are going to fuck tomorrow night. Looking at your canvas, I'm guessing this is going to be a marathon session. We're prepping all the beds tomorrow morning so that if she or Mary or both want to stay over, there will be places for them no matter who they want or don't want to sleep with. Just because the five girls you live with are open and ready for you and each other any time of the day or night, it doesn't mean that we automatically assume every girl who visits is going to be part of our harem."

"I don't know what will happen with either Eva or Mary," I sighed as I watched Kelly set up the camera. "I wish I'd thought to catch some of the preliminary work of the painting on video like you did with the one of Char and Sarah Lynn."

"We did," Kelly laughed. "You were so into your zone that you didn't even notice me slipping in to video snippets while you were doing the original drawing. I was in last night while you were painting, too. Oh, and I'll show you some yummy footage of Ariel bent over that stool Tuesday night while you plowed her. I got such a good licking after I showed her the tape that I thought I'd pass out!"

"Oh, geez! With you flitting around like you do with a camera, nowhere in the house is safe," I laughed. "We could have our own reality TV show."

"It would only air on adult cable," Kelly said. "Just having you running around with your dong flopping would get us an NC-17 rating. Now go back to work and be ready to fuck me into the mattress tonight. I'm beginning to see your concept for this painting in my mind's eye. Can't wait!"

Kelly was gone and I returned to the painting of Athena.

•◦•◦⟩ ⟩⟩(☼)⟨⟨ ⟨◦•◦•

I DIDN'T REALLY get back to painting Friday night after stir-fry. It was family night and my family all wanted a little care and loving. Not that I screwed everyone, but each of my girlfriends got held and petted—not just by me, but by each other. It was like we needed that time of bonding to reassure each other that we really were part of one family.

Kelly and I finally made it up to the Kat House after leaving our four other lovers all piled together in the big bed. What a sweet sight.

We started just holding each other and I thought we might just go to sleep that way. So much for fucking anyone into the mattress. But Kelly was just taking it slow and easy. Our little orgy Sunday night was frantic. Not only did every one of my lovers want to feel me come in them, they wanted to lick each other out and fuck as well. With so many of us involved in this relationship, it seemed that our lovemaking was always a little rushed so we'd have time for someone else and so no one felt left out.

Kelly wanted to slow down. Even when she did her camming, there was often a rush at the end to get her to orgasm. I was more than willing to take it slow. I wanted to kiss every inch of her body—find every freckle and love it. We spent an inordinate amount of time lying head to toe and sucking each other's toes as we got and gave exquisite foot rubs. Kelly rolled on top of me while we were in that position and began inching her way up, allowing me to kiss her ankles, shins, knees, thighs. She covered my legs with kisses and little licks as she moved upward and before long, her puffy pussy was at my lips as she sucked in my cock.

Kelly is the sweetest girl I've ever tasted. Literally. We toss around words like nectar and honey for a girl's lubrication but Kelly's lives up to the description. Her pubic hair is shaved up to the top of her slit, so her juice just makes everything from that point down slippery as hell. Combined with my tongue adding moisture, there was a total flood the first time she came. I drank down as much as I could and Kelly whined around my cock.

Sarah Lynn had taught the girls about squeezing the base of my cock hard enough that it delayed my orgasm. It was a little painful, but I had to admit that it gave me more staying power and the longer I could stay, the better it was. Kelly pinched my cock and held it as she rolled off and lay with her legs spread and her knees bent.

"Make love to me, baby," she said. "I want to feel you in me. My pussy is crying tears for want of your cock. Push. Push it into me."

Her heat surrounded the tip of my cock and I pushed. Feeling each slippery inch sink into her hot depths brought a loud groan from my throat. I think that just the act of pushing my cock into Kelly's pussy is almost as good as the orgasm that ultimately follows. The moment of orgasm is a mind-blowing clutching of all the muscles in my body as everything is focused on pumping semen into the waiting vessel. But before that is the feeling of that vessel wrapping itself lovingly around my cock, welcoming it home, sliding against me and caressing my length. Kelly is hot and can tighten her muscles to hold me in a velvety embrace. Ariel is tight and almost unyielding, but Kelly is tight and welcoming. As soon as I was in her, I bent my head and licked her nipples, perfect little points atop modest mounds that didn't slip to the sides when she was on her back like the bigger busted girls did. They rose from her chest, begging to be sucked. I gave generously and Kelly responded.

The inevitable climax of a long climb caught us by surprise, convulsing both our bodies. Kelly's legs squeezed around my waist and I drove as deeply as I could into her and let my come control my nervous system. As soon as I had enough breath in my lungs, I kissed Kelly and found her mouth every bit as welcoming as her pussy. We kissed deeply and I felt another surprising spurt pulled from my cock as more than an aftershock. Kelly's body reacted to it as well and we lost ourselves in the kiss, in the moment, in the love.

I'd do anything for this girl. Anything she asked.

·∘· ⇴ ⟆ ☀ ⟇ ⇦ ·∘·

I wasn't so tired Saturday morning that Grandpa wouldn't let me cut meat. That had been embarrassing on Monday. Kelly and I made love more than once Friday night but we both had to work on Saturday, so we didn't stay up all night. And somehow, sleeping snuggled up to my little redhead seemed to make my sleep even more peaceful.

Even my job was part of my education. Grandpa quizzed me on grades of beef Saturday as we worked on various cuts.

"What's the difference between choice and prime?" he asked as he laid out two slabs of ribs that we were cutting into steaks. Of course, this wasn't what we learned in class yesterday. Grandpa wanted meat grading on the cuts. Yesterday the ten of us in the Slaughtering class had worked in the feedlot on sorting the slaughter cattle before they went into the chutes. The steers and heifers were thirty to forty-two months old and their hides were marked by grade and expected yield. Then they got sorted and sent through the chutes.

After they were dead, skinned, and hanging, the hanging carcass was graded prime, choice, or select. Cattle that fell in the lower grades—commercial, utility, cutter, and canner—were separated out to be slaughtered by the night shift when there was no USDA carcass inspector on duty. Grandpa wanted me to tell him about the quality of the two rib eyes on the butcher block.

"This one is prime," I said confidently. When you had two laid out in front of you like this, it was easy to tell the difference based on a quick observation. "This rib eye is about eighteen or nineteen inches long and has a nice layer of fat over it. The choice rib eye is only about sixteen inches long and has a thinner layer of fat."

"And?"

"Prime beef is produced from young, well-fed beef cattle. It has slightly abundant marbling (the amount of fat interspersed with lean meat) and is generally sold in upscale restaurants or out of our butcher case," I quoted from my reading. "Choice beef is high quality but has less marbling than prime. It has at least a small amount of marbling. It's the type we'll cut to package and put in the coolers over there and in the freezer case. Both grades are good for braising, roasting, and grilling. We only sell select in the freezer case and in the lower cuts for stew meat, pot roasts, and crockpots."

"Good. Now let's talk about the difference in how we cut these for sale."

It was a good morning and I cut a lot of steaks. Grandpa marked the choice meat for me and I sliced the steaks at the thickness he marked. They were generally thinner than the prime steaks he cut. Still, by noon, my mind was on painting. I'd switched from cutting steaks and roasts to cutting up chickens. I was getting pretty good at deboning chicken breasts but I was thinking seriously about getting a new set of knives. A simple set of the four basic knives—boning, breaking, butcher, and cimeter—could easily cost me well over a hundred fifty dollars. Maybe I'd put it on my Christmas list.

I GOT HOME at two-thirty, almost frantic to get started on this new painting. I found that Mary was already there, sitting on the sofa drinking tea with Ariel. They stood up and all thought of painting fled from my mind.

Ariel was Ariel, of course. She was wearing a thong and a crop-top and bounced over to kiss me as soon as I walked in the door.

"I need a shower, sweetheart. I smell like a butcher shop."

"Yeah, but say hello to Mary first." I lifted my eyes.

She hadn't waited to take off her sweater—at least I assumed she started with a sweater. It was pretty chilly outside. The bodystocking she wore didn't have long sleeves. Instead, it had a couple thin straps that went from the boob panels up behind her neck. The front was fully opaque, but this time I let myself check for the piercings Sarah Lynn said she had. Sure enough, there was a little bump on either side of each of her thick, hard nipples. While the stocking covered the front of her, the side was laced all the way from her ankle to her armpit. The lacing exposed about six inches of bare skin all the way up her shapely side. In back, the stocking was opaque again. She wore a flouncy skirt with the outfit that hung to about mid-thigh. I was cued in on the idea that this was a crotchless stocking.

"Mary," I squeaked. "It's good to see you. I didn't really expect you to be here so early." She smiled and approached for a little kiss. I put my hands lightly on her waist over the laces.

"Hi, Jett."

"It's really good to really see you, really," I whispered.

"I thought I'd get here early and help get things set up. Hope you don't mind that I already took my things into your studio."

"I don't mind." I was a little glazed. The feel of Mary's skin beneath my fingers was electrifying. She stepped up closer and pressed her boobs into my chest as she gave me another kiss.

"You better get that shower. Your substrate will be here soon." *My substrate? Oh, yeah. I'm painting on Eva this afternoon. I almost forgot.*

"Sarah Lynn said to go upstairs and use the big bath. She's got your painting clothes laid out," Ariel said. *My painting clothes? I only wear… I* just went upstairs.

I could hear the water running in the shower when I got up there and Sarah Lynn called for me to come on and get in. I wasn't expecting her to be in the shower with me. That must have been why she wanted me upstairs. The shower downstairs is a little crowded for two people. She kissed me warmly when I stepped in, her wet boobs pressed up against my skin. I automatically caressed them and flicked her nipples with my thumbs. She caught her breath and kissed me more deeply, reaching down to stroke my erection. I'd hardened almost as soon as I saw Mary.

"I thought it might be a good idea to get you off before you start working with naked girls," Sarah Lynn said as she stroked.

"What a great idea."

"I didn't think of it until I saw Mary. Holy fuck, Jett." She turned her back to me and rubbed my cock up and down her butt crack. "I'm as ready as you are. Put it in me, lover." I bent my knees and Sarah Lynn guided my cock up into her steamy core. Yeah. She was as ready as I was.

When we were out of the shower and dry, she showed me a new pair of white boxer briefs. "Kelly thought you might need more support and more painting surface before you were done tonight. You know what she thinks of your briefs."

Yeah. She'd expect me to have this pair covered in paint before the day was over. That's Kelly.

Time to get this show on the road.

24
Athena Was a Virgin

AT EXACTLY three-thirty, the doorbell rang. Jasmine drew the honor of answering it. She was the only one in the house still fully dressed. As soon as Eva saw the rest of us, she took a deep breath and dropped her coat. It was all she was wearing.

"Okay then. Okay. I'm okay. Where do you want me to pose?" Eva wasn't quite hyperventilating but her being naked let us see the thin stream of sweat that dripped from her pits. Ariel ran to the bathroom for a washcloth and towel as I took Eva's hand and led her into the studio. She let out a moan when she saw Mary standing in a corner waiting for us to get settled.

You know, if Mary decided to open her legs, my entire family would be lined up as if it was a buffet. I think Eva would have been on her knees, as well.

"I've got things set up so I think you'll be able to relax and be supported while we work. It's a standing pose, but I've tested it a few times to make sure it's comfortable. Once we get started, we'll take a break every half hour so you can move around. Do you need to use the bathroom?" I asked.

"Not yet," Eva said as she let Ariel wipe her down with the washcloth and dry her. 'Just to make sure the paint will stick.' I noticed that by the time Ariel was finished, Eva's nipples were popped out erect. Well, that would just add an interesting dimension to the painting.

"I've got a nice pillow on the stool so you can just rest your butt on the edge. Did I get the right height?"

"Yeah. I guess so. It's pretty comfortable."

"Now the tough part will be having your right arm stretched out. I've got this little padded tripod that you can rest your hand on so you don't get tired. Your left arm will be held against your tummy. Yeah, right there. Curl your fingers into a fist. You don't need to clench them. Be as relaxed as possible. How's it feel?"

"Aside from the fact that I'm letting a boy put his hands all over my naked body while I try to stay still…"

"Isn't that the best feeling ever?" Sarah Lynn asked. She was wearing a pair of panties but that was all. I wasn't even sure it was a whole pair. You couldn't see the string in back that went up between her cheeks. I knew, though, that she'd put on panties so my come wouldn't drip out of her and down her legs. Just touching Eva to position her could have had me hard as a rock if Sarah Lynn hadn't drained me in the shower.

"It's not… um… bad exactly. I just feel so… submissive," Eva whispered.

And then the penny dropped, as Granddad would say. I'd gotten kind of pissed on Tuesday and laid down the law to Eva about me being the one who would decide things and that she was to be at the house at exactly three-thirty. You could have set a watch by the moment she rang the doorbell. And then walking inside she'd simply dropped her coat. She hadn't been wearing anything else. Within thirty seconds of ringing the bell at exactly three-thirty, she was naked and ready to obey my posing instructions exactly.

"I want you to point with your three middle fingers."

"Okay."

"Shouldn't that be 'Yes, sir'?" I whispered in her ear. She shuddered.

"Yes, sir," she whispered back. I placed a hand on her back to unnecessarily correct her posture and let it slide down to her butt. Then I got the painting I'd worked on all week and cross-checked it for her pose. Just about perfect. I moved the vertical easel behind Eva and pushed the painting up against her back. She caught her breath as the cool surface came in contact with her skin. I moved around in front to check the position and ran my hands freely over her body as I made sure the curve of her breast would be against the canvas. I had to raise the tripod her hand rested on to get exactly the exposure I wanted. All the time, Eva followed me with her eyes.

"I'm not going to work on your head right away," I said. "As long as it doesn't shift any of your torso or arm positions, you can turn your head."

"Thank you, sir."

"Now…" I began. I blew softly across her nipples and they hardened appreciatively. "While I'm doing the initial sketch, I want you to memorize this position. Think about where your wrist is on the tripod. Remember this feeling along your back where the edge of the canvas is." I traced the line where the canvas met her bare back and then continued across her butt. "Remember where your butt is resting here against the stool. Can you do that?"

"I'll try, sir," she squeaked.

"I need to take the reference photos now and then start drawing on this beautiful canvas you've provided me today."

I turned to get my camera and to turn the video on. Mary was still in the corner and I swear she was smirking at me. While I started taking as many reference pictures as I could from as many angles as I could, Mary collected her drawing pad and started to sketch. I made sure Eva was aware that I was taking a few closeups for my personal use.

Then I no longer had time to indulge either of our fantasies. I grabbed my Sharpie and began to draw on her skin. Athena began to take shape, standing proudly with her right arm outstretched, her spear thrust out along Eva's arm, ending in the point at her fingers. The figure in my background painting was maybe eighteen inches tall. The figure I drew on Eva was about halfway between that and life-size. Even while I was concentrating on drawing the figure I was about to paint, I wasn't at all shy about holding her breast steady with my fingers. Athena's skirt I drew right across Eva's pussy and watched as she moistened against the tip of my pen. The Goddess's feet were on Eva's thighs.

I stood back and looked at the drawing on Eva's skin, snapping more pictures from every possible angle. Then I reached over and turned off the video camera.

"Ten-minute break," I said. I stood right in front of Eva and traced her jaw with the tip of my finger. "You should use the bathroom this time and make sure you are fresh for the next session. You did a good job, my little substrate." I emphasized the sub and Eva shuddered.

"Thank you, sir. Ten minutes." She was off with Ariel as her personal assistant.

"How many orgasms do you think she'll suppress over the next four hours?" Sarah Lynn whispered as she pressed her bare breasts against my chest and lifted her lips to kiss.

"More importantly, how many do you think she won't suppress?" Mary asked. Sarah Lynn made room and Mary pressed herself against me and kissed me. It was the first time we'd had such a blatant expression in front of my girlfriends and I was worried until Mary turned her lips to Sarah Lynn and kissed her as well. "After watching that, I'm tempted to pose for you, too," she giggled. "Except I could never hold still that long. You'll have to find other ways to paint me."

⋆ ⟫ ☽ ☀ ☾ ⟪ ⋆

I'D BE USING multiple techniques with this painting and, while it was fun playing touchy-feelie with Eva, I had serious painting to do. I wanted to use this as my next Literature and the Arts project, so there was no room for me to make a mistake. Eva might have been a little disappointed that I wasn't taking quite as much time to get her posed as I had initially, but the next phase taxed us both. I used airbrushes to lay in the background. The scene I'd painted on the canvas showed a classic pose of Athena with a shield, her spear outstretched, glowing against a starry firmament. It was that glow and starry firmament that integrated Eva's body into the background painting. It had to be done in one sitting because I'd never manage to get her body into exactly the same position again, no matter how long I played with it.

I held her there for about ten extra minutes as I lifted soft flesh slightly to be sure I'd filled in the exact shape of her breast and arm and shoulder. I compensated her with a slightly longer break. I wanted to be sure the water-based body paint had integrated into the painting and was dry before I shoved it up against her again. Fortunately, it was fast-drying, both on the canvas and on her body. She and Ariel took longer in the bathroom this time and I wondered if my little pussy hound was snacking on the model.

"God! I see what you are doing now, Jett. I like it. It's subtle, but the outline of her body is just enough different from the shades and textures of the original painting that you can see her body against the stars. Beautiful!" Mary said. Jas beat her to my lips, but soon yielded and Mary gave each of us a very happy kiss while I stroked up and down her back. Her shoulders were bare and she leaned against me.

"You are worming your way into our hearts, Mary," Jas whispered as she kissed the blonde's ear.

"I don't want to be sneaky about it," Mary said as she pecked Jasmine's lips. "I was hoping that I was being obvious."

"We're enjoying the process," I said. My hand slid down her back and I squeezed her butt.

"Later," Mary whispered. "Where's Char? I haven't seen her all day."

"She came in with me from work and went straight to the kitchen. Saturday is her day for dinner," Jas said. "She's making naan, curry, dal, and half a dozen little dishes to go with it."

"Yum. I think I'll sit in the kitchen for this session," Mary said. "Maybe she won't mind if I sketch her there."

"She'll love it," Jas agreed. Eva and Ariel returned from break and I got down to serious work again.

•०·◈))C ☽ C((◈·०•

THIS TIME I laid in the large color backgrounds of the figure of Athena with the airbrush and then switched to brush work for the details. I was still learning fine control of the airbrush and was far more comfortable using a selection of sable brushes. Of course, this was a different experience for Eva, as well. The wet paint from the airbrush chilled her skin a little, but the sensation was really like having a cool breeze blow across your skin. My sable brushes tickled. Especially around her sensitive nipples, stomach, and pubic mound. I had to touch up her nipples a couple of times because it seemed they kept stretching out harder and more erect. Even plumper.

Most of the imagery was on Eva's right breast. That's where Athena's face and helmet were emerging. That also left her left breast bare, unpainted, and tempting. I finished Athena's face just before our next break and simply leaned over and sucked her left nipple into my mouth. Her gasp was heard in the living room where most of my girlfriends had moved. I laid my brushes on the table and ran my fingers up the inside of Eva's thigh, not quite approaching her suddenly wet lips.

"You're being mean to our guest," Sarah Lynn said. "Come to me, Eva. It's time for your break and I'll help get you cleaned up so you don't spoil the paint." Sarah Lynn took Eva's hand and pulled her toward the upstairs bathroom where I was sure Eva's needs would be well-cared-for.

Ariel, who had somehow lost her crop-top and panties during the afternoon, came up to me and rubbed herself all over my chest before jumping up a little and wrapping her arms around my neck and her legs around my waist. She only jumped high enough to reach my lips and that left her always-ready pussy rubbing against my cock through the one-time white boxer briefs I was wearing. There was almost as much dried paint on the underwear as there was on Eva's skin.

"If Eva won't fuck you tonight, I will," Ariel whispered through our deep kiss. "Less than a week not a virgin and my pussy is constantly weeping for you."

"Can I get another kiss, too?" Mary asked as she pressed close to Ariel and stroked up and down my little Asian girlfriend's back to where my hands were holding her butt.

"Yes!" squealed Ariel as she turned her head to accept Mary's offered kiss. Ariel managed to move just enough while not letting go of me that Mary could reach my lips while still pressed against Ariel and running her fingers over her bare skin. Finally, Ariel dropped down to the floor and took Mary's hand. "Would you like to draw a picture of me now? We can go upstairs to one of the bedrooms and I'll get in any position you want me."

"Yum! Sarah Lynn told me you were a tasty morsel. Let me get a fresh pad of paper and pencils," Mary said.

I was left speechless as the two girls left and I wondered if Mary would draw her or fuck her. Or both.

•·•❖ ❭❘❲ ☼ ❲❘❬ ❖•·•

I HEARD KELLY come in from her long day at work and she stepped right into the studio to see what the progress was. I progressed directly to kissing her. While I was at it, I undressed her.

"Mmm! Touch me, Jett. It's been such a long day." I was only too glad to comply with Kelly's requests. We were almost finished with the painting and I figured this would be the last session coming up. Then we'd have Char's delicious dinner.

"Look at this beautiful naked teenager," Mary said as she moved to join us. "Are you about to paint the finale?" she asked.

"Yeah. When Jas and Eva get back. Have you drawn enough of my girlfriends today? Ready to watch the last act?"

"I think I'll have to do Kelly later," Mary said as Kelly turned her face so they could kiss. As soon as that reached a break, Mary had her lips on mine again.

"Oh, honey, you can do me any time," Kelly said. "Just say the word. I'm going to run up and take a shower now, though. Wearing so many clothes all day makes me sweat." Kelly planted another kiss on each of us and then took off.

"You've been really… um… open today," I said as Mary closed on me for another kiss. She dragged my hand up to her breast and I felt the little bar through her nipple for the first time.

"It's been a… personal challenge for me," Mary said. "Not that I haven't been enjoying myself. I have. A lot. I'm always just on the brink of running out of the house screaming. But they've all been so sweet. They never gang up on me. They don't try to push me. Even Ariel, who was practically salivating, didn't make a move on me. She posed just as I wanted her and we talked while I drew. You've got five girlfriends and a model here and I think I've done thirty drawings of naked girls. I'm thinking I might manage to get you to pose and then I'd have a full set."

"Don't feel like you have to force yourself into a zone where you're not comfortable," I whispered. I still didn't let go of her hardware, though, as I gently tugged on it through her bodystocking. "We'll let you set the pace and the direction."

"I kind of like the direction you're tugging but your substrate is back. You should feel her up a little."

I positioned Eva carefully.

"You've been doing well today, my substrate," I whispered in her ear. She shuddered. "You've worked very hard for me."

"Thank you, sir," she gasped as I pulled her hair back into a ponytail and tied it. I arranged the wisps and held my hand in front of her eyes as I sprayed the hair into place.

"This is our last session. You are so beautiful."

"No one has let me look into a mirror on my breaks."

"It will be better to see it finished. You'll get to see the video of the stages once Kelly edits it. Now, I need you to stand for this session instead of being on the stool. You can stand for half an hour, can't you?"

"I think so. Can I still have my arm supported?"

"Yes. We're just going to have to adjust some of the heights so we can do the final pictures. When we're photographing, we'll take away the arm prop." I moved the painting up behind her again and worked on positioning it at the correct height to match her new position. It wasn't a big adjustment, but I used the opportunity to pet Eva farther down her butt and the back of her thighs. The fronts were now fully painted and I didn't want to risk smearing anything, but Eva relaxed her stance a little so I could slip between her thighs from the back and stroke once across her very wet slit. "I'll make sure you are properly rewarded when we're finished," I whispered in her ear. "Now close your eyes. I don't want to get paint in them."

And the final marathon session began. I painted Eva's face and hair so she was wearing a helmet. I reached for the makeup kit we'd put together after the session with Jas and began applying a stylization around her eyes and shaping her cheeks to match the painted visage of Athena on her torso. She was beautiful.

"Open your eyes," I said.

"Yes, sir."

As soon as I removed the tripod from beneath her arm, we started snapping photos. I'd made up a spear out of a closet pole and a cardboard point and placed that in her right hand so she grasped it just above the painted point of the spear on her arm. Kelly grabbed the video camera off her tripod and started the same intense survey of the finished artwork. The starfield fell away from the feet of the painted Athena and dissolved into Eva's lower thighs.

"Now step away from the canvas and walk directly toward me," I said. As she complied, Kelly and I continued to take pictures and video. At last,

I had Eva turn around and look at the canvas. Athena looked up into the heavens from the faint outline of her own form in the constellations. "We can go look in a mirror now if you'd like."

•∘•⟡ ☽ ☀ ☾ ⟡•∘•

Jas had loved her body paint. Ariel loved her body paint. Char and Sarah Lynn loved their body paint. Eva just stood in front of the full-length mirror in the hallway.

And stared.

She didn't move.

Char called us to dinner.

Eva didn't move.

"Eva, come and replenish your reserves," I whispered. There was something about her stance that cautioned me about touching her again, even to guide her to the table.

"Will this last overnight?" she asked.

"Unless you sweat. Or until you shower. The felt-tip that I used on you needs to be gently removed with alcohol. I have everything here that you need to remove it and I'll help if you'd like," I said.

"No," Eva answered. "I should go home now. If I stay… If I shower with you… We'll fuck. I am a goddess. I am Athena. Athena was a virgin."

Eva walked to the front hall, put on her coat, and left.

25
A Thief in the Night

"JETT? COULD YOU run me back to the dorm? It's getting late and I should have left when Eva did," Mary said.

"You can stay if you want to, Mary."

"Yeah. I know. Thank you. I'm… not really ready for that."

"You know, we'll never push you to do something you don't want to do. Let me put my jeans on and grab my keys."

"It's not about not wanting. In fact, it *is* about wanting. This has been a bit of a stressful day. You know?"

"If you want to talk about it, we can talk in the car."

Mary said goodbye to everyone and slipped her sweater back on before her jacket. She didn't get up close to any of the girls, though, and we went out the back to my car.

"Sorry I didn't want to play," she said as we pulled out and headed to campus. "I was fine as long as I was drawing or was with just one of your girlfriends. When everyone got together for dinner, I started getting anxious. It was just too much to have everyone so… close."

"I'll tell you that all five girls really like you," I said. "And so do I. But we don't want to put you in a stressful position."

"I know that and it's what makes me want to come back again." We rode in silence almost to her dorm with her head leaning back against the seat before she spoke again. "I'd like to make love with you, Jett. I experimented with a girlfriend in high school and I know I'm at least a little bi, so I'd like to mess around with your girlfriends, too. Especially Ariel. I could smell her arousal when we went off and I sketched her. I'm sure she could smell me, too. I just am not at a point where I could feel comfortable with all of them and I want to. I really want to."

We pulled up in front of the dorm and just sat there for a minute.

"I can't invite you up to my room because I know my roommate is in tonight and she's even more backward with boys than I am," Mary sighed. "Would you… Can I… Maybe we could have a goodnight kiss?"

"I'd love to kiss you, Mary. I think you've got very sweet lips."

I leaned over the seat and kissed her with my lips. I wasn't trying to push her into anything but after a few seconds, she opened her lips to me and the kiss deepened. When she put her arms around me, I took that as a sign that I could wrap her in a light embrace. She pulled away slightly and I thought I'd gone too far. She caught my hand before I pulled it away.

"You know what it means when I wear a skirt or shorts over my bodystocking?" she whispered.

"Are you telling me it's crotchless?"

"You could explore a little and find out," she whispered. She put my hand on her leg and I let it drift up under her skirt. Not only was the bodystocking crotchless, she wasn't wearing anything else over it. "I had a thong on most of the day," she whispered. "I took it off just before we left."

I found her pussy and began gently rubbing it. She was leaking and after a few strokes, my fingers slid between her wet folds.

"Yeah!" she sighed. She reached over to rub my cock through my jeans. "I saw how hard you got when you were playing with Eva. You didn't get soft while you were painting. I thought it was just because you were handling her boobs and her… crotch. But when you painted the helmet on her face and hair, you were harder than when you were sucking her nipple. Can I unfasten these?" She was already tugging at my snap and I helped, letting her open them fully and extract my cock from my painted briefs.

I sighed.

Having her stroking me while I dipped my fingers in her pussy was heaven.

"This won't take long if you keep doing that."

"If you put your fingers in me while you are playing with my clit, it won't take me long, either."

We went back to kissing and even when she stiffened, she didn't let up on my cock and I soon shot over her hand. We panted and moaned into each other's mouths and the sensation was just more intense.

"I'll try not to make you wait too long to put that in me," she whispered. "I'll see you Tuesday." She got out of the car, licking her hand, and ran to the dorm.

⁕ ⁕ ⁕

EVERYONE HAD GONE to bed when I got home. Kelly, Jas, Charmaine, and I all had to work Sunday morning. I went up to my room to get undressed before I went to the bathroom and found Sarah Lynn waiting for me. Before I could get undressed, she grabbed my hand and pulled it to her face.

"Ah, yes," she sighed. She cleaned my fingers with her tongue. "Give me some of what she got?" She helped me strip and found my wet, sticky cock. She immediately dropped to her knees to lick me and then stood up. "It isn't her juice on you."

"She kind of jacked me off while I did her," I said.

"Well, I'm not fond of the taste, but you can put it in me. Please, put it in me." I did and Sarah Lynn welcomed me home. "You know we won't push her, right, Jett? But I'd really like to lick her. I'd like her to make love to me. Ariel and Char couldn't wait. They were already fingering each other before your car had pulled away. Jas took Kelly to the other room and everyone could hear them when they came. It didn't take long. We're all hot for her and want to undress her and eat her."

"It might take a bit, Sarah Lynn. She gets overwhelmed when we're all around her."

"I'll wait. There isn't one of us who doesn't think she's worth waiting for."

As hot as we both were over Mary, it didn't take long to forget her as we made love and I came deep inside Sarah Lynn.

⁕ ⁕ ⁕

THE NEXT WEEK was pretty calm as we moved into October and cooler weather. I think Eva must have wrapped herself in tissue paper at night because she still had paint on her when I saw her Tuesday after class.

226

"Next time we use the permanent paints," she said. "I wanted to live in this skin as long as possible."

"It's looking a little tattered. This paint should really be washed off."

"I know." She opened her jacket to show that she had no shirt beneath it. "I've been showing it to everyone who would look but my nipples have worn through. You could come wash me now. I'm not as afraid of losing the Virgin Goddess anymore."

"Bad timing. I have papers for both 2D Design and Foundations this week. For some reason I didn't get any work on them done this weekend at all. I spent most of Sunday and Monday after work fine-tuning the canvas and putting the digital files together for Merck. Kelly's trying to teach me the video editing software."

"I know what you mean. I didn't get anything done all weekend either. I spent Sunday with my girlfriend. We found interesting places to pose and she took pictures of me."

"Nudes?"

"No. I was painted."

"Where?"

"Um… A few places around campus. The Lake. The steps of the Capitol."

"I hope you'll share them," I laughed. "And I do wish I could wash you. Please don't start thinking that I suddenly don't want to soap up your body with my hands and make sure every little nook and cranny is cleaned."

"Okay, bastard. I'm going to go take a shower and masturbate. Maybe I'll see you this weekend."

•○•◦❧ ⊃⊂ ☼ ⊃⊂ ❧◦•○•

MARY AND I were getting along… comfortably. There was never a mention of our play beneath her skirt, her adventures with my girlfriends, or where our relationship might go. We just let it float along. It seemed that neither of us had any difficulty casually touching each other, most commonly hand to hand. If I saw her beginning to tremble, I offered my hand. Sometimes she took it and sometimes she didn't. I didn't try to grab her.

After Thursday's class, we stopped to chat for a few minutes and her hand slipped easily into mine.

"Is it too much like being steady dates to ask you to a movie again this Sunday?" she asked.

"I've got a great idea! Can we see something that makes me think something ridiculous and then ask you if that's why you wanted me to see it?" I said with fake enthusiasm.

"It wasn't that ridiculous," Mary sighed. "I completely understand how you'd think that. I wonder… If I had proven to be…"

"Instead of fingering you to an orgasm, I'd have jacked you," I said firmly. "Really, Mary. By the time we got to that point, I was already your friend and already committed to… I don't want to say help or something but I was committed to you as your friend. Even if I'd discovered I wasn't that enthused about it, I'd still have done it."

"Did you tell your girlfriends that?"

I nodded.

"I'll bet you got fucked half to death."

"Three-quarters."

"Sometime, I'll collect the other quarter."

"You don't have to, Mary. I mean… I'm looking forward to being intimate with you, but it isn't a requirement in order for you to be my friend."

"Jett, I know that. It's all new stuff, you know? We're in college. We became friends. You reached out to me and I appreciate that, but I'm not thankful enough to fuck you. If I fuck you, it will be because we're both having fun and want to do it. Okay?"

"More than okay. What's playing Sunday?"

"Araby."

"Middle Eastern?"

"Brazilian."

"I'll pick you up at two-thirty."

Friday, I moved from the feedlot to the carcass hangers. We had to compare feedlot grading to carcass grading. Grading on the feedlot focuses on the value on the hoof. It's like trying to guess your Christmas present from the shape of the package. Only you get the shape, the weight, and even the texture when you push on the side of the steer. Grading the carcass focuses on actually seeing the thickness of the layer of fat, the marbling of the meat, and even the size of the rib muscle. Grading for the whole carcass is done based on the rib muscle.

What surprised us all was how accurate the feedlot grading was. These guys had the whole thing down to a well-practiced science in which they could objectively look at a steer on the hoof and project what the carcass would look like.

A lot of people assume—as I did—that there is someone from the USDA stationed at every slaughterhouse in the country who grades all the beef. The reality is that in order to be considered a USDA certified slaughterhouse, you have to get somebody trained on your staff and certified by the USDA to certify the meat. Yes, government inspectors spot-check the houses to make sure everything is being done according to spec, but the meat inspector is just another employee of the slaughter-house who has had special training. We were shown a machine they were testing that electronically grades the meat. It's a hefty investment, but as long as the machine is certified, your meat gets certified.

·∘·⇨ ⅀Ⅽ ☼ ⅀Ⅽ ⇦·∘·

ALL I WANTED when I got home was a shower and a nap. I'd be happy to move to the studio and paint after that. I'd try to be human enough that my girlfriends would want to spend time with me before we all fell asleep.

What I found was a wreck of a girlfriend sobbing on the sofa in the living room.

"You've got to talk to Char," Ariel said when I came in through the kitchen door from the garage. "I can't get her to tell me what's wrong but she looks and sounds miserable. Please, Jett. Please help her." Tears were running down Ariel's cheeks and I wondered if any of the others were here crying as well.

I sat on the edge of the sofa next to Char and tentatively touched her shoulder. She looked up at me and burst into even more tears. She did move, though, and threw her arms around me as she sobbed against my chest.

"Hey, sweetie. It will be okay. Tell me all about it," I said.

"I'll have to leave," she sobbed. "All I can do is go back to my bastard father. What else can I do?"

"Whoa! Why would you ever have to leave or go back to that man? We're here for you, Char. Tell me what's happening?"

"I… I was going to transfer the funds for my rent this month. My… my bank account… it's empty! I don't have any money."

"Oh, fuck! How did that happen? You've been depositing your pay each week, haven't you?" I asked. Char didn't make a huge amount, but I knew she and Jas made a weekly trip to the bank to deposit their paychecks and tips. I was pretty sure Char was barely making it on what she was earning.

"Of course I have!" she snapped at me. "I needed every penny to transfer to the co-op for my rent. It's gone! Everything is gone!"

That started another barrage of tears. I felt, more than heard, our other roommates come home. Dinner was beginning to smell great as Ariel cooked. Someone brought us a cup of tea. It seemed like it took forever to tease the story out of Char and she didn't want anyone else around her when she told me. Fortunately, I eat stir-fry one-handed with chopsticks. Char didn't let go of my left hand and scarcely pushed her food around on her plate with a fork. Finally, I took her to bed and closed the door behind us.

⋅∘⋅∙⇨ ⫯⫯⫯ ☼ ⫯⫯⫯ ⇦∙⋅∘⋅

"I DON'T WANT them to hate me," Char said. "I set all this up and was supposed to be the most financially responsible one among us. I'm supposed to be an accountant. How could I let this happen?"

"Char, I still don't understand what happened. Please tell me so I can help you."

"My mother… I wrote to her and told her I'd broken away and was living with my friends. She wrote back and sent me a check for five thousand dollars. Jett, five thousand! That would let me pay my rent and food here for six months while I built up more money from my earnings. I was so happy! Then I went online to my bank account this morning to transfer my monthly rent and there was nothing there."

"The bank must have some information. Money doesn't just disappear."

"My father," Char said weakly.

"How could your father get access to your account? He's not a signer is he?" I asked. She shook her head.

"I… When I turned sixteen I got my own bank account so my father wouldn't have to keep handing me money. He deposited fifty dollars a month in it and that's all the money I was allowed to have. Over the next two years it increased to a hundred dollars a month. The money was just transferred from his account to mine each month. Of course, when I left on graduation day, he stopped payments to me. I never realized that his transferring money meant that he had my password and I never changed it. As soon as he found out my mother had made a big deposit for me, he stripped out the account," Char said. "Now I can't pay and I'll have to leave. It's what he planned all along."

I was seething. Mr. Gupta had been pressuring Char to come back home so he could arrange her marriage. He called her at least once a week and harangued her about staying a virgin so he could get a decent price. She'd only told him that she was living with her girlfriends and never mentioned that I lived here, too. It would be just like him to make her penniless so she'd have to accept his offer.

And I was mad at Char, too. How the fuck do you have an online bank account and not change your password for two and a half years? Or forget that your father has the password? One thing was for damned sure, I was going to cross-check my bank accounts and encourage all the rest of us to do the same. I didn't think my parents would ever be as mean as Charmaine's father, but what would happen if they decided they wanted me to do something and wouldn't take no for an answer? What kind of hold did they have on me that they could twist until I obeyed?

But none of my anger was going to help the destroyed girl still whimpering in my arms.

"Honey, we're going to get through this. First of all, he stole money from you. You need to press charges against him. I'm sure there is some kind of fraud line you can call and the bank will back you up. I'll ask Granddad about getting a lawyer if you need one."

"But I need to pay…"

"Hush. You haven't told anyone else what happened, have you?" She shook her head. "God knows it took me long enough to get it out of you. So as far as anyone else is concerned, you were upset because your father has been harassing you again. I'll transfer the money for your payment."

"You can't do that, Jett! I can't let you pay my way."

"You'll pay me back when we get the money back from your father. I still have three more months rent-free because of the initial deposits, so I've been building up enough to pay my dues each month without actually paying out anything. At least until the end of the year, we're covered. You should tell your mother what happened, too, in case your father pulls something like telling the bank the money was intended for him to keep safe."

"That's just like something he'd do. I'm so embarrassed to tell my mother this."

"I know, but we'll work it out. How have you been doing with your job? Are you making enough to put aside rent?" I asked.

"I… was. This summer, I earned enough to make my way and save a little. Since school started and hours have been cut back, I wouldn't have made it without the money my mother sent."

"Maybe you should look for a different job," I suggested. "I know the waitressing gig sounded good when you started, but you've got some other skills you could use. For example, I'm going to suggest that our co-op pay you fifty dollars a month for keeping our books, paying the bills, and making sure everyone pays their rent. I'll bet that with your current classes and experience, you could find a part time bookkeeping job."

"I could do that," she said. A hard fierceness crossed her face.

"The very first thing, though, is to change your passwords."

We finally settled down and cuddled up for sleep. This wasn't exactly how I planned to spend my Friday. I hadn't gotten a nap, a shower, or any painting done. But I had this precious woman in my arms and I felt insanely protective of her.

"Jett," she whispered into the darkness. "You can make love to me. I mean really. I'm willing to give myself to you. Not just my ass."

"No," I said. Maybe that was a little too abrupt for her as she pulled away and rolled to face me. "Char, I won't make love to you when you are doing it out of a sense of obligation to me. What we've arranged comes with no strings attached. I won't be the kind of bastard your father is."

She looked hard at me and I thought she was going to argue but she nodded her head and pulled herself tight to me without saying anything. That's how we fell asleep.

26
What I'd Do for Love

MY MOVIE date with Mary to see *Araby* was fun. A factory worker is in a bad accident and a teenager is sent to his home to collect some possessions. He finds a diary of his travels. The rest of the movie is the kid vicariously living the journey of the laborer's life over the past ten years.

"It's all so futile," Mary sighed as we got in the car to go back to the dorm. "We snatch little moments of happiness out of a life of hopelessness and convince ourselves it is all worth living. It was beautiful and all too painful at the same time."

"My high school classmate killed himself," I said. "It was just at the time Jas and I were discovering sex. He was Sarah Lynn's best friend and she tore apart the police department in her commencement speech. After that, a bunch of us gathered at my Granddad's place and eventually, the six of us bonded and made our little family. Out of the ashes."

"You'd have gotten together anyway. Maybe not all of you. You might have needed a catalyst of some kind to get all of you into one unit, but…"

Mary looked into my eyes and held me there. She leaned forward and kissed me. It was soft and almost as sad as the movie we'd just watched. I gently put my hand on her shoulder and she stroked my cheek.

"Jett, I don't know that we have the kind of catalyst that will stick us together," she sighed. "That doesn't mean I don't want to try. I don't want to just have fun. You know? It doesn't mean I don't want to have sex. I just don't know if we have the bonding agents that will hold us together on the canvas."

"Spoken like a true artist," I chuckled. "We all like you, Mary. Maybe that's a drawback. You're sexy as hell. And funny. But we… I won't try to force you someplace you won't fit in."

"I don't think you'll have to do any forcing when it comes time to fit in me." Her mouth twitched and we slammed together in another intense kiss. Somewhere along the line, my hand landed on her thigh and started sliding upward. "Um… Jett, it's not a good time to be playing around down there. Not that I wouldn't like to, but it's messy."

"If we were someplace with a bed, I'd just say let's go get messy," I laughed. "Probably not the best idea clothed and in the car. And as much as I like playing around down there, that isn't the only reason I go out with you."

"Yeah. It's not a bad reason, though. I'm not, like, inexperienced, you know. It was pretty easy to have sex in high school. Guys couldn't wait to dip into the mystery girl who was always covered up. But no one really got interested in having a relationship with the 'nervous girl.' They couldn't relax. And they wanted me naked. I just couldn't do that. When the time's right, I'll get naked with you, Jett. I think. Just… you know… take it slow."

"Whatever pace you say, Mary. I'm sort of falling for you."

"You fall kind of easily. Remember, I've got to fall six times if this is ever going anywhere. We can kiss some more."

We did and Mary taught me about how she liked to have her nipples twisted with the bar pierced through them. We didn't make it all the way to orgasms, but we were damned exhausted by the time she got out of the car and went to her dorm.

•∘•❧))ᘔ ☀ ᘔ((☙•∘•

MARY'S PERIOD MARKED the beginning of what the girls called Shark Week. Over the next ten days, there was a constant exchange of girls who were bloated, horny, crabby, cramping, bleeding, bitchy, clingy, depressed, manic, and crying. As Jas referred to it, there was 'blood in the water.'

In my book, it was like trying to connect to a WiFi network without the WEP code.

"Don't touch me unless you've got a tampon crammed up your ass!"

"Rub my tummy. Not down there."

"Hold me."

"How can you be so stupid?"

"I'm hungry."

"Ow! Ow! Ow!"

"Fuck me, fuck me, fuck me."

I wasn't sure but what the longer we lived together, the worse it got. One played off another and seemed devoted to outdoing everyone else. And add to my five roommates, Mary and Eva, who seemed to be over to 'study' every night that week.

And forget about painting. "You're so selfish. I need you."

A guy needs a little recovery time between forays into the mine field of menstruating girlfriends. I called Derek and we got together for a latte Wednesday afternoon.

•°••°❖ ᗡᏟ ☼ ᏟᏟ ❖°••°•

"How CAN YOU stand it?" Derek laughed when I'd given him a rundown of circumstances at home. "I'd run out of the house screaming. You know there's an order of monks who make cheese in the next county. I hear they are looking for recruits. They take a vow of silence and you are only allowed one sentence a year."

"That is such an old joke," I moaned. "I'm tired of all this bickering about oatmeal."

"It just shows that no matter how you change your circumstances, you'll find something to piss about," he said.

"That's true enough. Just think: I could still be living with my mother."

I was really thinking about my family and how my mother was insane about sterilizing everything I touched and planning every detail of my life. Since I moved out, we had a much better relationship. About once a month, I took one of my girlfriends home with me for Sunday dinner. It was fun. Unfortunately, Derek went suddenly silent as he stared at his coffee.

"Hey. What is it?"

"Um… Dee and I spent a lot of time with each other—in each other's house—before this summer. It's not like we didn't know what the parents were like. But actually living together full time has its challenges." Derek sighed. "It's so different than I expected."

"Are you… like… living *together* together? Um… I thought you were in the guest room."

"Not anymore. I… um… We did it in August. Had sex. Made love. Moved into her room together."

"And her parents are okay with all that?"

"They practically strewed rose petals in our path. I tell you, Jett, they have been planning this with my parents for eighteen years. Maybe longer. Our parents were college friends, you know. We were practically conceived in the same bed."

"It sounds like you've got it all then. Your parents are paying for college. You're living with the love of your life. Her mom cooks and cleans for you. You live rent-free. What's to complain about?"

"It's weird to have sex every night down the hall from her parents and next door to her little brother. It's like they know what we're doing every time we close the door to our room. It's the kind of smile they have when we emerge again. I mean, they're right. We were having sex. I don't know how you can keep up with five girls. Dee and I have sex all the time! It's like we went through eighteen and a half years being close and loving and friends, and then we had sex and now that's all we ever do. *All the fucking time!*"

"I'd never have thought Dee was a nympho," I laughed. "Or that you were a sex maniac."

"That's the thing, you know? It worries me. Remember when we first got into *Minecraft*? We played all the time. Our parents confiscated the controllers until our homework was done and unplugged the Xbox at eleven at night so we'd sleep. Then one day I came in with my controller, ready to play, and Dee had *Final Fantasy XV* out. We never played *Minecraft* again. I'm afraid she'll be like that with sex. One day, I'll walk into the bedroom and start to undress and she'll say, 'Let's play canasta.' It will all be over."

"I think sex stimulates different brain-centers than games," I guessed. "You make it good for her, don't you? I mean, Kelly…"

"I screwed things up so badly with Kelly. Shit. I still feel like I owe her an apology or ten. I'm never going to treat Dee like that. We downloaded a book."

"What kind of book?"

"How to sexually satisfy your partner and have a lifelong sexual relationship. Our parents gave it to us."

"You're kidding."

"No. It was right after we moved out of your Granddad's place. We were in our blanket fort in the basement and my phone chimed that I had a new book synchronizing. We read it all that night and started downloading others. You know, the stuff we all did online was nothing compared to the kind of stuff that's possible when two people put their parts together IRL."

"I found that out. Maybe I need to borrow that book. But that was like back in June! And it took you until mid-August to put the parts together?"

"We did a lot of… um… experimenting before that. We found a dozen more books. Indian, Japanese, Chinese. They're all more interesting than the straight sex American books. We compared anatomy, methods of stimulating each other, positions. Then one night, we started kissing. Jett! They need to write a book about kissing! I mean, we had little pecks on the cheek and even a smooch on the lips before, but we'd been reading *The Kama Sutra* one night and for some unknown reason we just kissed each other."

"That has been an experience I'm loving at every opportunity."

"Yeah, but… The downside about how we were raised together, you know from sharing a crib onward, is that we were sort of like brother and sister. We'd seen each other, watched each other develop, and really loved each other. But we didn't get turned on by each other. Who'd kiss his sister? And when we started reading all the sex books, it was like maybe someday we'd find someone to actually do all this stuff with, but we didn't think it would be each other. Then that kiss!" Derek's eyes glazed over as if he was reliving the kiss right then. "Who knew how it connected everything. We made love all night long. I've always loved Dee. I just didn't think the sex stuff was part of it. Wow! Just, wow!"

"And now you've accepted the parents' plan for your lives, huh?"

"We're getting married at Christmas, Jett. Dee's pregnant."

I HAD A lot to think about. I went shopping and picked up five heating pads. I went back and got two more. It was silly of me to treat Mary and Eva any differently than my five girlfriends. I called the contact Ford had given me before he left to get some decent dope. I didn't want us routinely getting high, but if it helped my girls get past the pain of their periods, I could see a once a month pot party. I stopped by the Bath Shoppe and picked up half a dozen different kinds of bath salts and three bottles of massage oils. Then I picked up the girls' favorite Chinese noodles and chicken dishes and rushed home.

It was Sarah Lynn's turn to cook. When I walked in the back door, I found her standing in the kitchen, staring at a package of chicken. She winced as I watched her.

"Don't…" she started.

"Let me take over dinner, Sarah Lynn," I said. "I'd like to do that for you."

She burst into tears and rushed to hug me.

"I thought I'd make it through today before it started," she cried. "I didn't mean to get cramps today. I'm sorry."

"Honey, come out to the living room. I have something for you." I led her to the sofa and gave her a heating pad.

"Really? For me?" She kissed me and even though she tried to put something into it, she got another cramp and curled up around the heating pad.

"Aww! Me, too," Kelly whimpered as she came into the room. "Can I share?" I handed my redhead another heating pad and got an equally abbreviated kiss before she curled up on the other end of the sofa and snuggled against the comforting warmth.

I quickly unwrapped the other five heating pads and put them on the coffee table so the other girls could grab one as they got home. Then I rushed the recycling out and picked up my other purchases from my car.

"I smell Chinese food. Is Ariel cooking tonight?" Jas whined as she and Char came into the kitchen.

"This is a Jett special," I said. "It's designed to make all my girlfriends as comfortable as possible."

"I know what would make me more comfortable," Ariel said as she, Eva, and Mary walked in the living room door. "Please say you're going to get us high before we try to consume all that food."

"Your wish is my command, my little pixie," I said pulling out the baggie.

"Oh, yes! I'd give you a blowjob, but I think I'd gag. Toke me up."

I packed the bong and the sweet aroma filled the air. While the girls passed the bong, I ran back to the kitchen and heated all the food. Chinese food for eight costs about a hundred bucks—a quarter of my monthly food allowance. But if I could make my girls feel better, it was worth it.

"There are bath salts in the bathroom if anyone wants to soak. I have massage oil and will do your feet or backs. If you feel up to a shower, I'll shampoo your hair. There's only one of me, so you'll have to share, but I'll take care of all of you."

"I'm down to a slow drip," Mary said. "The worst is over for me, so I'll help Jett if any of you want that foot or back rub."

"I wish I felt good enough to thank you for that properly," Sarah Lynn said as she stripped down to her panties. "Please do my lower back, Mary. It aches so much." I laid our beach towels out on the floor and soon Mary and I had six near-naked girls stretched out, moving from one to another with massage oil. I needed to get every extension cord we had together so they could all keep their heating pads plugged in as we worked on them. As the food, pot, and oil gradually took effect, the girls mellowed out, shifted around, and eventually went to bed. I set about cleaning up our mess. I still had a bit of a buzz, but I'd been most concerned about how to treat my girlfriends and got most of my high from just being in the room. I took out the garbage, having wisely chosen to feed everyone off paper plates and with plastic forks. I'd just finished loading the washing machine with all our oily towels when I felt a hand on my back. I turned to face Mary.

"No wonder they all love you so much," she whispered. She leaned in to kiss me softly.

"You know, it was really a challenge this morning. They all seemed to want to rip me a new one. But I was talking to a friend this afternoon and I realized that… they're the most important thing in the world to me. It's not enough to love them. You. All. I want to take care of each and every one."

"Um… I hate to put another request on you then, but I didn't get any massage this evening."

"Mary, I'd be happy to massage you. Why don't we go up to one of the beds where we can be comfortable?"

"The three bedrooms are all in use with two girls per bed. But Kelly told me I could stay in the Kat House tonight if I wanted. Would that be okay?"

"Absolutely."

•·•·◈·)IC·☼·)IC·◈·•·•

WE STOOD A little awkwardly in Kelly's room. It looked like the set for a porn movie. Which I guess it was.

"Um… What would you like? Whatever you want," I said. I'd brought up the remains of all three bottles of massage oil, but with Mary still in what appeared to be a heavy-duty body stocking, I figured this was going to be a dry massage. She took a deep breath and reached between her legs to undo snaps.

"This is a two-piece," she sighed as the tension was released. "I get through my periods with less pain than your girlfriends because I have Prozac. That and this high-compression bodystocking help control the cramps. But… um… it kind of squashes my boobs. Could you… would you massage them?"

"Of course," I said. I reached for her and she stepped back. She unsnapped the crotch of her leotard and pulled it up and over her head. It took longer for her to get the sleeves off her arms than the body off her torso. I know because I was holding my breath the whole time. In front of me were the most beautiful breasts I'd ever seen. I couldn't believe she'd nailed a spike through the most perfect nipples I could even imagine. "God, you're beautiful."

"They might not be ready for quite as much stimulation as they were on Sunday, but I could really stand to have them rubbed." I sat on the bed and Mary leaned back between my legs. She immediately scooted forward again and turned to pull my T-shirt and jeans off. Then she settled back and I felt her bare back against my chest for the first time. I warmed a little oil in my hands and reached around her to begin a gentle massage of her chest.

I spent a fair amount of time just massaging her tits but as she leaned back into me and nuzzled her lips under my chin, I stroked the entire length of her torso and arms, up and down her sides, and across her shoulders. Mary had been shaking when she first leaned back against me but now there was no more than an occasional quiver of her skin. She'd said her nipples were a little more sensitive than they'd been on Sunday, so I didn't treat them roughly, but I spent a good bit of time tracing her bars with my fingers and trying to keep my own nipples from pulling inside out from thinking about being pierced.

Mary turned in my arms and pulled herself to my lips. We kissed deeply and intently as I shifted my manual ministrations to her back, pressing all the way down to the waistband of her tights. She purred and cooed as we kissed and she rubbed her oily breasts against my chest. There was no question that she could feel my erection against her stomach. In fact, I was pretty sure I was poking out the top of my briefs and smearing precome between us.

Mary slid down and dragged my shorts the rest of the way off my cock. She looked up at me and smiled. "You were so good to all of us today. This is just for you." With that, she lowered her mouth over the head of my cock and began a slow and exquisite blowjob. She teased me as long as possible before it was obvious I was beyond the point of no return. Then she swallowed me down as I pumped my week's worth of seed down her throat. My moan was probably loud enough to have woken all the girls below us if they hadn't been sleeping a deep, stoned sleep.

She kissed her way back up my torso after stripping off my briefs altogether and pulling me down so I was lying next to her instead of sitting up. We lay facing each other and kissing. That's how we fell asleep.

27
Euripides

EVERYONE WAS pretty mellow in the morning. I woke up with Mary's bare breasts still pressed against my chest, her lips near mine. Most of the time when I go to sleep with a girlfriend—even if we drift off holding each other—we end up in our own favorite sleeping positions, giving each other room in the bed. Mary seemed to relish being held in my embrace overnight.

And I loved it.

My left arm pillowed her head and my right hand explored her back and her butt. I slipped my hand inside her tights so I could touch the skin on her ass and she hunched her pelvis forward as I caressed her. Her left arm was wrapped tightly around me and I wasn't sure how her right arm was pinned under her until her fingers twitched and I felt them wrap around my cock.

"I need to get up and use the bathroom, Jett," she mumbled. "I just don't want to move from your arms."

"It *is* a weekday and we have classes," I sighed. "I just wish we could lie in bed all day making love."

"You're a dreamy lover but school beckons," she said, finally loosening her grip and rolling away from me. Those gorgeous breasts and their pierced nipples. I bent to lightly kiss each of them. "We'll get to the rest soon. It's something… I haven't felt rushed with you. I'm enjoying the anticipation, knowing that one day soon I'll be here with my legs wrapped around your waist as your cock slides in and out of my pussy. Are you anticipating that, too, Jett?"

"I can almost feel it. I'm loving the pace you've set."

"Okay. Now I really have to run down to the bathroom," she laughed. She popped out of bed and pulled my T-shirt on, catching her leotard up in her hand. She headed for the stairs.

"I need to go downstairs and get some breakfast ready for my lovers. They'll have a bit of THC hangover this morning."

And so it began. After I'd used the bathroom, I got out the blender and the fruit I bought yesterday. I scooped some protein powder into the almond milk and added strawberries, blueberries, and bananas. I had to make three blenders full, but by the time sleepy Eva got to the kitchen, everyone had a glass of the protein-rich smoothie.

By some miracle, I made it to my ten o'clock 2D Design class having gotten seven happy ladies off to their day of classes. Perhaps I'd jumped the shark last night, but I knew he was still swimming in the waters around my home for the rest of the week. It was hard to understand how women were at the mercy of a physical process that wrecked them each month. It wasn't always as bad as it had been this week but to some extent or another, they all went through the discomfort each month.

My professor for 2D Design was Lila Jones. The twenty of us in the class came from different disciplines in the arts as it was a core requirement but about a third of the students were graphic arts majors. Oddly, the fine arts students in the class were getting along better than the graphic arts students. Lila—she insisted that she went only by her first name and not by Professor—was a pre-computer graphic artist. She insisted that her students learn the principles of 2D Design without resorting to their computers. It involved a lot of sketching and some drafting. No computing.

The first few weeks of the class had been a survey of design over the centuries. In that way, it resembled my Literature and the Arts class. We started with design and motifs of Egypt, China, and India. Then we jumped into pre-Hellenic Greece and worked our way toward the present. There was a lot about the effect of the printing press on graphic arts as we made our way through the ages to the 'contemporary' arts. These were defined by styles and sometimes by influential artists. Names like Art Deco, Art Nouveau, Celtic, Chippendale, Queen Anne, and most importantly, William Morris. We quickly progressed to wallpaper and textile design.

"As we have seen as far back as the second millennium BC, the underlying principle of two-dimensional design is motif. The motif recurs throughout the decorative surface. In order for this to happen, it must be repeated, and that is the second principle. Finally, in the case of room-size design, we have match. Match is the second dimension of repeat. Motif, repeat, and match. That is your first lab assignment. As the practical portion of your midterm, you will present a repeating motif in both vertical and horizontal dimensions. This assignment is to be black and white, ink on Bristol, drafted and measurable. It should incorporate a style element that is reminiscent of one of the periods we have studied. All projects must be received by October twenty-fourth. You have two weeks. Use them well. Next week, we will begin the discussion of textile design and the effect of the industrial revolution."

Fuck! I'd completely forgotten that there was a practical portion of this class. All we'd had to do so far was sketch examples of each of the periods and styles we'd studied. Now I had to come up with some kind of motif and actually create what was essentially a black and white wallpaper pattern. This was going to be horrendous.

My day continued to go to hell in a handbasket as Mammam used to say. I thought of her every time I got in my car—the little Mini that she loved so much. Well, this time Merck was on a roll. I think he must have switched from pot to speed. If studying Homer was a long lyrical process, Euripides was a rock opera. I swear, he even sang parts of *The Bacchae*.

He stopped me after class and told me how much he liked my Athena project, hinting broadly that he'd like to watch me paint one of my models. Frankly, I think he just wanted to be in a room with a naked teenager and think it was legit. I told him I'd consider it and talk to the model when the time came. As if.

He hit me with a suggestion for our Euripides section. That was a first. He was really getting into my body paintings. Anyway, he asked specifically if I could take something from *Medea* and develop it into a statement about the strength and power of women. That was something Euripides was really into. He'd written *Medea*, *The Bacchae*, *The Trojan Women*, and several other plays about the strength of women and in support of women's rights.

"Of course, I'm not your inspiration," he said, still talking as fast as he had all through class. "You're the artist. I just saw a vision with no means of realizing it. Follow your own creative energy. But *Medea*. Yes. There was a woman for all ages."

The third project was also due for midterms in two weeks. Great.

And the hits just keep on coming. Blankenship was living up to his nickname, Blankety-blank. I was ready to fill in the blanks with a few choice obscenities. The bright spot was seeing Mary walk in and sit next to me. The smile on her face lit my own as we reached out and touched hands.

"Weaknesses," Blankety started as he walked into the room at exactly three o'clock. "You have weaknesses in your drawing." I glanced around. There had been over twenty of us in this class at the beginning of the term. Now there were fourteen. The bastard was living up to his reputation of weeding out students who couldn't take it. I might have been one of them if I hadn't bonded with Mary and entered into a mutual support pact. "Just in case you have forgotten your weaknesses, let me review them. You…" he pointed at a girl four seats over from me, "… smudge everything. There is nothing that would help your drawings more than an eraser. You…" pointing at the only other guy left in the class, "… seem to think this is a drafting class. Your pencils are too hard and ground to too fine a point."

And so it went on. He hit every single one of us with our 'isms' as he called them. He'd pointed them out often enough. Everyone cringed as we waited for him to turn his pointy finger at us. But even I didn't expect the criticism he directed at Mary. He'd always seemed to avoid directing too much of his wrath at her. This time, though, he went directly to the point. "You can't draw a straight line with a ruler." I saw tears spring to her eyes and was reaching for Mary's shaking hand when the son of a bitch swung and pointed directly at me. "And you can't seem to draw what's in front of you. You are wrapped up in reflections and shadows and never get around to actually drawing the fucking object."

My hand was still partly raised to touch Mary's even though my eyes were locked with Blankenship's. He was in rare form and I was giving him back every ounce of hatred I could muster. We were trying to bore holes in each other with our eyes.

And then I felt Mary's grip on my hand. She was still shaking but so, I realized, was I. I tore my eyes away from Blankety and over to Mary. I saw a determination there that filled me with my own defiance. Both of our hands settled as Blankety raved at another student. He appeared to be taking us randomly, but it was evident that he wasn't leaving anyone untouched. We would survive.

"Don't you leave this classroom, young woman!" he screamed at a girl who had burst out in tears when he called her a cartoonist rather than an artist. She'd stood to leave and he froze her with his words. "I don't lose people after six weeks," he growled, pacing the floor and pointing the girl back to her seat. She sank down in it. "Despite all your weaknesses, you have lasted this long; you can last the rest of the way. You stubbornly keep drawing no matter how I try to discourage you. You sit down in this class twice a week with a sketch book in front of you and a pencil in your hand, knowing full well that I'm going to blister your ass with my words. Why do you do that? Why do you take this abuse? Because you are artists. Don't you dare believe that means I'm suddenly going to become nice and compliment you on every scribble you make. You have a long way to go before you draw something that is praiseworthy."

I glanced around the room and noticed others were looking at their classmates as well. Perhaps we had some kind of perverse pride in having survived six weeks of his abuse.

"Most, if not all, of you will fail your midterm project. Those who pass will do so accidentally. Why? Because you have not yet learned to exploit your weaknesses. You can't exploit them without knowing them and over the past six weeks I have done my best to point them out to you. Your midterm project will be to draw a still life in black and white. The substrate and medium are your choice. The subject is your choice but it must be a still life. No life drawings, figures, or portraits. No landscapes or nature scenes. You will *create your own composition* and draw it, exploiting your weakness. There will be no further classes until the project is due. After you have failed the midterm, we will spend the next six weeks working on exploiting your weaknesses so that you become more than draftsmen and stand the chance of becoming artists."

We seemed to come to life about then. I could hear people shifting in their seats as the fact that there was meaning to the abuse we'd taken for the past six weeks sank in.

"Now," he concluded facing the 'cartoonist' who had nearly fled the class, "today is the last day to withdraw from class. If you can't take the likelihood of failing your midterm, go get it done. I'll see the rest of you on the 25th." Blankenship turned and left the classroom without another word and without waiting for questions from the three people who had raised their hands.

We were on our own.

∘∘∘⇨ ⟊⟊⟋ ☽ ⟊⟊⟋ ⇦∘∘∘

Apparently, everyone had received much the same messages in their classes because everyone was focused on studying for midterms. There were still heating pads clutched to stomachs but the mood in the house was more subdued than the angry pain of the previous night.

Kelly kept to her Tuesday, Wednesday, Thursday night camming schedule, even though her show was a little shorter and fully clothed. It was amazing to me how many guys seemed to really care about the fact that she had her period discomfort and did their best to cheer her up with tips. When she'd reached a thousand tokens, she took off her top and talked about how tender her nipples were during her period.

"The good news is that I'm not pregnant!" she laughed in response to one guy's commiseration over her condition. After an hour and a half online, she thanked her supporters and took her heating pad to bed.

Sarah Lynn had a stack of books on the dining room table where she was carefully planning out exactly what still had to be read and what had to be reviewed in the next ten days before midterms. I didn't envy her, but I wasn't stupid enough—or smart enough—to take twenty hours my first semester in college.

I would have one midterm exam in Foundations of Contemporary Art that would be filled with names and dates and movements. It was important stuff to know, but it was really nothing compared to the three projects I had upcoming. They were so different. Black and white wallpaper with a step-and-repeat pattern and a horizontal match. A bodypainting that represented the strength of woman as shown in Euripides' *Medea*. And a still life drawing that exploited my weaknesses.

I was in a world of shit. I sat down to start reading *Medea*.

•••

ALL OUR OBSERVATIONS in the slaughterhouse had been in the feedlot for sorting, shipping, and grading, and in the hanger locker where testing and grading took place. The grading process was one of the most important in processing carcasses. And it is different for beef than for pork or lamb, so we had to observe and were tested on all three. We weren't qualified to grade anything—that was another entire USDA training course—but we were tested on what the grades meant and how they were determined.

My next Friday class was the killing room. I think they planned the order of the observations to make us accustomed to seeing live cattle on one end and hanging carcasses on the other so we wouldn't be squeamish about seeing the transition. There's a mindset that is required. Outside there is food moving into the chute for processing. Sometimes it makes noise. It moves on its own. But it's food. Inside, the food no longer moves on its own. It hangs on hooks while other useful products like the hide are stripped from it for processing.

I watched a hundred cattle enter the stanchion one at a time, saw the bolt positioned precisely at their foreheads and watched the steer go slack as the bolt was triggered. It didn't really even make a noise. The carcass was already on a moving conveyer when it was stunned. As soon as it was out of the killing room, the hind legs were hooked and the carcass elevated enough that one of the butchers could slit the throat so the blood drained out as it crossed the collection trench. This is where the bloodiest part of the process takes place and where some of the most skilled butchers work. In a matter of fifteen minutes, the hide is stripped, the organs removed, the head and hooves removed, and the carcass split for grading and cutting.

Sharp knives and precision cutting.

Did I mention the blood?

•••

MEDEA WAS BLOODY, TOO. Okay, so it was written twenty-five hundred years ago. Were things really so bloody back then that this was okay? Granted, the woman was mistreated. I had to read half a book before I read the play in order to get the context. Everyone has heard of the heroic *Jason and the Golden Fleece*. His ship, the Argo, gave its name to the crew of Argonauts. Well, I'd only heard part of the story. It was Medea who saved Jason's life, killed the poison snake that guarded the Golden Fleece, betrayed her father, and then killed her own brother so they could escape. She was the daughter of a barbarian king and Jason married her. She had two sons.

But they had trouble finding a place to live after she killed Jason's usurper uncle. So, they arrived at Corinth where the Tyrant king Creon ruled. Creon had a daughter but no sons, so he decided that the heroic Jason, also a prince, would make a perfect heir to the throne if married to his daughter. Instant divorce by decree for Medea. She ranted and raved and Creon banished her and her sons from Corinth. That's really where the play begins.

I get it. This woman was wronged. Severely wronged. Her husband agrees to the divorce and new marriage to the king's daughter because then he'll become king one day. Medea, who saved his life, killed for him, and bore his sons, is summarily divorced, and sent into exile penniless with their sons. Hey, this is a cheating husband vengeance story in the making. Medea convinces Jason she is contrite and asks him to plead for his sons to remain in Corinth. She sends them with gifts of a golden robe and crown for the princess to make nice. Only the robe and crown are enchanted and not only poison her but cause her to burst into flame. King Creon rushes to his daughter and embraces her, getting the nasty stuff on himself, and joins her in a painful death.

Shit! Well, that stuff will get you hunted down, for sure. But Medea hasn't adequately wreaked vengeance on Jason. Besides, the children would be hunted down in Corinth for taking the gifts to the princess, so she kills her two boys and displays their bloody bodies to Jason, refusing to even give them to him for burial.

Then there is the great *deus ex machina*. Medea is saved by the gods and taken away in a serpent drawn chariot with the bodies of her children so she is beyond the reach of Jason, the Corinthians, and vengeance.

She murders the princess, the king, and her children, and *she* is the one the gods save? Jason is the villain?

I went to my sketchbook and started doodling out designs for my 2D project. I needed to get my head out of death and destruction. Somehow, even my straight black lines started looking like dripping blood.

⁕

I won't pretend there was no sex going on, even though we were all a little stressed out by our upcoming midterms. Saturday night, I'd taken Kelly out to dinner. I realized that the only one of my girlfriends that I was actually dating was Mary. I wanted to keep doing that, but I really needed to show the five I was committed to that I cared for them. And Kelly was a beautiful treat to go on a date with.

And surprised.

"You want to actually go out and be seen with me?" she said when I asked her out. "Like without a camera? I'm a slut. Why would you ever want to be seen with me?"

"Kelly, we've had this conversation before. You're a sex worker—that's not the same as a slut. You are a performer. You aren't out sleeping around with anyone who looks at you lustfully. You aren't a drunk or drug addicted gutter whore. You are my girlfriend and I'm proud to be seen with you."

We almost didn't make it out of the house but the whole point was to go out someplace nice for a date. Kelly looked absolutely beautiful. She wore a green dress that accented her red hair and green eyes. Her high heels brought her forehead just up to kissing height. And made the absolute most of her legs. I couldn't wait to have my hands on those silky-smooth thighs.

"I'm getting a lot of offers," she said.

"You want to date someone?"

"Not that kind of offer. In this business 'date' simply means 'fuck.' No thanks. There are producers contacting me to make movies. Would I like to audition for them? Would I consider a solo movie? How about a girl-girl movie?"

"Legit offers?" I asked. I could just imagine the guys next door deciding they wanted to make a porn flick and putting a video camera in their bedroom to tape every girl they could lure in.

"Some probably are. But what are they offering, really? You know, it's just like writers who self-publish. The only thing a big publishing company can offer them is better distribution. It's the same thing with getting a major porn producer to make a movie with you. They have better distribution. But I'm making some pretty good solo films by myself. I've even got one with Jas. I don't have the platform that will support more than I'm doing at the moment, but I've got some loyal followers. I need to build my cinematography skills and get better at digital editing before I really focus on expanding my market."

"What I really want to do is direct, right?" I laughed.

"Well, yeah! What do you think I'm in school for?"

"That's the thing, isn't it? You're a student. You're doing a good job of managing your work hours the same way that I manage going to the grocery store or Jas manages working at Applebee's. It's a part time job you're using to get your career established."

"I'm so glad you understand, Jett. I don't want a career as a porn star. I admit that I'm a show-off but I don't really want to spread my legs for a living long-term."

However, spreading her legs for me later in the evening was definitely on her mind. We touched and flirted all through dinner, then took a walk down by the shore where we held hands and stopped for long sensuous kisses. Back home, she eschewed the Kat House where Ariel and Sarah Lynn were having a playdate and came to my bed. I took a long time getting reacquainted with Kelly's trim body. I kissed and licked her little nipples and discovered anew how much she loved having her tummy kissed.

When we finally got to the part where my cock slipped effortlessly into her pussy, it wasn't at all like a porn flick. We were just two lovers completely lost in loving each other. In her online performances, she often used a vibrator or a dildo but it had done nothing to stretch her out. The tight, velvety sheath that encased my cock milked me for all the sperm I could give her as she cried out her pleasure.

I slept on my back with Kelly lying mostly on top of me. In the morning, before I went to work, she managed to get fully on top of me and slide us together again.

<h1 style="text-align:center">28
Still Life</h1>

I HELD CHAR IN my arms Sunday night as we cuddled in bed. We'd gone to a movie for our date. Not the kind of art film that Mary and I usually saw. Oh, no. Charmaine wanted to see the new Predator movie. There were only a dozen girls in a theater with close to a hundred boys. It's a guy flick. Ragtag bunch of soldiers—one token woman, of course—are all that stand between an upgraded Predator and the destruction of the human race. I had no idea that Char had that dark side to her.

"I want to be a monster," she said as we cuddled. She lifted my hand and bit it lightly. "They'd never get me that easily." She rolled toward me and continued nipping at me—my lips, my fingers, my chest. "My Predator would eat her way through them on my way to destroying my father. And him, I'd eat alive. I'd be sure he watched as I ate his balls. I'd slice him open carefully and pull out his organs to eat while they were still attached. They needed a female Predator. We'd never let the bastards get away." She bit again and I jumped back. She hurt. "Sorry, Jett. I'm not mad at you. I wouldn't hurt you." She kissed where she'd bitten and licked at my nipples.

"The lawyer's letter didn't help?" I said as I squirmed a little. She was working her way down toward my cock and I didn't want her in the organ-eating mood when she got there.

"He said he'd give me back the money when I agreed to come home and accept his choice for my husband. He says I'm costing him the bride price that is due to him."

"He actually has someone who would pay to have a forced bride? You need to tell the lawyer to go ahead with the suit. You'll get a judgment against him easily. This is America. You can't sell your daughter in marriage."

"Oh, he wouldn't. He'd pack me off to India where there's an old man who will pay for a young virgin bride. I'm almost too old for him, but I'm a virgin and he believes he'll be rejuvenated if he takes my maidenhead."

"I'm not going to let anyone take you away, Char."

"And you aren't going to take my virginity as long as you think I owe you."

"No. As long as *you* think you owe me."

"When I kill him, I won't owe you anymore."

"Char, you scare me."

"I know. I scare me, too. I keep thinking bloody thoughts. I can't help it. My counselor thinks it isn't that bad. She's in total denial that my father could be a real threat."

"I'm not. I'll do anything I can to protect you, Char."

"And I'll keep owing you. I'm glad I like having my ass fucked so at least we can still make love."

That's what we did. She slurped my half-hard cock into her mouth and started working it up. I'd flagged considerably once we got to bed and she started talking about being a monster and devouring her father. Of course, once she had her mouth full and quit talking about it, it didn't take long for me to get fully hard. And then it was a matter of Char backing onto my cock with her ass.

She was the only girl I'd ever taken anally. Kelly and Ariel had both offered but I could tell they were afraid of it. I wasn't sure even if I started fucking her pussy, that Char wouldn't still prefer anal. And, my God, she was active! Going gently into that tight little hole was not in the cards. As soon as I was positioned and started in, Char slammed back against me, driving my cock up into her. I wondered sometimes if the screams were agony or ecstasy—or if Char could tell the difference.

There was no doubt that she was turned on. I reached around and diddled her clit. It was drenched in her juices and slippery as all get out. And sensitive. I could definitely tell when she came because the pulsing was so intense my come was sucked out of my cock into her ass.

My cock kept pulsing as her ass kept clenching and relaxing on it. It softened a bit but was still caught tightly.

"Paint me, Jett. Paint me a demon so I can get it out of me. Please?"

•◦•◦⟩ ꐦ ☼ ꐦ ⟨◦•◦•

I HAD A pretty restless night. Not the least of which was caused by Char waking up and coaxing me into her ass again. Not that it required much coaxing. I was already spooned behind her with her breasts in my hands. She just wiggled enough that I hardened completely and then she guided me into the slippery channel.

But my dreams were haunted. Char wanted her demon painted and I needed to figure out a painting that represented *Medea* for my Literature and the Arts class. The two were coming together in my mind. If there was ever a demon in literature, it was the betrayed and scorned Medea. What Char had said sounded like it could have come from the mouth of the Greek heroine.

I thought about it all day at work, thankful that I had cutting gloves on, as sloppily as I was slicing meat. I could have lost a finger or two.

As soon as I got home from work, of course, I had to get started on dinner. Mondays were my night. I'd decided on a roast and root vegetables with a nice salad. I was so thankful my girlfriends were all meat eaters. Imagine a butcher with a vegetarian girlfriend. I'd guess that would be a short-lived relationship. There was no question they didn't want red meat for every meal and I was equally thankful for that. I'd go broke quick.

When I got the roast and vegetables in the oven, I started on my 2D project. This was a lot harder than it sounds. I actually used a T-square and triangle to draft out several scale models with the positions for the match and repeats. That was just the format. Kind of like setting the margins when you were typing a paper. The real issue was the design. It was to all be black and white and that can really be distracting.

I saw three paths I could take. The first was a real cop-out and I dismissed it as soon as I thought of it. I could do stripes. No match and infinite repeat. I had a feeling that I'd get exactly the grade that kind of effort deserved. There were other random match patterns. I could do a spatter but that didn't make any difference, but that was a cop-out, too. I put it in the same category as the stripes. Secondly, I could do a linear match so that the pattern was basically a grid of identifiable objects like diamonds, fleurs-de-lis, or any other linear repeated pattern. That would probably be the most commonly done project. It was easy. It was like the border on one of the Greek vases and could be seen in hundreds of wallpaper patterns. Finally, I could draw something that interconnected in an unusual way. It would need to be a pattern that wasn't immediately obvious, but that if you stepped back, you would see the repeat.

I was frustrated with trying to plot out a full-scale model, so I switched over to graph paper and just started doodling. On graph paper you could just draw and figure out the matches and repeats later. I blocked out a frame on a grid and drew a random line into it from the left. Then I plotted those points on the other side to create the same line as if it were going into the next grid. I was beginning to get the hang of drawing random lines on one side and repeating them where they would match up on the other. I progressed from matching straight across to shifting the pattern down. Then I started doing squiggles instead of lines. That was a little more challenging because you had to make the same shape. Still, it worked. Finally, I was drawing doodles and repeating them across the tile.

Dinner was ready before I had anything that I thought remotely usable, but at least I'd made progress. We all settled in to study after dinner and the tensions seemed to decrease as we leaned against each other, snacking on chips and soft drinks and trying to read or write. Sarah Lynn seemed to have it the worst of us, but she was taking a crazy course load. She had two papers and four full midterm exams. It's not that I don't like learning, but I'm not a glutton for punishment. Still, it was Sarah Lynn and I stayed up with her as she continued to study right through till midnight. Everyone else had gone to bed.

"What are you doing up?" she asked when she finally closed her book. "Do you have more to study for?"

"No. I just didn't want you to feel abandoned. I didn't disturb you, did I?"

"I didn't even realize you were here. You didn't have to wait up for me."

"I know. But you are working about three times as hard as the rest of us."

"That's not true. Maybe for schoolwork, but you hold down a job thirty hours a week. If anyone deserves…"

"Don't go there. We're a mutual admiration society. Can I hold you in bed tonight? Just to hold you."

"Jett, what do we do to deserve you?"

"I ask myself every day what I do to deserve you. I don't want anything to spoil what we have together." We got ready for bed and brushed our teeth. Neither of us wore anything to bed but that didn't mean we were ready for anything but sleep.

"Is that why you haven't had sex with Mary?" Sarah Lynn asked. "Are you afraid it will spoil what we have?"

"I don't think I'm that noble. I'm not going to push her and we haven't really had much opportunity to do anything more. I mean, I was ready for a lot more when she sucked me off the other night."

"It will come together. And when it does, don't worry about us. We're hoping she'll sleep with us, too."

"Really, Sarah Lynn. What did I do to deserve you?"

"You waited up for me and asked to sleep in my arms."

⚬•◦◦❖ ⟩⟩⟨ ☽ ⟩⟨⟨ ❖◦◦•⚬

We didn't have drawing Tuesday and Thursday this week, but I met Mary before our class time and took her home with me.

"I feel like I'm freeloading dinner off you guys. I need to chip in," she said as we tossed our bags in the studio.

"I paid the guest fee. We agreed on a rate for having dinner guests early on."

"I'll pay it. I'll pay you back!"

"Your contribution will be welcome, but the truth is that everyone wants to invite you for dinner, so we all toss a couple bucks in the pot when you come over."

"Do you do the same for Eva?"

"Um… She is different."

"She just wants to sleep with you and not everyone."

"Do you want to sleep with everyone?"

"Not at once."

"Maybe that's the difference."

We laughed it off and after we got sodas, went into the studio.

"What are we going to draw?" I asked.

"We don't have to draw the same thing. I brought a couple things, but you know he's really after us to make a composition, not to draw something," Mary said.

"He made such a big deal about using our weakness that he hid the real purpose, didn't he?"

"It's the first project he's given us that we had to create our own subject. He was very specific about what it could and couldn't contain."

"He wants us to compose a still life. Nobody thinks that's what the class is about. Which is why everyone will fail."

"Or we'll focus on creating a great composition and fail the drawing. Lose-lose. Let's work on a composition."

It took us until dinner before we'd accumulated two piles of things to draw and had a table set for each of us. Mary had spent a lot of her time in the attic with Kelly and brought down an assortment of sexy objects Kelly said she could do without for a few days. I was surprised to see a pair of my painted underwear in the collection that also included a dildo, a lacy bra and a camera that Kelly had just replaced with a higher resolution model. Mary attached the camera to her laptop and focused it on the collected sex toys and underwear that she kept rearranging.

I'd created a sort of kitchen scene. I used my cleaver, boning knife, a kettle, my cutting glove, and some vegetables. I wanted a roast in my composition as well, but I didn't have one and would need to add that at the last minute. As a last-minute inspiration, I grabbed my marble cutting board and laid the objects out on it as if I was getting ready to fix a stew. What I liked about it was that it subtly reflected things that were set on it, as did the blades of the knives and the side of the kettle.

"To get the effect you are going for, you need a liquid spilled on the cutting board," Mary said as she eyed my composition critically.

"Blood," I said.

"What?"

"When I throw a slab of meat down on the marble and cut into it, there will be blood running out onto the marble. That's not only going to provide a reflective surface, it's going to give a difference in tone as well. The biggest problem is going to be getting the right angle for the reflections I want. That and keeping things fresh enough while I'm drawing. The blood won't reflect after it's dried."

"Nice. With the colors, you're going to have to paint this, too. Now tell me about mine."

"I like that you've concealed all the straight edges," I said. "Even the keys on the computer are occluded. I think I see what you are going for. I know that you could blend things with paint, but in the drawing, your um… shaky lines are going to be masked. You chose a frilly bra and panties and the paint splotches on the underwear change the shape of the outline. The dildo isn't completely revealed, so as long as you have a couple of edges, you don't have to worry about outline. The tricky part is going to be the image on the screen but you've set it up so the camera's angle is different than your artist perspective so inconsistencies can be easily accounted for. I like it."

"The tricky part is really going to be that I will never get the same composition twice and I need to have my computer for schoolwork," she sighed. "Every time I set this up, I'll be starting from scratch."

"How much time do you think you'll need to draw it?"

"To lay in the basic outlines, it will take maybe three hours. I could do the detail work from imagination if I need to. Do we have three hours or should I just snap some pictures and set it up to draw the next time?"

"We don't have any time constraints as far as I'm concerned," I said. "I'd like to do a couple of detail sketches to start with. Try to identify my areas of reflection and focus. I don't know how you're feeling, but I'd cut my morning classes tomorrow if I need to sleep in. We could take all night if we wanted to."

"And could stay awake. I'm wishing I'd cut my classes this morning so I could stay awake all night. I think I've got three hours in me, though, if you want to go to work on it now."

We agreed and each got out our drawing materials. Before we got started, I turned and gave Mary a long sweet kiss.

"Good luck."

"You sure you want to draw?" We laughed at the idea of what we could be doing but were both too intent on getting this project right to distract ourselves from what we needed to do.

-o·-❖ ⟩⟨ ☼ ⟩⟨ ❖-·o-

Two hours later, my eyes were crossing. It shouldn't have been too difficult to stay awake. It wasn't all that late. Just a bit after ten. But I'd been studying my composition so intensely that I kept seeing different shapes in the reflections. I'd sketch a particular reflection—say the shape of half an onion reflected in the curve of the stainless steel pan—and then I'd see the shape of the knife overlaid on it. My sketchbook was filled with unrecognizable doodles as shape was overlaid with shape.

Then there was the movement.

Mary and I weren't exactly sitting next to each other, but more at right angles in order to have adequate space for our compositions in the little room. We were working with easels and large sketch pads. When I glanced over her shoulder, I could see that she was making good progress. It wasn't that her hand was actually shaking, but she made short quick strokes with her pencil and the style was perfect with the objects she was drawing.

I started sketching her back. She'd discarded her sweatshirt when we started drawing and was sitting on it. As I scanned down her back, I realized she was in a crotchless bodystocking made obvious by the portion of her butt that was exposed. That kind of finished any productivity that I was going to have. Just that little bit of ass that was exposed took all my attention.

The other thing I became aware of was that Mary's left hand was in her lap as she drew with her right. And it was moving. I wondered if she was shaking and just trying to keep it still by holding it between her legs. But her legs weren't clamped closed. They were spread wide apart. I was glad I'd finally managed to put blinds up on the studio windows. At this time of night, the guys next door could all have been gathered on their porch with a clear view of her crotch.

There was no mistaking it now. Mary was playing with herself. Certain strokes with her pencil were accompanied by increased vibrations of her other hand. I was torn. I wanted to be respectful and maybe this was a vital part of her process. At the same time, I wanted my hand in there helping. Her drawing looked about finished as far as the shapes were concerned. She had already begun to lay in detail that she mentioned she could do later.

I laid a hand on her thigh. She jumped just a little and then relaxed completely, continuing to draw as she spread her legs even farther. I took that as an invitation and moved my hand toward where hers was still busily vibrating away. It was met by her hand and I could feel some of the tremor there, but she pulled my hand between her legs and pressed it against her moist sex. I got the message and began exploring, sometimes vibrating on her little nubbin and sometimes dipping deeper as she continued to draw. Her breath told the story of her increasing arousal and she left my hand to do its own exploration as she laid her wet fingers on my cheek and pulled me forward and down.

The position she cranked herself into couldn't have been that comfortable, but she twisted her butt on the stool so her legs were parallel to the easel and her shoulders were still more or less facing it. Her pressure on my face and neck were definitely pushing me down between her legs. In a few wordless moments, I was face to pussy.

Fuck! I'd explored her pussy with my fingers a few times and got her off, but I'd never been down where I could see it up close and personal. The promise of the shape we'd seen outlined in her tights was totally fulfilled. She was beautiful. With the amount she'd been playing, she was already open and puffed up with plentiful juices running down onto the sweatshirt she sat on. I leaned forward and tasted her for the first time. She moaned, but her pencil never stopped moving on the drawing.

And then I was lost in her scent and flavor. I just wanted more and more of her in my mouth. I managed a finger into her opening as I tongued her clit and discovered something I hadn't been fully cognizant of when I was touching her in the dark. The bars through her nipples weren't the only piercing she had. As soon as my tongue found the bar through the hood of her clit, I started playing with it. Of course, when I'd been exploring with my fingers, I'd been focused a little lower but now I discovered she was even more sensitive to having the bar flipped with my tongue than direct stimulation on her clit. I remembered all the ways she'd shown me that she like the nipple piercings played with and started doing the same things with the clit hood piercing. I tugged at it with my teeth, flicked it with my tongue, even managed to twist it a little. I pressed my finger inside her and scraped around the front of her vagina as her moans became more pronounced.

Her hand pressed against the back of my head, letting me know she didn't want me to stop, even though she was still drawing. I wished I could see how she was managing to draw while she moved progressively toward orgasm. She was amazing. A new flood of juices flowing over my fingers and into my mouth let me know she was near. I vibrated my tongue against her clit and then grabbed the bar with my teeth.

Mary's pencil fell to the floor as both hands pulled my head into her crotch. A high-pitched keening issued from her mouth as her body went rigid and even more juice flooded from her. As long as she kept the pressure against my head, I kept licking and finger-fucking her. And she kept coming. *God! I'd do anything to have an orgasm that lasted that long!*

She pulled my face up at last and began kissing me and licking her love juice from me. Eventually, I withdrew my finger as well. I really wanted to replace it immediately with my cock, but I'd stayed dressed while I was drawing, totally unaware of Mary's state. As soon as my fingers were free, a hand pulled them up and away. It took a second to realize it wasn't Mary's hand. Sarah Lynn pulled my fingers to her mouth with one hand and used the other to strum her own clit while Mary and I kissed and then Mary turned to kiss Sarah Lynn.

"So hot," Sarah Lynn moaned as she pulled my fingers from her mouth so she could kiss Mary. She pulled my hand down to play with her pussy and Mary caressed her bare breasts. Sarah Lynn soon reached her peak and we all leaned into each other to support ourselves.

"Maybe I could spend the night tonight," Mary whispered as her breathing slowed to normal. "I like being sandwiched between you two."

As we started toward bed and bath, I glanced over at her drawing. Part of it was pretty sketchy, but the section with the dildo and lacy thong were intensely detailed. There was a passion there that I'd missed in her other drawings. I wondered if that was what her real weakness was.

29
With My Teeth in Your Heart

I WOKE UP WITH my cock wedged up against the cheeks of the world's most beautiful butt. Not that I've seen every butt in the world, but I couldn't think of anything more beautiful than this one.

After we'd brushed our teeth, Sarah Lynn and I peeled Mary out of her body stocking. Then we cocooned ourselves in bed with the blonde beauty sandwiched between us. When Mary stopped shaking, she got active. I got the most explosive two-girl blowjob I'd ever had—and with my living arrangement, I'd experienced playful girls teaming up on me before. Mary and Sarah Lynn were exploring each other as well as me and doing their best to delay my orgasm. When the inevitable came—me—they managed to swallow down everything I spewed out, licking up the spatters from each other's faces.

Before I could flag, Sarah Lynn mounted my cock and about a second after she was seated, Mary lowered her exquisite pussy with the clit hood piercing onto my mouth. We were pretty frantic in our lovemaking. Both girls were primed and I wasn't sure how many orgasms they were having. I know I felt fingers join my tongue to pull at Mary's piercing and there was a hand wedged into the space where Sarah Lynn and I were joined. I was just along for the ride of my life. Eventually, we were all exhausted. I reluctantly pulled my tongue out of Mary's pussy as she slid down between Sarah Lynn and me. There were shared post-coital kisses and we spooned together.

My waking in the morning wasn't the first. Sarah Lynn had rolled to face Mary and the girls' boobs were pressed tightly together as they kissed and their fingers worked their pussies. That caused a gentle rocking against my cock and I joined in. It was active and I was thinking I might slip down far enough to slide into our lover. Everything seemed to be well-lubed and I was gliding between her cheeks. I wasn't sure I'd have time to penetrate, though, as I was getting incredibly close to an explosion. We were all going to need a shower soon.

Whether it was me going too deep or Mary thrusting too high, the tip of my cock caught and wedged in her asshole. She gasped and clamped down. That triggered it, but she'd pinched the head of my cock and the passage was so tight it was almost painful to spray the pressurized contents of my balls into the little opening. Both girls screamed and there was a fluttering of her asshole that resulted in another strong spurt before she pulled away.

"Oh, God! I'm more than willing to fuck you, Jett, but don't go in there! At least, don't go any farther in there. That was pretty intense. Wow!"

"Did he pop your anus?" Sarah Lynn cried. "Jett!"

"It was an accident. And I didn't really go inside. You have powerful butt muscles, Mary."

"Yeah. Well, that was… intense. I guess I said that, but it was so… intense."

"What happened?" Sarah Lynn asked.

"You know how when a guy comes in you, sometimes you can feel his cock pulsing at your vaginal opening and rarely you think you can feel his come in your cootch. For me, anyway, I'm usually too far gone in my own orgasm to be aware of what he's spraying. That's why I enjoy giving a blowjob now and then. There's something about being able to actually feel the pulses and spurts in your mouth. This was a lot like that. He shot his load through the most sensitive part of my asshole and it was just intense. I could feel every spurt entering my body. And now my body is thinking it has to eject what entered through the exit. But it was… wow!"

"Come on. We'll grab a quick shower and make sure you're cleaned out before the other girls hit the bathroom. Jett can go downstairs. Maybe after your shower you could make some bacon. Could you, honey?" Sarah Lynn asked as she kissed me and moved my new girlfriend toward the upstairs bath. I had to laugh, Sarah Lynn said she'd even give up men to have Mary. I didn't think that would be necessary.

"Yeah. If bacon is what my lovers want, bacon they shall have. I suppose I'd better make enough for everyone."

"You know how that smell wakes everyone up!"

· · · · · · · · · · · · · · · · · · · ·

THE ONLY PERSON in the house who wasn't excited about bacon was Char. And it wasn't that she was vegetarian. Her father had blatantly abandoned everything Hindu except the idea that he could sell off his daughter, apparently. So, she was raised in a meat-eating household. With her own renewed interest in the religion, she was evaluating what she ate and we'd talked about the humane killing of food when I went to the slaughterhouse. So, there was nothing specific that she felt banned her from eating bacon, but she just didn't like pigs. Different strokes for different folks.

I sat with Char Wednesday evening and showed her some of the sketches I'd done of unleashing her monster. She got very excited over the ones that were more monster-like and less animal-like. I'd started out thinking I'd do a snarling wolf or something like that. She liked the ones that were truly otherworldly.

"And blood," she said. "I should show the spirit of Kali. She's the destroyer of evil forces and is often pictured with a bloody head in one of her hands and her tongue hanging out. She is the dark one." I was getting a bit of education about Hinduism as Char explored further. I wasn't really sure how much faith she put in the various gods. She certainly wasn't following a specific doctrine. But she'd made a little shrine to Shiva on one corner of the buffet in the dining room and had a batik of Ganesha for a window blind in the bathroom. No one seemed to mind when these little touches showed up. Kali wasn't a stretch.

I remembered Char talking about eating her father's organs in her dark fantasy and it reminded me of a phrase in *Medea* that I'd nearly passed up. Of course, I had to re-read the whole damn play before I found it. Fortunately, that only takes an hour or less. I found the quote the next morning and checked with Merck after class to see what he thought.

265

"In many ways, that summarizes exactly what Euripides was trying to get across. Women were—still are—a little frightening. Sure, a man took pleasure from mating, but a woman created life inside herself, raised it, and nurtured it. That's why Medea says, 'I would rather take sword and shield into battle three times over than give birth to one child.' Euripides paints a picture here and in *The Bacchae* of women who are the frightening monsters of men's nightmares. Go with it."

My sketches took on a bloodier aspect as the monster I would paint held a bloody heart in its maw.

•◦•✧ ⟫C ☽ C⟪ ✦•◦•

FRIDAY AFTERNOON WOULD be when we started the painting. I was taking the weekend off work to do the three massive projects. I didn't know how long it was going to take me to paint Char. She'd agreed—requested—demanded—to have me use the permanent body paints except on her face. That meant we didn't have to complete everything in one sitting. I had no objections at all to having Char naked with me for a few days.

Jas took on the responsibility of making sure the canvas was prepared, so to speak. She bathed Charmaine and shaved her bare below the neck. Char usually trimmed her bush enough to wear sexy panties or a swim suit but seeing her pussy completely bald was breathtaking. Her legs were smooth and silky. And when I managed to tear my eyes away from her snatch, I discovered that she'd plucked her eyebrows bare as well. On the other hand, her hair hung below her shoulders and was puffed out to form a black halo around her face.

I had prepared a more literal canvas, blocking out the general area where the monster would emerge from the darkness of the goddess. In the Athena project, Eva had seemed to simply step off the canvas. This time I intended that the monster emerging from Char would interact with the monster on the canvas, a sort of mirror image. Char joined me and we started working. All we managed to get done before Ariel's stir-fry dinner was generally blocking in the background fields.

Mary was working in another corner of the studio. She'd set her still life up again and was focused on adding detail to her drawing. I wouldn't even get started on mine until Sunday. I surreptitiously glanced over to see if she was getting herself off while drawing, but she was wearing a full bodystocking that had no crotch openings. Those things had to be a real pain when she needed the bathroom.

After dinner, we worked for another two hours. The face of the monster was beginning to emerge on Char's chest. I slept with her that night, not even cognizant of where Mary slept. Char pressed her ass against my cock until I was buried inside and we attempted to sleep that way. It didn't work. Neither of us could hold still when we were connected like that and she cried out an orgasm as I flooded her dark passage. We tried to stay connected after, but as soon as we stopped moving and started to fade toward sleep, I softened and fell out. In the morning, Char got me plugged back in for another round. Usually, her ass could only take one drilling about every week or ten days.

"As often as we can this weekend," she whispered. "I want to feel the connection. Your hands will paint the monster on my body. Your cock will fill me with the monster inside."

And Saturday, the monster took shape.

•๐•๖ ⟅⟆ ☼ ⟅⟆ ๖•๐•

EVERYONE SEEMED TO agree that this was Char's weekend. Even when Eva came over to run the video camera while Kelly was at work, she didn't attempt to take any focus off Char.

"If you fuck him in that paint, he might not survive," she whispered to Char.

"We each have our own expression of desire and intent," Char said. "Jett found yours and revealed it in Athena. He's found mine in the monster. This might just be what I need to purge it from my soul."

And I fucked her ass again that night. Twice.

•๐•๖ ⟅⟆ ☼ ⟅⟆ ๖•๐•

SUNDAY MORNING, THE painting on Char was finished but I had a lot of work yet to go on the canvas. Unfortunately, I had other projects to work on and I needed to put a slab of meat on the table for my drawing project. I had fresh vegetables for the arrangement and had polished the kettle, the marble cutting board, and my knives. In my experimenting, I discovered that a slightly higher angle worked well, as if painted from the perspective of the chef leaning over the counter to prepare the stew. That meant I could have liquid in the kettle which gave both additional reflection and distortion to the cut potatoes and carrots I put in the kettle to start.

It took about two minutes for the meat I cut to bleed onto the marble. It was important to me to capture the difference in tone of the different reflections I was composing. Broth in the pot reflected differently than blood on the marble which was different than the steel of my cleaver.

To complicate matters, the heat went off as soon as the temperature outside reached our first frost. Of course, no one was coming out on Sunday to check the furnace. We all had sweatshirts and long pants on. Char was most upset since she hadn't put clothes on at all after the paint dried. When it got too cold for her to run around naked, she dressed in a beautiful outfit her mother sent her. It had baggy harem pants and a mid-thigh tunic in a colorful fabric. She said it was called a *Patiala salwar* suit. It was sexy as hell.

I still had my cutting glove on and was moving pieces of meat around with the tip of my cleaver when someone started pounding on the front door. It didn't sound friendly. I headed out of the studio as Kelly came charging in, dressed for work. She grabbed the video camera we'd been using to record Charmaine's body art and followed me to the door with it running.

I opened the front door and a large dark man, obviously Indian, practically knocked me over as he charged in. He was followed by two younger men. *Shit! This could only be Char's father and brothers.*

"Rajani! I've had enough. Where are you?"

He started into the house and I braced myself to block him. One of the younger guys pulled a knife and waved it at me to get out of the way.

I'm not a really physical guy. I'm in good shape from tossing around animal carcasses at work, but I'm sure not a fighter. I'm a meat cutter. And I know about knives.

The guy was not prepared for me to reach out and grab his knife by the blade, twist, and break it off. Cheap Chinese steel. Buy American, dude. Of course, if I didn't have my cutting glove on, that little move would have put me in the hospital with a whole bunch of stitches and nerve damage in my hand. Like the other guy. Seeing his partner disarmed, younger guy number two—I assumed they were Charmaine's brothers—drew a knife as well. Before he got the blade all the way open, I stuck the broken blade clutched in my gloved hand through the back of his knife hand. His knife fell to the floor.

"Get out of our way," bellowed Char's father. "I want my daughter and I want her now."

"Go to hell!" Charmaine yelled as she pounded down the stairs and into the living room. "I'm not going anywhere with you."

"You're my daughter and you'll do what I say!" He lunged past me and grabbed hold of the sleeve of her tunic. Char jerked away from him so fiercely that the sleeve ripped right off.

"Aahh! You want to rip my clothes off, you foul dirty man? Let me help you!" I think they call it hysterical strength. Char grabbed the neck of her tunic and ripped it down the front. She tore it off and Mr. Gupta fell back a step. Her brothers gasped. I swear the monster on her chest came to life. "I am not your daughter! I am my mother's vengeance on a pitiful greedy little thief. I will never submit to you. Think how you'd explain the dead body of the husband you sold me to. Think how you'd explain the hanging remains of your sons who never learned to stand up to you for anything decent. And think how you'd beg of me to finish killing you as I devour your liver in front of your eyes. Come near me or my family again and I will kill you!"

Her chest was heaving as Char worked herself up in a rage. Mr. Gupta was fixated on her chest.

"Tattoo! Rakshasa! You have become a demon!" He backed away, pushing his sons toward the door. He just kept pointing at her and gibbering.

"Tell me, how does it feel with my teeth in your heart!" she screamed. "I am coming for what is mine. I will sever the head from the body that opposes me. Flee for your life, old man! I am coming for you!"

Char's father and brothers fled. I thought for a moment that she'd actually chase them. She took two steps toward the door and then collapsed on her knees. We swarmed around to give her support as she continued to scream through the open door at the retreating figures of her father and brothers.

It took a few minutes to get things settled down. Char stood up and pushed the *Punjabi* trousers off her hips. They fell to the ground and she stepped out of them before she turned and grabbed my head to drag me down for a kiss that sucked the air out of my lungs.

"Take me to bed and fuck me. Now, Jett! I'm through preserving the virgin out of fear of my father."

"Char…"

"I don't owe you anything anymore! I've slain my own monster. Now fuck me!"

⁘ ⇨ ⅅℂ ☼ ⅅℂ ⇦ ⁘

Eva had warned Char in jest that if she fucked me with this paint on, I might not survive. I was a little concerned about that myself.

The painting started on Char's pussy lips. I suppose it's a cliché, but sex is the seat of a woman's power. Most men—and some other women— will do anything for the gift that lies between a woman's legs. And it is the home of the miracle of life. The seed goes in that hole and the fruit of the woman's labor comes out of it. A child. We are fascinated by it, thrilled by it, turned on by it, and frightened of it. No other thing in the universe can so completely cripple a man to its service.

So, the smoke arises in gray wisps from the lips of her temple. Wisps float randomly to curl around her sides, but before the gray smoke reaches her navel, scaly legs emerge—a kind of Lamia, the child-eating monster of Greek mythology. The monster was inside, painted with a degree of transparency in the lower section so it looked like it was near the surface of her skin. But, of course, the real focus was between her breasts where the head of the monster broke through her skin with her heart in its mouth and blood dripping from the wound. I'd abandoned the idea of an animal like a wolf emerging. This had humanoid features distorted into a mask of rage with fangs in the meat of the heart and eyes that bugged out of a sloping forehead. The words Char had thrown at her father were the quote from *Medea* when she flaunts the dead children at Jason. "Tell me, how does it feel with my teeth in your heart!"

Let's just say that it was a frightening, ugly, beautiful piece of art. And when Char descended on me, it looked like I would be devoured.

She was passionate. Dominant. Demanding. Loving. When she lined herself up over my straining penis and slammed down, I bent before breaking through an incredibly rigid barrier. Blood flowed from our joining like the tears from our eyes. I tried to move and adjust myself so I wasn't causing so much pain, but Char held me tightly forcing me deeper still.

We both had to overcome the pain. Char's hymen was thick and tough. Breaking it had hurt both of us. While we lay there recovering, we began to kiss and the kissing got other parts moving. Before long, we were thrusting and picking up speed. The muscular inside of Char's vagina grabbed at my cock and molded to its shape, holding me snugly as I pulled out and pushed back in. Before long, joy had replaced the pain as we pounded our sex together and mounted to a pinnacle of lust that swept us into oblivion.

I woke with Char's weight fully on top of me. Char isn't fat, but she's a big girl. It's not like waking up with Ariel or Kelly on me. I couldn't bear to push her away, so I rolled until we were side-by-side and my cock slipped from her folds. She opened her eyes with a drawn-out moan.

"I said that if my pussy felt better than having you fuck my ass, I might die. I did."

"Me, too. But we lived through it. That was incredible, Char. I love you."

She pulled at me and continued to roll until I was on top of her.

"Kill me again, Jett. Kill me again."

30
Midterm Break

WHEN CHAR and I ran for the bedroom after the confrontation with her father, Jas and Sarah Lynn looked at the bloody meat in my studio in disgust. They determined—correctly—that I would not get back to painting that still life before the meat was spoiled and the blood dried all over everything, so they did the practical thing and turned my composition into beef stew. We ate it for dinner that night. I would need to go to the store and get all new produce and meat for the still life in the morning and start over.

Worth spending Sunday loving and fucking the monster Char? You bet.

Kelly got home mid-afternoon, much to our surprise.

"You're home early," Ariel said. "Is everything all right, honey?"

"I quit," Kelly snapped back. "I have to edit that video! I've been thinking about it all day. That was one of the most awesome things I've ever seen." She ran up to Char, cuddled up next to me on the sofa where we were taking a break, and kissed her. "You are my idol! I want to worship you from the wisps of smoke at your pussy lips to the maw of the beast emerging with your heart. You are incredible!"

"Kelly, don't you need your job?" Jas asked. "Can you afford to just quit it?"

"In three nights a week online, I make twice what I can earn at the store in a weekend. If I add a weekend performance instead of going to the store, I'll make up the difference in no time."

"You're doing so well, Kelly," Char said. "You are the kind of woman I want to be."

"You are your own woman, baby. I love you. But right now, I have to go edit that video!" She took off. Char and I finished our snack and went back to bed.

•·◦··◦·⇨ ☽☽ ☼ ☽☽ ⇦·◦··◦·•

Monday, I got all my props together and drew my still life. This turned out to be an expensive drawing. But the result seemed okay to me. Mary came over around noon to work on her drawing and we had a great conversation while we were completing details. While I was battling demons on Sunday, Mary had taken Eva to see another art film at the Pyramid Theater. It was about two boys who were friends in the Middle East but grew up in different religions. Sounded intense.

"So, will you go with me next week?" she said. "The preview looked incredibly sexy. It's in Chinese. The wealthy young man seduces the beautiful seamstress and makes her his mistress. She has a life of luxury and pleasure until the man's father shows up with a bride he's selected for the man. Of course, once the guy is married, he can't keep his mistress any longer and no one will have anything to do with her."

"Yeah. That sounds real sexy," I moaned.

"Trust me. I want to see it with you, not Eva."

I guess my drawing was adequate. After the emotional intensity of Sunday, I found it difficult to focus on the reflections. I was just too drained. My wallpaper pattern, however, had turned into a simple masterpiece. I drew cartoonish cows grazing in a field. They were as large as I could support with the size of my tiles and had a simple half-tile drop to the pattern repeat. It wasn't complex, but it covered all the fundamentals required for our 2D final. I liked it well enough I thought of painting my one blank studio wall with the pattern.

Tuesday evening, we all gathered after dinner for the premiere of the video Kelly edited for my Literature and the Arts project. *Wow!* She time-lapsed the painting so you could see the monster as if it truly emerged from her chest. It was beautiful and terrifying. But then the scene cut to her father bursting in. Kelly had managed to artfully cut my brief knife battle. She focused on Char's confrontation. She'd been all but unnoticed as she filmed and slipped around so she was shooting almost over Mr.

Gupta's shoulder as he grabbed Char's sleeve and tore it off. When Char ripped off the rest of the tunic, we all gasped involuntarily. I understood how her father had assumed it was a tattoo. The paint rippled with her skin. The bounce of her breasts sort of made the mouth look like it was chewing. When Mr. Gupta turned to leave, there was a genuine look of terror on his face. And Kelly zoomed in on the face of the monster as Char called out, "How does it feel with my teeth in your heart?" And that's where the image froze.

"Yes!" Char yelled as she stood and pumped her fist in the air. Her bouncing breasts highlighted the vision we'd just seen on the screen. Once we had heat in the house again, she had refused to wear any clothes when she was home. Every one of the girls had bent her head to worship between her legs.

I took the project to class with me on Wednesday and Merck wanted to run the video before I even left after class. He was practically jumping up and down when he saw it.

"How did you get players to act so realistically?" he demanded. "It captures the entire spirit of the wronged woman and the broken man."

"They aren't players. That was her father and brothers trying to take her to force her into a marriage," I said.

"Jesus! That man will never bother her again. I want to play the whole tape for the class tomorrow. Will you agree?" Char had already given permission, so I agreed. I was getting a rock-solid A in this class. I needed to take Kelly to bed tonight. Her video editing was making my projects come to life.

•○•⇨ ⅠⅠⅭ ☽ ⅠⅠⅭ ⇦•○•

When I got home, I could smell Char's Wednesday night curry. *Yum!* I stepped into the kitchen and wrapped my arms around her as I nuzzled her neck. She was, of course, naked. I squeezed up against her bare butt.

"You can still fuck me there, even though you have my pussy now, too," she said as she leaned her head back against my shoulder and rubbed her cheek against my neck.

"Oh, yes, my love," I whispered. "In fact, now that I have all of you, I'm thinking when we take the paint off, we should plan a trip around the world."

"You have all of me. But tonight, I have a date with Ariel. I promised to help her with her math. I think she just wants to show me how many orgasms she can count up to."

"I bet after three she loses track," I laughed.

Our doorbell rang and I left her in the kitchen so I could answer the front door. There was a UPS guy on our porch with a cart full of boxes.

"I have a delivery for Rajani Charmaine Gupta," he said. "I need a signature here."

"Does it have to be hers?" I asked.

"I don't care whose. As long as someone takes delivery." The guy was completely bored with his job. I signed the electronic receipt and he took off. He didn't offer to move the boxes from the porch into the house. Six boxes and an envelope. And they weren't light.

"Char!" I called. "There's a delivery here for you. Did you order something?"

She came out of the kitchen like she was still floating on the cloud emanating from her pussy. The monster was looking sexier every day. We'd have to remove it this weekend, or maybe Monday after I got home from work. I could see that some of the smoke paint had been rubbed off her pussy from repeated contact.

"What's all this?" she asked. I handed her the envelope and she tore the stiff tab from it. Inside was a letter and she read it out loud as I listened.

> *Rajani,*
>
> *Don't hurt your brothers! Please! I have left them with the house and enough to live on for a year. I do the same for you. Enclosed you will find a check for $5,000 that your mother sent to you. A second check for $10,000 matches what I have given your brothers.*
>
> *I packed everything from your room that would fit in boxes. All your possessions. If you want any of your furniture, the boys have been instructed to help you move it. Please don't hurt them!*
>
> *I have returned to India to try to make things right with your mother. May Shiva add a blessing to our meeting. Please do not follow me. I wish you no harm. I will not return to bother you again.*
> *Ranjit Gupta*
> *Once your father*

She shook out the envelope and two checks fell into her hands. She just stared at them. *Shit! What's the right response to a woman when her father has just fled the country in fear of her?* I wasn't sure what to do. She solved my dilemma by lifting her lips and kissing me softly.

"I can pay you back now."

THERE WERE ONLY nine of us left in Blankety's class on Thursday when we put our drawings on our easels and waited for his scathing remarks. Mary took my hand and we started breathing together.

"It's out of balance. These items need to be shifted to the right. Or you could change your perspective slightly and get a better view of the cup." Wow! That was almost instructive! I glanced over at the girl he'd commented on and she looked relieved.

"I sincerely hope you take better care of your clothes than this pile of laundry shows! Photographers can take a thousand photos of random collections and expect to get one that will make them famous. You can't afford to do that. You need to actually stage your composition and not depend on random chances." Well, he was still being critical, but there were actual hints of helpfulness. I noticed I was the only male remaining in the class. Less than half the students we started the semester with.

"Learn from classic art but don't try to replicate it! You will never paint the same bowl of fruit as Cézanne. Ask yourself what made this still life famous in the first place? That is what you should try to replicate, not the exact position of each piece of fruit."

"Bloody!" he said over my shoulder. "Are you a serial killer?" I couldn't help myself. I laughed. So did Mary. "I fail to see the humor in that. You must have an unusual kitchen. The background looks suspiciously like drapes. You are so focused on this tiny detail of reflection that you've missed the setting. Open your eyes further and capture the scene, not just the detail."

Shit! He's absolutely right. After all the work I'd done to capture the depth and reflection in the blood, the knife blades, the kettle, I'd pretty much run out of time and blanked in the background so my objects looked suspended in space. And he zeroed right in on it. He'd moved on to Mary's drawing. Her hand gripped mine tightly.

"I'd never have thought this of you. Surprise is good." He looked over at my drawing again and then back at Mary's, bumping into our joined hands. He sighed. "It is okay to be influenced by each other if you are influenced by the strengths instead of the weaknesses. If you are going to draw with your hands held, you must be critical of the other's work. This…" he pointed at the reflection in the computer monitor, "…is not your style. While this…" pointing at the detail in the lace panties "…very much is. The composition, however, is balanced, has good contrasts, and leads the eye on a constant pattern of exploration. You pass."

We all sat in semi-shocked silence. Did that statement mean none of the rest of us passed? He'd warned us that most would fail. But all of us but Mary?

•◦•✦))C ☼))C ✦◦•

"Hey, you two," Eva said as we came out of Blankety's class. "You survived the first half of the semester. How'd it go?"

"I think I hate him more now than the first time he blew his damned whistle," I moaned.

"I'm not all that fond of him either," Mary said. "It was like he was intentionally using me to shame the class. Now everyone hates me, too."

"Can I have this hand?" Eva asked, nudging my left hand. The right was still in Mary's. I shifted my backpack slightly and took her hand. "You'll never like Blankety, but he'll make you a better artist."

"There are fewer than half of us left that started the class," I said. "I really feel bad for those who dropped out."

"Those who got out early probably shifted to another unit. It's a required course for Studio Arts majors and the work from that class will be one of the first things reviewed when you apply to switch to a BFA. But not all the instructors are as abrasive as Blankety."

"I have to admit I'm learning things."

"What are you doing over break?"

"Break?"

"Classes don't resume until Wednesday. This is our fall mid-semester break," Eva said brightly. I groaned. I'd taken last weekend off work so

277

I could complete my projects. That meant that Saturday, Sunday, and Monday, I'd be in the grocery store for eight hours a day.

"I guess I have Tuesday off then," I moaned.

"Why don't we have a little party tomorrow night?"

"I could run it by the girls."

"I already did," Eva laughed. "We only need you and Mary to agree." Mary squeezed my hand. "I'm in."

"Well, there you have it," I said. "All the women in my life want to have a party. I guess we're having a party."

"Don't be a sourpuss, Jett. I promise we'll have fun," Mary whispered. *Mmm. Fun with Mary. I could live with that.*

⋯∘⟢ ⟅⟆ ⟡ ⟅⟆ ⟣∘⋯

I GOT HOME from a tough morning at the slaughterhouse. Even though I'd had my last class of the semester at the university, my Friday Farm to Table course was still the next day. There was no break from that. And this Friday, we had each been instructed on exactly how to use the stunning bolt and pull the trigger. Over the course of the morning, I'd killed three steers. Each steer we were responsible for, we followed through the bleeding, skinning, and sectioning phase. The only thing that kept me balanced was Blankety's comment about me being a serial killer. I was thinking maybe I should take him a package of steaks for our next class.

When I got home, I smelled something strange. It sure wasn't Ariel preparing Friday night stir-fry.

"What is that?"

"Fun and games," Eva answered. She, Ariel, and Char were stirring bowls of colored glop.

"Guess what!" Char said, bouncing over to me. "I got a new job!"

"You did? That's great! What and where?" I hugged the naked girl to me. Her paint was significantly worn and I'd promised that when I got home, I'd remove it.

"I saw a posting for a ten-hour-a-week bookkeeping job and they hired me on the spot. I quit Applebee's!"

"Is that going to be enough?"

"With the money I got from my parents, I'm good. It's such a relief." She was rubbing up against me and I could feel her heat right through my white canvas butcher clothes. "Would you like some relief? I was just helping out until you got home."

"Let's go. I owe you a good scrubbing."

Char already had the materials laid out, including towels covering my bed. Of course, I couldn't start working on her until I was out of my clothes.

"The instructions say you have to give me a thorough massage and eat me out first," Char said.

"The instructions said that?"

"Well, they didn't have the 'eat me out' part in them, but I figured if you were rubbing vegetable oil all over my tits and pussy, you could just add that part without any strain."

Yes, indeed I could.

It took about three hours to go through all the stages of getting the paint off her body, including oiling her paint, scrubbing it with shampoo, showering, and then cleaning her off with alcohol. By that time, Sarah Lynn was home from her last final and stripped to join us on the bed. Char immediately moved her to the center and began oiling her body.

"Oh! What are you doing?" Sarah Lynn squealed as the oil dripped onto her breasts.

"Giving you a little of the treatment Jett just gave me," Char laughed, moving up to kiss our girlfriend.

"You're getting me all slippery."

"Yeah. Now I'm going to use you as my own slip-and-slide." Char mounted Sarah Lynn and began sliding her whole body up and down. It looked like fun, but it was obvious that the scene had shifted and I wasn't needed to help with their little after-finals relaxation.

I wandered downstairs to find out what the mystery goop was that the girls were working on. I could hear Kelly's laugh from the kitchen and saw Jas in the living room struggling to move furniture back against the walls.

"Let me help," I said, running to the end of the sofa.

"Oh, God! Thank you," she said. We got the sofa off to the wall and Jas rushed into my arms to kiss me. "Yum! You still taste like Char."

"Or vegetable oil. I suppose I should go take another shower."

"Oh, we'll all be getting showers soon enough," she said. That was cryptic. The front door opened and Mary came in with a large bundle in her arms. I ran over to take it from her and gave her a little welcome kiss.

"I got it," she sighed. Then she looked me over. "Getting prepared already?" she asked. I realized I hadn't dressed before coming downstairs and between Jasmine's kiss and Mary's, I was at a little more than half-mast. Mary didn't hesitate, though. While I held the heavy bundle she'd given me, she reached down and stroked my cock up to full rigidity while she kissed me again. Then she bent over and kissed the head of my cock. "Looks like we're ready to party now."

"Um… what am I holding in my arms instead of you?"

"The drop cloth. There isn't room in the studio for all eight of us, so we needed a cover big enough for the whole living room."

"We're going to paint?"

"You started something, Jett. Now everyone wants body paint. And we all want to paint you," Jas said. She helped me get the bundle of canvas out and we spread it over the whole living room floor. It was bigger than the room and ran up and over some of the furniture.

"How big is this?" I asked.

"The biggest they had," Mary said. "Twelve by twenty-four. I figured we could always use a big piece of canvas. Especially, since I know you are still planning the super performance piece with Eva. Any idea when you'll do that one?"

I turned to look at Mary and found that she was as naked as Jas and me. *Oh, shit!* My erection became painful. I stepped over to her and tentatively held out my arms. She was shaking slightly but immediately folded herself against me. The kiss we shared this time was destined to carry us to bed as she ground her pussy against my stiff cock. I could feel the bar through her clit hood rubbing up and down my cock. I felt another pair of arms reach around me and found Jas up against Mary's back, squeezing her between us.

"God! That feels good!" Mary sighed. "Sometime tonight, Jett—if it's okay with the others—I want to feel this moving inside me."

"At the rate you're going, it won't wait till tonight," Jas giggled. "If you want, lie down in the middle of the floor and christen the new drop cloth. I'll help."

"Mmm. As tempting as that is, I'd like the first time to be in bed. I wouldn't mind your help, though, Jas." Mary twisted in our arms until she was facing Jas and my cock was snuggled between her nether cheeks. The two girls shared a deep kiss that kept me sliding up and down that luscious crack.

The doorbell rang.

"Pizza's here!" Jas called out. "Does anyone still have clothes on?"

Eva came out of the kitchen. She wasn't wearing much, but it was more than anyone else.

"Damn! Late to my own party," she said. "Is the delivery boy cute?" She went to the door in her bra and panties to accept the pizza delivery. "Do you need any more tip than this?" she asked the delivery boy while pulling off her bra. We heard a garbled reply and then she came in and Eva closed the door. She was flushed… and topless.

"I bet that was the thrill of his life," Jas laughed.

"Her," Eva squeaked. "And she just had to reach out and pinch my nipples."

"Let's eat so we can play," Kelly said as she brought soft drinks into the living room. Eva stripped off her panties and flung them in a corner with her bra. Ariel brought bags of chips from the kitchen while Char and Sarah Lynn came downstairs with their hair still wet from the shower. I looked around at the seven naked girls sitting with me munching on pizza. There was no chance that I was ever going to soften tonight.

I'm a pig but couldn't help but wonder if I could dip my dick in all seven twats tonight. And then die happy.

•·•◆ ⅅⅭ ☼ ⅅⅭ ◆•·•

"SHOULD JETT GO first or should we save him for a happy ending?" Ariel asked when we'd cleared away the boxes and cans.

"Um… What are we doing?"

"Body paints!" Eva said. "I can't believe none of your mothers ever let you do this! Of course, I had to call my mother and get the recipe." She had a glass bowl of red paint in one hand and blue paint in the other. Ariel and Kelly held green, orange, yellow, and purple. All the primaries and secondaries.

"Wow! You all really want to go through the process of cleaning all that paint off?"

"Jett! These are kindergarten paints. They're made with baby shampoo, cornstarch, and food coloring, mostly. So, when we've had fun painting each other, all we have to do is shower!"

"I can't believe my mother didn't use this trick to get me to shower more often!" I said. "What do we use for brushes?"

"These are finger paints," Mary said.

Holy fuck!

We played. It started with a little face painting. Fingers just aren't made for doing fine designs like butterflies, so my insect ended up looking like a multicolored blob on Ariel's cheek. Spirals seemed to dominate the early designs we tried. Eva managed a reasonable representation of Indian warpaint on Sarah Lynn's face. Jas cheated and wore a thick coating of lipstick that she used to leave lip prints all over Mary's face and then had enough left to plant at least one kiss on each of us, though not all on faces.

I couldn't see the print she left on my butt.

And then it was a free-for-all. We attacked each other, ganged up on each other, and played intimately with each other. I heard Kelly whine out the first orgasm and saw Eva with her fingers in the fire crotch.

Char started spitting in front of Mary.

"Oooh! Don't lick after you've painted! It's nasty."

"Are you saying my pussy is nasty?" Mary laughed.

"No! The shampoo. I'm just going to have to use my fingers to play with this little toy you have between your lips instead of my teeth." Mary gasped as she lay back and Char manipulated her piercing and drove two fingers into her.

"My pussy hasn't been painted yet, Jett," Eva said. "I don't think it would taste nasty."

"Do you want me to paint it or lick it?" I asked.

"Yes."

There was no question about the order of those activities. Eva lay back and spread her legs so I had easy access to her juicy and tasty slit. I wiped my hands on a damp towel so I could play with her pussy while I sucked it. I'd run my fingers through her channel when we were painting her Athena, but as suggestive as Eva always was, we hadn't really been intimate.

I couldn't call licking her to orgasm anything less than intimate. It was almost supernatural. Eva saturated the canvas beneath her butt with love juice when she came. It was so yummy that I didn't stop licking until she'd pumped again. I crawled up her body, smearing the paints on her torso against my own chest. Before long, my cock bumped against the wet lips I'd just licked. Eva looked into my eye pleadingly.

"Not yet, Jett. Please? I want to, but let's save it for when it's just us and special. Please?"

Even when you're right at the gate and ready to take the plunge, when a girl says no, it means no. I lifted myself enough that the tip of my cock came out of her slit and up against her mound. She sighed and pushed so that my cock slid up her wet slit onto her belly.

I came.

31
Of Pain and Pleasure

ASIDE FROM the sex, playing with our body bath paints was giggly fun that made us feel like kindergartners. My cock was kept hard and then striped like a pride flag. Kelly's red hair was plastered together and painted green. Ariel had collected paint on her body by the simple means of rolling around on all of us. The canvas tarp under us was a spattered smeared colorful mess. But the most fun was showering and making sure everyone got clean before bed.

And that's how I ended up pressed against Mary in my little shower cubicle downstairs, washing her hair and making sure every speck of the colored shampoo was rinsed from her beautiful body. And when our faces were clean enough to not get soap in our mouths, we spent most of our washing time kissing. As we rinsed the soap down our bodies, our lips followed, kissing every possible nook and cranny of exposed skin.

We'd come close to climax half a dozen times as I tugged and twisted on her piercings as she directed. She tugged and twisted on my cock in delightful ways. But we didn't push each other over the edge. We got out of the shower and dried ourselves in the cramped little three-quarter bath. And we kept kissing.

"Use the Kat House," Kelly whispered to us at the top of the stairs. She pressed her naked body up against us and kissed each of us passionately before she slipped into my bedroom where it appeared all six of the girls other than Mary were gathered on the big bed. I raised an eyebrow at Mary and she tugged my hand toward the attic stairs.

Kelly had made up the room as a simple bedroom with no elaborate sets. Her props for camming were all neatly stowed. I cross-checked the cameras and her computer and everything was turned off. Mary and I stood in the middle of the room, kissing and caressing each other.

"They're being awfully nice about a strange woman taking you away to have sex," Mary said.

"You're not that strange, Mary. And I think they're all hoping they will have a time with you."

"A couple of them already have," she giggled. "When that little Ariel sets her mind on a pussy, it's almost impossible to distract her."

"I've heard she's the best at cunnilingus in the household. She's just as devoted to fellatio."

"I kind of enjoy that, myself. If you are interested, though, I sort of had a different idea tonight. Make love to me, Jett. I've been obsessing about it."

We lay down on the bed, trying not to let go of each other as we scooted ourselves into position, and trying to not stop kissing. Mostly, we succeeded. We were lying on our sides with our arms wrapped tightly around each other and our bodies pressed together from lips to toes.

"As nice as this is, it isn't the easiest position," Mary said. "Be on top of me so I can feel your weight pressing me down." We rolled and Mary thwarted my natural instinct to support my weight on my arms by holding me close to her. Her legs wrapped around mine, opening her center. I could feel the heat of her sex against my cock and pulled back enough to lodge the tip at her opening. It took a couple tries to get lined up correctly and then I just started sliding into her. Her grip tightened as I penetrated her depths. We held there.

I felt the slight tremors in her body relax and calm, our mouths continuing to devour each other. And then we began to rock together. Locked together the way we were, we could only move our pelvises, exercising lower back and ab muscles to work together. It didn't give us a pounding sensation and we moved only a couple of inches apart and back together. But those couple of inches were the most stimulating I'd ever felt. It was as if all the tremors she had previously had concentrated in her vagina. It was like being wrapped in one of Kelly's vibrators.

I could feel the metal bar at her clit pressed into my pubic bone and shifted left and right a little so it moved with me. Apparently, that was the right move and the stimulation of the bar against her clit brought Mary up and over the peak of a climax that sucked the air out of my lungs. The vibrating, clamping, and fluttering of her vagina around my cock pulled me along with her.

I had to roll us to our sides again so Mary could breathe but I let go of her only enough that I could pull the blankets up around us. When we rolled, she clamped her thighs together, trapping my cock in her.

We both knew that in the course of the night, I would slip out of her. We'd have to shift our arms out from under each other or they'd be numb. We'd stop kissing as we drifted to sleep. We knew all those things, but with the blanket pulled up snugly around us, we ignored them. We breathed each other's air, warmed each other's body, and held each other close.

·०· ०⋟ ꊂ ☽ ꊁ ⟨०· ·०·

CLASSES RESUMED ON Wednesday and we were as lost in the pressure as we had been during the rush to midterms. I'd enjoyed one day off on Tuesday, having had to work Saturday through Monday. Jas had to work, too. Kelly and Charmaine had both quit their day jobs. Kelly did a long online performance Saturday afternoon that had her fans teasing her with a new vibrator she inserted into her vagina. Each time a viewer tipped, the vibrator would turn on for an amount of time determined by the amount tipped. Tipping a token gave her a one-second buzz. Tipping ten tokens gave her a ten-second buzz.

Ariel had no piano students over the break, so she was constantly into mischief. She had sailed through her exams and just wanted to play. Fortunately, Char had blossomed sexually in the past week with her monster paint. She took Ariel firmly in hand and introduced her to anal play. Ariel was in heaven.

Poor Sarah Lynn used the official time off to study. I couldn't believe the size of the book she had to read for Constitutional Law and the Organization of American Government. She did get a break on Monday when the skies cleared and the weather took a jump in temperature. Eva took her to the little airport on the edge of town and they went flying in a two-seater airplane of some kind. I'm not sure what happened up there, but when they got back home Monday, they spent a good bit of the night locked in a sixty-nine and screaming out orgasms.

Mary spent time on Monday giving Jas a long slow massage that left my first girlfriend sated and limp as a noodle.

But, as I said, school.

We found a subtle change in Blankenship's class. He was still as caustic and critical of our drawings as ever but he spent more class time talking about what makes a good drawing. The first half of the semester had all been materials and techniques. The second half seemed to be more focused on composition and art. I wasn't fond of having every drawing I did ridiculed, but I had to admit that I was learning to be a better artist.

Studying Virgil's Rome was a bit of a drag. I don't know if he was just more boring than the earlier writers or if it was just that the *Medea* painting on Char had been so intense that anything would have paled. I managed to convince Sarah Lynn to pose for me by having her lying on her back while I painted Romulus and Remus on the twin hills of her breasts, nurtured by a wolf and overlooking an interesting perspective of Rome that extended just to her slit. Lying on her back, she could still read her textbook. The photography for this piece required careful cropping and I decided not to show Merck the video because to get the right perspective, the camera looked straight up Sarah Lynn's pussy.

I didn't think it was the most successful piece I'd done by a longshot, and Sarah Lynn was happy to get in the shower and scrub the paint off her body. Merck was satisfied, but disappointed that there was no video. Dirty old man.

•◦•◈ ⊃⊂ ☼ ⊃⊂ ◈•◦•

MARY DIDN'T MOVE into our house. She was a frequent visitor and shared her loving with all the girls as well as with me. She had to really psych herself up to be with everyone at the same time, though. One or two of us at a time could make her happy. And we made love together whenever we could. It wasn't always missionary position but Mary really liked to be squeezed. Once she was out of her ever-present bodystocking, she wanted the security of being held tightly. If she was being pressed into the bed by my body weight, that was good. If she was being pressed between me and Kelly or any one of the other girls, she was happy. And lacking either of those, if she had a heavy blanket over her while she rode me, she was good with that.

"Mary, whatever inspired you to get your nipples and clit pierced?" Kelly asked one night while we were lying in bed and she was playing with Mary's nipples. Mary was happily sandwiched between us.

"Frustration," Mary said. "Pain and pleasure are tied together. I'm not into discipline or anything like that, but when I'm at the peak of pleasure, a little pain jolts me into an intense orgasm. I found that out by accident when a guy bit me a little harder than expected during sex. And there's also the point where a little irritation becomes arousing, like what you're doing now. If you keep that up, I'm going to eat you again."

"Maybe Jett would get behind your idea if we sixty-nined. You'd like him behind your idea, wouldn't you?"

Mary growled and swung a leg over Kelly's head, settling her pussy on my redheaded girlfriend's mouth while she drove her own mouth between Kelly's legs. I hadn't seen much of this view of Mary and I liked it. A lot. I got behind her and Kelly positioned my cock at Mary's opening as she licked both of us.

•∘·❖ ❨❩ ☽ ❨❩ ❖·∘•

AND THEN CAME Dante. Merck was all over the poet of Florence and had a thousand slides he showed in class. He talked about how the three-part masterpiece of Dante Alighieri—*Divine Comedy*—was in many ways a metaphor for the city itself. What got me was that even though I didn't much appreciate Virgil's *The Æneid*, Dante used the Roman poet as his guide through the levels of the afterlife.

I don't know if it was Dante's poetry that was so exciting or simply that Merck's excitement was infectious. I had *Inferno* downloaded on my phone and was reading it as I walked between classes, on my break in the grocery store, while I cooked dinner, and before I went to bed.

Not that it was easy reading. I just got caught up in all the Renaissance glory of Firenze and couldn't wait until I could go walk those streets.

"I sometimes wonder about Dante's sex life," Merck said in his lecture on Tuesday of Thanksgiving week. There were no classes for the rest

288

of the week and I had only Blankenship's torture session to go before I was free for a while. Merck was on a tear. Dante's sex life?

"You've read *Inferno* now. Trust me, it is the best of the three parts. *Paradiso* is a yawn. In very little literature is there such joyous description of everlasting damnation as in *Inferno*. It's exciting. When Dante climbs out of the lowest circle of hell where Satan gnaws on Judas and Brutus, you're left with a chill that says, I'd like to go there," he said. "What kind of sick depraved man writes a description of hell that gives you a hard-on?"

The class was laughing as Merck flashed up a few slides of *Il Boccalone*, a gargoyle of a terrified man on the roof of Florence's cathedral.

"The frustration of hell in *Inferno* is that the souls are separated from their bodies. Dante fully believed that even the damned would be resurrected one day and reunited with their souls. Then the damned would have perfect suffering because the body and soul would be together. Note, Canto Six:"

> *"Quanto la cosa è più perfetta,*
> *più sent il bene, e così la doglienza"*
>
> *"As the thing is more perfect,*
> *The more it feels of pleasure and of pain."*

"The idea is that the souls without their bodies are less than perfect. So that even the suffering that they are under is less than the suffering that will be endured after the judgment. Pleasure is more perfect, but conversely suffering is also more perfect."

We had Thanksgiving weekend to complete our projects for Literature and the Arts. I wondered if Mary would cooperate with me. The more perfect a thing is, the more it feels of pleasure and of pain.

•◦•❖ ⊃⊂ ☼ ⊃⊂ ❖•◦•

THANKSGIVING WAS GOING to be a little weird. My family wanted me to come home for the usual gathering of grandparents, parents, and me. Sarah Lynn and Charmaine had no home or family to go to. Ariel's parents expected her to join them on a family trip to Orlando to take her younger brothers to Disney World for the week, despite the fact that she had two days of classes that week. Sondra gently suggested to Jas that maybe we'd like to have the families over to our house for Thanksgiving dinner and she'd gladly come and help cook in our kitchen. Kelly's mom suggested we order a complete Thanksgiving dinner for everyone from the co-op and charge each person a share. That was actually a pretty good idea. None of us were enthused about cooking or going to our homes.

Except Eva. This was the first year that she planned to fly home for a holiday. It would take her most of the day to fly her little plane to Virginia with the number of stops she planned and then a whole day to fly back. She said she wanted to do it over Thanksgiving because the weather became more unpredictable as we got deeper into winter. The forecast for this weekend was good all across the Eastern US. I appreciated her desire to fly, but it was really beyond me. How could you spend a whole day isolated in a little bubble in the sky and not go stir-crazy? I'd have to investigate that more, but not while there was still snow on the ground.

And Mary. She lived the other direction and wasn't planning to go home until Christmas. That suited me just fine! She'd stay with us for the weekend.

We finally negotiated an agreement with the involved relatives. Eva and Ariel would be missing. My folks, Jasmine's mother, and Kelly's mother would chip in for the food and Grandpa would order everything complete from the Deli at the grocery store. Including paper plates, napkins and plasticware. Granddad brought over a couple of long banquet tables and folding chairs from his church on Wednesday afternoon and we spent the day cleaning and preparing for guests.

And it wasn't too bad. Introductions were made, since none of the adults knew Mary. We had to update everyone about Charmaine's father abruptly leaving the country. Of course, we all had to tell about our progress in our first semester of classes and I had to show a couple of my new paintings and drawings. We didn't show any of the photos or videos of me painting Eva, Char, Sarah Lynn, Ariel, or Jas. I just showed the canvas of Athena and my still life drawing.

I noted, however, that Jas took just her mother upstairs and showed her the art video and photo. She told me later that she didn't show the porn film version. Sondra was shocked, but also thought the artwork was stunningly beautiful, especially the final photo composition with Jas sitting like a goddess on the rock by the lake.

Kelly's mother, on the other hand, stayed after most people had left for the day and viewed all the videos, including Jas and me. She gave us detailed critiques, mostly aimed at Kelly, on the theme and direction of the videos and how we could make money off of them. Siobhan is a very sexy woman, like Kelly. She insisted she was officially retired from the industry and had a respectable job but she was an eager consultant and very proud of what Kelly was accomplishing.

We survived having fourteen sit down for dinner, talking to parents, and generally being polite. And we had enough leftovers in the fridge to last us the weekend without cooking.

◦·◦ ◦❖ ⟡ ☾ ⟡ ❖◦ ◦·◦

"So, LET ME get this straight. You want to do a figure painting of me, stretched out naked on a bed," Mary said as she examined my rough sketches. "While Kelly films my naked body, let's not forget. Then you want to move the canvas up against me and paint me, dissolving into the canvas. Ambitious at all?"

"Um… I know it's a lot of work. Mary, I'll happily pay you as my model if that helps. But the whole line about perfection enhancing pleasure and pain… You're perfect."

Mary reached out and took my hand. She tugged at me and I followed her to the front door where we put on our coats and boots and went out for a walk. It was pretty cold and we walked close together just holding hands in silence for a while. When we got to the main cross-street, we turned and headed toward downtown, looking at the newly lit Christmas decorations. There was a big tree lit up in front of the courthouse and, in defiance of political correctness, a nativity scene. We stopped there and Mary turned to offer me her lips in a long deep kiss.

"I don't know what our relationship is, Jett," she sighed. "Are we just fuck buddies? Am I a girlfriend? I know I can't be your one and only. I would never want to break up the house. Everyone has accepted me as one of you. In fact, every single one has tasted me and I've tasted her. I like it. I'd have never thought that I could be so comfortable with so many people around, but even meeting your families today didn't freak me out too much. But just lying there, exposing myself… It's going to take something a lot more intimate than money to pay me for that, Jett. Someone's going to have to keep me from freaking out and moving to a different state."

"Mary, I don't want to put you under that kind of stress. I can ban everyone from the studio, including Kelly, while we paint. Or I can get a different model or scrap the project altogether and do something else. I don't want you to feel that I'm pressuring you to do something you don't want to. I can't help it, though, that I think you are the most beautiful woman I've ever met and I want to paint you."

"My suffering will be a pleasure if you love me a little."

⋯∘⋗ ⅠⅠⅭ ☽ ⅠⅠⅭ ⋖∘⋯

THE REMAINDER OF the weekend was intense. The first thing we realized was that the studio was too small. We got out our living room sized tarp and spread it right over the top of the sofa. I didn't want the furniture well-defined in my setting. It was only there because I couldn't float my model in space. I made sure there were adequate pillows that Mary would be comfortable and could get back into the pose easily.

And then there was keeping Mary calm. My precious roommates jumped in to help. Whether it was just sitting beside her and chatting or getting between her legs and licking, by noon on Saturday I had a painting that I considered respectable. I could work on smoothing out details without Mary actually being there posing. I'd captured the perfect expression on her face while she was coming with Sarah Lynn between her legs.

As soon as the portraiture part of the project was done and we needed to let it dry for an hour before I started the body paint, Mary dragged me to the bedroom and attacked. I've been ridden hard by my girlfriends before, but this was a new experience with Mary. The inside of her vagina… well, it's different than the other girls. It's squishy and hugs my cock like Mary's bodystockings hug her form. When I pull back, it sucks at me and tries to hold me in. And when I come, I can feel her entire body vibrate through my cock. There's just nothing like it in my experience.

When we'd sated each other and I'd held Mary tightly to me, we were finally ready to start the body paint and dissolving background. Mary opted for permanent body paint like Char had anyplace from her shoulders down. I thanked her profusely. I knew this was going to take more than one day and sleeping in the temporary paint—even as careful as Eva had been—guaranteed a lot of touch up the next day. I offered to put off doing her upraised arm and hand until the second day for temporary paint, but she said she didn't mind showing the permanent paint on her hands.

I positioned the canvas behind her and posed her so she completely covered the figure behind her. Airbrush and blending were all we got done in the first two sittings. This time, I wasn't as concerned about blending the canvas as I was about blending Mary. I wasn't trying to conceal her gorgeous body. I wanted her perfect breasts exposed with her piercings. I wanted her eyes bright and visible. I could even see the glint of light reflected from her clit piercing. But rather than a contrast between her body and the canvas, I needed to make her edges disappear. It took a long time, but when that part was done, her hip, thigh, hand, and shoulder disappeared into the canvas.

We spent all day Sunday as I did the patterns of her flesh breaking into dust and floating away.

And all Sunday night, we made love.

32
Sex Doll

HAVING HAD Thanksgiving weekend off work, I still had to be back on Monday morning. I had progressed far enough in my training that I could open the meat department by myself. Most of the early morning work was stocking the coolers and making sure meat was tagged with special sale prices if it had been on display in a cooler for more than 48 hours. After a holiday weekend, there was little left in the coolers and I needed to move a lot of previously frozen meat out of the meat locker into the refrigerated cases.

After the coolers were stocked, I went to work on fresh cuts. I had a dozen chickens to cut, pork loin to turn into chops, and Choice beef to make steaks, roasts, and filets out of.

The time all seemed to blend together as I cut and sliced.

"Aren't you about ready to go home?" Grandpa asked. I hadn't even noticed he was there until he spoke. I was butterflying some thick pork chops to be stuffed this afternoon as shoppers came by to pick up dinner items.

"Home? What time is it?"

"Almost two o'clock."

"I've been here… Have I been the only one in the meat department today?"

"You got the entire Thanksgiving weekend off. I needed to give others some comp time."

"Alone? You let me do this alone?"

"And from what I've seen, you've done a fine job." I washed my knives and put the chops in the locker for Grandpa to pull and stuff later. He led me out in front of the coolers to inspect what was wrapped and ready. "It's good to know that I can depend on you to do the work and understand the process. We have just the right amount on display and I can get the chops stuffed and the chicken breasts seasoned for the afternoon rush. This is what makes us different, Jett. SuperFoods doesn't have a custom cut meat department like we do. Their cooler stock is delivered by truck from the warehouse each morning. They don't do any Prime cuts. I don't know how long we'll be able to compete in this market, but this is our niche. You're helping me maintain it. Now go home to your women and get some loving." He slapped me on the back and I grabbed my coat to go home.

⋅∘⋅⟶ ⟩⟩⟨ ☼ ⟩⟨⟨ ⟵ ⋅∘⋅

I WAS THE only one home when I got there. That wasn't unusual on Monday. It was my night to cook and everyone else had classes. The house was filled with the aroma of the turkey stock I'd put in the crockpot to simmer all day. I'd need to pick the carcass and cut the vegetables in a little bit. But first I took a detour through my studio.

The painting of Mary was on my easel and the living room had been cleaned up. There were still some fine details in the portrait that I needed to finish but I'd do those after dinner. I was filled with a sense of tenderness and pride when I looked at that painting. I was no more nor less in love with Mary than with Jas or Kelly or Sarah Lynn or Ariel or Charmaine. There was something about painting one of my lovers that was almost more intimate than making love. Of course, doing both was best!

What surprised me, though, was that I was still wrapped in the warm feeling of my grandpa's words of praise. I didn't think it was possible, but I was as proud of my work in the meat market as I was of my painting. I'd managed the department for a whole day and did it well. Not only was I an artist with paint but I also had a marketable skill.

Tomorrow, the feeling of pride and accomplishment would fade as I immersed myself back into the world of art and my passion. It might even be gone by the time we finished dinner tonight. But for now... *I guess I'll go finish the soup and get ready to feed my girls.*

MERCK WAS PLEASED with the painting. He was blown away when Mary came into our class, stripped off her clothes, and lay on the desk in front of the painting to pose.

"As a thing is more perfect, the more it feels of pleasure and of pain," she said. She maintained the pose through a thunderous round of applause and then grabbed her clothes and ran out of the room.

"This is what we mean by the *influence* of Literature on the Arts," Merck lectured. "It is not replicating a scene, but letting words flow through the artist to inspire artwork. Is Blackburn's *Inferno* an illustration of Dante's *Inferno*? How could you be so dense as to think that? It is an artwork inspired by a piece of literature. But not just the literature. This work was equally inspired by the model." He was really on a roll.

"That inspiration comes in different forms. Look, for example, at Giambologna's *Rape of the Sabine Women*, two hundred years after Dante's *Divine Comedy*. Did Giambologna read and interpret Dante's work? Not likely. But the Florence of the Renaissance had been so profoundly influenced by the poet that a world of art had burst from it."

He pointed at my painting and applauded, as did the rest of my class. It was a little embarrassing, but I was also really proud. Mary slipped back into the lecture hall fully dressed and all but unnoticed as she took my hand. This wasn't her class, but she'd decided to join me on this Wednesday. We had drawing on Tuesday and Thursday, but no classes after this one on Wednesdays.

"As our last section in this course, we are going to take a look at the influence from the other direction. Our next subject is not an author or, in the strictest sense, an artist. We are going to look at the influence of a printer in Venice named Aldus Manutius and use as our example of his work, the book by Francesco Colonna named *Hypnerotomachia Poliphili*. We could, of course, have talked about Gutenberg and his various inventions that made the printed word a feasible medium. But Gutenberg was only the mechanics of reproduction. With Aldus we have the art of the book. The fifty-year span from Gutenberg's invention to the innovations of Aldus are referred to as the *Incunabula*, or the cradle of printing. As

Gutenberg's Bible marks the beginning of that era, *Hypnerotomachia Poliphili* marks the end. You have a few reproduction pages in your text, but I want you to read the first chapter for discussion tomorrow. This is a short section describing the morning Poliphilus wakes up in his dream, but I assure you, reading this English translation from 1592 will challenge your interpretive ability as much as reading the Greek poets."

·•·◆ ⟩⟩C ☼ C⟨⟨ ◆·•·

"YOU DIDN'T!" KELLY squealed. "You just ran into the room and stripped? I can't believe how brave you are!"

"I thought Merck would swallow his Vape," I laughed. "Mary, you were—and are—spectacular! I'll bet the janitors have come-stains all over the room to clean up tonight. Male and female."

"It was just… I had to do it. When I'm in front of that painting, I feel like I am becoming one," she said.

"Wait! I thought the painting with you in front of it was all these flakes of you floating off into space," Ariel said. "You're becoming one with the universe?"

"That's one way of looking at it, but…" She stood and stripped out of her bodystocking. The paint was beginning to fade but was still clear enough that we could easily see the image. "When I looked at the photos and video, I had a strange sense that all those particles weren't floating off of me, but they were coalescing on me. I was being made whole from the fabric of the universe. I am not fading out of existence but fading into it. I'm solidifying. Becoming one."

·•·◆ ⟩⟩C ☼ C⟨⟨ ◆·•·

I HAD A term paper to write comparing a specific aspect of modernism with a counterpart in postmodernism and how it influenced my own work. Foundations of Contemporary Art was not my favorite class by a long stretch. It was almost impossible to self-analyze and suggest that my own art was more modernist or post-modernist. It was certainly influenced by both philosophies and the artists that were used as representatives.

One aspect that intrigued me, though, was the rise of performance art in the postmodern era. A few years ago, an artist named Marina

Abramović had spent the entire length of her exhibition at MOMA in New York sitting in a chair across the table from another chair that visitors, one at a time, could sit quietly in. From all the reports I'd read, it was an intense experience for those who chose to sit across from her while those who chose to just walk past saw nothing significant. She sat a total of seven hundred thirty-six hours during exhibition opening times!

On the other hand, everyone knows and loves Bob Ross. He started in the eighties on Public Television, supposedly teaching people to paint. It's true that you can learn a lot from him, but every lesson is truly a performance. Even more now that his performances have been transferred to YouTube. He was only active for about fifteen years, but because his performances were video-taped and digitized, he continues to instruct and entertain almost twenty-five years after his death.

I'd never considered it, but I was as much a performance artist as these two. I'd started painting publicly through Skype conversations with my friends while we chatted and I painted in my underwear. My most recent works had all been videoed and played in front of my classmates.

I set to work structuring my paper.

⋯◈ ⟊ ☽ ⟊ ◈⋯

My 2D FINAL project was to structure a surface composition that could be displayed in a gallery. This was very different than the wallpaper exercise at midterm. We needed to determine an object and draw, paint, or otherwise decorate it with two-dimensional art.

I laughed out loud when I thought about having one of my painted models on display. In a way, that was what I was doing with my Literature and the Arts projects. I was creating a 2D Design on a delightfully irregular surface. I couldn't really exhibit one of my girlfriends, but I got to wondering if I could paint a mannequin. I had a feeling that most of my classmates would go down to the local pottery shop and paint a vase. There's a reason there are so many still lifes of vases with flowers. They hold still. Georgia O'Keeffe is said to have claimed that she preferred painting flowers to painting people because the flowers held still and didn't talk back.

I had to figure this one out carefully.

BLANKETY WAS A pain in the ass as usual. The nine of us who had survived the midterm were still subjecting ourselves to his abuse twice a week. Our drawings had become more complex and he'd warned us that the final would be the most complex yet. When he announced it, we all regretted having stuck it out.

"You have finally figured out that a significant part of drawing is the composition itself, but your little brains haven't grasped more than the surface. You still draw technically as if you were tracing outlines. Composition has depth and meaning. An object can be broken down into ever smaller objects. Shadows, reflections, highlights. It is only when all those bits come together that you truly have a drawing. I have tried to chip away at your intense egos all term. You keep putting them in front of your pencil and drawing on them. Strip them away."

Drawing on our egos? Yeah. Every time he attacked me, I strengthened what he attacked instead of getting rid of it. Was I going about it all wrong?

"You have two class sessions next week and one week thereafter to complete your final project. You are to create a composition. I suggest you make it simple. You'll end up scribbling as it is. The drawing will be on twelve-by-sixteen paper substrate. You may choose the graphite or charcoal you wish, but the substrate must be compatible. Draw your composition and bring it to me on the nineteenth."

That was it? This was a simple project and we could have done it the first day of class.

"Oh. Yes. Your rendering of the composition is to comprise smaller objects. If you see a reflection that looks like a basketball, draw a basketball. If a shadow looks like a sinister man waiting in a dark alley, draw a sinister man waiting in a dark alley. Every object in your composition is to be composed of other objects. Look deeper than the surface."

The bastard!

•·o··◦❯ ⫷ ☼ ⫸ ❮◦··o·•

I WAS FASCINATED by Aldus Manutius and the end of the *Incunabula*. In a lot of ways, it paralleled the development of modernism and postmodernism, but in the compressed timespan of fifty years. I supposed this would be repeated in every shift over the ages. In fact, I guess that's what Merck had been saying all term. Before Akhenaten and after. Before Homer and after. Before Euripides and after. It was beginning to make sense.

"Some people have speculated that Colonna hid a map to a secret treasure in *Hypnerotomachia Poliphili*. We can write that off because if there had been such a thing, Aldus would have kept it to himself. When he decided to start a printing business, he needed funding. His solution was to move to Venice, find the richest man there, and marry his daughter. Instant funding," Merck said as we laughed. "Aldus was a cagey businessman and knew exactly what he wanted. We can't slight him for his vision, even if we doubt his ethics."

Merck projected a page from another of the books printed by Aldus, a 1501 edition of Virgil's *Aeneid*.

"Let's look at one of the things Aldus initiated. Prior to Aldus, nearly all the printing done in the first fifty years of the art used German Blackletter or Roman type. Aldus was, in fact, influential in codifying the character shapes of Roman type, the use of inscriptional capitals with Carolingian minuscules, and even stabilizing the letters of the alphabet itself. That Roman was easier to read than Blackletter was obvious, but both had the common problem of the block of lead type being the width of the character. Aldus needed a font that would cram more characters into the allotted space so he could make smaller books rather than only printing books that needed a library table to support them. Enter a punchcutter named Francesco Griffo. He created a font we know today as Italic type. Aldus claimed credit for the typeface since Griffo worked for him, but he did eventually admit Griffo was the designer. The significance of Italic type is that the letters overlap the base of neighboring characters so the spacing is significantly compressed."

He switched slides back to a reproduction page of *Hypnerotomachia Poliphili*.

"Aldus abandoned the use of religious texts and bulletins as the only subject for printing. He was a secular humanist and sought to bring classic works of Greek and Latin authors to the attention of the masses. Yes,

Homer, Euripides, Virgil, and even Dante. Common people did not have large libraries where they could read books on tables, hence the advent of the octavo size book, roughly the size of our current trade paperbacks. A technological advancement, yes, but one that opened the world of books and reading to common people who could put a book in their saddlebag and read under a tree. Aldus brought reading and secular texts to the masses."

⋯⟡ ⟩)C ☼)C⟨ ⟡⋯

"It's brilliant, isn't it?" Mary said when she arrived on Friday afternoon. "What shall we draw?"

"Blankety's project? It's torturous. He doesn't want a final drawing, he wants a composition of a thousand tiny drawings," I moaned.

"That's just it! Everyone sees things differently. If I look at an old-fashioned watch with a dial and hands, I might see an entire composition of gears and levers. But you might look at the same object and see circuit boards and rushing electrons. We'd draw the same object but with different references."

"I see the sense. It's just a *lot* of work," I said. "On the other hand, we could both draw the same thing, couldn't we? Create one composition that we can both interpret in our drawing?"

"That's what I was thinking. I'd rather not draw bloody meat, but we could create about any still life. It would be fun to do a project side-by-side like we did the midterm." I reached over and took her hand, pulling her to me for a kiss.

"I can think of a few projects we could do side-by-side that would be even more fun." We kissed long and deep. Something was different. "Have I correctly noticed that you aren't shaking as much lately? Did you get some new medication?"

"Well… sort of. I have a biofeedback therapist, you know? The past week, I've been incorporating my coalescing as one into my biofeedback. I've been meditating each morning to visualize my body coming together from the particles of the universe. You really opened a new avenue for me."

"That's amazing."

•◦•◆ ⊃⊂ ☼ ⊃⊂ ◆•◦•

"Ariel, would you be willing to be painted again?" I asked at dinner.

"Of course! I hoped you'd paint me again. After all, I was the original canvas." That was true. The first time I'd painted on someone's body, it was hers. But the concept that Aldus had essentially engineered a new artform with the popular book just made me think of Ariel and her combination of music and engineering. This time, I would be creating something that I planned out, though, instead of just doodling. "What do I get to be?"

"A sex doll." Everyone laughed.

"I thought you were going to paint her, not just display her," Sarah Lynn said. "She's already a sex doll." Ariel stood up and pirouetted in place, displaying her naked body to all of us at the table. We applauded.

"I feel so left out," Kelly sighed. "You've painted everyone but me."

"I paint your insides every chance I get," I said. "And I sign your mound each time."

"Yeah. I just… You know."

"I have one more painting project that I need to do," I said. "I wanted to ask if you'd help me, but I don't want to take any more time away from your performing and school work. You already do so much."

"What do you want? I'd love to help! In addition to recording and editing the Ariel Sex Doll project."

"I have a 2D project to do."

"I'm a little flat but I'm not two dimensional!" she huffed.

"I think turnabout is fair play," I said. "I want to paint your underwear."

"What???"

"You've been collecting my painted underwear for like three years. I want to paint yours. While you are wearing it."

"Oh, my! Um… Could we do it live in my chatroom?"

"Oh! Now there is something that I could use to enhance my paper on performance art, too!"

•◦•◆ ⊃⊂ ☼ ⊃⊂ ◆•◦•

"Will you paint my pussy?" Ariel asked as I slipped into her.

"I'll sure be painting it with come," I sighed.

"I don't know why I waited so long to have sex with you. I love this feeling. I want to ride you every day. I just want to bounce on your cock all the time."

"I've been having sex with you since the week of graduation," I whispered. "Don't ever think that my licking you isn't sex. Don't think that my painting you isn't sex. In fact, don't even imagine that listening to you play the piano isn't sex. Anything I do with you is sex, Ariel. I can't help it. Just thinking about you is sex."

"Think about me. Lick me. Paint me. Listen to me." Her cadence picked up with the rhythm of her bouncing on my cock. "But most of all, put your hard cock in my little pussy and fuck me. I love being your sex doll, Jett. I. Love. It!" She exploded on top of me and I exploded inside her. I could see in my climax blindness exactly where her gears were turning as she bounced her way to seconds.

$$33$$

Performing

ARIEL WANTED PERMANENT paint when I showed her my design. I didn't think that was a great idea. Her entire body would be covered, including face and hair. We finally agreed that from her neck down I would use the acrylic paint but above it would be watercolor. I promised she would still look like my sex doll.

I was thankful she was willing to do the acrylic. And thankful she was a small girl. It was going to take us days to finish this project. I thought how in my initial interview the professors had said they would teach me to slow down. I guess this was my first lesson. Ariel had also agreed to 'perform' in my Literature and the Arts class. I told Merck when he asked that not all my models would be willing to come to his class naked, but a couple of unique girls would transform for the class.

"Anytime. Not only is your artwork stimulating to look at, it is giving me an opportunity to connect different aspects of the literature to its influence on the art world today. You've really captured something with this body art. Have you figured out a way to exploit it? Not that I think art should be exploited commercially, but artists need to make a living. And the artwork needs to survive. That's the biggest problem with performance art. It is fleeting. Once the performance is gone, so is the artwork."

"We *are* doing videos. I'm working with Kelly on how to make the videos truly salable. We plan to open a YouTube channel over the holiday. We just don't have time to do the setup while we're doing classwork."

"I understand you hold down a part time job as well?" Merck asked.

"Yes. And I'm completing a certification course as well. Thankfully, that should be over by the end of summer. It's normally just two semesters, but I'm dragging it out over four because I can't do that and the work at the U as well."

"What kind of certification?"

"I'm working toward becoming a butcher."

Merck just stared at me. He started to say something two or three times, but finally just shook his head and left.

I never thought cutting meat would give me so much satisfaction.

⋯∘⋅◇ ⫶ ☼ ⫶ ◇⋅∘⋯

"I JUST CAN'T stand the thought of drawing a bowl of fruit," Mary complained. "I mean, I understand why food and table settings are the most common subjects for a still life. It's stuff everyone has around. And I like the wine bottle and glass for their reflections, but can't we figure out something more original than a bunch of fruit and cheese on a cutting board? Something more relevant to life as we know it?"

When Mary got wound up, there was no one more passionate. That wasn't only in bed, but in our drawing, as well. We were staring at our first attempt at a still life composition. I agreed that we'd set something up that was attractive. It was a cutting board with a few slices of cheese, cold cuts, and a glass of wine. Boring. We'd even sketched it out from different angles and it was a good composition. Caravaggio could have assembled the exact same still life in 1600.

"This isn't us," I agreed. "It should say something about our world. You got that on the midterm with the objects from Kelly's Kat House. I even got it with the bloody meat and stewpot. They were things that were relevant to where we live."

"Vases of flowers and bowls of fruit were everyday objects to classic artists. What are our everyday objects?"

We started a tour through the house and snapped pictures on our cell phones of things we saw. A stack of books. My car keys. The makeup tables the girls had put in one bedroom. The bed with a pile of pillows. Our mismatched dinnerware. A pile of laundry being sorted. The spice rack in the kitchen. A laptop. A camera.

Something dawned on me and I turned and snapped a picture of Mary.

305

"Hey, we aren't supposed to do portraiture," she laughed. I showed her the picture.

"The one thing none of us are ever without," I said. "Our cell phones."

"Yes! A story. We need a story to tie it together. Cell phone. Makeup. A mirror. Glass of wine. We can do this!"

⚜

"They convinced me to work Saturday and Sunday through the holiday," Kelly said. "The store is a zoo but I don't feel like I can just walk away. Besides, that means that I still get an employee discount through the holiday. This one is pretty!" She held up a cute and very brief, lacy set of bra and panties. I'd never shopped for girls' underwear before and when she held it up in front of her, I blushed.

"Um… I'd love to see you in that," I squeaked. "But it won't do for the project. I need enough surface area that I can paint it."

"Yeah, I know. But plain white bras and granny panties are so boring!"

"They won't be when I finish painting them on you."

"Oh! That sends chills down my spine. Maybe we could do that as another performance. Instead of painting the underwear, you paint me. Paint a really pretty bra and panties right on my bare skin. Maybe a garter belt and hose, too. Wouldn't that be fun?" Kelly giggled. I imagined it in my mind. I wondered if she'd turn off the cameras before I fucked the paint off her.

"I wish I could exhibit you in the gallery. I'd make that my project. Is there anything like this that isn't bulky and padded?" I asked, holding up a plain white bra that looked like a bulletproof vest.

"Over here. I think this is what you want. They are really made for girls like me with not much chest who don't want to wear a bra in the first place." She showed me a lightweight nylon bra that all but disappeared against her skin.

"I think that works. I'm going to have to do something to stiffen it into your shape, but I think I know how to do that. Panties?" She showed me a plain, nylon pair of panties.

"These are a classic brief," she said in her best sales clerk voice. "The waist is above the navel and provides just a little support for the lower tummy while it snugly conforms to a woman's intimate curves."

"I'll buy it," I laughed. "Better get two sets in case I mess one up."

⋯∘⋅✦ ⊃⊂ ☼ ⊃⊂ ✦⋅∘⋯

"Can you see my pussy in this position?" Ariel asked.

"Not yet. We're just working on the cover of the book right now. Believe me, your pussy will be a featured attraction when we open the book. Can you hold that?"

"Yeah. It's not difficult. But you'll paint the sex doll part, too, won't you?"

Ariel really wanted me to get to painting the sex part. It was funny that she turned out to be the horniest of all my girlfriends. I don't think she ever had a day without someone's tongue or my cock in her pussy. And she dove between the other girls' legs with wild abandon. Mary agreed with the other four that Ariel was the best pussy-licker ever.

This part of the project let me apply a lot of paint very quickly with the airbrush. The shade of 'leather' I'd chosen was just slightly browner and darker than Ariel's skin tone. I'd carefully put plastic wrap around her neck so I wouldn't get any acrylic spray above her shoulders. It would also make a good clean edge for the book. Of course, the spray was just the base coat. After her break, I touched up edges when she folded back into her little ball. Then I started adding texture and the indentation of the spine of the book where it joins the cover. The gold letters I applied to her back, right down the spine, might have been a little more explicit than the Colonna book, but I felt that 'Sex Dreams' captured the spirit of the work and I could fit that on Ariel's back. It took the rest of the day to stipple the texture and do the lettering. I still needed to do the front view of the book, the edges of the pages on her lower legs. I thought I might be able to do that before doing the sex doll on the inside of the book, but first, I had to fuck Ariel.

It was no chore.

⋯∘⋅✦ ⊃⊂ ☼ ⊃⊂ ✦⋅∘⋯

Getting Kelly's new outfit prepared for painting *was* a chore. The problem was that the nylon underwear was limp and even when I put acrylic paint on a test patch it didn't stiffen enough to support itself. It fit

307

her sexy form perfectly, but once it was off, it just collapsed. Not sexy at all.

We ended up painting polyurethane on the bra and panties while she was wearing them. Well, that had its own problems because I didn't want to cement the garments to her body and didn't want her sensitive skin affected by the strong chemical either. Plastic wrap and a well-ventilated area came to the rescue. At the risk of being seen by the boys next door, I opened the two windows in my studio and put the box fans we'd used this summer in them. This was going to blow some of our precious heat right out into the freezing night, but there was nothing I could do about that.

I rubbed Vaseline onto Kelly before wrapping the plastic around her so it would seal down like a second skin. It was Kelly's shape I wanted. I didn't want a bunch of wrinkles and textures disguising it. She put the bra and panties on over this and I painted them with polyurethane. We both wore face masks to keep from inhaling too much of the toxic fumes.

The hardening of the underwear all had to be done at once, so Kelly had the longest posing session of any of my projects. She had to keep her legs spread, as well, so I could paint her crotch. The one thing I'd decided that made it more tolerable was that I would only be doing the front, not the entire piece. We realized pretty quickly that if I did the whole thing, she wouldn't be able to get it off without breaking it.

It took two hours working as quickly as I could to get the bra and panties coated and set hard enough that we could remove them. It was a good thing we'd used Vaseline and plastic wrap. The wrap had mostly solidified into the poly.

•◦•❖ ⊃⊂ ☼ ⊃⊂ ❖•◦•

"ARE WE SATISFIED?" Mary asked. With the girls' approval, we'd moved one of the small makeup tables down to the studio. On the table were an assortment of makeup, an old cell phone that still turned on but had a shattered screen, a glass of wine, and my car keys. We'd positioned the table and ourselves so that we had completely different perspectives on the composition and so that the mirror reflected something different in the background. Not only was my perspective from the left but it was also from my full height, so I was looking down at the composition. Mary was working from the right and almost straight on at the table. We'd debated a long time about what to show on the cell phone and decided that it was much better to show a text message than a photo.

It was close to eight o'clock at night by the time we were satisfied with the composition and our perspectives. We drew all night long.

•◦•◦❖ ⊃⊂ ☼ ⊃⊂ ❖◦•◦•

THE PAINTING OF the sex doll took two more days. It was a combination of mechanics, art, and sex. Ariel is beautiful and petite. Part of my task was simply to exaggerate her natural attributes. She had previously waxed her lower labia, but in preparation for our project, she'd had the whole thing waxed. Her lips opened at even the suggestion of a touch and various girlfriends ran in and out with tissue to dab away the moisture so I could paint. By the time I had finished painting those outer labia and the surrounding area, Ariel had come twice.

The result of my efforts was an enlarged and detailed gash, a big clit painted at the top of her slit, the outer labia painted into glistening red inner labia. It was almost as if someone held a magnifying glass at her crotch and the image blossomed. I moved up and did the same thing with her small breasts. She had more on top than Kelly did, but was still a conservative B at best. I used highlights and shadows to create deep cleavage, enhanced her nipples—which cooperated by popping out to an incredible erection—and painted the surrounding area to make it look like she had twice the amount of breast flesh that she had. By the time I was finished with that part, she looked like she had double-Ds.

That night she chose to have Sarah Lynn explore her new, enlarged equipment with her tongue while I went to the Kat House for a live performance with Kelly.

•◦•◦❖ ⊃⊂ ☼ ⊃⊂ ❖◦•◦•

"GUYS, I KNOW you fantasize about fucking me. That's what I'm here for. I love the tribute pics with your come splattered on my photos—keep sending them! If you want comments about your cock, though, be sure to send a nice tip with the picture," Kelly said. She worked her virtual audience and I heard the chimes ring that indicated tips were coming in.

309

"You want to know what is happening tonight? I'm going to get fucked after cam by the only cock that ever gets real-life access to this pussy. This is my boyfriend. You all know him online as Kat's Coal. But before I get to do that, I promised that he could paint me. Sort of. Coal, come over here and get your Kat ready to be your pussy."

I moved into the frame but didn't say anything. Kat was the performer. I was just an artist. I started by slowly removing her top and running my hands all over her little boobs. There were a lot of tip chimes as I pinched her nipples up to maximum erection. The chatroom couldn't really see that I was also rubbing Vaseline into her skin. We wouldn't be using any additional plastic wrap but I didn't want to take a chance of the acrylic bleeding through on her. There was a bit of text chatter on-screen booing me when I put the new bra on her. Kelly just told them to be patient and she'd be completely naked later in the evening.

Once the bra was in place, I started painting. The first thing was to paint it out and blend it with Kelly's skin. I even had to put a little spray of freckles across the upper slope and very carefully painted her nipples the way I remembered them from sucking on them earlier. When I was finished, you could barely tell the bra was on her. Then I started decorating it as if I was creating a tattoo on her breasts. The tattoo was of two dragons, tails wrapped to the outside of her breasts and heads rising up between. I'd decided to make this as purely tattoo-like as I could. It was all fine black line art.

When I was finished with the bra, I moved to her waist and tugged her short skirt off, showing there was nothing but Kelly under it. A lot of tip chimes again as I massaged and opened her pussy while she moaned. Once again, I used this time to spread Vaseline over the entire area, even in her tightly trimmed red landing strip. The guys hated it again when I covered everything with the stiff panties but I noticed there were more than twice as many in the chatroom now as there had been when we started. Kelly spread her legs to accommodate the stiff fabric between them and once I felt the panties were securely in place, I repeated the process of blending them into Kelly's natural skin tones.

When I'd finished painting her pussy, navel, and fiery red landing strip, Kelly looked like she was naked again. The guys loved it.

We'd searched hundreds of images of women's lower stomach tattoos under every variation of the search terms we could think of. There were basic patterns like scrollwork, flowers, birds, mottos, roses, skulls, hearts, butterflies, cartoons, unicorns, Teletubbies, flames, tigers, snakes, shooting stars, guns, Medusa, feathers, Northwest Indian totems, and warnings. One I recognized from my reading of Dante: 'Abandon all hope, ye who enter here.'

We finally agreed that it would be spread wings on the sides and a laurel wreath crowning her landing strip. When I'd finished the paint job, we took several photos and the guys tipped generously.

"Anybody want to see me naked now? Eight-token tips mean leave the artwork on. Nine-token tips mean take it all off. You've got five minutes to vote. Come on, guys. Who wants to see my pussy up close and personal?" The chimes started ringing immediately. It was no contest, really. Several voted to leave the artwork, but the vast majority voted to strip.

I took no chances of ruining the artwork, so I cut the straps on the bra and carefully removed it. Once it was off, of course, I had to massage Kelly's breasts and clean the Vaseline off them. I was surprised to hear how many guys tipped just watching me maul her little nipples. I cut the legs of the panties and Kelly spread wide so I could lift the stiff material out from between her legs. And then I massaged all that part of my little redhead lover.

"Coal, I'm so turned on and horny. Rub my little clitty, please. Look, I'm dripping after all that attention." Kelly grabbed the handheld camera and moved it down to her crotch where I started manipulating her clit and dipping my fingers into her hot wet channel. "Remember, guys, if you come before I do, pay the fapping tax. Let's finish this session with a bang." We took our time as more and more tip chimes rang. Then Kelly's chimes rang. She bid her chatroom goodnight and turned off the cameras.

Kelly and I didn't get to sleep very soon.

•◦•◈ ⟫ ☼ ⟪ ◈•◦•

My first 'final' was to turn in my drawing for Blankety. We all sat in the classroom with our drawings in front of us. He didn't really say anything as he looked at each of the nine drawings. The silence was spooky. We all expected his scathing critique. He stood between Mary and me and looked from one drawing to the other. He bent down to look at them from about center of the artwork and continued to swing his head from one to the other. I couldn't even reach over to take Mary's hand because he was between us. It seemed like he was taking a long time.

"I see," he finally said. He walked up to the front of the class and gathered his things. Just before he walked out the door, he turned back to us. "Well, you all passed." Then he left.

·•·•✦ ⊃⊂ ☽ ⊃⊂ ✦•·•·

I'D CAREFULLY TRIMMED the bra and panties so that only the hardened and painted portions were left. Then I suspended them the exact distance apart they had been on Kelly. All the people in the class were given fifteen minutes of the exam period to display our work in the mini-gallery. It's great that the gallery has everything available and assistance for getting art properly displayed. I had two fishlines dropped from the overhead grid and hung my creation at Kelly's height. Then we all walked around and judged each other's work.

I passed that class, too.

·•·•✦ ⊃⊂ ☽ ⊃⊂ ✦•·•·

MERCK GAVE ME the final presentation in the Literature and the Arts exam period. I carried Ariel in and set her on the desk at the front of the room with her back to the class.

"Sexy Dreams," I said. "Looks like a good book, to me. Better than all those religious tracts. And look! It's so tiny and compact, I could carry it in my saddlebag." The class laughed at my presentation as I pivoted Ariel on her butt to face the class. She looked like the page edge of a book. "It would take a lot to copy my sexy dreams," I said. "I'll release the latch and see what's inside." The latch was Ariel's head that had been painted only that morning. When she raised her head, the class laughed as it was obvious that she was a doll. I'd painted her with the same exaggerated features that were waiting when I opened the book. Big eyes, cherry-red lips puckered in a perpetual O, and rosy cheeks.

But when I opened the book, they all gasped. First, I pressed her right leg out the same as I would open a book for reading. I think they were expecting the inside of a book instead of the bright red gash of Ariel's sex and the big boob. I moved to the other side and spread her left leg out, opening her fully. Not all the glistening between her thighs was what I'd painted.

The class had still only seen the squatted opening between the pages, though. I took Ariel's hands and she pulled herself upright. As she unfolded, the painted gears and cables that connected her joints appeared, framing the sex doll within. When she was standing straight with her feet a little more than shoulder width apart, she began a little mechanical doll dance that got her turned in a full circle so the class could see the paint job on her entire body. They applauded.

I reversed the process, taking hold of her hands and letting her lower herself back to the squat position. Then, one at a time, I closed her legs. There were a few sighs as that over-exaggerated sex disappeared from view. I lowered her head and she was once again, just a book.

"What a good read," I sighed. "I think I'll take this book home and look at it more closely."

34
Holiday

WE WERE through! No more classes for a month. It seemed like the entire town emptied out in twelve hours. The campus was deserted. The house next door was empty. The guys had carried suitcases out to their last exams and didn't come back. I saw all three blonde bimbos from two doors down load into a Ford Focus that looked like it was dragging bottom under the weight of everything they packed with them. I didn't know where they were headed, but I hoped they made it.

I got out of my final in Slaughtering at ten on Friday morning. It was a written test and didn't take that long to complete. I was glad to have that class out of the way. Next semester… Well, that was going to be another tough one as I'd be in class five days a week at eight o'clock in the morning. Nothing like starting your day right with food prep.

Mary and Eva were both with the girls when I got home and everyone was dressed casually—meaning not at all. I got stripped out of my clothes as soon as I walked in the back door and joined the pile of girls under all the blankets in the house in front of the TV for a day of movies. We hadn't had a day like that in months!

Ariel was still sporting all her paint below the neck, but before getting to bed last night she'd shampooed it out of her hair and off her face. She'd been daring, however, and we were surprised when the Dragon Lady fixed our dinner Thursday night. Ariel demonstrated her whole unfolding routine and her mother made her repeat it three times while she walked around the little pixie and looked at the paint job. She clapped with delight at the transformer-like performance. I was afraid she'd be offended by the blatant sexuality of her daughter exposing her enhanced genitals and breasts, but the Dragon Lady laughed and looked at her from every angle. Then she demanded that Ariel play the piano for her before she went home and told her she had to wear clothes when she came home for the holiday.

Even without the face makeup, Ariel was taking every opportunity to fold and unfold for each of us Friday. The paint on her labia was mostly worn off.

"I have to fly out tomorrow," Mary said. "I hope I can stand this."

"Where's home?" Eva asked.

"It's a short hop. I live in the town of Fridley, which is really a northern suburb of Minneapolis. Can you take me to the airport tomorrow, Jett?"

"Sure, I can. Want me to fly home with you, too?"

"Would you?"

"I was kind of joking, you know."

"Yeah. I'm going to miss you all. I'll probably lock myself in my room for the next month."

"That sounds terrible," Sarah Lynn cried. "Jett, you should go visit. Maybe you should go for New Year's Eve and then bring her back to us." There was a chorus of assent and I started to seriously consider it.

"I don't want to take you away from the family on New Year's Eve," Mary said. "But would you mind a guest here until classes start the twenty-second? Maybe for a couple of weeks?"

"Any time," Ariel said. "In any bed."

"I think I'm jealous," Eva said.

"We're just getting started," I said. I took the naked girl into my arms and kissed her deeply, the movie forgotten. "Whether we are lovers or not, I am going to have you naked in my arms frequently this term. I'm going to touch you and every inch of your body will obey my commands. We are going to make a great artwork this spring and I will paint you," I whispered in her ear. She shuddered and I could feel her skin ripple all the way down her body as I stroked her side. She moaned a minor orgasm as I held her. I moved my hand down toward her pussy and found a head between her legs. "I think everyone is willing to help you out a little, don't you?" I kissed her again and squeezed her breasts as Ariel lapped at her pussy. Her next orgasm was neither minor nor quiet. "You are my substrate," I breathed. She moaned again.

"So, when are you leaving and coming back, Eva," Jas asked as if a massive orgasm had not been occurring right beside her. She nudged me out of the way and kissed Eva. Ariel crawled up on top of me and offered me her face to lick clean of Eva's juices.

"Oh… Uh… I'm…" Eva had a hard time catching her breath. "I'm flying to Virginia on Sunday. I wasn't going to come back until the eighteenth, but if you'd like to do some more sample painting, I could come back a week earlier. If you want." She looked at me.

"I want," I whispered. She shuddered again.

•○•⇨ ℭ ☼ ℭ ⇦•○•

The immediate concern was getting all of us where we needed to go for the holiday. Mary flew out Saturday morning and Eva on Sunday afternoon. We went out and got a small Christmas tree for our house on Saturday afternoon and decorated it with any miscellaneous objects from our childhood that we could find. It was mostly lights that I got at Lowe's on sale with some red balls and tinsel.

Sunday night, my dick kept switching between Ariel's and Kelly's pussies. They kept me going most of the night and when I was exhausted, they kept each other going. Then, Monday morning, Ariel's mom picked her up to spend three days with the family. She'd be back on Thursday but would leave again on Friday for a family ski trip to Tahoe for a week. We'd get her back on the sixth.

Kelly's mom arrived at noon. She and Kelly were spending a mother/daughter holiday and Kelly admonished me to watch her Christmas Day special. She said it would really be special. Once we'd all greeted Siobhan and made sure they had everything they needed, Jas, Char, Sarah Lynn, and I went to my parents' house.

•○•⇨ ℭ ☼ ℭ ⇦•○•

"We thought maybe we could get you to visit more often if we put a bigger bed in your room," Mom said as we stood staring at the king-size bed that about filled my old bedroom. "Since you have a painting studio

316

in your new house, we didn't think you'd mind sacrificing your painting area in here."

"Mom…" I started. Here she was planning my life for me again. Sarah Lynn squeezed my hand. *Yeah. So what?* "Thank you, Mom. Some number of us will try to visit more often if we can. At least during breaks. We could almost all fit in this bed."

"You don't need to give me the details. Just tell me how many towels you need in the bathroom."

°○·◇ ⊃⊂ ☀ ⊃⊂ ◇·○°

We had a quiet exchange of gifts for the family on Christmas Eve. Mom and Dad included a little something for Char, Sarah Lynn, and Jas. Jasmine's mom and Ray joined us as well. There were little gifts for us to take to Ariel and Kelly. It was really sweet and even I felt kind of sappy and emotional.

On Christmas Day, of course, the grandparents all arrived to fill out the Christmas dinner table. With eleven of us at the table, I think we were the biggest group that Mom and Dad had ever entertained.

"It's too bad Ariel and Kelly couldn't be with us," Granddad said. He still stopped by our house a couple of times a month just to check on maintenance. He'd helped me put up the storm windows we found in the garage a couple of months ago. You'd think that would be something the landlord would do! "And what's that cute blonde's name? Mary?"

"Oh, yeah. She's cute," Jas giggled. "We're going to send Jett to Minneapolis to capture her and bring her home."

"Dear me," Mom said. She looked genuinely worried. "Should we have gotten the California King instead of the regular one?" Everyone stopped eating and then all burst out laughing. There was a little choking and liquid coming through the nose. I quickly took Grandma's mimosa to get her a fresh one.

"I'm not that fond of orange juice, Jett," she said sweetly. "Would you mind just getting me a gin and tonic?"

"Of course, Grandma," I laughed. "It's much easier." I think I was only eight when I learned to make Grandma's gin and tonic.

"So, what are you going to do with all your vacation time?" Grandpa asked. "Want more hours at the store?"

"I could use some hours," Sarah Lynn said. "My schedule this term really didn't leave me any dependable time I could work. I've cut a couple of hours from the schedule for second semester."

"I'm picking up three more hours with that damn Farm to Table course this term," I said. "It meets every morning at eight. Grandpa, couldn't I have done this course at the store like I did the first semester one?"

"I wish. There's too much cooking involved in this course. You'll also cover the grading, costing, and yield estimations that I can't effectively teach you at the store. Better you take this one in a class. I take it you don't want extra hours, then."

"I'd like some during the break. I might have to cut back once school starts. I'll have two classes on Mondays."

"We'll work something out."

•०•०✦ ⅅⅭ ☼ ⅅⅭ ✦०•०•

WE MADE IT back to the house on Boxing Day—not that we celebrate it but our parents had been watching *Downton Abbey*. We watched Kelly's special on Christmas night. She had cute antlers on and a red nose. The real shock, though, was seeing the reindeer tail attached to a butt plug. I didn't think Kelly had ever put anything up there.

"You know what this means, don't you, Coal?" she'd said. Then she wiggled her ass around in front of the camera.

"You'd better practice," Char said as she backed up against my erection. Sarah Lynn and Jas continued to watch as I slowly sawed in and out of Char's butt. When Kelly started using her Hitachi, though, Jas and Sarah Lynn went to work on each other. It was a fine climax to our Christmas holiday.

As soon as we walked in the door on Wednesday, Kelly was all over us, kissing and hugging.

"Did you like it?"

"That was really sexy."

"Did it hurt?"

"Not much. A little at first, but I got used to it."

"I want to try it."

"Let's go order some!"

318

Well, I was left alone pretty quickly but Santa's little elf entered the living room. Siobhan O'Rourke is only a slightly older version of Kelly. She has the same bright red hair, the same stature, and the same tiny titties. I'm not sure why I was thinking about Siobhan's titties, other than that they weren't really hidden very much by the thin fabric of her elf-suit.

Nothing was.

"Siobhan? That's a pretty revealing outfit."

"Hmm. It is, isn't it? This is what I get for spending the holiday with my daughter. I try to coach her a little and I end up mimicking her. Don't mind me. I'll just go get some dinner ready for everyone. I have to go back to work tomorrow and we didn't really have much of a Christmas dinner with just the two of us. Will Ariel be back today?"

In answer to that question, a cold burst of air from the living room door was accompanied by Ariel's bright voice singing out, "Honeys, I'm home! Fuck me!"

"I think you've been called," Siobhan laughed. The rest of my afternoon was well-occupied.

•◦•◆ ⟆ ☾ ⟆ ◆•◦•

"ABOUT ME GOING to Minneapolis," I said to my five lovers in bed on Thursday night. Ariel was leaving again in the morning for a ski trip with her family to Tahoe. "I don't think it's such a great idea."

"I agree," Sarah Lynn said. "We were just dreaming and wanted Mary to know that we'd like her back as soon as possible even if we—or you—had to come and get her. I talked to her this morning and she'll fly home—I mean here—on the third. That will give us almost three full weeks with her before school starts."

"That's a relief. You know I want her back as much as everyone else does, but the cost…"

"I can tell how much you want her back. The evidence has been in my hand ever since you said her name," Sarah Lynn said. "Now it's time to plant the evidence in me."

I moaned as Sarah Lynn settled her hot spot around my cock. She was in a lazy fucking mood and I enjoyed her little movements as we continued to discuss Mary's arrival and how to organize things.

"You know, I only use the attic for performing and special liaisons," Kelly said. "It seems like a waste, but I don't want to be separate from everyone else. Will there still be room for me down here?"

Sarah Lynn continued to move on my cock as I reached an arm around Kelly and pulled her to us. We both kissed our girlfriend for a long time before answering. My breath was getting a little short.

"I… We will… always have a place for you in our beds," I managed. "You are in our hearts. Nothing could displace you from our beds."

"I just love you all so much." She leaned over and sucked one of Sarah Lynn's nipples into her mouth and I felt the responding spasm in her pussy. My cock jerked and I guess my fingers twitched in Jasmine's pussy. I'm not sure what the connections were between our little chain reaction and the gasps I heard from Ariel and Char.

"Do you really want Jett in your pooper?" Sarah Lynn asked. "That butt plug looked hot with the tail attached, but even when I get mine, I don't know yet if I want to use it." Sarah Lynn shivered and the vibrations notched up my come rocket another degree.

"I want Jett to have all of me," Kelly sighed. "I don't have much in the way of boobs for him to lay his cock between, but he can have every hole any way he wants it."

I didn't know how to respond to that. Kelly was renewing her offer to me and I wanted all of her. It wasn't just that I wanted blowjobs, fucks, and sodomy. I wanted Kelly. But just at the moment, Sarah Lynn was picking up the pace a little and I was about to pop in her pussy.

"Kelly, I love you," I gasped out as I erupted.

"I love you, Kelly," Sarah Lynn echoed. Three other lovers paused in what they were doing and echoed our sentiments.

"I love you all," Kelly said. "Sorry I got all emotional. 'Tis the season."

·o· ·⟡ ꓛꓛ ☼ ꓛꓛ ⟡· ·o·

IT TURNED OUT that it was the season for all the girls and one by one they started their periods over the next few days. Ariel took off with her parents so she didn't add fuel to the fire. The others, though, seemed to have a milder time than some cycles as far as the cramps went. Mostly everyone was kind of sentimental and wanted to cuddle together. Granted, often with a heating pad.

I picked up a lot of extra shifts over the New Year holiday and was getting in the rhythm of preparing the butcher case, the coolers, and the freezer each day. Grandpa or one of the senior meat cutters still took care of the prime cuts, but I was getting good at cutting and packaging the choice meat. There was one day that I forgot to put the absorbent pads under the meat before I packaged it in foam meat trays and shrink wrap. I caught it before there was too much blood in the cooler but I had to clean the cooler and repackage about thirty pieces of meat. Other than that, though, work went fine.

Sarah Lynn picked up several shifts as a cashier and felt like she had some spending money at last. Her scholarship and grant paid tuition and housing, but it's nice to have a little cash in your pocket for a cup of coffee now and then. Our parents had always been self-indulgent, stopping at Starbucks once or twice a day, eating out often, and buying whatever toys they wanted. For Mom, those were kitchen gadgets and the newest cell phone. Dad liked electronics and had about five computers and tablets. He was talking about getting a new 3D printer that he could use to actually print a crown for a tooth. He swore it would completely revolutionize dentistry.

The net result was that we didn't always make good use of our money. I never thought twice about buying paint, brushes, canvas, or other supplies whether I really had a need for them or not. I took a look at my bank account and was really shocked to see that I'd gone through half of the money I'd gotten for my paintings last spring. I tried to figure out what I'd spent so much money on and couldn't. I didn't have a full ride at the University but only paid about fifty percent of my tuition and fees. I contributed my share to the housing and food fund, but I worked half-time and couldn't see why I didn't have more money.

I felt bad about Jas. She had limited scholarship support and was hustling tables at Applebee's almost thirty hours a week. Her mom helped, but Sondra didn't make all that much at her job and still lived in the same apartment she'd moved into with Jas when her husband was killed in Afghanistan. Jas got some kind of stipend to help with college from the government, but it always seemed like she was struggling.

Ariel's parents made things easy. Maintain a 3.5 average and practice the piano two hours a day. Then she gets her college, room and board paid for and an allowance.

Kelly was making more money than any of us, I think. But she was also complaining that tuition for spring semester was going to wipe her out and she hoped she could save enough over the next six months to pay for fall tuition and keep living with us. I was a frequent visitor to the Kat House upstairs, and the amount of clothing, toys, and electronics in her room was probably equal to the rest of the house combined. I know her mom helped get her started, but I didn't think Kelly was managing her money any better than the rest of us.

The rest of us except Char.

Char was working on a year-end accounting of everything we put into the house, how our money was allocated for food, rent, utilities, and maintenance, and what each of us could claim on our taxes. She was really a whiz with the accounting stuff and was doing great at her new job. She'd received some bad advice from our high school guidance counselor who told her she could enroll in a certificate course in business and get everything she needed for her chosen profession without getting a degree. It turned out that wasn't true. After her first term, front-loading the pre-reqs for her biz cert, she was told she needed to follow the curriculum for an accounting degree. The educational requirements didn't bother her as much as finding funding for a four-year degree did. Still, she'd recovered the money her father stole and he added another ten grand. She budgeted every penny of her own as carefully as she managed the finances of our household.

Since Mary and Eva didn't live with us, I had no idea what their financial circumstances were. They didn't seem to be hurting, but all of us kept that kind of thing hidden from everyone else. They could be eating ramen noodles every day for all I knew.

I kept looking at all my paintings and the projects I'd completed the first semester. I was proud of it, but I wasn't selling anything. I didn't really even care about selling anything except that I needed to pay for painting stuff. Of all the projects I'd done this semester, only *Athena* and *Perfect Pain* were anywhere near marketable. Without Eva and Mary painted in front of them, they just seemed to be lacking something. I realized how important my meat cutting certificate would be to my livelihood and considered adding another course for the spring. I just couldn't imagine carrying more than the nineteen hours I was scheduled for, though.

I made it a point to make love to all four of the girls present in the house over New Year's Eve and New Year's Day. I'd fucked Ariel thoroughly when I cleaned all the paint off her body on Thursday before she left town. We were all sad to see the sex doll disappear, but Ariel convinced us there was a sex doll under the paint as well.

The sex was a short-term antidepressant for all of us as we looked at our year-end finances.

35
Plotting the Finale

I GOT HOME FROM work Thursday afternoon and walked right into the arms of a beautiful blonde in a black bodystocking. Jas had picked her up at the airport and sandwiched her between us as we hugged.

"When did you get in?" I asked around our kiss. She was shaking in my arms.

"Just before you got here. I'm sorry I'm shaking. Airports and planes are really stressful for me."

"I wish I could stay to help you destress," Jas said. "But I've picked up some extra evening shifts at the restaurant and need to get going." She slipped around Mary and we each got a sweet kiss before she left.

"Thank you for picking me up, Jas. We can cuddle later," Mary said. Jasmine's smile was brilliant. She kissed Mary again and was gone.

"How can I help destress you?" I asked.

"I had visions of getting here and lying naked under a pile of writhing naked girls with your cock stuck in me," she giggled. "Eventually, I stressed out over imagining that. I'm glad it's just you and me for a while. Can you just hold me?"

I was happy to hold her close, whether we were naked or not. We decided to lie on the bed and inevitably fell asleep.

•·◦·❖ ⊃⊂ ☼ ⊃⊂ ❖·◦·•

"Ooh, someone yummy is with my lover," Kelly whispered as she slithered into the bed behind Mary. Mary pushed her head back and rubbed against Kelly's shoulder as she sighed. "Will you share him?" Kelly asked.

What? Someone yummy… Will you share him?… Him?

"You know I'd always share with you, Kelly," Mary answered sleepily. Her shaking had calmed and she pressed her hips forward into mine. "Do you mind me sharing you with Kelly, Jett?"

"I thought it was me sharing you," I said, a bit bewildered.

"Oh, that works, too. But Kelly is my girlfriend and I always share my lovers with her."

"When did this come about?"

"About thirty seconds ago," Kelly giggled. "Love you, Mary."

"Love you, too, Kelly. We haven't really gotten around to doing anything to share but sleep. I feel so much calmer now that I'm here," Mary said. "I hope my little idiosyncrasies aren't too stressful on you all."

"We've survived both Ariel's emo phase and her sex doll phase. I think we can survive a little anxiety on your part."

"Let's not forget Char's monster phase," I laughed.

"And Sara Lynn's disowning by her family," Kelly agreed.

"And Kat Mon Dieu's sex shows online," Mary laughed. "I watched you every night you were on."

"I know. You were so sweet. It took me all of ten seconds to figure out who 'Bodystocking' was."

"I wasn't trying to hide." Mary's stomach growled loudly and we all laughed.

"Oh, yeah," Kelly said. "I was sent up to fetch you for dinner. Maybe we should go downstairs and feed you, baby."

Our meals during the break were a bit more haphazard than our normal schedule. We were all trying to put in extra work hours and people weren't always home at mealtime. Sarah Lynn had brought deli food from the grocery store for dinner this evening and we combined that with some of the leftovers from our holiday meals. Those were about gone now, too.

"I don't have a job to go to before school starts," Mary said. "How about if I pick up some of the cooking while I'm here."

"You're our guest!" Char said emphatically. "We wouldn't ask you to cook!"

"Char, I'm hurt," Mary said, sticking out her lower lip. "I agree that I don't live here all the time, but to think you only consider me a guest…

Really, I'd like to make a regular contribution, even after school starts. I'm living in the dorm, but in November and December, I ate half my evening meals here. And slept here a third of the time. You have to let me contribute or I can't keep coming over. And I really want to keep coming." We all looked at each other. Sarah Lynn broke first and spluttered out a laugh.

"You heard her. We need to keep Mary coming. I volunteer to go first!"

"You guys!" Mary laughed. "Well, okay. That, too. But please?"

"Girlfriend, we will accept your participation," Kelly said. "But right now, I have to run and get ready for my Thursday night bath show. You can scrub my back if you want."

"If you didn't have cameras running, I'd crawl right into the tub with you."

"I'm sorry, Mary," Char said. "I didn't mean to imply that you weren't part of the family. You know I love you, too."

"And since Jas is working until ten and Ariel is skiing with her parents, that just leaves Char, Jett, and me to make sure you keep coming tonight," Sarah Lynn said.

•○•⇨))C ☼))C ⇦•○•

"So, here's what I think," Mary said as we sat in the living room Saturday night. Kelly had finished her Saturday matinee and Char had cleaned up the kitchen after Mary's lovely meal of poached chicken breasts. Jas and Sarah Lynn drew night shifts at Applebee's and at the grocery store, so it was just the four of us. We had been discussing what to do with Eva when she returned next week and that led to my proposed painting project. "Paint her into a wall," Mary concluded.

"That's kinky. What, like 'The Cask of Amontillado'?" I asked.

"That might make a good Halloween painting," Mary laughed. "No. Let's find a venue that will let you paint your masterpiece on one of their walls instead of trying to haul around a life-size canvas. You'd have to have a canvas that was at least six-by-six to do this painting. How are we going to get it to the venue, even? It was almost impossible to get the three-by-five of me to your class. And I know you wanted to do more with my head and face than would fit on the canvas."

"That's true. What kind of venue would let me paint their walls?" I asked.

"Think of it in terms of a mural. You want to use an airplane or flying theme with Eva. Where would be better than an airport," Mary said. "When I flew in this week, I noticed there was a lot of wall art at the airport."

"Would they even let me into the airport with paint supplies and allow Eva to strip and be painted? It doesn't sound like a very friendly performance space."

"I wasn't thinking of that particular airport. I was thinking of the one Eva flies out of. It's a small airport out on the west side of town, but it has a really active flying community. I think there's an airshow near the first of May to celebrate the thaw and start of private aviation season. People fly in from all over."

"How do you know all about that?" Kelly asked. "That's amazing."

"Eva took me flying once this fall. I think she took Sarah Lynn one weekend, too. She's always hunting for someone to fly with her. Anyway, security is not quite the same out there as it is at the commercial airport. Not that there isn't any, but it's really a recreational airport. Families come out during the summer to eat at the café and just watch the airplanes land."

"It sounds worth investigating," Char said. "Jett, how big a wall could you paint?"

◦·◦❖ ⊃⊂ ☀ ⊃⊂ ❖◦·◦

ARIEL ARRIVED HOME on Sunday afternoon. I think she managed to fuck everyone in the household by bedtime. It was hard to believe this was the same emo girl we all knew in high school with all her angst and shyness. She'd changed her tight skinny jeans and band T-shirts for nudity and was a sex maniac. Once she got in the house and got her clothes off, Ariel was a bundle of energy and joy.

And sex. Did I mention sex?

"Will you paint me again?" she begged. "I just want to let you paint anything on me that you want to!"

"Come here and let me lick you some more," I growled as I crawled across the bed.

"Yes?" she squeaked. "Are you going to make me come again? Please?"

"Yes. And there's something else I've wanted to explore for a while." Ariel looked alarmed and scooted up on the bed pretending to get away from me. I grabbed her ankles and pulled her back, bending her legs back so her butt rolled upward.

"What do I have that you haven't already explored?" she asked in a tiny voice. "You lick my pussy all the time. What else… OH! Oh, God! Oh, God!" Ariel screeched as I rimmed her asshole with my tongue. I managed to wiggle a thumb into her pussy and rub her clit with my fingers as I lapped and explored the sensitive little star of her ass. She started squirming all over the bed as orgasms swept over her. She held her own knees back to make sure she was as wide open as possible and I used the opportunity to switch hands on her pussy and shove my very wet and lubricated thumb up her back channel.

Ariel shrieked. And passed out.

"I don't believe it," Sarah Lynn sighed. "You knocked her out. I thought we'd be going all night."

"Don't count on it being over," Mary laughed. She curled up behind me and spooned against me. Sarah Lynn, who had been mauling and sucking on Ariel's nipples, scooted around the bed, and spooned against Mary. I gathered Ariel in my arms and we all went to sleep. At last.

•०• •❖ ⊃⊂ ☾ ⊃⊂ ❖• •०•

EVA ARRIVED ON Tuesday and we had a full house. Seven girls—mostly naked most of the time—and me. I was still putting in extra shifts at the grocery store, but they were all early shifts. I got to work at six-thirty and was home by three. I guessed that would get me in shape for my eight o'clock meat cutting course this semester. At least I wouldn't have too much in the evening. My last class on Monday and Wednesday would be out at five-thirty and the rest of the week I was off at two unless we had a symposium. Looking at the second semester Literature and the Arts syllabus, though, told me that it wasn't going to be an easy session. The course would cover the Renaissance with Shakespeare and Michelangelo through the Modern period with T.S. Eliot and Picasso. I figured it was a good idea to start lining up my models and projects for the term.

"So, Eva, how much paint do you want to get on you this term?"

"You still want to do the big project at the end of the term, don't you?" she asked.

"Yeah. We're thinking of talking to your airport about doing it there during the fly-in in May."

"Mother's Day. We'll just be finished with finals. So, it's not for a class, right?"

"That's right. I actually want to do a performance piece that we can advertise and make some money from. Sarah Lynn and Mary want to coordinate with you on getting the project set up."

"Okay. So, I've got a pretty heavy schedule this spring because BFA auditions are in April. I could do some little projects, but I don't think any of your Lit/Art projects qualify as little, the way you've set yourself up with Merck. I'm sure you'll have one due right before spring break. As long as I can get some flying time in—assuming the weather cooperates—I'm good to do a project just before or during spring break," Eva said. Her brow creased and she looked at me.

"What is it, Eva?"

"I… uh… Even though I'm not posing all the time… Could I maybe… Jett, I still want to hang out here. I'd like to do… maybe a little more than that. If you'd let me."

"Are you asking permission to be intimate with my family?"

"Yes, sir. And with you."

"You know that everyone in the family decides for herself who she wants to have sex with. You'll have to work that out with them." Eva glanced nervously at Ariel and my little pixie was almost beside herself with glee. "As to me…" I was about to find out if I'd read Eva correctly or if she'd storm out of the house and our lives. "I might reward you for good behavior occasionally. If you are good and obedient." Such a powerful shiver came over Eva that I thought she might have had an orgasm. That or she'd contracted Mary's essential tremors and I was sure that wasn't possible. She looked me in the eye and quivered.

"I'll do my best, sir," she whispered.

"Come here and let me taste your lips."

•·•❖ ꒰꒰ ☼ ꒱꒱ ❖•·•

I WAS DETERMINED not to have sex with Eva until at least after classes started again. That didn't stop my girlfriends. Especially Ariel.

I still needed four models for spring term.

"You need to talk to the bimbos," Jas said as she stretched next to me on the bed. "I'm sure they'll be back this weekend. Classes start Tuesday. Better talk to them before the boys next door get them too drunk to think."

"That might be the only way they'd agree," I said.

"Oh, I think they'd be willing, but we might have to put in a stock of weed and Fireball for during the paintings. Or wait! Do all three of them in some kind of Baroque setting. Let them unfold as full nudes like you did with Ariel," Jas said. "We could sell that as a feature film on Kelly's site. If we offer them the same deal Kelly gave me for my film, they'd get a tidy sum. We could ask the guys next door to fuck them on camera so you don't have to put your penie in their skanky twats."

"Hmm. Maybe I should make it a group scene and paint the guys into it as well," I said. I was doing a lot more advance planning for my projects this term than I had last. "Jas, I love you, you know that?"

"Yes. But I love to hear you say it. I love you, Jett."

"Our life isn't exactly what I imagined it would be when I convinced you to pose for me in a hotel room."

"You know, my imagination still ran along the lines of Disney princesses. This house… We've made it a home but it doesn't quite measure up to the castles of my dreams."

"You measure up to my idea of a princess, though," I laughed. "I just want you to know that even though we're surrounded by other girls who all want to have sex with us, I still think of our first time in that hotel room almost every day. It's hard to keep it in perspective sometimes. I love you."

"Jett, what we have is so much better than if it was just you and me. There were a few twinges of jealousy when we first started inviting others into our lives. I mean, Sarah Lynn came right out of left field when she just mounted you and went for a ride. If I hadn't had Kelly's tongue lapping my snootch, I might have gone ballistic. But think how much more difficult things would be if we were depending on just each other for everything in our lives. We wouldn't get half the cuddling we do and not even a quarter the orgasms."

My fingers had been busy smearing Jasmine's juices out of said snootch and all over her little love button and she was thrusting at me, trying to find the tip of my cock. I helped her and slowly slid into the depths of my first lover.

"I love being in you, Jas. I want to make love to you all night long."

"I'm willing. Keep me awake. I don't have to work until eleven tomorrow. Push in again. I love to feel you opening me. I love knowing that in a few minutes—or maybe a few seconds—you'll spray that yummy love juice into me."

"You can taste it down there?"

"No. But as soon as I scream out my orgasm, Ariel is going to run in here and lick it out of my snootch and feed it to me. I do love that girl's tongue." We laughed softly and I could feel the walls of her vagina clasping my penis. I backed and filled again. And again.

"I'm close, love," I whispered. "I can never hold back when I'm in you. I love feeling your snootch grab hold of my penie."

"Come, Jett. Come and I'll come and then Ariel will come and then we'll start all over. Oh! Yes! I feel you! I'm…"

Two minutes later, Ariel was between Jasmine's legs making sure she was extra clean for our next round.

⋅∘⋅❖ ⊃⊃⊂ ☼ ⊃⊃⊂ ❖⋅∘⋅

"Hey, you," I whispered in Eva's ear. She was in front of her laptop trying to organize her portfolio.

"Um… Hi. Uh… sir." Far from bursting out after permission to have sex with any of the girls who wanted to, Eva had become more quiet and shy. Only keeping the house warm encouraged her to join the family's partial nudity. She sat at the dining table wrapped in a fluffy bathrobe with her laptop but I knew it was all she wore. "You… um… want me? At all?"

"I won't interrupt work but if you can pause for a while, I want you."

She slammed the lid of her laptop down and jumped up to sit in my lap.

"I… I… You haven't… I didn't think… you wanted me," she stuttered.

"Didn't think I wanted to caress these beautiful breasts? Suck these tight little nipples. Kiss these tender lips? Desire is not lacking." I opened her robe and explored her body with my fingers and my lips. Eva moaned and clutched my head as I sucked her nipple into my mouth.

"What would you like, sir?"

"I would like you to get dressed so we can go out."

"Dressed? You mean… You're not… Dressed?"

"Before I reward your good behavior, I want to know how obedient you are. Put on a bikini under sweats that are easy to get out of. Then grab your coat. We're going for a drive."

"Yes, sir." Eva was disappointed that I wasn't simply ravishing her body, but at the same time I could see a glint of excitement over my commanding her and the obvious implication that wherever we were going, she would strip to her bikini. Char and Mary had worked together to contact the airport and make the initial presentation. I had an appointment with the facilities manager this afternoon. I packaged up my laptop and got my coat on so I was waiting by the back door jingling my keys when Eva caught up. I scowled at her.

"A little slow, aren't we?" I demanded. She hung her head.

"I don't have a bikini here, so I had to borrow one from Sarah Lynn. It's winter."

"Did you ask permission?"

"Yes, sir."

"Then let's go."

Eva rode quietly and nervously next to me in the Mini. I was really going to have to consider a bigger car sometime in the near future. We had no way to transport all eight of us. She didn't say anything but twisted at her fingers, watching out the window to see where we were going. She caught her breath when I turned in at the airport.

There are no commercial flights in and out of the Municipal Airport. Even the name was a misnomer since the field was not actually in the city. The regional airport on the north side of town had been annexed before it was even built. There was only one runway at Municipal but it was a mile long. It had been plowed but there was almost no traffic with our unpredictable weather. It had snowed on and off for the past five days. Most of the aircraft and business out here had to do with training and recreation. A few private business flights came in but there was no car rental office so it was difficult for passengers to get to town unless someone came to pick them up.

"Show me your airplane," I commanded. Eva got the first smile on her face I'd seen since my first instruction. She grabbed my hand and excitedly took me out to a hangar. A side door was unlocked and we went in. Lights were on in the hangar and a man looked up from under the cowling of a small airplane when the wind came through the open door with us.

"Eva!" he called. "I was beginning to think you don't love us anymore."

"Johnny, you know that isn't true. School's been a bitch and I was home for the holiday. How's my baby?" she asked running to the mechanic.

"She's next on the list," he said. "When are you going to buy her?"

"I think I only owe you another five thousand hours of labor," she laughed. "I wish I owned her instead of that piece of junk car I have. But if I didn't have the car, I couldn't get out here to fly."

"And if you lived in the apartment we offered you, you couldn't get to school," he said. "Who's this handsome boy you have with you? Planning to take him up high?"

"This is my… an artist who wants to paint me out here. Johnny Lewis, meet Jett Blackburn. Jett, this is the best airplane mechanic in the country."

"Your flattery will get you everywhere, girl," Johnny said as he shook my hand. "So, you're the artist? Does that mean our own little Eva is the model you intend to paint?"

"Yes, sir. It's nice to meet you."

"Jefferson is waiting in the office. We'd better go see him."

"Wait. You know each other?" Eva said.

"First time we've met, but the phone lines have been burning up the past two weeks. That woman who's been negotiating… Charmaine?… She is some dynamo. Can't wait to meet her!"

⋯◈ ꓱꓱ ☼ ꓱꓱ ◈⋯

OUR MEETING WITH Jefferson Wright, the airport facilities manager, went well. Eva was surprised and embarrassed when I told her to strip to her bikini so I could show what I had in mind with her positioned against the wall. She was red in the face when I showed the video of her Athena performance.

"I'd certainly pay to see that," Johnny said. "What do you think, Jeff?"

"We'll have to run it by the board but I think the idea will fly. What's the bottom line, Jett?"

"Zero," I said. "Charmaine has done a lot of prep work and investigation of the airport and the event. She believes I can make a solid profit based strictly on donations for the performance over the weekend."

"You. What about Eva?" Johnny asked. "Are you paying her?"

"That's a different matter. I was hoping that you might arrange some flying time for her in exchange for performing that weekend," I said. Eva gasped as she looked at me. Johnny and Jefferson exchanged a look and smiled.

"I think we could make a fair exchange for that," Jefferson said. "Pending board approval, you've got a date."

36
Back to Class

EVA LITERALLY bounced in her seat all the way back home. As soon as she was in the car and it was warm, she shed her jacket and sweatshirt. Her bouncing in just the bikini top was distracting from my driving.

"I can't believe you got me ten hours of flying time for my 'performance' that weekend! I love you!"

"You'll have to work nearly thirty to earn them," I laughed.

"Do you know what that works out to as an hourly wage? More than you make at the grocery story, for sure! Jett, I just can't believe you did this for me! I really… Can we make love, Jett? Please?"

•◦•◆ ⊃⊂ ☽ ⊃⊂ ◆•◦•

MARY LOOKED UP at us when we walked through the kitchen door. She smiled when I winked at her. Eva was stripping just inside the door. Not down to her bikini, but all the way.

"We're going to have sex!" she shouted. "We're going to do it!" She ran for the bedroom.

"Must have gone well," Mary laughed.

"I might have to clean the car seats."

"Haven't had to do that since our first date, have you?"

I walked over and pulled Mary into my arms for a long kiss.

"And always willing for a repeat performance," I said.

"Go satisfy the substrate," she laughed. "We can go out Sunday if you want."

"It's a date."

335

"WHAT WOULD YOU like, my model?" I whispered when I shed my clothes and approached the bed where Eva was stretched out. Over the holiday, she'd cut her hair into a little pixie bob. It was a good style for her oval face and generally thin features. Lying on her back, her boobs flattened slightly but the nips were still perky and sat proudly on top of hand-sized mounds. I'd chuckled a little when she was posing at the airport. She never quite popped out of Sarah Lynn's bikini top but it was just big enough that we all caught glimpses of her nipples in certain poses. That was probably what convinced the two older men to give her so many flying hours in exchange for the performance. Dirty old men.

Eva had shaved completely before I did the Athena painting and maintained a bare pussy. It was glistening with her moisture as I sat beside her on the bed.

"I would like to please you," she whispered back.

"Do you doubt that you are pleasing to me?"

"You… um… since I got back and you kissed me… until today you didn't touch me at all. I thought… I was afraid you were disappointed… didn't want me."

"Eva, I'm not all that experienced with this stuff. You look around and see my five roommates and Mary and you think I must be some kind of sex powerhouse or something. I've only been sexually active for about eight months. There's a lot I don't know about how to please a woman. Especially a woman like you. You gave me the opportunity to explore something new in my own life, too. I've always just taken things as they came. You even asked Sarah Lynn's permission before you asked to have a painting date. I'm just not very dominant."

While I talked, I touched her cheek and drew my fingers across her lips. She kissed them and I continued down her chin. I didn't grab at her boobs but trailed my fingers down between them and continued toward her heat, pausing a moment to trace her navel. The whole time, I was looking her in the eye and ignoring what my fingers were doing. Her breathing sped up the lower I stroked.

"But you gave me an opportunity. I'm exploring what it means to be an artist with a human canvas. You asked to please me? You do, my substrate. You are a blank canvas and I will paint a masterpiece on you."

I finally slipped my finger between the lips of her pussy and stroked from her opening up to circle her clit. I believe she levitated off the bed. When I rolled over on her and pushed my cock into her pussy for the first time, we both flew toward the sky.

·o· ⋄ ↹ ᛞᚲ ☀ ᛞᚲ ↶ ⋄ ·o·

THE GIRLS DUG into managing my art subjects for this semester. Having successfully negotiated Eva's and my engagement at the airport, Char was the one who took the lead, inviting the three bimbos over for dinner Saturday night. That is how I ended up 'demonstrating' my art technique on the naked bodies of Barb, Terri, and Syl while we were all stoned out of our minds.

We didn't do a huge production, I just painted on their tits and tummies.

There is a phenomenon called the freshman fifteen. It is the inevitable packing on of fifteen extra pounds during freshman year. For some people, it is followed by the sophomore fifteen, the junior fifteen, and the senior fifteen. I guess that's why so many people go back to their ten-year high school class reunions unrecognizable to their classmates. We'd all succumbed to some extent, though our meal planning and cooking schedule meant that we had a better chance of not packing on too many pounds. I'd put on five. Jas, Char, and Sarah Lynn had put on a few, but not nearly fifteen. Ariel burned off calories having sex so fast that her Asian figure was still slight. And Kelly… *Damn!* Kelly was sexier every day. She worked out at the university fitness center after class each day and her tight, toned body was no heavier but slightly shapelier than it had been the first day she sent me a naked selfie when we were fifteen.

All that to say that the three bimbos—I really need to stop calling them that or I'll slip up when we're working—the blondes from two doors down had definitely packed on some weight. A steady diet of alcohol and snack food will do that to you. I don't think any of their household cooked meals, so they ate at the student union or McDonald's. They weren't fat,

337

but their curves had definitely become rounder and softer since we first met in September. I liked it. They were almost Rubenesque.

"This is fun, but if I don't get fucked soon, I'll die," Syl said

"We don't loan Jett out," Sarah Lynn jumped in. "He has seven of us to satisfy as it is. I thought you were playing with the guys next door."

"Yeah. But they aren't here. Why didn't you invite them to the party?" Terri asked.

"We can do that when we do the painting, if you want," I said. "We didn't want you to be uncomfortable when we were introducing what we wanted to do."

"Hell, give me another Fireball and you can paint Reggie's cock in my twat," Barb said. "You're only young once and I plan to get as much dick as I can. Sure you don't want a little of this, Jett?" She spread her legs in front of me and pulled her labia open.

If a girl is shaved and plans to entice a guy into her pussy, I think she should have shaved recently. Barb looked like a guy with a two-day beard and I imagined her pussy would feel like sandpaper against my cock. I declined.

"We'll negotiate something with Reggie and the guys. Remember, we film everything in order to get the short videos you saw earlier. If we film you fucking, we'll release it on a porn site," Kelly said. "And we'll be moderating the amount of weed and alcohol during the session. With a project this big, it will probably take six hours to get you all painted adequately for the scene."

"So, aside from the weed and a good fuck, what do we get out of it?"

"We're putting together a YouTube channel for Jett's artwork," Sarah Lynn said. "We'll be able to record hits for individual videos and pay according to popularity. That video won't include any graphic sex, but it will include you being painted like the videos we showed you earlier. You'll get a bitcoin payment for each hit."

"Porn is a different thing entirely. If we reach an agreement to do some serious sex, we'll either pay you a percentage or a flat fee. A percentage split among half a dozen actors might not be much," Kelly said.

"Have you done that before?" Syl asked. Kelly looked over at Jas. She sighed.

"I did one. It's the only one we've released," Jas said. "I've made seven hundred dollars from my cut."

"Shit! I could use seven hundred!" Terri said. "Can we see your film?" Jas nodded and Kelly queued up her Egyptian goddess vid. We all watched but the three blondes were glued to the screen. Seeing Jas in her paint and her expressions of ecstasy was something I'd never get tired of watching. She was just so beautiful it made me want to bundle her off to bed again. When the video ended, the girls turned back to Kelly and me. They had tears in their eyes.

"I think I'm drunk. I'm getting all emotional," Syl said. "That was just so beautiful."

"Can you make us look like that?" Barb sniffed. "I want to look like that."

"Our technique and editing has gotten better since we did that one," Kelly said. "The acting is what you'll bring to the set. And the boys."

The girls left and I watched as they turned left instead of right and went up the steps to the guys next door.

I'D ALWAYS BEEN first out of the house on Monday mornings because I started work at six. It was almost a luxurious feeling to sleep later and not have to be to class until eight. Two extra hours to sleep in the arms of my lovers. Everyone was pretty exhausted after our Saturday encounter with the blondes. I could only imagine what the actual painting would be like once the guys got involved. We'd have to do the whole painting in a canvas-covered living room in order to have six in the painting. There would be a lot of digital backgrounding and post-production work. I'd have all I could handle just painting their bodies as nymphs and satyrs.

I walked into my Protein Identification, Fabrication, and Utilization class as the first class of spring semester. I wasn't sure what this was going to include since the first term that I took in the summer really focused on being able to identify primal cuts and figure out how to cut them into marketable cuts. Grandpa had handled the instruction on that course for me in the store. The setup in our new class was a stainless steel kitchen. There were eight of us in the class and we were each assigned a work station.

"If you came here to learn to cook, you're in the wrong class," Mr. George, the instructor, said. "The college has cooking classes. Go enroll in those. Oh, we will cook things, but this class is focused on the commercial preparation of meats for use in the home. In other words, how do you advise a customer on the cut of meat and preparation when they are shopping in your store? We will also look at the various ways you can prepare cuts so all a customer needs to do is take it home and heat it to the right temperature. We specialize in the boyfriend's seduction of his girlfriend, the working woman's satisfaction of her man, the single mom's providing for her children, and the old-man-living-alone-in-a-trailer-park's fantasy of being rich and loved. We'll learn what makes a pot roast pre-seasoned with seven cents worth of spices sell for a dollar a pound more than an unseasoned roast. You will learn marinating, rubbing, pounding, cubing, kebobbing, stuffing, wrapping, and seasoning. You will learn proper cooking temperatures, recommended grades for each use, and combination of vegetables with various proteins. Now, let's get started."

I glanced around at the other seven in the class. We were evenly divided between men and women but I thought I was probably the youngest in the class. I recognized two who were in my slaughtering class, but I wasn't on the standard two-semester-and-out program, so I seldom overlapped with the same people. As hard as this class looked to be, it still sounded interesting. I was looking forward to applying principles from this to the cooking we did at home.

•ı• •❖ ꓲꓵꓒ ☀ ꓲꓵꓒ ❖• •ı•

MERCK WAS HIS usual high and entertaining self as he started the term with a slide-show of Michelangelo that was focused mostly on the 'pristine' chapel, as he called it.

"If in your ventures, you decide to visit and study the art of the Vatican, plan on spending at least a month. Half of that time will be spent waiting in the incredible lines to see the chapel. And do not assume you will be able to take good photographs as the light varies by time of day and weather conditions, you will be constantly jostled by sightseers like yourself who want a selfie with 'The Creation of Adam', and a priest will intone, 'Please be silent,' every five minutes. For that matter, security people will shout 'No photo!' at you if they so much as see you with a cell phone in your hands. Photography is prohibited, though you might sneak the occasional shot. If you bring binoculars, you might be able to focus on one or two of the paintings on the ceiling. Binoculars, I say, because the ceiling is seventy feet above you and you will get no closer." Merck was having a good time showing the slides.

"It took Michelangelo four years to paint the ceiling and another six to paint *The Last Judgment* on the altar wall. We are told he was under duress when he painted the ceiling, being called off the sculpture of the tomb of Pope Julius the Second, for which he had previously been commissioned. Jealousy among artists and architects resulted in Michelangelo being set up to fail at a medium he'd never used before. Nonetheless, he made his own suggestions and modified the original scope of work to include the entire chapel rather than just twelve panels of the apostles. And what he placed there! For example, contrary to contemporary Christian and Catholic moralities, a majority of the four hundred or so figures in the chapel are naked and Michelangelo has no difficulty painting both male and female genitalia. In the central scene, *The Creation of Adam*, we see that only God is clothed—presumably in glory. But what is this? Who is this naked nymph with God's protective arm around her? No one knows? Is it Eve? Mary? Sophia the goddess of wisdom? A female angel? God's mistress? Well, it is too far up in the heavens to be easily defaced as were many frescoes close enough to the floor for later censors to paint in clothes or paint out unholy details."

It was a fun lecture and I wondered what else was hidden in the frescoes of the Sistine Chapel. In our brief tour, we found that Michelangelo had changed the design of the original commission and instead of the twelve triangular panels being portraits of the twelve apostles, they were portraits of the twelve prophets who prophesied the coming of Christ. Seven of those appear in the Old Testament. The other five were the classic female sibyls referenced back in Virgil's *Æneid*.

"I'd still like to attend one of your painting performances," Merck said to me as I was headed out of the lecture hall. "I know you compress hours of work into the short videos you produce. I'd like once to get the whole experience."

"I'll see what I can do," I said. "I think one of the pieces this term will include both male and female models, so there might not be as much embarrassment about having a man who isn't engaged in the process watching them." *Dirty old man.*

⁃o⁃ ⁃◈ ⁋⁊⁌ ☼ ⁋⁊⁌ ◈⁃ ⁃o⁃

"I HAVE COMBINED my two Drawing I classes into this single Drawing II class. I am assuming that the weak have been eaten by predators and we needn't wait for them. I am also assuming that you are sufficiently toughened that I can chew on you without further losses. This term, we will be focused on composition, illusional space, perspective, proportion, and form." Blankety continued to lecture for the rest of the first hour of our two-and-a-half-hour class. Then he unveiled a doll house and told us to work on the technical rendering of perspective. He wanted us to plot the vanishing points, horizon line, and angles of each element. We were to leave all our working lines on the page. We were not to do any shading or detail work. That, he said, would come later.

⁃o⁃ ⁃◈ ⁋⁊⁌ ☼ ⁋⁊⁌ ◈⁃ ⁃o⁃

"JETT, YOU KNOW Andi Michaels, right?" Mary asked as a girl followed us out of Blankety's classroom.

"I'm sorry we haven't really talked," I said. "We're always so crushed after this class that we don't seem to be in a very social mood. It's nice to officially meet you, Andi."

"Yeah. It's great being known as the cartoon girl," she snorted. Just before our mid-term, Blankety had pointed out all our faults, suggesting that Andi's drawings were all cartoons. She'd nearly run out of the class. As far as I could tell, she was nice and certainly nice-looking if a little plain. "You guys are so lucky to have each other," she continued. "Mary's the only person in class I knew at all and that's only because we had the same Western Culture class."

"We didn't know each other at all until we sat down in class," I said. "I'm sorry I haven't reached out to more people."

"Um… Mary showed me a video of the project you did using her as a model. It was really cool. She mentioned that you might need more models this semester. I'd… uh… it's not like I'm all wild about getting naked and having my body painted, but I guess I'd be interested enough to talk about it if you want."

"What time's your ILS course tomorrow?" I knew Mary was enrolled in the Western Culture: Science, Technology, Philosophy course. I just assumed Andi was, too.

"We get out the same time you do," Mary said. "Two o'clock."

"That's a relief. Why don't you come over for dinner and meet the gang?" I said. Andi smiled. *Hmm. I could work with that.*

I GOT HOME Monday night to realize that we hadn't redone our cooking schedule to accommodate our new class schedules. I used to get off work at two and be responsible for Monday night dinner. Getting home at six with no food ready and none scheduled threw everyone off-kilter. I quickly looked in the fridge to see what we had available and what was quick. I had a flank steak in the freezer that I planned to use for teriyaki sometime. I grabbed it and immersed the plastic package in warm water.

"Mary, could you do me a favor and run down to the convenience store?" I asked. "I had no idea that I'd be on dinner duty tonight. We really screwed this up."

"Sure. What do you need?"

"Tortillas, shredded cheese, and salsa."

"Back in a jiff," she said, taking the twenty-dollar bill and my car keys.

I grabbed an onion and some peppers and set to work slicing them up into strips. Our first class this morning had itemized a long list of prepared foods that were common in grocery stores. Fajita kits were one of them. I didn't have a kit, and I didn't have time to marinate the steak, but I had cayenne pepper and hot sauce. While the peppers and onions caramelized in the skillet, I sliced up the partially frozen meat into two-inch strips. I sprinkled them lightly with cayenne and seasoned salt. As soon as the vegetables were suitably soft, I tossed the meat in the skillet to brown. By then, Mary was back with two dozen tortillas, cheese, salsa, and she'd added sour cream and guacamole.

It was only a little past six-thirty when we sat down to eat and discuss our schedules so we could determine a new cooking rotation. I hadn't seen Eva yet this week and she wasn't with us tonight, so she didn't get put on the schedule. Mary was listed for Tuesday nights and had contributed to the monthly food budget.

"I switched my meal plan at the U to the lightest they have," she said. "It's enough to give me breakfast and lunch. I'm over here almost every evening, even if I don't spend the night. So, I'm contributing the balance of what my food budget would be."

There was some discussion about whether that was too much, but we also saw this as Mary making a commitment to our family.

37
The Garden of Earthly Delights

"BY THE way, we have a guest coming for dinner tomorrow. I'll pay the guest fee. She's a potential model for one of my class projects," I said after dinner as we were getting our schedule set. "I don't mind cooking again."

"What's she like?" Sarah Lynn asked.

"I like her," Mary volunteered. "I told her about Jett's project and what I did. She's in that kind of tremulous stage of deciding if she can or can't do it. I can tell you right off that she has no designs on Jett or anyone else at the moment."

"What's she *look* like?" Char asked.

"About five-seven. Nice shape but I don't think she's a supermodel. She always dresses nicely. Shoulder length brown hair. I think it was brown eyes. Mary?" I asked.

"Yeah. Brown. Dimples. Probably about a thirty-five C if I had to guess. Waist might be a little thick but if so, she disguises it well. I haven't seen her nude so I can't give you dirty details," she laughed. Gee, it was nice to have Mary sitting down with us and so relaxed.

"How far will she go?" Kelly wanted to know.

"There won't be any porn with this and she's sure to be nervous if someone is moving around with a camera while I'm working. Once I'm done, I think she'll be okay with the camera circuit because she won't really be recognizable."

"What are you thinking of doing with her?" Jas asked. There were a few titters around the table.

"Not that!" I said harshly. Then I smiled at her to let her know I wasn't mad. "I'm trying to come up with some representation of the Age of Reason. That would be next after spring break."

"You're planning things way ahead this semester," Sarah Lynn said.

"I didn't have any idea what I was doing last semester and only managed to come up with ideas and inspirations as we covered them in class. This is a harder semester. The Wednesday class is a discussion group, not even in the lecture hall. And the material overlaps. I was going to start with something from Shakespeare and then do the blondes for a Rubens Baroque painting come to life. But Shakespeare and Rubens were the same year, even though Shakespeare was considered classic and Rubens Baroque," I said. "It's a good thing I actually looked at Merck's syllabus."

"But you were going to do Ariel as Shakespeare's Ariel!" Jas exclaimed. "Does that mean you won't be able to do that?"

"I suppose I could, but I came up with an even more appropriate theme from Hieronymus Bosch. He's a Dutch painter of about the same time as Michelangelo and much better at the human figure in painting. He did a famous painting called *The Garden of Earthly Delights*."

"I'm going to be a sex doll again!" Ariel said jumping up and down. *I think I'll just get her a trampoline and have her bounce naked in front of me for a few hours a day.*

"Probably, in one way or another. I want to keep the theme of a triptych, more or less, but you will definitely be the centerpiece. I read the description on my phone as I was headed from Lit to Drawing. There's a great phrase here." I thumbed my phone to Wikipedia and read. "An erotic derangement that turns us all into voyeurs, a place filled with the intoxicating air of perfect liberty."

"I like voyeurs. I want to fill them with intoxicating air," Ariel said. I had a feeling this would be an interesting project.

"And then we do the Baroque porn with the blondes and the boys next door. Or whoever they entice to be their partners," Kelly said.

"That's going to be a logistic nightmare," I said. "I'll have to get each of them painted before I put it all together. And I'm going to have to use acrylic or it will all run off of them as they get sweaty together."

"I have to get 2257 Compliant Forms filled out and signed by each of them," Kelly said. "It certifies their age, legal names, consent, and compensation. I had to fill one out in order to perform online, too. We've all filled them out even though Jas and I are the only ones who have actually performed explicit sex acts on video. And you, of course."

"I hope they are all okay with this," I said. "Um… We'll need at least two cameras going, right?"

"Yeah. Anybody want to volunteer?"

"I was just thinking… Merck has been bugging me since he saw Jasmine's video to let him come to a sitting. Since this one doesn't involve any of us and they don't really know our crews, I just thought maybe it would kill two birds with one stone to have him be a cameraman."

"That is so kinky to have a professor film porn in our home!" Sarah Lynn said. "You rock!"

•o• •◇ ⊃⊂ ☼ ⊃⊂ ◇• •o•

THAT FAST, WE were into the semester and it seemed like there was no time for anything. We were all studying late into the evening so we wouldn't get behind. Jas was picking up multiple shifts on the weekends because she couldn't work during the week with her class and study schedule. Ariel had picked up two additional piano students and was deep in a full load of principles of mechanics, statistics for engineers, math, and engineering graphics. And she was taking Mandarin Chinese Language for her Liberal Arts elective!

Sarah Lynn was piling on the credits again with courses in International Relations and Statistics for Political Research. Of course, she had a math course, an English Comp class, Russian Language, and having completed a course on the principles of aeronautics last term, this term she was focusing on principles of naval science. That was her course 'just for fun.'

Kelly was even coming downstairs after her evening chatroom session and instead of seeking immediate sexual gratification, she was cracking a math or Spanish book. She'd finally declared herself as a Communication Arts Major with a focus in Radio-Television-Film. She had some courses to make up because her first term had been exploratory.

And Char had met with her adviser over the break and had been encouraged to enter the Integrated Master of Accountancy program.

347

When she'd explained her circumstances, the adviser had really gone to bat for her and got her some more financial aid. That really relieved some of the economic pressure she was under, but she had to maintain a 3.5 GPA in order to keep the support. She was studying Economics, Psychology, General Business, and Speech Communications this term.

Suffice it to say that bedtime had been pushed to about one a.m. on the average and I had to be at an eight o'clock food prep class. This was a crazy term.

"How ARE YOU going to approach it?" Mary asked. We'd been working on the latest Blankety project, entirely on applying mechanical perspective to drawing of irregular objects. It was a long and tedious project but I was learning something beyond the basics of vanishing points and horizons. I guess it was helpful. And the project allowed Mary and me time to just talk while we worked. It was far more technical and we didn't tend to get in the same zone that we did when actually drawing or painting something. Of course, she was asking about my upcoming triptych with Ariel.

"The Bosch painting is an inspiration, but I'm not going to try to replicate it. I mean, it has a little of everything in it. Gluttony, bestiality, fornication, homosexuality, interracial, music, drunkenness, and a progression from innocence to depravity to punishment. I'm not as interested in that as in the concept of *The Garden of Earthly Delights*. Especially when it comes to Ariel."

"That girl is the embodiment of earthly delight," Mary laughed. "You wouldn't have to paint anything. Just take her on stage and strip her."

"The thing is, she'd love that!" Once Ariel came out of her shell, sex had competed successfully with music and mechanical engineering. It was almost like she had a triple major. "I'm thinking of doing an actual garden scene with flowers and such sort of growing out of her."

"Sounds kind of boring."

"Unless I apply Blankety's final project last term with it."

"The shapes… Oh! Create all the flowers and highlights and shadows out of other shapes? That could be interesting."

"Especially if all the shapes were… um… sexual in nature. I mean, can't you just imagine Ariel's body covered in flowers that were actually made of little vaginas and penises?" I asked. Mary raised her eyebrows and put her pencil down.

"Speaking of vaginas and penises, did you notice that I wore a skirt today?"

It didn't take long to verify why she was wearing a skirt. As we kissed, my hand slid up under the hem and found the open crotch of her bodystocking. It didn't take long before I was standing between her legs as she sat on her stool. My cock sank into the spongy wetness of her pussy and we both sighed at the feeling.

I'd noticed that over the past month or so, sex among the family had moved from utter spontaneity to the last thing we did in bed at night, assuming everyone wasn't too tired. That wasn't just me having sex with the girls, but the girls with each other, too. Having a little afternoon delight with Mary in the studio was a treat beyond imagining.

I pulled the top of her stocking down her arms far enough that I could release her breasts and could tug and twist her nipple barbells while we kissed and I plunged into her. The one-piece bodystockings like this one were meant to be put on at the feet like hose and then pulled up the body until she could put her arms in and adjust it around her shoulders. This one was new. When she took her sweater off in the studio, I discovered the entire stocking was mesh with a pattern of roses woven into it. The sides were a more open weave and it was only a series of half a dozen straps that went over her shoulders. I had to be careful when I lowered it because the barbells caught in the mesh and her nipples poked through.

I suppose I looked ridiculous standing between her legs with my jeans around my ankles and my butt flexing as I pushed in and out of her. I didn't care. I wasn't doing this for anyone else's entertainment. I was totally caught up in the way Mary's pussy sucked at my cock as I pulled out, trying to get me to thrust back in. I was glad she got so stimulated with her nipple play because there was no way I could get a hand between us to play with her clit in this position. She whined into my mouth as she came, clamping and releasing on my cock with that incredible soft pussy. She hadn't quite made her second release when I erupted in her and I almost lost my balance when my knees started shaking. Mary jammed a hand between us and grabbed her clit bar to twist and pull. She managed to get her cookies before I shrank out of her.

"We don't do that anywhere near enough," she whispered. "I wish Ariel was home. She'd love this little snack."

•୦•⇨ ⊃⊂ ☼ ⊃⊂ ⇦•୦•

"Um… I don't know how to ask this," I stumbled. We'd been in class for two weeks and my first project was due in just another ten days. Ariel as the garden of delight. But I needed models. "We're lovers and I don't want to make it weird."

"What could be weirder than having seven girls who love you and love each other?" Sarah Lynn asked. "You're not planning to propose to any of us, are you?" Dee and Derek had gotten married in a private ceremony at Christmas, but they were having a party reception for their high school friends on Valentine's Day—at Dee's mother's suggestion. We were all thinking about it.

"No. I… um… Well, the concept for Ariel's Garden of Delights is that I paint it all out of… um… pussies and cocks. And… um… I need models."

"Jett? You want to draw our pussies?" Char asked. She clamped her legs together. What a contradiction. She'd been hesitant about giving me her vagina cherry but was not hesitant to give me her mouth or ass long before. But I wasn't going to push anyone.

"Yeah. I guess that's what I need. Not just pussies but breasts and lips, too. Nothing that would be recognizable in the painting, but sexual body parts."

"Haven't you stared into my snootch enough times to memorize it?" Jas asked. "If you'll lick it when you're done drawing it, I'll do it."

"Yeah, me, too," Sarah Lynn said. "Same terms."

"Oh. Uh, sure. I need pictures in various stages of arousal. Mouths in different expressions. Lips pursed, lips slightly parted, lips in an O, tongue hanging out… You know."

"Nipples erect," Mary picked up. "Nipples soft. Nipples pierced." We all laughed. "I'm in."

"Oh, yeah. When you put it like that…" Char said, "You should probably draw my asshole, too. Closed. Open. Dripping come."

350

"How about dicks?" Kelly asked. "You can't just paint her out of pussies. It would be much sexier if you were getting both together."

"Yeah… um… It's going to be difficult enough to paint the blondes' boyfriends up as satyrs, if you know what I mean."

"I got you covered." We all looked at Kelly trying to get her to explain. "I get like fifty dick-pics a week. In all stages of arousal, including spurting come. Circumcised, uncut, skinny, fat, short, long, hard, soft… I got you covered. Since I know the sketches of our pussies are just reference pieces, I don't think pictures of dicks would be any worse to use as references."

"I just hope nobody gets on my computer and starts finding pictures of dicks," I sighed. "Thank you, Kelly. And thank you all."

"Wait!" Ariel said. "Does my pussy get to be in it, too? I mean, more than just between my legs?" We all laughed. I reassured her that her pussy would be prominently displayed.

•ο•⚬➤ ⊃⊂ ☽ ⊃⊂ ⬅⚬•ο•

"Jett? Don't you like my asshole anymore?" I'd just plunged into Char's pussy and felt that velvet glove close around my cock.

"Hmm? Uh… What?"

"You haven't done me back there since, like, Christmas. Don't you like it any longer?"

"I… uh…" I slowed down and looked at my Indian lover. "I kind of assumed that now that we were doing sex normally, you wouldn't want to substitute your ass. Isn't this okay?"

"Oh, it's okay. But I never offered you my ass as a substitute for my pussy. I offered it because I liked it."

"Really? God, yes! Next time you're prepared, let me know and we'll definitely do it that way. I loved coming in your ass."

"I'm prepared every time I come to bed with you, honey. Just do me."

My eyebrows shot up and she nodded. I pulled back out of her pussy and lodged my cock against her little pucker. She gripped my shoulders and I sank into her like I was passing through soft butter. *Oh, God!* No one had mentioned anal sex again since the night of Kelly's Christmas special. I loved bouncing against her hot, buttery butt. I chuckled. *Butter butt.* I figured I'd better keep that one to myself for a while.

Besides… Char.

•◦•✦ ⟠ ☀ ⟠ ✦•◦•

Wʜᴇɴ Kᴇʟʟʏ ᴡᴀɴᴛᴇᴅ me to come to the Kat House for her pussy drawing, I assumed she must want to broadcast it to her chatroom. She didn't usually log in on Mondays, though. But all I needed was a sketchpad and pencil. It wasn't like I was painting anything. When I turned to face her, she was on all fours on her bed, looking back at me over her naked butt.

"Kelly, I'm going to draw your pussy, you know?"

"You don't like this view? I looked through your drawings of Char, Ariel, and Mary. You got different pussies in different stages of arousal, but they are all from pretty much the same perspective. You need not only different pussies, but different views. Take a close look and tell me if you don't like what you see."

Fuck! I liked what I saw with her upturned freckled ass pointed at me and her pussy flowering open beneath it. I kept her in that position when I gave her the reward.

•◦•✦ ⟠ ☀ ⟠ ✦•◦•

"Dᴏ ʏᴏᴜ sᴛɪʟʟ love me?"

"Yes. I love you more all the time."

"Even with all the other girls who love you?"

"And who I love. No matter how much crazy stuff we do, I still keep coming home to you."

"Put that to music! You'll have a hit country tune." Jas laughed and I felt her insides vibrate with her joy as I slid deep again.

"Sometimes I worry that you aren't being satisfied. I should be with you more often," I said. "Are you okay?"

"If you were with me more often, I'd have to cut back on how often I'm with Kelly. Or Ariel. Or Char. Or Sarah Lynn. Or Mary."

"And Eva?"

"Oh. I'm not sure I could cut back my time with her much more. Don't get me wrong. I like Eva and she is willing to play with all of us when she comes over. But it's pretty obvious that she's only really interested in you. I'm not even positive about that. Her head's always kind of in the clouds."

"What a great theme. Her head's in the clouds. I might name the airport painting that."

"Yeah. But the point is that I'm happy, Jett. I love you so much it squeezes out of my eyes sometimes. I go hunting for little romantic memes on Facebook. But I love all our girlfriends, too. I can't wait to go walking in the park with Mary or argue some obscure point of jurisprudence vs. the media with Sarah Lynn. Or to go down on them. And Ariel. You know that as soon as you leave a deposit in my snootch, she's going to run in here to make a withdrawal, right?"

We laughed and I felt that delightful ripple around my cock again.

"I don't think she'll need to wait long," I rasped.

"I bet she sucks me off of you before you pull out of me," Jas whined as her own orgasm mounted.

⋆⋅☽ ☾⋅⋆

ANDI CAME HOME with Mary and me after class Wednesday. I just figured she was getting used to the environment or maybe wanted to ask questions about the project she'd be part of. Not that I'd thought that far ahead yet. We tossed our bags down and I went to get us pops from the fridge.

"So, Jett… um… Mary said you need… um… sex organ models. If I volunteer, you won't like try to touch me, will you?"

"Andi? I never even thought to ask you to model that way."

"Yeah, but I thought maybe if I did that, nothing that happened when we do the bodypainting would bug me. It's not like anyone around here is going to recognize my quim. My boyfriend is at IU."

"Ouch. That's hard to be in a long-distance relationship."

"It's working out okay so far. I suppose no girl has asked him to get naked so she can paint his body yet."

"Andi, when we do that, I obviously have to touch you some, just to get paint on you. But I'm not on the make. I've got all the girlfriends I can handle. So the answer is, 'No. I won't touch you if you want to model for the 'sex organ' sketches.'"

"Okay. I'm ready. Unless you need me shaved. I figured I'd have to do that for the other project, but I didn't shave for this. I'm kind of hairy."

"I think that would be a great variation to have in my sketches."

Mary took her up to the bedroom where I'd been doing most of the sketches and when Andi was ready, she called me.

I started with sketches of her lips and tongue and then moved on to her prominent nipples. She kept pushing the sheet down as I needed access to her body. I paused to do a quick sketch of her navel, which was popped out just a little, unlike the deep indents of my girlfriends' navels. And then she unveiled her delta and the slit beneath. I lay on the bed between her legs with her pussy about a foot in front of me and started sketching. A faint scent of arousal wafted toward me and I asked her to part her lips a little for the next sketch. She did.

I should be used to this view. Kelly and Jas had been sexting with me and doing mutual masturbation on Skype for three years. We'd been lovers and added Sarah Lynn, Ariel, Char, Mary, and Eva—all of whom I'd had up-close and personal views of from this angle. But a guy just can't lie down and stare at a new girl's pussy for the first time and not have a response. I was folded in half under me as I got stiffer and stiffer. I ignored the pain and just focused on the pussy. I was impressed with the directions her hair grew and wondered if she'd combed it before I was called. It wasn't the tangled mess she prepared me for, but a fluffy frame for a beautiful pussy.

Fuck!

"We're all done," I said. "Thank you for helping me out, Andi. It was beautiful. I really appreciate it. Thank you."

I got out of the room and saw Ariel coming out of the bathroom. I grabbed her hand and pulled her into one of the other bedrooms, much to her surprise. As soon as I closed the door, I dragged my jeans and underwear down, letting my cock spring out straight at last.

"Suck!" was all I could get out of my mouth. Ariel's face lit up and she swallowed my cock.

38
New Models

I CONVINCED MERCK TO let me present my project on the Monday after Valentine's instead of on Valentine's Day when they were due. I explained that my model had difficulty making time to be painted until the weekend and that we needed to film at a controlled time and location. He was hesitant. I played my trump.

"Um… I'm preparing a Baroque rendition of the Bacchanalia next. It's pretty complex because there are six models involved. It would be really handy to have a second pair of hands on the video camera. Would you be interested?"

"Oh. Sure, I'd love to help out. Women?" I nodded. "That would be… What's the date you plan to do that one?"

"I think we'll do it the weekend of the twenty-third. None of these models will come into class. The whole production will be on video. In fact, I plan to project an image of Poussin's *Bacchanal before a Statue of Pan* at the beginning, then fade into my own rendition. From there, we'll have the figures come to life."

"That sounds incredibly ambitious."

"Uh… How do you feel about porn?"

"I'm not sure what the point of your question is. I've nothing personally against it, but I don't think the administration would be pleased if we showed any in class."

"Well, these painting sessions sometimes get a little rowdy. And the models are all… um… intimate with each other already. I can't swear that they won't get a little carried away in the excitement. We plan to just keep filming and use what we can." Little lie? Not really. We just intended to use it all.

"Are you…?"

"No, not me, nor any of our crew. Only the models. Hope you're good with that."

"I think I can work with it." He might have been breathing a little heavily.

"Okay. See you Monday."

"Oh, yes. It will be fine to put off your *Garden of Earthly Delights* presentation until Monday the eighteenth."

Whew!

⋅∘⋅⇨ ⟆⟅ ☾ ⟆⟅ ⇦⋅∘⋅

I'm a glutton for punishment. That's the way Granddad described my relationship with seven women. It's what I thought of myself when I stood outside the classroom where Blankety was concluding his Drawing I class Thursday afternoon. I wondered how many people he'd lost from the class after six sessions so far this semester. I was actually going to ask him for a critique. *Fuck!*

At exactly five o'clock he walked out the door of the classroom and I fell in step with him as he swept out of the room and down the hall. I felt like Harry Potter trying to get a word with Snape. *Why am I doing this?*

"Professor? I was wondering if I could ask your opinion on a project I'm doing for a different class." He turned and scowled at me.

"You know my opinion. Sophomoric. Big dreams for a small talent. Too much focus on the reflection and not enough on the subject. Probably the wrong pencil and paper. Barely in a class that would be considered art."

"If you would look at it, sir, I'd appreciate it. I'm trying to improve." *God! What an obsequious idiot I am!*

"The indignities that I have to put up with at this so-called school," he muttered. "Sit down and give me your scribbles," he said as we entered his office. I handed him my sketch for *The Garden of Earthly Delights.* "Pervert!" he snarled when he looked at the sketch. "I knew that the minute you grabbed the hand of that disabled girl who sits next to you and worships you. She's the only one in the class who has a real talent." I was seething but I vowed to learn something from his irrational rantings

356

about my shortcomings. "Is this what you really want? To dress up a woman as if she is simply a cunt waiting to be plundered? Ninety-five percent of the people on this campus would try to hang you. Four-and-a-half percent wouldn't get it and the remaining half-percent would shake their heads and say, 'too bad about what happened to Jett.' The composition is flat. If you are going to mimic great art, you need to find the depth. Making flowers out of genitalia is fine but what kind of flowers?"

He turned to his whiteboard and grabbed a marker. While looking at my sketch, he quickly outlined it on the board. In thirty seconds, I could see Ariel take shape and, in a minute, flowers bloomed from her in the shape of the cunt garden. The only real difference was that he gave her bigger boobs. He tossed the sketch back on his desk and started highlighting things with a red marker. I'd been in his classes since September and this was the first time I'd seen him draw. It was amazing.

"First, composition. Making the flowers into a flowering vagina is okay as far as it goes, but where are the thorns? Where is the Venus Flytrap? Where are the bees pollinating the garden and threatening to sting? You can't have the earthly delight without the earthly peril. Second, the depth. The closer the viewer gets to the work, the less he should see the obvious and the more he should see the shapes it comprises. Each flower should be a compilation of smaller units. And don't limit yourself to genitalia. Free it up. Symbols of fertility. Third, focus. If you maintain the style through the entire composition, it will all blur together. Something needs to stand out. Perhaps the eyes. Render them as photographically as your little skill will let you. Let them peer out from the overwhelming backdrop of the garden."

He turned and glared at me, shoving my sketchbook across his desk. I couldn't say anything. He'd torn it apart and put it back together in three seconds. I barely got my cell phone up and snapped a picture of his whiteboard before he started erasing it.

"Redraw it and show me the new rendering in three weeks."

"I have to paint it for my class next weekend."

"I don't care what you paint. I care that you learn to draw. Bring me a rendering that shows you know both the subject and the story. Then draw it again. By the end of the term you might have an acceptable drawing."

I didn't say anything else. I wasn't going to argue or defend anything. I was going to try to learn what he taught. He wanted me to render this again and again. I'd do that. I picked up the sketchbook and walked out. I realized that was one of his moves. When you are finished, just leave.

•◦•◦❖ ⅅⅭ ☽ ⅅⅭ ❖◦•◦•

BOSCH'S TRIPTYCH IN the Museo del Prado in Madrid is nearly seven feet tall and thirteen feet wide. It must have taken forever to paint it and that clued me in on the scope of the project I'd proposed at the airport. I needed to get a rendering for that project done and get out there to lay in the base soon. Doing a project that big was going to be a monster task.

Doing my own garden triptych was almost as daunting now that I'd been ripped to shreds by Blankenship. I picked up the materials I'd need after my morning class on Friday and spent most of the day assembling the pieces at Granddad's. He had a pretty good shop and was always willing to help me if I needed to build canvas frames or some other odd thing. When he realized what I wanted, he even used a router to cut notches for the hinges and then we both sanded the surface I'd paint on. It was three-sixteenths-inch clear birch plywood and I attached a one-by-two frame on the back to stabilize it. If it ever became a major work of mine, I'd eventually have to come up with a scene for the outside, too. The center panel was three feet square with the two side panels half as wide. When fully open, it would be six feet wide and three feet tall.

It barely fit in the Mini.

Before the day was over, I'd put a primer coat on the wood and was back to work on the sketch. If Sarah Lynn hadn't slammed a book shut in the living room at two a.m., I'd probably have pulled an all-nighter. Some Friday date night!

"Jett, take me to bed," Sarah Lynn demanded. "You have to be at work in four hours."

"Fuck! I didn't even realize what time it is. Thanks. Let's go, honey."

We got our teeth brushed and fell into bed next to Jas. My cock twitched when I thought about making love to either one of the girls, but we ended up just cuddled together sound asleep.

At five-thirty, I left the two holding each other and went to work.

I WANTED TO get right to work on Saturday, but I was so tired after I left the grocery store that I came home and collapsed in bed for a couple of hours. I woke up to Sarah Lynn nibbling her way across my chest.

"We were too tired last night. Are you awake enough to enter *my* garden of earthly delights?"

"Mmm. Your garden is causing my stalk to sprout," I laughed. "I love you, Sarah Lynn."

"I love you, too. Now lie back and let me plant your sprout." She pushed me down on the bed and straddled my erection, sinking onto it as I held her breasts. She moved with me in a gentle wave motion that brought us slowly up from our sleep state to full sensual awareness.

I was still kind of in awe of Sarah Lynn. She wasn't the prettiest of my girlfriends, but it's hard to think a girl who's riding your cock isn't pretty. She was as smart as all the rest of us put together. She was about the most daring person I'd ever met. And she was a natural leader. We never made a big deal about our decision-making process in the house, but if there was a disagreement, we automatically turned to her to arbitrate. When we came to an agreement, we looked to her to validate it. I'd begun to see the sense of her studying political science and wondered if the US would be ready for a female president with a husband and six wives when she ran for office.

She was in that lazy sliding mood this afternoon. She leaned into my hands and kissed my lips as she alternated sliding up and down my pole with grinding her clit against my pubis. And we kissed. I petted her breasts and moved to her butt. My hands slid up her back and around to her breasts again before returning to her butt. She pressed down against me, flattening out on my chest, still seeking my lips and my tongue with her own. Her movements and my own only amounted to an inch or two of withdraw and insert, but it was all that we needed.

And as we kissed we climaxed.

It wasn't one of those screaming orgasms that were often heard around our house. It was more like a deep sigh as we emptied ourselves into each other—literally or spiritually. I held her against me as we dozed again for a few minutes in deep satisfaction. Finally, she pushed up off of me, relieving my breathing but also leaving me with a sense of separation. She looked into my eyes and kissed me again.

"I know it's difficult right now. For all of us. But if we can all just keep having these little moments of connection, we'll survive the term. You have big projects this semester. We're all overloaded with course work. We need each other."

I WAS IMMEDIATELY presented with a problem. If Ariel sat in front of the board for the painting, she'd be at the bottom and I'd need to fill all the rest above her with plants and sky or something. I wanted her more central in the vertical and horizontal space—not quite in the middle, but only slightly below the center. Of course, she was happy to help me. It involved getting naked and painty.

I started with her on the sofa and worked on the pose I wanted. I wanted a languid and inviting pose that said, 'lie down on me.' And I realized that in addition to wanting her stretched out and open to me, I wanted my POV to be higher, looking down on her, as if I'd just come across her lying in the grass. We moved into the studio and I rearranged things so I could lay the whole six by three panel out on the floor. I was thankful that Granddad had insisted that we needed cross-bracing for the center panel to keep it from warping. Without that, even as light as she was, Ariel would have cracked the three-sixteenths-inch plywood when she lay down in the middle of it. I wasn't sure how I was going to get her in this position when the piece was displayed for class, but this was what it needed.

Once we were satisfied with the pose, I used water-based paint to spray around her and establish the shape of her body on the board. She was truly a little green nymph when I was finished and had to lie still until the paint was set so she didn't smear it when she got up. When that was done, I had her body shape on the panel and I could draw in the line art without her actually posing until the triptych was done. Then I had to shower and clean her and love her. That took the rest of Saturday night.

"THE MODEL AND artwork have consented to allow the class a closer view under two conditions. Please stay at least three feet away and do not attempt to touch. Please keep comments respectful. If you would create a line on the left side of the classroom and file past, we won't rush the viewing. Please keep moving though so everyone gets a chance to view the artwork."

Merck's entire class had gasped when we opened the triptych. Ariel had practiced dozens of times Sunday evening after the painting was all done. Of course, we couldn't completely close the panels with Ariel inside but we had them partially closed as she sat scrunched up in a ball. We set the whole thing up on a piece of Astroturf and when I pulled the drape off, you couldn't really see exactly what the project was.

Then Ariel unfolded, pushing the panels out to the side while I stabilized the piece from behind. When it was fully open, Ariel relaxed into her pose in front of the painting. She'd insisted on permanent paint again, but I refused to do that to her face. I cut all my morning classes Monday and did her face and hair. The result was that she was actually a kind of reflection of the scene on the triptych. I couldn't suspend her in the pose in front of where her image was, so it looked a little like she had slid off the painting onto the turf, leaving her impression on the wood.

It took nearly half an hour to allow everyone a chance to get a closer look. I noticed several who made their first pass and then got back in line to see it again. And there were a few who seemed more interested in examining Ariel than the artwork in general. The comments, however, did remain respectful as people pointed out the various shapes that made up the painting and talked about how it changed as they got closer to it. Terms like 'erotic' and 'sensual' were bandied about but I also heard 'indecent' and 'porn' mentioned. I figured I'd managed to reduce the number of people who wanted to hang me to about fifty percent.

I also noticed there were people who weren't actually in my class who filed by the painting. My adviser, Professor Wells, came through the line with Blankenship. Neither one of them said anything to me or commented while they viewed, but their heads were together as they walked out of the lecture hall.

When the class viewing was finished, Sarah Lynn and Jasmine wrapped Ariel in a robe and boots and a blanket. They took charge of getting her home safely from campus. I folded up the triptych to pick up from Merck later. With a huge sigh of relief, I headed out to walk across campus for Blankety's drawing class. A tall girl with a tan, dark hair, and deep brown eyes caught up with me.

"Excuse me, Jett?" she called. I stopped and waited for her. "Can I walk with you? I'm Rania. We've never talked but I've been enjoying your artwork in class all year. Wish I had creativity like that. Anyway, I wanted to know if I could ask you questions about your art… mostly. Anyway. Do you mind?"

"Hi, Rania. It's nice to meet you," I said. She was striking. I wouldn't have started by saying beautiful, but she was. At first, I thought she had a big nose, but it was just that it didn't have a deep indent at the eyes beneath her brow that most people of European descent seem to have. It ran straight and slender directly from her brow to narrow nostrils. Her lips were full and her chin made her whole face a little triangular. But not in a bad way. Just looking at her made me want to draw her. "What kind of questions can I answer for you? I've got about half an hour to make it to my next class but I'm happy to have company on the walk if you have time."

"I do. What inspired you to do body painting?"

"It was kind of an accident," I laughed. "Ariel, the girl in the painting today, saw me doing some pseudo-Asian doodling with inks one day. She stood beside the painting and as we were joking around, I sort of continued with the ink over onto her. We got into it and by the time we were done, I'd covered her whole body with doodles. Some of them were pretty cool. I guess that's what started it."

"She just happened to stand by your easel naked while you were painting?"

"Um… well… We've known each other for a long time. She's a real free spirit. Usually that means free of clothes."

"I envy her. I mean… not being naked with you… I mean… Do you have sex with all your models?"

Holy shit! That came out of the blue. What was I supposed to say to that?

"I'm sorry. I mean… We haven't seen all the women you painted live but even in the vids Merck showed the class, there's a kind of intimacy and I just needed to know if a woman has to have sex with you in order to be a model."

"Oh. Sure. I think I understand." Was this woman saying she wanted to model for me? *Yes!* "My first models were all women I already had an intimate relationship with to one degree or another. Not necessarily having sex exactly. At the time. But it was much easier for us to get started since we were already familiar with each other's bodies. But I'm expanding on that now. The next piece I'm doing, for example, involves three women and three men and I'm not presently nor at any point in the future going to be involved with any of them on an intimate level. Then I have another model lined up for later in the term who has done some posing for me but we'll do a body paint scene after break. We aren't really interested in each other sexually either."

"Could I model for you?" she asked breathlessly.

"Do you think you could do it?" I asked. "I mean, I'm not suggesting that we would, should, or even could have sex but putting paint on your naked body is in itself an intimate act."

"I get that. I thought about it a lot last semester and seeing your *Garden of Earthly Delights* today just lit a fire. I just wanted to be sure that getting my body painted didn't mean I had to have sex with you. I'm sure you're nice and all, but I don't know you well enough and I'm not into random hookups. Could I?"

"I think we can arrange something for after break. Maybe you could come hang out with us some and even pose for some of the painters in my family. We can play it by ear and see if you are comfortable."

39
Baroque Porn

IT WAS not my finest hour, painting a rather sloppy rendition of Nicolas
Poussin's *Bacchanal Before a Statue of Pan*. It had everything except the
people. I even painted in the statue. I chose the Poussin for a number of
reasons. First, it was a pretty easy backdrop to paint. Kelly convinced me
to invest in a blue screen and some lights. She owned all the other production equipment, including the high-end computer her mother started
her with. We'd shoot the entire video in front of the blue screen and then
replace the blue screen with my rendering. So, the rendering was blocked
out on a canvas board at forty inches wide and sixteen inches tall. It
had to be wider and taller than the portion we'd show at the beginning
because camera angles would require the background to shift slightly.
Kelly just told me not to worry because her editing software would take
care of that. *Okay. Good.*

Second, in Poussin's painting, the actors weren't so bloated or
Rubenesque that they wouldn't appeal to my generation. Which also
meant the girls wouldn't be horrified by how fat they looked. I'd met the
guys when they all came over to sign their papers and get briefed by Kelly.
She laid down the law that there was hard work to be done and they were
getting paid for it. I didn't realize that, but Kelly was putting up over
two grand in salaries for them. I sure hoped we sold a lot of this video.
These guys were all well-experienced boning the girls but had never done
it on camera. After I assured them all that I wasn't gay, they agreed to
be painted as satyrs like I showed in my rendering. The fact that when I
painted them, they all got erections went without comment.

Third, the actors in the Poussin painting were all at least partially clothed so, unlike the Rubens and the Breughel renditions, it looked more like the party was just getting started instead of like they were all drunk and sated or passed out at the end. That worked well for both the girls' initial modesty flares and to let us work up to what we'd get in the porn. We might have a little video to show in class before things got past the #safeforschool tag. They all understood, though, that it was a lecherous and debauched party and they'd have to act drunk. We told them they could take a quick break on the porch to toke up if they wanted but not to overdo it.

Of course, in addition to the background rendering, I needed a few props and 'furniture' pieces. The green Astroturf had worked well for Ariel's base, so I got a piece that was large enough for the actors to perform on and decorated it with more leaves, a few plants, and couches for the actors to fuck on. Char went shopping with me at several second-hand shops to get pieces of fabric and props that we could use. The acting area would be twelve feet deep—the width of the turf carpet sold at Lowe's—but like the blue screen and the background painting, it ran the full width of our living room. I sprang for an extra two hundred bucks worth of foam padding to put under it.

I was getting pretty good with my airbrush. The guys all came in on Thursday to get painted. They laughed and joked but every one of them got a hardon when I painted their thighs and stomach like the lower part of a goat. I suppose Ariel running the camera, still in her Earthly Delights paint and nothing else, might have had something to do with it as well. The guys were impressed with their new six-pack abs and hairy chests and arms. They did a bunch of posing for Ariel along with a few lewd comments before we finally told them to go home and we'd see them Saturday.

The three blondes came in about noon on Friday and they were a lot raunchier than the guys had been. They wanted to tease and play as much as to get painted. Kelly ran the camera and shook her head at their antics. Barb, in particular, kept thrusting her hips at me while I was padding her stomach and asked for bigger boobs as she shoved them into my hands.

"You know, you keep teasing like that and none of us will be responsible if Jett gets turned on and molests you," Kelly said. Barb just laughed.

"What do you think I want?" she sneered. The sneer went away when I shoved two fingers up her twat and started thumbing her clit until she screamed out an orgasm and collapsed back into her friends' arms.

"That was good," Kelly said. "I managed to get a sound level reading on you when you come so I can have it adjusted correctly when you get fucked tomorrow."

"Oh, God! I didn't think you'd just… Fuck! I haven't had that good a come all year. Can I have you as my partner in the video?"

"Huh-uh. I've already painted your boyfriend." The other two girls teased a little but were more circumspect and I didn't molest them. I was a little worried, but we had their agreements, releases, and the whole exchange on video. Kelly assured me that there would be no repercussions after the three girls left with rounder bottoms, bigger boobs, soft tummies, and gashes that looked like a chimp in heat.

I took Saturday off work so I could direct the makeup on their faces. Kelly and Char took the girls and worked their magic with theatrical makeup that would totally disguise them. Ariel took over for Kelly when Merck arrived and she had to show him how to run the camera she'd assigned him. Sarah Lynn joined her as the other camera person and Kelly blocked out the acting areas, camera sightlines, and range of motion. Merck was going to mostly be on a tripod in a stationary position while Sarah Lynn would be the roaming camera. Both were told that because of the blue-screen they had to be careful of where the top of their shot was so it didn't get up on the ceiling. They were also told that they needed to keep their cameras horizontal and not shoot up or down. If Sarah Lynn wanted a low shot, she had to get down on the floor to get it, not just point the camera down. Sarah Lynn had been practicing a lot lately and her camera had a horizon line that showed up on the screen so she could tell if she was level. It was a lot like shooting animation cels except we were using live action.

Merck came to join me as I was painting the beards, eyebrows, and hollowed cheeks that would disguise the guys. I had goat horns on headbands they weren't sure of until I arranged their hair and sprayed it black. Suddenly, they all thought they looked too cool for words. I stood back to survey them with their loincloths concealing phalluses in various stages of arousal and Merck did a visual survey with the camera. Then we headed to the living room where the set was.

"This floor is soft AF!" Don said. I had no idea which girl which guy was paired up with or even if they were paired or just a free-for-all. I'd learned their names, Don, Lou, and Sam, just two days ago when I painted them. I guess Barb and Reggie had a falling out and he was eliminated from the party. They were into saying a lot of things out loud that people normally only used online. Whatever. One had made a comment while I was doing their faces this morning and another actually said 'LOL' instead of laughing.

The girls were finally ready and paraded out of the dining room where they were getting made up. The job Ariel, Kelly, and Char had done on them not only disguised them but made them beautiful in an otherworldly way. I wasn't even sure which was which when I looked at them.

"Sis, you are so snatched," Sam said coming up to one of them. "Let's get this show on the road so we can fuck." I glanced over at Merck but the comment seemed to roll right off him. He was panning around with his camera in the limited range he had. I saw him step back a little to look at it and then crank the height down slightly. I wondered how well he'd keep his objectivity once the clothes started coming off.

"Okay. If anyone needs a break—restroom, smoke, drink—now's the time," I said. "We'll be shooting the static scenes first. You'll be doing various tableaus, freezing, and we'll photograph. In this part, I'll be interfere between scenes to direct where you're to stand, sit, or lie and what you are doing there. Then we'll take another break. When we get back from that one, Kelly will direct you through some warmups and will get you rolling for the video. From that point on, we'll be shooting for anywhere from an hour to an hour and a half with no more interruption than we have to. Don't worry about dialog. We'll cut around it if need be." All six trooped out to the front porch and I saw the air turn blue with smoke. Whatever. Merck stepped out back to have a few quick tokes on his vape. As long as I could get them in position, I didn't care what they did to get themselves ready. After the front porch, they hit both bathrooms and came back ready to go.

I had several tableaus ready to put them in that would slowly tell the story of the party getting wild. That would include losing some pieces of clothing and getting hands involved, but it wouldn't involve exposing the guy's dicks or girls' pussies or having any real sex. They cooperated and Kelly handled her digital SLR like a pro. This also gave us a chance to test the lighting and adjust for shadows. The blue screen behind them had to stay blue. I made sure the tableaus were also opportunities to get individual shots of the actors and with their preferred partners so each could have pictures after we released the video. Kelly had given them all instructions on creating social accounts under their stage names and not linking them to their regular accounts. We'd give them each a profile pic as soon as the shooting was over.

Things got gigglier as the clothing started to come off. Breasts got groped and dicks got handled. The loin cloths were all tented. We got the stills done and gave them another break. A lot more smoke filled the porch and when they opened the door to come in, we could all smell the weed.

"Okay, this is the video portion. Everybody get your costumes back in the shape they were when we started. We'll be starting from the same position as the tableau we started with before. That's what Jett's arranging. When we start filming, we'll hold in that position for a minute to give me material for titles. Then I'll call action and you'll start to wake up and go through a lot of what we did in the stills. If you don't remember the exact sequence or positions, don't worry about it. You're at a party, the wine is flowing freely, and everyone is getting horny. Don't rush it, but the pace is going to be on your back. If I need to speed it up a little, I'll do it with cuts. That's why we have two cameras running. When you really get into it, I doubt I'll need to say anything, but if I do, don't bother to look up at me. Just do what I say and keep going. You ready to party?"

"Partay!" they responded and the cameras all clicked on.

Not being porn professionals, I half expected the guys to pop in five minutes and be worthless for the duration. But apparently all six of them had watched an adequate amount of porn to know the sequences. We shot for an hour and a half. And then we shot pussies dripping with the evidence. They'd all chosen to go bareback and come inside, even though we gave them the option of using condoms and coming anywhere. Well, each of the guys had at least two money shots and all the girls got painted. The various screeches of the girls indicated they'd all managed to get their cookies at least a couple of times as well.

I'd prepared a clean-up kit for each of them that included instructions for removing both the face paint and makeup and the body paint. Finally, they were gone and I heard them agree to order pizzas down at the girls' house.

We all breathed a big sigh of relief and decided to order our own pizzas.

•ᴼ•ᴼ⇨ ⅠⅠⅭ ☽ ⅠⅠⅭ ⇦•ᴼ•ᴼ•

"You're producing porn here," Merck said, still a little dazed from the day's work.

"Well, I guess we did today. It will be up to Kelly to determine if it's marketable or just a fun afternoon. Frankly, we invested about four thousand dollars in this project, so I hope we get some return."

"I'll buy a copy," he said. "Are they all like this?"

"First and only," I said. "I know there won't be another like this all term, but I thought you'd enjoy this one the most."

"You guys want a hit before the pizza gets here?" Sarah Lynn asked. "I'm tired boots."

"Oh, God! You're talking like them," Merck moaned. "I've never felt so old in my life. I didn't understand half of what they were saying and was shocked at the other half. I'm supposed to be the cool prof who's just one of the kids."

"Oh, don't worry," Sarah Lynn comforted him. "You're slick. What other professor would spend his afternoon filming students making porn?"

"None who are still employed," Merck groaned. I passed him the bong and he took another deep drag.

•ᴼ•⇨ ⅠⅠⅭ ☽ ⅠⅠⅭ ⇦•ᴼ•

"A Kat Mon Dieu Production, staged by Kat's Coal. Starring Torrid Starling, Blue Delight, and Robin Clouds. With Bud Flicker, Tom Swift,

369

and Big Hardy." We all read the titles when Kelly finally got the video all edited. I'd turned in the eight-minute R-rated version for class on Wednesday. The X-rated version was hot. We got into some interesting positions as we acted out a few of the scenes being played before us. Barb was the leader of the gang and certainly the most willing to do any sexual item with any of the men or women in the group. The scene with Don plugging her doggy-style and Sam with his dick in her mouth was enhanced by Syl under her licking away at Don's balls. But the show stealer as far as all of us were concerned was the intensity of Lou and Terri as they truly connected. They'd created a subtle chase, staying in the background for most of the first fifteen minutes. Lou would approach and offer her wine but when he bent to kiss her, she'd turn her head to the side and move away. Somehow as she moved, her costume loosened. He reached across Sam and Syl in a basic missionary and caught Terri's shoulder. The dress fell, exposing her breast.

Merck had proved a sharp cameraman. Even though his camera provided the wider-angle shots, setting scenes as Sarah Lynn moved in for closer views of the various sex acts that the others got right down to, he seemed to always have Terri and Lou in the center of his lens, occasionally zooming in on a particular interaction between the two, like when Lou poured a little wine in her shoulder indent and lapped it up. That was when Terri's other shoulder slipped and the dress fell to expose both breasts and Lou's hand slipped up her side to cup one while he drank.

Kelly had done a masterful job of cutting in the backdrop I painted. I wasn't sure exactly how this whole blue screen stuff worked, but it shifted behind the actors as the camera angles shifted or zoomed. The hour-and-a-half of two cameras shooting no less than eight explicit sex acts and a few sexy scenes that weren't explicit sex was edited down to half an hour in which a painting seemed to come to life and a bacchanalia ensued. Most of the last ten minutes, after Barb, Don, Sam, and Syl had already had multiple explosions, was devoted to Terri and Lou finally consummating their playful romp.

Another of Kelly's clever ploys was that the audio we recorded during the taping was muted, only coming up at key points where there was wet slapping of genitals against each other or a girl's wailed orgasm. All of the miscellaneous grunts, movement, comments were missing. Instead, Ariel had recorded a soundtrack of Bach Fugues using her new electronic keyboard to mimic a pipe organ. It was amazing!

With the credits and stills cut in, we had a damned professional video. Merck bought the first copy.

And somehow, my cock found its way into seven wet pussies that night. Sometimes only for a few strokes as we all played and rolled around on the Astroturf and sometimes to a most satisfying conclusion.

⋅ₒ⋅ₒ❖ ⟁ ☀ ⟁ ❖ₒ⋅ₒ⋅

EVA WAS BECOMING more involved in planning out projects as the term moved toward spring break. The Astroturf was proving to be a great investment as I prepared to paint her as Gulliver staked to the ground by miniature Lilliputians. This was going to be a portrait rather than body painting. The tiny people swarming over her body would all be Eva. The drawing would all be images of her tying herself to the ground. After the intensity of doing *Baroque Porn*, we all needed to rest a little. I wanted to do this study as an adjunct to the airport wall that would show her flying. And after we'd done the posing session and drawing, I had a rare opportunity to take my time making love to Eva.

"You know, when I asked you to paint me almost a year ago, I didn't really intend to become a lover at all," she whispered as I bathed her nipples with my tongue. She gasped as I nibbled a little but kept talking. "I kind of went wild my freshman year and slept around. I did some parties that I don't even really remember except that my pussy and ass were sore for days afterward. While everyone went south for spring break, I flew to a little airstrip up at Ashland on the shore of Lake Superior. It was cold and snowy and a risky flight at that time of year. But I had to go. There's a meditation center up there that I spent five days at. Most of it was crying by the shore for what a mess I'd made of my life. When I asked you to paint me, I was desperately trying to see what I'd become."

She pulled me on top of her and guided my cock into her steamy center. For a few minutes we just kissed and slid together. I sensed that this was all part of what she wanted to tell me and that I should just stay focused on loving her and not try to say anything. We hadn't come yet but weren't trying to reach a peak, just staying connected, and enjoying the union of our bodies.

"Instead, you painted me as Athena. You didn't show me what I'd become but what I could be. I fell in love that day, Jett. Not with you but with my future."

I kissed her deeply. Kissed the tears from her eyes. Kissed the neck she stretched up to give me. And as we moved slowly together, we found release. It was a burst of light that let me see a glimpse of my own future. I could hardly wait to paint Eva at the airport.

•◦·◦❖ ⊃⊂ ☽ ⊃⊂ ❖◦·◦•

I HADN'T FORGOTTEN my assignment from Blankenship. I did two new sketches of *The Garden of Earthly Delights*. Ariel was always willing to pose for me, whether I needed her to or not. I had a veritable library of sex organ sketches and photos at my disposal for reference. And having Ariel pose was always like foreplay.

But I was really trying to understand what Blankenship was ineptly trying to teach me. I could see from his quick sketch on the whiteboard that he had incredible control and talent. But the only way he could communicate was by deriding and criticizing. I was determined to get through that to the nut of the lesson.

"This subject is obviously too complex for your little brain to grasp," he said as the intro to my second meeting with him. He sighed and then began sketching out small details of my drawing on the whiteboard as he criticized them. He was so fast at his criticisms and sketches that the depth of his understanding was almost missed. His eyes had to be phenomenal to pick out the details that he did. He would glance at my sketch and then turn his back and reproduce a portion on the whiteboard with incredible accuracy as he described not only the elements, but the latent emotions that weren't given rein.

After two sessions, I was tasked with developing a larger version.

"Not life-size. Save that for playing with your girlfriend. I want a drawing that captures the emotion. I want to see it right after spring break. You *are* planning to study and work over the break, are you not?"

"Yes, sir. I have too many projects and need to work at my job to stay ahead of expenses."

"Your job. I believe you mentioned you were a serial killer. Please don't get blood on this drawing. We'll deal with that later."

I left his office feeling overwhelmed. Again.

40
Liberty and Death

IT LOOKED LIKE spring break was going to kill us all. I worked every day, but only a five-hour shift. Grandpa had me putting what I was learning in my Proteins class to work by preparing 'ready to cook' meats for the butcher case. I did kebobs, seasoned roasts, stuffed chicken breasts and pork chops. You name it. I even got a couple special orders. Easter was very late this year—only two weeks before the end of school—but people were already planning their meals. Two customers who tried my stuffed porkchops asked if I could prepare a larger stuffed piece, like a leg of pork or lamb, to cook for their Easter dinners. We took the order and Grandpa said he was proud of my progress.

Then I had Dostoevsky to read. Fortunately, *The Idiot* is one of his 'shorter' works at only 650 pages. I was a month away from the project for that in Merck's class, but I knew I'd never finish the book if I waited to start it. Mary really surprised me, though, when she suggested a final project for that unit.

"Would you, really?" I asked. Wow! We'd talked about it once months ago, much to my embarrassment.

"Yeah. Either you'd need to use your imagination a little or maybe I could borrow Kelly's double-dildo. But, you did those sketches last fall. I think you could develop it nicely in relation to the book."

"You know it still goes," I said. She looked at me curiously. "If you were trans, I'd still be just as much in love with you."

"I have my own little issues you need to cope with. We'll just imagine that one."

And then there was the airport. I spent about three hours a day prepping the wall where I'd paint Eva in May. The painting would be fifteen feet wide and ten feet high. I needed to get all the background in before we could ever do the live performance of the painting.

I wished I could say 'finally' when it came to drawing the larger version of *The Garden of Earthly Delights*, but I still needed to work on my next project for Merck. I'd planned to use Mary's and my drawing classmate, Andi, as the model for that painting, but she took off for spring break in Florida. I discovered Rania was local, though, having gone to a different high school than we did. She agreed to do the Age of Reason portrait of the Statue of Liberty after I explained what I wanted.

In order to get the full portrait of my nude Statue of Liberty, I needed a canvas eight feet tall and three feet wide. I'd never transport that to school, so I used the time-honored method of doing two canvases four feet tall and three feet wide. I would have to cheat the background image a little and her torch would probably stick up above the canvas, but I wasn't going to go any bigger than that. This was an instance in which I had to do a background painting of Rania in one pose and then hide it with her body paint portrait in front. It was kind of a shame that I'd be hiding her beautiful skin tone in gray paint. It was going to take all week.

•०··⇨ ⊃⊂ ☽ ⊃⊂ ⇦··०•

WE STARTED SATURDAY right after classes were out for the week. Everyone liked Eva's *Earthbound* drawing earlier in the week and I was relieved that I hadn't really been slinging paint that week. Sometimes you just need a break. But Saturday afternoon, I was going to work with Rania for the first time.

"I'm a little nervous," she said as soon as she was inside the front door.

"Oh, Rania! You are so beautiful," Sarah Lynn jumped right in. "It's so nice to finally meet you. I'm Sarah Lynn. Come in and relax for a bit. There's no need to be nervous. We won't bite."

"I'm a little relieved already. I mean, I've walked across campus with Jett a few times and he's told me about... um... your family here. I was afraid I might be... I don't know. That people might not like me coming here to pose."

"Hi, Rania. I'm Char. We're used to Jett needing models. We've all done it, so we know how much hard work you have to put in and how

375

embarrassing it can be. Would you like tea? I have my own Chai recipe that is sure to relax you."

"Thank you, Char. You're so sweet. You were the *Medea* monster, weren't you?"

"That's me. Dear Jett let the monster out and I'm almost a normal girl now." Char left to get tea and Ariel came bouncing into the room. She isn't real big up top, but she sure knows how to bounce. And, of course, she was stark naked as usual.

"Hi, Rania! I'm Ariel. I get to show you that you aren't the only one likely to be nude today. Any of us might forget our clothes at any time. We're pretty relaxed around here. Jett won't get naked unless you encourage him to. He works in white briefs that Kelly collects."

"You! You were *The Garden of Earthly Delights*! And the *Sex Dreams Book*! You are the inspiration that got me to volunteer for this. I absolutely adored your pieces." Rania hugged Ariel in her enthusiasm.

"You probably remember Mary, too," Ariel said as Mary walked into the room bringing some cookies as Char brought the tea. So far, I hadn't said a word to my model. The girls had taken charge of getting her comfortable.

"Oh! Hi, Mary. I'm Rania. You were the girl exploding into the universe, weren't you? I feel like I'm walking among legends."

"I prefer to think of it as coalescing from the universe into the person I am," Mary laughed. "These little butter cookies are my favorites. Help yourself."

"Are there others of you?"

"Kelly and Eva are upstairs finishing up a project. They'll be down soon," Sarah Lynn said. "Eva was *Athena* and *Earthbound*. You probably won't recognize Kelly because her project was for a different class. Jett painted her underwear while she was wearing it."

"Oooh. That sounds as interesting as the body paint. Um… What about the wild ones who were in Bacchanal? There were guys in that, too."

"Yes, but they aren't part of our family group. Like you, they just came in to work on a single project," Sarah Lynn explained.

"They looked like… Well, like maybe we only saw part of the video. They were so ready to have sex it was a little scary."

"That's not really our normal mode," Sarah Lynn continued. "It was a special project that they wanted to do that went a lot further than Jett's classroom rendition. Maybe someday you'll want to see it, but it's not the kind of thing that will get you comfortable for posing. Just be assured that the girls were all with guys they knew and trusted and none of us were involved except in painting them and videoing. We can get wild but it's for our own consumption, not the public."

"So, what do we do today?" Rania asked turning to me.

"Oh, hi, Rania. I didn't realize you were here," I laughed. "Welcome to our home."

"Have we been ignoring you, love?" Ariel asked as she planted a kiss on my cheek. I patted her butt and she wiggled it in my hand.

"No. It's been just right. I wanted to make sure you were comfortable with the environment and the family before I started in on you, Rania. I hope you aren't too overwhelmed."

"Not at all. This is exciting. What's first?"

"Well, there are two parts to the project as I explained. You'll just pose for the first part and I'll sketch and then paint. But before I can do that, I need to have your outline in the second pose on the canvas. So, I'll get you right up against the canvas in the pose that we'll do when I body paint you and I'll spray your outline. I'm going to give you safety goggles to make sure the paint doesn't get in your eyes. When I do the body paint, I'll be doing your face with a brush and makeup instead of spray. I think that is all we'll be able to do today other than a few poses and reference shots to make sure we know what we're doing for the rest of the week. As soon as we're done, of course, you can shower and get freshened up. We have all the right shampoos and things that will take the paint right out of your hair and off your body."

"Whoo. I… guess… It sounds like a lot of work. I think… I'm ready to get started," she said. "I assume this is um… when I undress?"

"Why don't you go into the studio to get started? Any of us… I mean the girls… will help you if you want or we'll leave you alone. I'm not going to watch you undress, Rania. I'll come in when you are ready to pose."

"Yeah. Um… Ariel? You were such an inspiration. Would you come in with me?"

It took about two and a half hours to get the poses set and recorded and to do the spray work on the canvas that would show me exactly where to paint the background image. When we did the final, of course, the spray would be repeated since I'd be painting all the background over it. It took another hour for Rania to emerge from the shower. If she had taken someone in with her, she could have gotten scrubbed faster. Then again, the shower might have taken longer. Rania was truly a lovely woman.

And she had a subtle ethnic quality that made her perfect for a Statue of Liberty. She might be mistaken for any number of different heritages like European, Native American, Latino, Mediterranean, or even Hawaiian. In truth, her mother was Lebanese and her father was of German descent. It had been a good genetic mix to bring about this beauty.

We had dinner and talked about the project and whether Rania needed to shave her pubes. Personally, I liked the fluffy dark bush between her legs. But, as I'd mentioned to Andi when I sketched her, for the painting it is just easier to paint skin than hair.

"Um… I've never done that. I've trimmed up for a bikini, but… Maybe I'll go to a salon to have it done," Rania said.

"If it's just *help* you want, I'll help," Ariel said. *I bet she would!* "I've had mine all waxed at a salon every six weeks for the past nine months. It's a little raw the first few days after and hurts like hell. I'm thinking I might have my hair lasered this summer. But I help all the girls here who shave," she said brightly. Now that was something I didn't know. In fact, most of what happened in the girls' bath upstairs was a mystery to me. I was only occasionally invited in to share a bath.

"Really? Um… Let's talk about it later. That's really sweet of you, but it seems so intimate."

"You'd rather have a stranger be intimate with you than one of your new friends?" Ariel responded.

"Tomorrow, we'll work with the background pose," I said to change the subject. Just imagining Ariel between Rania's legs was getting me stiff.

"I'm going to have you get in the pose we resolved today and then I'll sketch it directly on the canvas. What I want to do is get your head as near to the same place as possible, even though the background painting will be not quite life-size. You're a great model, Rania. We'll take breaks whenever you need them, but I expect to get the sketch all laid in tomorrow."

"If you don't mind, I'd like to do a few sketches as well," Mary said.

"I want to do a watercolor, if it's okay," Eva added. "We'll stay out of your way, Jett."

"With Kelly doing photos and some video, maybe you should move into the living room in front of the blue screen," Sarah Lynn suggested.

"I really hate to take over the living space again," I said. "It's not fair to the rest of you."

"We can just arrange the furniture so it's like a theater. It's not like any of us mind watching you paint. Nor looking at your nude models," Sarah Lynn laughed.

"We all started out—or at least the five of us before Mary and Eva joined us—watching Jett paint via Skype. We'd all sit in front of our computers and chat while he stood in his underwear and slung paint at the canvas," Kelly said. "Just so you know, I get the underwear from this project. I've got a new pair for you, Jett."

I sighed. Rania was getting sucked in.

⋅∘⋅⇨ ⅅⅭ ☀ ⅅⅭ ⇦⋅∘⋅

THE REST OF the week was mostly wash, rinse, repeat. I'd work from six till eleven, grab lunch, and head for the airport. Often Eva and sometimes Mary would come out with me to help lay in the background on our performance project. Whichever joined me, there was always a photo record and some video shot. Then I'd get home around three to see Rania waiting for our session. Sometimes we'd take a break for dinner and then continue, but usually we ended before. After dinner, I would do some additional work on the painting or on the drawing for Blankenship. Then I'd read. Nothing like Dostoevsky to put you to sleep. I usually managed to read until at least eleven before snuggling someone up close to make love and sleep. The girls were figuring out who got what position with whom. I just went to bed and loved whomever I was with.

379

"Are you sure?" I asked again. Rania had just told me that she wanted to do the pose in our class on Monday when it resumed. "I mean granted that Ariel and Mary have appeared live in class with the artwork, but they didn't know anyone in that class. After you do this… Well, everyone will know it's you. I can't disguise you that much. You're just too beautiful. And you'll know… you'll know every one of your classmates has seen you naked."

"I'm not an exhibitionist, Jett. It took me all the courage I could muster to take my clothes off here the first time. But… I've seen what you are doing with this piece. Patrick Henry declared to the Virginia Convention, 'Give me liberty or give me death.' It was the declaration of a revolution. Our country was founded on the concept that death was the alternative to liberty. But you are showing that in abandoning the age of reason, we brought the two together. Death is liberty. Liberty is death. I believe in what you are saying. And I don't think the message will be clear unless I step off the pedestal in front of the class and leave them with just the image on canvas. And I saw your sketches. You have the one of Liberty leading the people from the French revolution. I'm sure some Puritan insisted that they couldn't have a bare-breasted Liberty in New York Harbor. But that's the one you should paint. And how you should paint me."

"With your breasts bare?"

"And unadorned. Paint the dress on the rest of me, but don't even gray out my breasts. Let them see flesh coming through the statue."

Rania's passion was intense. Delacroix's image of Liberty was certainly more passionate than Bartholdi and Eiffel's stiff Lady. To put the Delacroix image of sixty years earlier in the pose of Bartholdi's guardian of the shores would give the image a power that I'd only imagined. I turned and hugged my model.

"Oh, I'm sorry," I said, jumping back from her naked body. I was working shirtless and having her bare boobs pressed up against my skin gave me an instant reaction. She followed me and pressed herself against me. I relented and just enjoyed the contact. A lot.

"Well, let's get the paint on the canvas, partner," I whispered in her ear.

I knew the body response. I'd seen it in a video months ago. The instant of impact. The head thrown back. The leg jerking up as the arm is flung to the side. Lonnie's death was coming back to haunt me again. It took four sessions to paint the canvas. Her body was stripped bare, no fancy costumes painted on or around her. In the outstretched hand, a high-power rifle replacing the torch, in her left hand, not the stone tablet with the date, but a ragged parchment of the Declaration of Independence. On her breast, the single billowing wound of death.

I'd finished everything except her face. We'd tried a hundred expressions and snapped digital photos of each one, but none was right.

"It needs more surprise," I posited.

"No, I don't think she has time to be surprised at death," Rania said. "I just don't know how to get the moment of agony. The sudden end of her dream. The climax of life in death." We sat there a few minutes and I watched different expressions cross her face like she was trying on feelings. The video was running to capture anything we thought of that could be useful if we watched it again. "I need to take a few minutes break. Do you mind?"

"Of course not. This is hard work. Every bit as hard for you as for me. Take whatever time you need."

She was gone longer than I expected as I reviewed the still photos we'd taken. One was close. I could probably work with it. In the video of Lonnie's murder/suicide, his face had been out of the frame. The cathartic painting I'd done of it had no background and simply faded off at the edge. I'd never really seen the face of death—and, I suppose, I hoped I never would.

When Rania returned, she was flushed. Ariel entered the room right behind her. Rania immediately went to her pose.

"Run the camera, Jett. And take lots of stills. I think we have it." Once she was in the correct pose, she shifted enough to spread her legs and Ariel crawled between them.

Oh. My. God! I think they'd been working up to this in another room during the half hour she'd been gone. Ariel began licking Rania, whose face began a wide progression of expressions that I captured in both video and stills. It was tempting to point the camera down to Ariel's lithe tongue parting the folds of Rania's sex but I kept focused on her face from exactly the angle that I would paint it. The contortion, the rictus, the agony, the release.

The little death.

As Rania cried out her orgasm, I snapped photos as quickly as the Digital SLR could capture them. And I knew that we had the right expression.

•o·•❧))C ☽))C ❧•·o•

Merck agreed to let us open the class on Monday after break, even though projects weren't due until Tuesday to give those who never thought about it during the break a chance to write something up the day after they returned. Merck was a pragmatist.

Rania and I had worked on her body paint for two days after she decided to go with permanent paint. The result was a grey translucent gown through which one could see every curve and hollow of her lower body and her arms. She held the equally gray torch and tablet as props and I did a sweeping gray wig held in place by her crown. The gray makeup on her face seemed to thaw to flesh tones as it neared her chin and neck, only the gray shoulders connecting the gray arms to the body. Because we were doing a live performance of this piece, I had to do a full body paint around the back as well as the front. It was long and tedious to make it look like folds of fabric flowed around her.

Kelly cut her morning classes as well so she could set up a camera at exactly the correct location to get the full impact of the piece. We had to check angles and positions several times and rope off the half dozen seats in the lecture hall that were directly between the camera and the artwork. Sarah Lynn showed up just before the class and took our second video camera to shoot incidental footage, including the reactions and responses of the class.

"What we have been discussing for a semester and a half is how the literature and art of other ages has affected that of contemporary artists. Mr. Blackburn took that to heart and created contemporary art pieces using his own special medium of the human body, video, photo editing, and canvas painting," Merck reminded the class. "Keep in mind that your artwork, papers, essays, short stories, poetry, skits, and assorted conversations have not been focused on recreating the period but using it as a launchpad for *your* creativity. Jett has asked that his piece, titled *Liberty and Death*, be presented without further comment to let you establish your own interpretation. If you would please settle yourselves for this short performance, we will begin." Merck stepped aside and we changed the lighting in the room so that only the lights we brought from home were on. Then I opened the curtain.

As we practiced, Rania held her pose for over a minute in silence as students shuffled a little to get a better view and a few whispers were passed. I mentioned that she was a great model. She could hold a pose almost as well as one of those living statues you see at fairs and panhandling on street corners.

Then she moved.

At first there was shuffling, thinking the performance was over—even a couple people applauding as she walked straight forward. But as she turned to leave, there was a collective gasp. She turned and walked behind the piece and it seemed like she'd left her shadow on the canvas. In the shadow was not the statue, but the model stripped naked of all paint and pretense. She threw her head back in a grimace of death as blood sprang from her chest, the high-powered rifle raised in her hand worthless against the reality of dying and the Declaration of Independence in her left hand, a tattered shred of her dreams.

41
Beatitude

ARIEL WENT home with Rania 'to help clean her up and get the paint off.' We didn't see her for two days.

"AAGH! YOU'RE HOPELESS!" Blankenship screamed when he saw my thirty-inch rendering of *The Garden of Earthly Delights*. "How can you create something with such detail that is so flat? Don't you listen in class? The whole point of perspective is to create depth and direction. Stop thinking of the horizon as a point out in the distance. The eye creates the horizon. If the world was truly flat, it would still fade in the distance and cut off at the point where your eye focused. Just because you have chosen to look down at your subject doesn't mean there is no horizon or vanishing point."

He scratched out a drawing of Ariel on the whiteboard so quickly I was amazed at how much it looked like her. Then he drew a line in red across the drawing and right between her eyes. He drew a second that cut between her breasts, and a third right through her pussy.

"Decide. Which is the focus? Where do you want the viewer's eye to begin? This drawing looks like a wallpaper print. There is no depth. No illusion of space. One, perspective. Two, overlap. The shapes you've created are all complete, interlinked like the pieces of a picture puzzle. Nothing is behind anything else. Three, size. You have objects of different sizes, but none of the sizes seem related to how far away they are. They are merely different sizes, not different distances. Four, placement. The eye works from a foreground at the bottom to background at the top. It is simply the way humans see. There is no differentiation of closeness or farness as you move from bottom to top or top to bottom. Five, value. You are back to drawing precise even objects without shading or color differentiation. Six, detail. Everything in the drawing is done with the same level of detail. Objects that are farther away are seen with less detail than those that are close. Everything in this drawing is just as precisely drawn and detailed. Flat. Flat. Flat!"

Fuck!

"Two weeks. Same size. Bring it back showing illusional space."

I picked up my drawing and shoved it in the portfolio. We scowled at each other a couple of seconds before I turned on my heel to leave. I didn't say anything. Sessions with Blankety, like his class, weren't discussions.

·º· ·◈ ꒰ꕥ꒱ ☼ ꒰ꕥ꒱ ◈· ·º·

THE LITERATURE AND the Arts discussion group, however, comprised small groups of a dozen out of the class of nearly a hundred that met together to talk about the topic being covered in class and respond to each other's representative projects. Wednesday was beat on Jett day. *Fuck! My project is over already.*

"You liberals are all alike. Everything is about gun control. Well, the second amendment guarantees us the right to bear arms. It's not about murdering. It's about protecting ourselves from a government that becomes a tyranny. If you take the guns away from Lady Liberty, only the tyrants and criminals will have guns!" declared one of the guys in the group.

I hadn't realized there was anything about gun control in my painting. I owned a rifle. Granddad made sure I knew how to use it out on the farm. It was a moderately low-power .22 caliber lever action rifle, but it was still a rifle I used to shoot at squirrels and gophers out in the fields. I painted the picture with the most popular mass-shooting weapon in the country because that's the most popular mass-shooting weapon in the country. Even if I thought there should be a ban on their manufacture and sale, it didn't mean I was unarmed.

I didn't get a chance to say anything.

"You and your rights," a heavyset girl next to me spat at him. "All you have is rights and no reasons. This discussion was supposed to be about the Age of Reason and instead we're talking about a pornographic portrayal of one of the most sacred symbols of American freedom, desecrating the most precious document of the Revolutionary War. Was it really necessary to have her breasts bared? To show a view up her crotch as she fell back when shot? This stuff is indecent and your model should probably file charges against you for molesting her. She's one more #MeToo exploited by a man in the name of his creativity."

Molesting Rania? You've got to be kidding. The closest contact I had with her was one hug. The rest was all at the end of a brush or a spray of paint. She'd been a collaborator on the piece. That expression of death on her face was *her* orgasm instituted at *her* suggestion without my help. Still no chance to answer.

"I'd trade freedom for security," a quiet girl with a bandana on her head said. "As a woman, I'm constantly afraid. I looked at the painting and felt that was my life. I expect the bullet, figurative or literal, at any time. It could be a rape, a closed door, a fanatic preacher, an offended brother, or a US Congressman. In the name of freedom, we've lost all form of being secure in our lives."

"You're an immigrant," another said. "You came here for freedom. But that isn't what you really want. You just want someone else to take care of you. The painting is a clear message that the Statue of Liberty is no longer an unguarded invitation to plunder our country in the name of Freedom. We've closed the gates."

What the fuck? I didn't say anything for the whole class time. It was just too much. Did I mean anything they were saying? I had only one message that I thought I was giving. Liberty equals death; death equals liberty. It's personal. I never thought it would affect so many others in different ways.

Left-right. Conservative-liberal. What's the difference? We have the vicious on one side and the humorless on the other. They both want to control our lives. *Fuck 'em.*

•·⊰ ⅃⊂ ☼ ⊃⅃ ⊱·•

"What are you making, Jett?"

"Stuffed chicken breasts for dinner. Friday's my night now. Um… you kind of missed yours Tuesday."

"Oh, shit. I forgot," Ariel mourned. There was something of her old emo self in that expression. I set my knives aside and washed my hands.

"This will wait a few minutes. Tell me about it," I said as I led her to the living room. It was only noon and I was getting a head start on things for the evening meal using one of the prep techniques I'd learned in my Proteins class.

Ariel hesitated a moment when I sat on the couch and then cuddled up on my lap. She pressed her face against my chest and I had to struggle to hear her whisper, "I'm in love."

I somehow had a feeling she didn't mean with me. Or with any of the girls in our family.

"You and Rania really hit it off, didn't you?"

"Yeah. Oh, Jett, she's wonderful! So gentle and loving and dominant. I want to be with her and obey her and be anything she wants," Ariel said. "I don't know what to do."

"I never imagined Rania was bi," I mused. "Well, I should have realized that when she brought you into the studio to lick her out."

"She's not bi. She's a lesbian. Pure, gold star, lesbian. She has no interest in men at all."

"Really? I'd never have guessed. She doesn't seem… well, when we worked together, we really got along well. She didn't seem to have anything against men."

"Why would she? Being homosexual isn't equivalent of being either misogynist or misandrist. Far more straight people fit in those categories than gay people. You automatically jump to the conclusion that if she isn't interested in *you,* then she must hate men." Ariel scowled at me and started to pull away. I held on.

"Please don't think that of me, Ariel. I'm sorry about my reaction. You're springing a lot on me at once and I don't know how to respond. We all love you, too. Telling us you've fallen in love with someone else hurts and I didn't mean to lash out at you."

"And I love you! That's why I don't know what to do. Rania is not only lesbian, she's very monogamous. She'd never fit in among our family like Mary does. She couldn't even be tolerant of multiple relationships like Eva is. What am I going to do?" Ariel started crying in earnest and I rocked her back and forth on my lap.

"It sounds like you are leaving us," I whispered. "I'm sad, Ariel, but I only want what makes you happy."

"But I'm happy with you, too. I don't want to give up seven sex partners for one, even if she knows, like, ten times the number of ways to satisfy a woman."

"Really?"

"You would not believe how she can make me feel!"

"I guess you need to choose."

"Why? Why can't I have both? We've never objected to you bringing home a potential or actual new lover. The girls all assumed at first that Rania was just interested in you and we'd never get a lick at her. The reality was she was interested in just one of us… but it wasn't you. But if you can have an outside lover and it's okay with us, why can't I have an outside lover?"

"Will Rania be satisfied with that?"

"I don't know! But I haven't made any commitments to her. I still love you, Jett. I still love Sarah Lynn, Jasmine, Char, Kelly, Mary, and Eva. Do you still love me? Am I still your little sex doll?"

"I love you, Ariel."

"Then let's put your hens away and let your cock out to play."

⋅∘⋅❖ ⫷ ☽ ⫸ ❖⋅∘⋅

I BARELY MADE it back to the kitchen in time to get dinner ready. Ariel was voracious. Rania might have been loving on her and had techniques that were far superior, but apparently, she didn't have a cock. And Ariel produced enough juice from her pussy that I was nearly drowned by the second time she came and my cock slid effortlessly into her tight little pussy when she mounted me. *I just love to watch her bounce!*

"Jett, you've come in my mouth and in my pussy. Why haven't you ever taken my ass?"

"What? I would never hurt you like that!"

"But I want it. I've wanted it since the first time you pushed your thumb into my little hole."

"I wouldn't want to do that unless you were prepared," I said. "Char is the only one I've done that with and she always prepares first."

"Char is always prepared. She told me that if I wanted that, I needed to always be prepared. I push my butt plug in every day before I leave for school and wear it inside me, stretching me to receive your cock, all day long. I always keep myself clean and cleaned out before we go to bed. Even this afternoon. I wasn't just peeing when I went to the bathroom. I'm always ready and you never take me. I'm your sex doll, Jett. I have three holes."

"I… You… Really? Now?" I wasn't making much sense to myself, but my cock had hardened in Ariel's hand as she talked to me and I was definitely ready. She nodded and started to turn over. I held her on her back as I crawled between her legs and shoved my cock in her pussy.

"That's not my butt!" she laughed.

"No. I'm just getting a little extra lube. I want to look at your face. I want to see your eyes when I push into your bottom. I want to watch your mouth stretch as I stretch your asshole with my cock. I want to feel your pussy juices running down your crack onto my cock to keep me lubricated when I fuck your ass."

"Yes, Jett. I'm ready. Yes!"

I pulled out of her pussy and pushed her legs up onto my shoulders. Ariel is extremely flexible and can be a little pretzel if she wants to. As her ass rolled forward, my cock slipped down. I didn't need my hands. I could feel the pulsing opening against the head of my cock as I moved against her. Such a tiny butt held in both my hands. I pushed.

Ariel began to whine as I applied more pressure. I was afraid I needed more lubrication or that I was just too big. Then there was a sudden relaxation and the head of my cock slipped past her rectal ring and Ariel's eyes popped open almost as wide as her mouth.

"Okay?" I asked. She couldn't say anything, but just nodded her head. I bent to kiss her and my cock slid in a little farther. She whined into my mouth and clutched my arms to pull me forward. Deeper. I thought of Char's butt as being buttery when I slid into her but Ariel's was a furnace. I was about three-quarters into her when her eyes popped open with a gasp.

"There! There! Stop! That's as far as you can go. Stop! That's as deep as I am." I pulled back a little.

"Do you want me out?"

"No! But don't go any deeper than that. I can feel you hit the bend in my colon. You can't push straight any farther. It hurt when you hit it. But don't stop fucking my ass now that you've started. Now I want to feel everything. I want to feel you coming up my poop chute." Ariel pushed a hand down between us and began furiously strumming her clit as I pulled back and moved forward again, careful not to pound into her too deeply.

It didn't make a difference. Being in my little Asian lover's bottom was ramping me up fast. Such an incredible feeling.

"Your sex doll has three holes and you can have them all," she chanted. "Fuck my mouth, fuck my cunt, fuck my ass. Fuck me over and over again. I'm going… again… I'm…" The rhythm of Ariel's fingers on her clit changed and I could feel the pressure increase as she started a wordless scream of orgasm. When she came, her ass relaxed and clenched and repeated over and over again. I pulled back and pushed into her one more time to the limit she had set and started spraying my come on that bend in her colon. Yes!

I was fine with her having an outside girlfriend. Especially, if I continued to have access to this!

•◦•⟡ ⅀⅀ℂ ☾ ℂ⅀⅀ ⟡•◦•

"I DON'T KNOW. I'm thinking the crucifixion theme isn't going to work," I sighed. Mary cuddled up next to me and guided my hand to the piercing in her left nipple. We were seeing more of each other since she was with us for dinner at least five nights a week and we shared our drawing from hell class. But it seemed like we had less time to be intimate with our late study nights and projects. This evening, we'd been going over my plan for painting a transsexual crucifixion scene to accompany the themes found in *The Idiot*. That got us to comparing male anatomy—mine—to female anatomy—hers—and trying to figure out exactly where her cock would originate if she had one. Eventually, we were cuddled together on the couch just touching each other and making out.

"What's the biggest problem?"

"Well, the unit is basically the transition from realism to impressionism. First off, it's rare to find a crucifixion scene among the romantic impressionists. We're talking Cezanne, Monet, Manet, Degas, and Renoir. They are more likely to paint a picture of a picnic where everyone is happily sitting around a blanket with food and all the women are naked."

"Gustave Courbet started that. Real subjects painted in a new and sometimes erotic way. Lips held inches from nipples. Direct view of hairy crotch. Casual embraces. Why not go with a romantic scene with our trans Christ that foreshadows crucifixion? Sarah Lynn can put her lips next to my nipples. You can show my cock right above my pussy slit."

"That's more futa than transgender, but we could go that way. I wonder what I can come up with."

"Come up me, lover. It's been too long since I've had your cock in my vagina. I know life has been crazy lately, but I want you, too. Do you still want me, Jett?" I could feel her tremble beneath my fingers and detected a bit of anxiety in it, not just the tremors she so frequently had.

"I want you, Mary. Let's go to bed."

⋅∘⋅⇨ ⊃⊂ ☽ ⊃⊂ ⇦⋅∘⋅

I DREW. I painted. I wrote papers. And for my 3D class, I even made a hanging mobile. I made kebobs, stuffed breasts and porkchops, teriyaki marinated beef strips, and tied roasts, fully seasoned and ready for the oven. And we studied.

By the end of the first week of April, I had a sketch that I felt was appropriate for my painting of the hermaphrodite Christ. I liked the concept better because it was in keeping with Christ. He was supposedly a complete human and a complete god, 'fully human and fully divine,' the way the church put it. So why not fully man and fully woman? This time, there would be no body painting. I was doing a canvas. Not even a really huge one, but the setting was reminiscent of the pastoral scenes of Monet and the sensuality of Courbet. I used Sarah Lynn, Jas, Kelly, and Eva in the scene as Mary's picnic companions or disciples.

I didn't need them all at once nor all the time so everyone was able to pose a while and then go do their own work. I started painting and just used my own normal freestyle strokes. I wasn't trying to mimic the impressionists but was using the subject matter of both the painters and of Dostoevsky to create a contemporary scene with my own social commentary.

I was relaxed painting this. I decorated three pair of underwear for Kelly while I worked on my first piece of truly flat art since I started bodypainting. Yes, my rendition of *The Garden of Earthly Delights* was progressing, but even though I was now using shading and getting more depth in the drawing, it still wasn't paint. I was painting a piece I'd decided to call *Beatitude*. That would give it a Biblical name without really calling attention to who was who. Nonetheless, I figured at least half my class would be offended and the other half wouldn't get it. But I figured everyone in my class hated me already so what the fuck. No matter what Dante said, I figured you went to the same hell if you killed one person as you did if you killed a dozen.

Unlike the excitement and tension of *Liberty and Death*, I was having fun with *Beatitude*. Each of my girlfriends got at least one orgasm after a posing session. And usually, so did I. Sometimes they were in the middle of the session.

"Kelly, let me see what this position looks like," I said casually as I moved her right hand over Mary's pussy. She looked at me and grinned as she started fingering our girlfriend.

"Let me know if I should be higher or lower so it looks like I'm stroking her cock, too," Kelly grinned.

"Higher," Mary squeaked. "Just… yeah… right there." I didn't sketch or paint anything while Kelly was getting Mary off, but as soon as she finished, I slid my hard cock into the well-prepared channel. *I love being in Mary!* I loved her up to another orgasm and then Kelly straddled her to get some kissing in. I pulled out of Mary and slid into the fabulous tightness of my redhead camgirl. *I love being in Kelly.* Am I getting repetitive?

•·•⇨ Ⅻ ☼ Ⅻ ⇦•·•

BLANKETY WAS STRANGELY quiet as he looked closely at my new drawing of *The Garden of Earthly Delights*. I'd come to realize a few things over the past weeks. I still hated him, but I was learning. I was learning more from this exercise than I was from his classes as he led us through each phase of creating composition, illusional space, perspective, proportion, and form. He set my drawing on a display easel at the end of his desk and sat down. *No drawing? Did I do it?*

"It's almost art," he sighed. *Oh shit.* "Your model—I saw her when you displayed the painting in Professor Merck's class. He was kind enough to invite me, no thanks to you. She is five feet and one inch tall and weighs one hundred six pounds. Why can I not tell that from your drawing? You have managed to show distance, shape, texture, but I can't see the form. Oh, it is here in parts of the drawing, but this flower—is it weightless? It doesn't even bend the stem. Is this thorn sharp? It looks like a paper cutout, flat on the drawing instead of pointing at me. Here, you have almost captured an appropriate chiaroscuro, but with its intense contrast between light and dark and the rest of the image's dullness, it looks like it is jumping from the page and is the only thing real. This carefully concealed yet delicately exposed female is what needs to lift from the page. I should be able to reach out and lift her with my hands. I should feel the size of her breasts, the depths of her sex, and the weight of her body with my eyes. Yes. It is *almost* art."

He turned to a stack of papers on his desk and started reading. I packed the drawing in my portfolio and left.

··o··o◆ ⟫⟪ ☽ ⟫⟪ ◆o··o··

Beatitude was displayed at the front of the class with half a dozen other paintings and drawings and several students stopped to look at it on their way in. I wasn't the only artist in this class. I'd just made a splash by bringing nude models into the room with me. A little conversation sprang up around it. I think that most people moved past too quickly to identify that the central woman with arms outstretched along the back of a park bench also had a cock that was partially erect. Of course, just below that was an open pussy. Her knees were spread apart, but her feet were crossed one on the other.

She whispered in a woman's ear on her right, their breasts nearly touching at the nipple. On her left, a woman was close with lips almost touching the pierced nipple of that breast. At her right knee, a woman knelt with hand outstretched but not quite grasping the stiff cock. And behind the figure, a dark beauty stood, running her fingers through the blonde hermaphrodite's hair as if it were a halo around her head.

It was a peaceful scene, despite reflecting a crucifix position with the women kneeling around her and an angel tending her head. When Merck projected the much bigger than life images of the drawings and paintings that had been displayed there were a few restless comments as more people grasped what they were seeing. Not enough, though, to relate the painting to the fact that the next day was Good Friday.

42
Alien

I **CUT MY** protein class Friday morning and went straight to the store. I had four large pre-orders for Easter to prepare and then I needed to get smaller dishes ready for the people who would wait until today and tomorrow to start planning Easter dinner. I don't know who figures out what food is appropriate for what holiday. Some of it I understand—like butterflying thick rib steaks to put in special heart-shaped grilling tins for Valentine's Day. We'd sold a lot of those. But who decided that Easter should be a ham day? Although it seemed that lamb was a big seller for the weekend, too.

Of course, not everyone can either afford or use a full ham. If you go down to Walmart, you can buy about three cuts of ham. A ham steak is a center cut of a whole ham. It's the best, tenderest, and meatiest piece of the ham and has just one center bone. It's usually half an inch to an inch thick, but commercial processors try to maximize the sale by cutting it into quarter-inch slices. That means that the butt and shank halves of the ham that are sold are labeled 'butt portion' and 'shank portion.' Neither one has the best slice included. The butt is meatier and fattier and is difficult to carve because it includes not only the leg bone, but also part of the pelvic bone and joint. The shank portion is a bit more popular just because it is easier to slice. It's also not as fatty and tastes a little sweeter.

We didn't deal with smoked hams behind the butcher case. Mostly, they come from one of the big processors completely tied and shrink wrapped. Some things you just can't compete with locally. But all day Friday, I deboned, sliced, tied, and stuffed hams and pork legs.

The bones that we didn't package for sale in the freezer case for soup, I took home with me—with Grandpa's blessing. I set our largest soup kettle on the stove and dumped all the bones in to simmer overnight. Saturday, I would pick the meat, strain the stock, cool it so I could skim the fat. I also put a big pan of navy beans to soak. By Saturday evening, I had ham and bean soup slow cooking for Sunday dinner. A little cornbread and some greens and we'd be all set.

In the meantime, I still had to cook dinner Friday night, after which Jas and Sarah Lynn decided to make a Jett sandwich between them.

Ah woe is me. I have such a hard life.

THE RESPITE WAS brief. After work on Saturday, I had to head to the airport. Mary joined me and we filled the wall with clouds, birds, and airplanes. The big weekend paint performance was just three weeks away.

That also meant that finals were just two weeks away. I went to classes Monday morning filled with dread. Proteins just kept chugging along like normal, though we were told that our final would include both a written and a practical exam. The written would include recipes, seasonal questions, and marketing terms. The practical would include identifying cuts, listing practical uses, and being given a recipe to prepare for sale.

My 3D class was as unpleasant as usual and the exam promised to be a narrow escape for me. We'd studied sculpture all term and had been given different assignments with modeling clay, foam board, wood, and found objects. Only one or two people in the class were actually studio artists in sculpture. The rest of us limped along with lame projects like making a face out of found objects.

Current Directions in Art was a jack-off class as far as I was concerned. We were supposed to learn to look at and analyze various artworks. What was the artist's motivation, intention, and process? What was their relationship to the development of contemporary art? To me, it was a lot like the discussions of *Liberty and Death* in my Lit class. Everybody had their own passionately argued position about what the piece meant. 'The exposed breasts were a classic invitation to suckle at the nurturing mother after the birth of her nation.' Get real. Rania had awesome breasts. I wanted to show them off.

Blankenship was out on Monday. That was so unusual that we just stood around in the classroom waiting for twenty minutes. I hoped he would be in for my review of *The Garden of Earthly Delights* on Tuesday. I'd reached a point with it that I doubted everything. I kept trying to think of what he would criticize next. Every time I passed the piece, I found something else to touch up a bit. Frankly, I'd had no idea that drawing could be so complicated. All my drawings up to this time had been pretty much as a basis for paint. This was the first time I was considering the drawing to be the end product instead of a step in the process.

Merck gave us the info for our last project. It was the first one I'd need to worry about because his three-hour exam slot was on Monday. That's when I'd get to present Andi. She'd agreed to do a few test passes, but didn't want me to use the acrylic paints on her. She wanted to be able to take a shower afterward and have it gone. That meant that I'd have to paint her in the morning before our exam. Unlike *Beatitude* that was presented only as a painting on canvas, *Princess* would be presented only as body art. The early 1900s were really when Modernism took hold. Part of that was the cubist movement in art and the rise of science fiction in literature. Picasso and Edgar Rice Burroughs. A painting on the Princess of Mars as if she were rendered by Picasso.

⋅∘⋅⇒ Ⅻ ☼ Ⅻ ⇐⋅∘⋅

I entered Blankenship's office at exactly five-thirty Tuesday afternoon. I'd been coming for these private reviews all term now. I couldn't remember having ever spoken since the first one. I didn't need to knock. Blankenship ran by a clock in his head. If my appointment was at five-thirty, I was simply expected to enter at exactly that time and listen until he dismissed me.

I set my drawing on his review easel and sat across from him to listen to his scathing critique again.

He sat at his desk with his arms folded and looked at the drawing. He pursed his lips as his attention was caught by one thing or another. He squinted one eye then the other. He stood and walked toward the

397

drawing, going so far as to pull out a magnifying glass at one point and examine a cluster of flowers growing from Ariel's pussy. He scanned the whole picture from up close again and then paced back to the other side of his desk and looked at it again.

I was getting frustrated. Usually by this time he would be ranting about one thing or another. He'd jump up and draw a section on the whiteboard in a better rendition than I had on the paper and then tell me why mine was inadequate. He was driving me crazy with his silence.

He nodded once and sat at his desk. He started going through papers and picked up a stack to start reading. That was an accepted sign that our session was over. I packed the drawing in my portfolio and turned to leave, still expecting him to snarl some derogatory comment at me. Nothing.

I left his office.

I guess his version of the Thumperian principle was 'If you can't say something nasty, don't say nothing at all.'

Ariel had dinner ready and we all sat when I got home. We ate and there was the usual chitchat about our day. It was a little strained because Rania had joined us and no one was exactly sure how to treat her. She just didn't seem like someone trying to take our girlfriend away from us. Until after dinner. Once dishes were cleared up, Ariel left with her.

I went into my studio. Sarah Lynn and Jas were studying in the living room. Kelly had her Tuesday night chatroom show at eight o'clock. I was still in shock a little, I think. I put the drawing of *The Garden of Earthly Delights* on my easel and lifted the tissue covering that kept it from getting smudged. I picked up a pencil to correct something and then laid it back down. If something still needed work, Blankety would have screamed it out at me. I pulled out a can of permanent spray fixative and carefully treated the drawing. What was it Jesus said on the cross?

It is finished.

•○·◇ ⫶⫶⫶ ☼ ⫶⫶⫶ ◇·○•

"THAT STUFF STINKS," Char said from behind me. She wrapped her arms around me and hugged me from behind as she looked past my shoulder at the drawing. "I loved the painting, but it wasn't as… I don't know…

special?... without Ariel all painted up in front of it. The drawing is complete. I love it." She squeezed me tightly and I could hear her breath shudder as she drew it in. "Are we losing her, Jett?"

I turned and pulled Char to me. She was just wearing a T-shirt and I stroked her soft back as I hugged her. "I don't know, honey. Do you think… Was it really good for her to be our sex doll? I think we've been seeing a little of the manic side of Ariel's emo persona the past few weeks. Since Christmas. Maybe Rania will help bring some balance to her."

"I know it's almost impossible to keep a group like we have together," Char said. "I really love all our lovers. I'll be so sad if she is never with us."

"Let's hope it doesn't come to that."

"Kelly's show has started. Let's go watch it in bed and make love."

That's an idea I could get with.

•○•◦❖ ⟩⟩C ☾ C⟨⟨ ❖◦•○•

"Two weeks. Your final project is due here on the eighth. Your task is to create a composition and draw it. Subject matter is open, but I strongly suggest you *not* do a figure drawing. We have not studied the unique aspects of figure drawing and you would just be guessing. Still life is yet beyond the reach of most of you. Your drawing is to be a finished work of art. It is not a drafting nor a sketch for a painting or future work. It is to be thirty by twenty, portrait or landscape and should be ready to mount for exhibition. You will show in this work of art that you have learned the principles and application of composition, illusional space, perspective, proportion, and form."

We were just a minute from the end of class and no one would have time for a question before he walked out the door. At least I understood the assignment, but I was exhausted just thinking about it. Blankety stopped in front of me on his way to the door.

"You have passed your final," he said, pointing at me. "You needn't return."

And then he was gone.

Fuck!

•○•◦❖ ⟩⟩C ☾ C⟨⟨ ❖◦•○•

"I HAVE TO see your final," Andi said urgently as we walked out of class with Mary. Everyone was looking at me suspiciously. "If you've already passed, seeing what you did will show me what I have to do. I'll strip and you can smear paint on my body. With your hands if you want to. Just let me see what you have drawn."

"I'd like to see it, too, Jett," Mary said. "I'm not sure it will tell me anything about what *I* have to do, but I'd like to celebrate with you. You are the only one in our class who knows he passed."

"Well, come on home with me. You know Blankenship once criticized me by saying I took advantage of you and that you were the one in our class with real talent. I just kept enduring what he said and trying to learn from it." I wrapped an arm around Mary. I couldn't wrap an arm around Andi, too, because I had my portfolio and supplies in that hand. She solved it by putting her arm across my shoulders as we headed home.

TRUE TO HER word, Andi stripped and asked me questions about the drawing while Mary and I applied paint to her body. Sometimes with our fingers.

"I don't think I have time to do a drawing like this for the final," Andi sighed. That might have been because I was drawing circles around her nipples and reaching in to pinch them occasionally. Or it might have been because of my drawing.

"I agree," Mary said as she painted Martian antennae on Andi's cheeks. "I'm glad he didn't show this to the class as an example. Everyone would have quit."

"I nearly *did* quit," I said. "I don't think he's expecting this from anyone. It's taken me all term to put this together. And I endured private humiliation from him every two weeks to get here."

"I see what he means about all the dimensions of the drawing, though," Andi continued. "It really looks almost three dimensional. I wouldn't expect that from a drawing that is all smaller drawings. Especially one that's all pussies and cocks."

"He said he wanted to be able to feel her breasts and tell her weight in his hands as he picked her up," I said. "I think he meant by looking at the drawing. Or maybe he's just a perv. I'm glad I'm not doing that drawing now, though. I was trying to make flat art look three dimensional. Here I'm trying to make a very three-dimensional girl into flat art." I'd whited out Andi's entire right side and was drawing a profile view of her breast in place of the straight on view I covered. It was kind of hard to keep my hands focused on painting instead of just playing with her tits. And pussy. I was putting a huge painted gash on her pussy lips similar to what I'd done with Ariel before Christmas. Somehow, I kept having to push her pussy lips around with my fingers in order to get the paint in the right places. Sometimes I sort of brushed her wet folds and along her clit. All in the name of art. I was sure Andi was going to recite this activity as her #MeToo.

"All right. That's all I have time for tonight," she declared, stepping away from me. "Take some pictures and then get me showered and clean." This was a practice session and Mary and I had both been pretty playful. I snapped a couple dozen pix from different angles, including one up between her legs. I was surprised but willing when she grabbed my hand and took me into my bathroom with her. That has the smallest shower stall. "Come in here and scrub all this icky paint off me, you lech." That was all the encouragement I needed to strip and let my hard cock lead me into the shower with her.

I scrubbed her, making sure I got the paint out of every little nook and cranny. I think cranny is another word for pussy. When she was rinsed, she leaned back against me and pulled my hand back down to her dripping core.

"You've been making me sloppy for the past hour and a half. Now use those fingers and get me off." Your wish and all that. In this position it was easy to reach into her twat and diddle an incredibly hard little nub, alternating between that and shoving my fingers into her hot box. My other hand wrapped around her to continue playing with her sensitive nips. She wasn't interested in kissing but stretched her neck to the side while I nibbled on it. My cock was tight in her ass crack as she came and slumped back against me.

"That was great," she said as she opened the shower door and stepped out. She grabbed a towel and glanced back at my cock waving in the air.

"Isn't it polite to return the favor?" I asked.

"My boyfriend is five hundred miles away. I needed help. You've got girlfriends in the next room. You don't need me."

Well, fuck!

WE MADE IT to finals week and I painted Andi in the morning to take her to the Literature and the Arts final in the afternoon. The girl was proving to be a real tease and wanted me to get her off each time I painted her but didn't want to do anything with me. *So, I'm going to turn down the opportunity to finger a hot girl's pussy to orgasm just because I can't put my cock in it? Really?* I assumed I'd have to take her home and shower her again when class was over.

When we left the room, a big guy stepped out in front of us in the hall. I mean big! He was about six-six and probably weighed two-fifty. He had blond wispy hair that was already thinning and a light beard. For as big as he was, he wasn't particularly threatening. He was kind of soft and round. He grinned and I had to think he was a big teddy bear.

That was confirmed when Andi shrieked and threw herself at him. He easily lifted her up by her butt cheeks and started a messy kiss.

"Dennis! You got here in time to see me! I'm so happy you're here."

"I couldn't get out of Bloomington until about midnight and drove straight through. You look amazing!"

"Jett, this is my boyfriend, Dennis Witt. He's going to wash all the paint off every part of my body and find exactly where you stuck all your sprays and brushes."

"Hi. Glad to…"

"Can we have sex while you still have all the paint on? It would be like sex with an alien," Dennis said, ignoring me.

"Yes! Getting painted was a real turn-on. I got off every time I got painted and every time I cleaned up. I want you. I want you so much!" They were already ten steps in front of me and moving fast toward the exit. Dennis obviously knew where he was going and didn't set Andi down as she kept slobbering kisses all over him.

To each his own.

Thursday night we were all finished with our finals and gathered in the living room. The bong was out and we were feeling pretty mellow. Even Rania had come to join us. Andi and Dennis had taken off the previous day, right after Blankety's final presentation. She did okay, I'm happy to say. Jas was leaning against my left side with Mary curled up in my lap. Rania was leaning against my right side with Ariel curled up in her lap. Friday, everyone was headed to the airport to start the three-day performance of *Flight*. The basic background was laid in but all the detail still had to be done. Eva, of course, would be part of the performance and part of the art as I painted her into the wall. She also planned to help paint along with Mary. Ariel was going to furnish music periodically on her keyboard.

"Are you nervous about tomorrow?" Kelly asked Eva. They'd experimented with several ways to get comfortable on a bunch of cushions on the floor and ended up with Char and Sarah Lynn as a backrest. Kelly was taking the night off from her Thursday bath show.

"Yeah, but no," Eva responded. "I think excited is more like it. Jett has painted me twice and tons of people saw the results. Granted, I didn't do live performances like Ariel and Rania, but we've been getting ready for this all year. I can't wait."

"What are you doing this summer?"

"Flying. I'll be working at the airport all summer. Jett negotiated ten hours of free flight time for my participation this week and I work for lessons. Once this weekend is over, I'll be a fixture out there—in more ways than one."

"And you're sure you want to do the full acrylic paint job?" I asked. I could change to water paints if she really wasn't comfortable.

"The only part I was worried about was my hair. The wig was a great idea. I don't want anything else to be smeared over the next week or two. Even my face."

We passed the bong around again, all relieved to have the school year over and done with. Rania was wiggling next to me and I turned toward her. She was in a deep kiss with Ariel but Ariel was squirming to get closer to me.

"What's up, you two?" I asked as Ariel's hand slipped between Mary and me to press against my chest.

"Guys, um… Rania asked me to move in with her. And um… I said yes." We'd all gotten accustomed to Ariel running off to spend nights with Rania over the past few weeks. The announcement wasn't a surprise but it was still a little sad. There were shouts of encouragement and congratulations and 'We'll miss you.'

"Wait!" Rania said. "Wait. That's not all. Ariel, you went right to the hard part first."

"What is it, Rania?"

"I don't want to take Ariel away from you. I've fallen deeply in love with her and a little bit with all of you. But I'm not cut out for life in a… household like this. I'm not body shy. I can run around naked with you. Jett, I'd like you to paint me again. Maybe paint Ariel and me together. But when it comes to going to bed at night or being intimate, Ariel's the only one I'm interested in. We talked about it a lot and she was willing to ask you all if I could move in here, but that just wouldn't work for me. But Ariel is in love with you all and I can't ask her to give up the special feelings she has with you. That includes the way she feels between your legs when she's licking, sucking, and fucking." We all kind of laughed at that but I wasn't sure what she was saying.

"What are you asking, Rania?" Sarah Lynn said for all of us.

"We'd like to be sort of an extended family. You know, have our own place to live but be able to come here, either together or separately, to be with you and connect. And for Ariel that really means to connect. I'm monogamous. I don't want to be intimate with anyone else, but hugs and kisses of a family are what make the world go round. And I'm not really a jealous person. Ariel is polyamorous. She wants us all and I want her to be happy."

"What she's saying or asking," Ariel said, "is if I can still come over and make stir fry sometimes and get my pussy licked and fucked by my wonderful boyfriend and girlfriends. Can I still be part of the family?"

There was a bit of a love fest as Ariel got passed around to all the members of the family to receive their affirmation of her welcome. I put an arm around Rania and gave her a little hug.

"You're really something special, Rania."

"Thank you, Jett. But it's not me that's special. It's her. I'm just in love."

43
Flight

THERE WERE logistics that needed to be handled at the airport. Warning signs were posted indicating that the wing we were working in may include nude models working on the new mural. There was a red rope pulled across the entrance to our hall and down the left side so people were guided into the performance area but couldn't come into the area where we were painting or modeling. Char had the primary responsibility of monitoring the entrance so she could warn parents with their children in tow about what was happening. Jas monitored the other end of the hall. Both girls had buckets for donations.

Rania ran errands, spelled other workers, and brought us food and drink. She was also the number one escort of our nude model when she took breaks, though she was often accompanied by one or more of the other girls. Ariel played music whenever anyone was painting and it filled the hall. Her mother, father, and little brother all came out to see the project on Saturday. I'd only met her father a few times. He was devoted to his family from a financial and support perspective but I found him rather aloof unless he was talking to people he considered his peers. The children weren't. The Dragon Lady, on the other hand, managed to get under the rope and investigate what we were painting as closely as she had investigated the various art I'd painted on Ariel.

"When will you paint my daughter again?" she demanded.

"Um… not sure. I think I'll do a painting of her with her girlfriend this summer." Having just been introduced to Rania, Dragon Lady glanced over to the two of them. Eva stepped down off the platform and Rania rushed over to give her a robe and escort her to the restroom.

"Paint them as a fierce Chinese dragon. I can see it in them and want to see it in person."

Sarah Lynn and Kelly were operating cameras. We were collecting a terabyte per day of images. Kelly was going to edit the whole thing into a PG-13 acceptable DVD and offer it for sale at the airport counter.

On day one, Mary worked on more background detail while I sprayed the outline of Eva in the positions she would take as I painted her. The shadow painting on the wall would show her rising from a rendition of her *Earthbound* drawing at the right, running toward the left, and leaping into the sky. In some ways, it would look like those pictures that show multiple frames of a person in motion by using stop action photography. I think it's called a Marey-wheel. We had a series of steps we could move in to give her height in the various stages.

The worst part on Friday was the fact that Eva really looked a mess. I was using colors that were tones of the background as it changed. So, in the first outline, she was nearly all green. In the last one she was all sky blue. We had to pause for fifteen minutes between each pair of poses to let the paint dry, both on the wall and on Eva. As I had done with Rania when I sprayed *Liberty and Death*, Eva wore goggles and a breathing mask for all the spray work.

•◦••◈ ⊃⊂ ☽ ⊃⊂ ◈••◦•

"I'm such a mess!" she said when she finally got a look in the mirror. We knocked off at dinner time and went home after picking up food at a Taco Delight. I was glad that with Eva, Rania, and me we had three cars since there were now nine of us to be transported.

"Jett, is all this necessary to keep?" Char asked. She held Eva and stroked the line where her wig had shielded her hair from the spray.

"No. I will probably have to blank her all out tomorrow with a fresh coat of white and start painting from that," I sighed. The splotchy, multi-colored spray job was an unintended side-effect. I should have used water paint for this.

"That's not fair," Mary said. "You don't really want her all sprayed white. Her natural flesh should show through. Let's remove all this from her tonight. Do you mind, Eva?"

"Mind? Oh, hell, no. But it sounds like so much work. I volunteered to wear the paint all weekend."

"But this isn't really part of the paint I want you wearing," I said. I liked Mary's idea. "Let us take care of it, if you're okay with all of us touching you."

Before long, we had Eva stretched out on the floor and were working through the process of oiling and wiping her body and then using alcohol to clean up the remnants. With eight pair of hands on her—even Rania participated in this—the work went more quickly and there was a little touching that wasn't strictly necessary to get something clean. Eva was writhing on the towels we'd spread out by the time we were finished.

"Come with me, my little substrate," I whispered in her ear. "Now I want to bathe your beautiful body and enjoy it in the shower." Eva shuddered and followed me to the shower.

I scrubbed the oil from her body with Dawn dish detergent and then a gentle cleanser in my tiny shower. It kept us pressed together as I worked. When Eva started to wash me, I pushed her hands away.

"Don't get in the way. I need to fully prepare my canvas for tomorrow's painting. People just don't realize how much work it is to prepare a surface like this. It's not enough for it to be clean. It needs to be stimulated so it is receptive. And I need to be completely familiar with what I am going to paint. I need to touch it—all of it. I need to see how it responds." As I continued to whisper all about how she was simply my canvas and I needed to prepare her, I touched her all over. I rubbed and lightly pinched her nipples until they were solid peaks on her breasts. I kissed her. I probed her depths. And finally…, "I need to see now if she is truly as receptive as I want her to be," I said as I bent her forward and slid my cock into her wet pussy. For the past two hours, Eva's body had been handled and stimulated to the point of climax repeatedly. When I pushed my cock into her, she went off like a skyrocket. The screaming went on so long as I plundered her pussy that Sarah Lynn opened the bathroom door to make sure we were all right. I just kept fucking and Eva kept coming.

Eventually, so did I.

Sarah Lynn, Jas, and Mary rode with me in the morning. Eva had succumbed to the attention of all my girlfriends after our shower last night and it was a miracle any of us were out of bed in time to get to the airport in the morning. But Eva rose this morning simply glowing. We were all excited about the work we'd be doing today.

"Can I ask… Well, I guess I am asking," Mary said. "With Ariel moving in with Rania, does that mean there might be room for one more in your house?"

I looked over at Mary, riding shotgun, and grinned. In the mirror, I could see Sarah Lynn and Jasmine with smiles splitting their pretty faces.

"So many things to consider," Jas sighed.

"Yes. I suppose we should try to fill the empty space in our nest," Sarah Lynn added. "But where would we ever find someone compatible with our mostly naked, free-loving community?"

"Someone who's beautiful and fun and loving…" Jas said.

"And willing," I concluded. "Willing to be loved and to love. Willing to contribute. Willing to cook on occasion."

"Willing to be fucked by four horny girls and our boyfriend on a regular basis."

"Willing to sit on my face while Jett pounds me."

"Willing to paint pictures of us."

"Where will we ever find a roommate that meets all those requirements? We're so hard to live with."

I glanced over at Mary and she was trying to keep from grinning as she raised a hand and wiggled her fingers.

"Yes, Mary?"

"Me?"

"We love you, Mary. Will you come live with us this year?"

"How soon can I move in?"

One of the things about taking two semesters of Literature and the Arts with Merck, Foundations of Contemporary Art, and Current

Directions in Art, was that I looked at a lot of art. From the earliest times, art has shown mythical creatures. When we studied the Egyptians of Akhenaten, we saw various paintings of part human, part animal gods. The Greeks were constantly turning men or women into animals. Like Artemis changing Actaeon into a deer. And their own combined beasts like the sphinx and centaurs. I'd painted a monster emerging from Char. Char had a little shrine to elephant-headed Ganesha. Michelangelo painted angels on the Sistine Chapel. And angels continued to populate both religious and secular art well into the 1700s. And even then, we took an eagle as our national symbol. Harry Potter's house was symbolized by a Griffin. Hagrid had all manner of mythical beasts in his menagerie.

With Eva, I was creating my own mythical creature. She wasn't a bird, but a colorful and fully feathered angel.

In preparing for this, I'd studied birds and how their feathers laid on different parts of their bodies. I learned which feathers were for protection and which were for flight. I'd looked at every rendition of an angel with wings to see how the artists portrayed the feathers on the wings of cherubs and seraphim. It would take me the better part of two days to feather Eva.

And both for the performance and my own entertainment, I wanted Eva naked all the time. As an excuse, I started by painting her tail feathers.

I'd gotten pretty good with my airbrush over the past few months of experimenting on my girlfriends and models. I laid in a mottled brown from her mid-back down, even spreading her cheeks a bit so I could spray into her crack and right around her little hole. She moaned when I sort of accidentally pressed against it with my knuckle to hold my hand steady while I sprayed. Then I switched nozzles on the airbrush for finer detail of the shadow and highlights of the individual feathers. Finally, I used a fine brush to define edges and make the feathers pop into three dimensions.

As I worked, we also took frequent breaks so we could walk around and keep our blood circulating. I was using a small platform for Eva to stand on while I painted her lower body and would eventually stand on it myself when I needed to be a little higher than her for the shoulders and face. When we were on break, she always put a robe on, but when she was posing, she was naked whether the part I was painting required it or not.

I noticed a guy who flew in early in the afternoon hanging around with a cup of coffee. Eva noticed, too, and ran to meet him as soon as I'd draped her robe over her shoulders for a break.

"Steve! You flew in for the festival!" she shouted as she hugged him across the rope barrier. I couldn't help but notice that she hadn't belted her robe together.

"No, I flew in to see the artwork taking shape. God! You're even more beautiful than last summer, girl."

"Being a model and a… uh… substrate has given me motivation to stay in shape."

"A great shape from what I can see. And I see most of it."

"Steve, I want you to meet Jett," she said calling me over to her. "Jett is my ma… artist. He tells me what I need to do to make beautiful art. Jett, this is my dear friend, Steve. He was my first flying instructor. You know what they say. You never forget your first."

Rania looked over Eva's shoulder at me and cocked an eyebrow. I'd caught both references as well.

•◦•◦❖ ᗪᑕ ☼ ᗪᑕ ❖◦•◦•

"So," I whispered as I worked my way up Eva's back later in the day, "your first?"

"Um… Well… um…"

"Listen to me, my little substrate," I said as close to her ear as I could get. I casually touched her breast as I turned her so her back was fully to the viewing area. "You are a free bird. You needn't be worried about any relationship you have. If you come home with me tonight, I am going to eat you to orgasm and fuck you to another. I'm not painting your pussy lips today. But if you choose to spend the night elsewhere, I'm still not painting your pussy lips today."

"Jett… I love you. Thank you."

"Now, little substrate, I am going to give you wings."

And that was what I spent the last part of the day painting.

•◦•◦❖ ᗪᑕ ☼ ᗪᑕ ❖◦•◦•

As it happened, it was never an issue. I didn't see Steve around when we finished the day but Eva never hesitated about gathering up her things and bringing them home with us. She'd spoken with her old lover at every break. I was sure they'd worked something out.

"You chose to come home with us," I said as we finished dinner. Eva had spent a good bit of time using a hand mirror to look over her shoulder into the hall mirror as she examined the golden wings, mottled brown tail feathers, and tan feathering over her butt and legs.

"How could I resist my artist offering his substrate such pleasure?" she whispered to me. "But… um… tomorrow night, I might go flying."

"For now, why don't you come to my nest and let me ruffle your feathers?"

I painted soft downy feathers that faded to her skin at about mid-thigh. I brushed the softness of her mound and pussy lips in such a way that they nearly disappeared. I completed the plumage on her arms from the flight feathers on the back to the pinion feathers of the front. Then I proceeded to the brilliant red plumage of her chest and stomach. This plumage pressed up the sides of her breasts a bit, but not up as far as her nipples that I left bare and exposed.

Under her chin, the feathers subtly blended to her own skin tone and disappeared. Finally, I began the process of sculpting her face. I was not turning her into a bird. Eva has good bone structure in her face that only needed accenting a bit to bring out the strength and beauty of the angel I was creating. When the paint and makeup were applied, Kelly helped me put on the new blonde wig and style it in a heavenly manner.

Quite a crowd had gathered for the finale of our performance. An announcement had been made throughout the terminal and outside by the hangars. The recreational pilots all came in to watch Eva's transformation completed. I led her once again to the little platform we'd used for much of the painting and people applauded as I turned her in a pivot on the stand.

"Now, ladies and gentlemen, we come to the conclusion of our performance. This is flight!"

I led Eva to the background and she took her position lying at the right edge. She held each pose for about thirty to forty-five seconds and then moved to the next of the stations we'd outlined on the wall. Each time she moved, it looked like she'd left her shadow behind. We had the different height platforms moved into position and she seemed to take off into the sky by the time she hit the last one, balancing on one foot as the other stretched out behind and her winged arms stretched forward. We held that position for longer as Kelly moved in with the DSLR and photographed the concluding scene of *Flight*.

The applause was as thunderous as a hundred people in an enclosed space could make it. I led Eva again to the small platform in the center and had her pirouette and bow. Ariel approached from the side and received her round of applause. All my girlfriends and Rania gathered around us.

Jefferson Wright, the airport facilities manager, joined us to shake our hands and make an announcement.

"The performance this weekend of this artistic crew and our own young pilot, Eva Rice, has helped make this year's fly-in festival one of the most successful we've ever had. Over a thousand people in six hundred eighty aircraft flew in this weekend. Another five hundred visited from the ground to watch the planes and the art. We are happy to give this angel Eva a certificate for ten hours of flying time and instruction for her participation this weekend."

That got a good round of applause. Eva was beaming.

"Jett Blackburn and his crew volunteered to do this painting and performance for just tips. I want to tell you he and members of his team have been out here every weekend for a month preparing the wall, painting much of the background, helping us with promotion, graphics, and general inspiration. I hope you have all been generous in placing tips in the canisters at the entrances. The Airport Association has decided to also tip Jett and his crew with this check for five hundred dollars. The mural behind us will stand as a major part of the character and charm of our airport for years to come."

I was pretty blown away to receive the extra contribution.

"Would you like to fly, Angel Eva?" Steve asked as the rope came down and people began to mill about to get a closer look at the art on the wall and, surreptitiously at Eva's feathers.

"May I be excused, sir?" she turned to ask me. The rest of us were getting our supplies put away and things cleaned up. I guessed the remaining eight of us could make it in two cars.

"Yes, my substrate," I said as I petted the feathers on her butt. "But you'll probably want to put some clothes on—for at least a while. These feathers look good on you, but they won't keep you warm."

"Thank you, Jett. I love you," she said. She gave me a deep kiss and grabbed her robe to head to the bathroom to change. "See you guys later in the week!"

·o·⇨ ⅅⅭ ☀ Ⅽⅅ ⇦·o·

"I THINK YOUR little bird has flown," Sarah Lynn said as she took my left hand to walk to the car.

"Like the swallows to Capistrano, she'll return," Mary said. "Not forever and not all the time, but she's got two more years of school left now that she's been accepted on the BFA program. She's got wings but she knows she can fly both directions."

"And we have a new roommate!" Jas said as she pushed Mary into the tiny back seat of the Mini with her. The two girls clasped each other in a passionate kiss.

·o·⇨ ⅅⅭ ☀ Ⅽⅅ ⇦·o·

I LOOKED AT my bank balance and no matter how hard I worked, it was always getting smaller. I looked at my work from the past year and only saw three or four potential pieces that I could sell. Of course, we had the videos of each performance piece, but they weren't getting a lot of hits on our YouTube channel. We didn't have as many subscriptions for that as we had hits on *Baroque Porn*. We'd made thirteen hundred on tips from *Flight*, but after Char deducted materials cost, we put the remaining seven-fifty directly into the household account since everyone contributed.

Our landlord tried to raise the rent on the house when we went to renew our lease because it was a much nicer place to live now than it had been when we rented it. Char was prepared and showed the before and after possession pictures of the property and the condition it was in when we started. She then pulled out a copy of our lease that said the property must be left in the same condition in which it was acquired.

"We will be happy to restore this property to the condition it was in when we took possession last summer," she said primly. "If we do not have a lease at the same rate as this one, we will do exactly that."

The agent we'd talked to last year smiled.

"I told him he'd lose money if he tried this. He might have gotten away with a cost-of-living increase that matched other rents in the area but he had to get greedy. I prepared the alternative lease already. This one is identical to the one you signed last spring."

Char read it anyway, comparing it line by line to the previous lease. Once she was satisfied, we signed it. We were on the hook for another twelve months.

•◦•✦ ⟡ ☀ ⟡ ✦◦•

As the anniversary of Lonnie's death approached, I couldn't see any appreciable change in the world. The five, six, seven, or eight of us who had made this extended family had found a way to insulate ourselves a little, creating our own little bubble. No charges had been brought against the police for shooting Lonnie. Two officers, a supervisor, and a medical tech were dismissed from their jobs for attempting a sloppy cover-up. I guess if it hadn't been sloppy, they wouldn't have been caught.

It was like Derek and Dee's little blanket fort in the basement. They'd sent out pictures of the two of them with their little baby, still in that blanket fort. In her parents' basement. Where they lived. And probably would for the next ten years.

I'd voted in the last election because I was eighteen and I wasn't going to let some idiot get in office just because I didn't vote. But we still elected a fucking Nazi. The world seemed to be stuck in a time loop somewhere between stupid and insane. What did I know? I guessed I'd just ignore it for another year if I could. I'd hold the ones I loved close at night and pray they came home each day.

I had only three more courses left for my meat cutting certification. College classes were out a month before high school, so I got in for the first summer term. If I started working full time at the grocery as a newly certified meat cutter, I could start at about twelve dollars an hour—better than minimum wage, at least. That was about $25,000 a year but I'd have to cut back on my class schedule. I thought I'd net about twenty after tax and social security. Maybe a little less. Well, I could make it half time this year as long as no emergencies came up. A thousand a month would cover expenses and a little of my tuition. I don't know what I'd have done if I'd ended up continuing to support Char last fall.

The world was a crappy place and I wasn't a great help. If Lonnie was alive today, I figured he'd still kill himself. I just hoped that somehow maybe my art could contribute to making it better. It didn't seem I had much to show for it right now.

But Jas, Sarah Lynn, and Kelly promised a party to remember this weekend to celebrate a year together. With the amount of weed and alcohol they've managed to put in, I'm guessing it will be a party we won't be able to remember. Right now, they've suggested I refresh my memory of their pussies. Time to party.

An Interview with author Devon Layne

KEEPING HIS IDENTITIES separate is sometimes a challenge, but author/
editor/designer Nathan Everett attacks the challenge of interviewing his
alter ego, author Devon Layne, with precision borne of living a double
life for years. Here's what Devon had to say to Nathan upon the publica-
tion of the Signature Edition of *Drawing on the Dark Side of the Brain*.

NE: I'm back with author Devon Layne. We've been sharing quite a lot
of headspace recently, so we'll try to keep our personalities separate
for this interview. Let's start off with a general question about the
book, *Drawing on the Dark Side of the Brain*. How did you come up
with that title?

DL: There is a well-known and still very popular book written in 1979
titled *Drawing on the Right Side of the Brain* by Betty Edwards. It
focuses on accessing the intuitive and artistic aspects of the right
hemisphere of the human brain. Back in 1993 or 1994 I had the
opportunity to attend a three-day workshop taught by Ms. Edwards
and truly saw a leap in my drawing ability—which is not as impres-
sive when you realize I started from zero.

When I conceived the idea of an artist whose drawings and
paintings changed people in profound ways, a play on that title just
sprang to mind, *Drawing on the Dark Side of the Brain*. The one
thing I regret about the choice is that it sounds more ominous than
I really wanted to write. Yes, people are changed by what he paints,
but not necessarily to the point of dying or being cursed. Many are
strengthened and encouraged by the paintings.

NE: Where does *Drawing on the Dark Side of the Brain* come in the
opus of books you've written?

DL: Kind of in the middle. I have sixty erotica books out and *Drawing on the Dark Side of the Brain* is somewhere around thirty or thirty-three. It was originally released in 2018.

NE: How long did it take to write it?

DL: A long time, actually. According to my notes, I started it in June of 2017 and was still writing the last chapter when I started posting it in July of 2018. The eBook version came out in December of 2018. I have never released a paperback until this Signature Edition.

NE: Was there a particular inspiration or set of beliefs you wanted to challenge in this book?

DL: I think so, but I'll have to paint some history as well. Back in 2005-2009, I worked in mobile technology. So, it was natural when my daughter turned thirteen or fourteen to get her a cell phone. Among all the other 'reasons' for a teen girl to have a phone, I wanted to see how she would use it. I was astounded when I looked at the itemization of her phone bill a few months later to find she had sent 10,000 text messages! 10,000! In that month, I'd sent a dozen. It was my personal wake-up that the times, and the youth were changing.

My daughter was at the tail-end of the millennial generation. You know, though, there's a lot of overlap in the generations, even though the census tries to clarify the specific years of each. Gen Z is said to be 1996-2013 and Gen Alpha from about 2013 to present. I didn't want to jump too far into the future with this story, but I realized that the significant change I saw between even my daughter's generation and the later Gen Z was remarkable. Those born in this century have always known a digital life. They have been *connected* practically from birth. They all know how to use their phones, computers, and the internet in ways my generation only imagines. I call those born in the 21st century "Digital Natives."

At the same time, I was hearing my generation and Gen X complaining online (and sometimes in person) about the lack of respect the 'modern kids' had for their elders; how they should have their phones taken away from them and be sent outside to play; how they were too protected and had to have a trophy for everything they participated in. In general, the world was going to hell in a handbasket because of the current generation. They seemed to miss that the people who needed the trophy were their parents, not the kids.

I was sick of hearing the current generation being bad-mouthed all the time. My interactions were far more positive. But kids were not only facing new technology every day, but a world that had run away from them. Despite people calling for a return to technical education and good jobs like plumbers, mechanics, and carpenters, jobs were scarce. They were constantly told they needed a college education and that became a requirement for even entry-level positions. It felt hopeless. They would never be able to afford a house. They might live with their parents for years. They would never be able to pay off the crippling debt of a college education that we uniformly told them they had to have. And with that sense of hopelessness came a distrust of authority, a confusion about societal roles, and a lack of commitment to any individual or career.

I wanted… I *needed* to show an honest picture of what life and expectations were really like for digital natives.

NE: You think they will end up in polyamorous relationships that share a house with half a dozen sexually active partners?

DL: There are things that sell. And by sell, I don't mean for money, but for readership. I did find people in more open relationships, but polyamory is seemingly an option for the prurient mind rather than for the reality of today's generation. At the same time, I can see that relationships change. Dating is different than it was, even in my daughter's teens. Much more happens in groups rather than one-on-one. I believe the common conception that teens are more sexually active than in my generation is far-fetched. I find them more reserved, more confused, and reluctant to engage intimately with a single other person. And our society makes that even harder.

NE: What came first for you: the plot or the characters?

DL: This was one in which they converged. I didn't actually know who the long-lasting characters would be until I was well into the story. Each time I introduced a character, I did a background check on him or her. I had to answer what kind of person this was, what race and ethnic background, what life dreams, what insecurities.

But I had—not exactly a plot—an overall theme for what would happen. Jett Blackburn, a name I got from my telephone exchange when I grew up, painted pictures that changed people. Profoundly. Sometimes terminally.

I had no idea how that talent would evolve toward body painting, how he would learn meat cutting as a skill he could market, how the original five women would attach themselves to him and how another would come into their circle as one left. That all evolved from their background checks.

NE: It's been seven years since you released the original and you are just getting around to releasing the paperback as a Signature Edition. Are you planning a sequel?

DL: Um… I think so? At the time of this interview, that is in my 'we'll see' stack, but it is a lot closer to the top than it was right after I finished the book. I was writing into the future when I released the book with the action taking place in roughly 2020-21. We didn't know what was going to happen to our world the next year. But now I have that history to deal with as I write their next year in college. Covid was one of the defining events of Gen Z and Gen Alpha. I can't ignore them. So, the answer is yes, I plan a sequel. It could take as long or longer to write than the original.

NE: We're all holding our breath!

DL: I hope you have good lungs.

NE: Has writing this book changed your outlook on life at all?

DL: I think I identify with this generation and the problems they face more now than ever. I'm pissed at my own generation for dismantling the support systems we had in place, for constant inflation of property values, for prioritizing personal wealth over universal welfare. I mean welfare as the well-being of everyone, not as a government program giving away money. Things like health care. Affordable housing. Decent food on the table.

I find that I, too, am struggling with those very issues. I can't afford a house, or even a decent apartment. I live a nomadic lifestyle in a travel trailer and find more and more retirees living on the road because it is cheaper than settling anyplace. Healthcare is a constant issue. Will Medicare cover my dental bill? My glasses? What happens if I'm in serious trouble, like fighting a-fib for four years and then getting a pacemaker for my heart last year. I live alone, so even the issue of what to eat and when to buy groceries comes into play.

And now we face a world and a nation that threatens our Social Security. The values we were raised with are being torn apart—not by the digital natives, but by our own generation. It is a depressing time and I join that generation in its post-apocalyptic despair.

NE: Ouch! I felt that. Is writing a kind of spiritual or therapeutic practice for you?

DL: I have frequently stated in the past that I don't write for a living; I write to live. To that extent, I think writing gives me purpose and hope for the future. At the same time, I don't try to deal with my mommy-issues, my heartbreak, or my personal psychological issues. Some of it finds its way into my character's lives because they are real people to me, but I don't think of my writing as therapy.

Often, in fact, my writing wrenches deep emotion out of me and I'm very angry about it. Sometimes angry at characters who act insanely. Or stupidly. I think, 'If you had just asked for a little help…' or 'Everyone knows you don't run into a blind alley at night.' And then the characters pay the consequences. I don't.

NE: Any last hints about what might be in the sequel?

DL: Jett will become a full-fledged butcher, but it won't be in his grandfather's store. The mega-corp mentality will take a toll. There will be more conflict and some really good artwork. And then they'll all be locked down together.

NE: Thank you.

Devon Layne

www.ingramcontent.com/pod-product-compliance
Lightning Source LLC
Chambersburg PA
CBHW070306310726
48976CB00005B/1589